The House on the Water's Edge

The House on the Water's Edge

CE Rose

hera

First published in the United Kingdom in 2021 by

Hera Books
Unit 9 (Canelo), 5th Floor
Cargo Works, 1–2 Hatfields
London, SE1 9PG
United Kingdom

Print ISBN 978 1 80032 781 8
Ebook ISBN 978 1 912973 76 7

Look for more great books at www.herabooks.com

Printed and bound in Great Britain by Clays Ltd, Elcograf S.p.A.

1

To my beautiful Emily, who makes everyone smile.

Prologue

Distant sound breaks through her sludge of deep sleep. A baby is crying. No, not crying but bleating and whimpering, imploring and scared. Her instinct is to help but she's too frightened to move and she doesn't know why.

Fractured images trickle back. A smiling family portrait; the rippling River Bure. Shadowy eyes that watch her. A presence at a door. Someone bad, very bad. And her own fist, tightly wrapped around a glinting object.

A knife? Oh God, is that really a knife?

She forces herself out of the black tar of the dream. It's a nightmare, that's all. She has to be brave and just look. Nothing will be there. Nothing. That white face was just a symptom of her fragmented psyche; if she peers into the gloom, she'll see.

Gently talking to herself, she blows out the trapped air and steels herself to move. She has to do this; she mustn't show weakness or illness or look odd. But... but the seeping coldness is there, isn't it? She really can smell it. A geranium-like stench, metallic and coppery and sweet. Which means they'll soon come too, vibrating, humming and buzzing; seething, teeming, *invading*.

Covering her nostrils and mouth, she shrinks into a ball and tries to block out the terror, but the mewling is still there, becoming louder and shriller, more and more insistent.

Oh God, the baby! She thrusts through the darkness; she must save the child. It's not any baby, it's hers.

Part One

Chapter One

'Ali? Mum's dead.'

That was my sister, breaking the news all the way from Canada.

It was the last day of June, a raw humid day, waiting for rain. The front door was open; the telephone yelled. I toyed with the idea of ignoring the call, but put down the watering can on what felt like the final peal.

'Ali? Mum's dead.' Said without preamble. 'She died at lunch time, three minutes past one. She was driving to Wroxham and crashed into another car.'

My mother had died and as I stared at the delicate veins garnishing the pink and lilac petals of the wilting plants, my thought was: *why does Laura always find things out before me?* Laura, my older sister and my shadow, even though she lived three thousand miles away.

'Joan Hague called to tell me the news. She's upset, so she asked me to contact you. She thought it would be better coming from me, what with the baby and all.'

Said as though I was mentally frail; Laura had no time for children. *'I've only had a baby. I'm not ill or inept, for goodness' sake!'* I wanted to protest. But in truth I didn't feel great; though over a month had now passed, I was still exhausted from the birth – stunned, in fact. I was still so sore I could only sit comfortably on one buttock.

'God knows why the police phoned the Hagues first but… Are you all right, Ali? You're not saying much.'

'What happened?' I asked.

It was all I could think of saying. The forlorn-looking cat basket was still by the garage from Wednesday's trauma. Laura's words didn't feel real; they couldn't be real. Mothers didn't die on sunny Fridays.

'She was on her way to the hairdresser's…' Laura began.

This I knew. Mum was coming to visit us tomorrow. She was driving the five-hour journey from Norfolk to Manchester to see her grandson, and stay for a week. She'd suggested it on Monday, but all I'd thought of was meals and fresh sheets and dusting. I could barely get myself dressed and out of the house each day; cleaning and entertaining seemed impossible. 'Mum,' I'd said, trying to keep the panic from my voice. 'That's fine. But you will come as a helper and not as a guest, won't you?'

'Yes of course, love. I can't wait to cuddle little Joe again. And it'll be so nice to have plenty of time for long chats.' I'd heard her intake of breath. 'In fact, there's something I really need to tell you… do you have five minutes to talk now?'

Oh God, I'd cut her off. Impatiently too. I didn't have *five minutes*; I hadn't had a flaming second spare since Joe was born. 'Let's save it until Saturday. OK?'

Laura talked and I drifted, the flowers still parched, the air solid through the gaping front door. On the way to the hairdresser's; a banal way to die. Of course that's what Mum would be doing; hair was a priority if she was going somewhere special. Her *impossible hair* got worse in the heat and this June was so hot. Like others would search for a church on holiday, the first thing she'd find was a salon – not for when she was there, but to look smart for returning home. *Respectable hair.* For the doctor's or the dentist, for the theatre or meals out. For visiting her new grandson and me.

As a helper, not as a guest. What an awful thing to say.

And Laura was still speaking. 'We don't know everything yet, but it looks as though she unexpectedly pulled out of a side street and was clipped by a car going too fast along the main road. You know what those country lanes in bloody Norfolk are like. I told Mum to take more care so many times after the whiplash, but she said not to worry, that she'd live forever.'

Laura's tone was efficient, irritated almost, and I was silent as random thoughts continued to waft by. I'd cut Mum off the last time we spoke; I'd deliberately not answered her three or four calls since then. But I'd thought I'd be seeing her in person very soon; I'd bought in plum jam, malted bread and blue-topped milk especially. And her favourite ice cream, still hiding deep in a carrier bag somewhere. Who on earth would eat them now? And my sister was right; Mum had promised to take care. She'd said she'd drive carefully and be here for us forever. Only she wasn't. Laura had just said she was dead. We were orphans, Laura and me.

Orphan. Did it still count when one was thirty-five? I tried the word a few times in my head; orphan, orphan, before testing it out loud. 'I guess we're orphans now,' I said, not really believing it.

Laura's voice cracked then. Laura, my proficient big sister who never cried. So I knew it must be real, even though I didn't *feel* it.

'It's just so horrible, Ali. She was alive when the ambulance got there. But she wasn't wearing a seat belt, so you can imagine the injuries… They put a medical brace on her neck and she grasped it with her hand. To pull it off, I suppose. But her aorta had ruptured. There was nothing they could do. Oh God, I hope she wasn't in pain.'

I watched Melissa from the house opposite lock her newly painted front door, climb into her car and reverse it smoothly onto the cul-de-sac. As she drove past, she lifted her palm in greeting, but all I could see behind a shattered windscreen was her slumped body, her face scored with pain, her hand clutching a collar. And blood, of course, congealing blood. Always that.

I blinked the image away. For God's sake, who the hell had felt the need to tell Laura that?

'Ali, you're very quiet, are you still there? Tom Hague is sorting everything out for us. We're lucky to have him. He'll know what to do as an ex-copper, and I can't just jump on the next flight. My diary is full up for weeks...'

My proficient and capable sister was back. Part of me was angry – couldn't she just do something loving and spontaneous for once in her life? But the other part was relieved. It seemed easier to cope when Laura was Laura. Besides, I didn't have the energy for an argument.

'Laura, the baby is crying. Can we speak later?' I asked instead.

Chapter Two

Joe wasn't crying. He was, I hoped, still snoozing where I'd left him. Before Mum had died? Now there was a thought.

Automatically holding my breath, I crept into the lounge to check he was still breathing, still living and undamaged from being left in a car seat rather than laid flat in his cot. Loving him dearly but still feeling that sharp stab of guilt: the guilt I wasn't finding motherhood a breeze; the guilt of struggling to cope with breastfeeding; guilt for allowing him to sleep curled in a chair; guilt for being almost joyous he was sleeping and not whimpering, not demanding, not needing.

What did Mum often say? No; *had* often said. '*Be kind to yourself, love. No one is perfect. We all make mistakes.*'

And there it was again, the image of 'me before Joe', a flash from a court case which had hounded me since his birth. As a prosecuting barrister I had stood robed and bewigged, proud and judgmental, and made my closing speech. '*Ladies and gentlemen of the jury, in cases involving the death of a child, there remains a temptation to believe that no mother could possibly be responsible for it. But you have heard from the experts that this baby was shaken…*'

I had nodded my approval at the jury's verdict. Guilty. They'd found there was a 'non accidental head injury' to the poor, dead baby; the 'triad of injuries' had been duly proved. So she was convicted, that woman, that grieving mother in court. Shaken baby syndrome, as they used to call it. Had she done it? Possibly. Probably. But the *why* was the thing. I had judged her; we'd all judged her without considering the why.

I stared at my infant's face. Asleep, this child was faultless; the little red spots on his cheeks had gone, his blond hair was growing and he was finally putting on weight. He was a treasure, an unspeakably beautiful gift. I was lucky, very lucky. I knew this completely, but at times it was difficult to *feel* it. Like a mother's death… My mother's death. Oh God, should I call Miles? But it was gone three; he'd probably be in court.

I'd phone later, I decided, I'd try him at five.

I imagined his rich, testy voice. '*I'm in a conference, Ali, can't it wait?*' he'd reply before I'd squeezed a word out. But in fairness, it was understandable; I'd rung umpteen times even before Joe's birth, each lonely antenatal appointment worse than the last. From discovering I had no rubella immunity at ten weeks, to a worrying blood result at twelve; from high blood pressure at seven months to signs of pre-eclampsia at eight. Then, after a difficult birth, I'd struggled to breastfeed and Joe developed colic.

It had felt like reproof, little Joe's revenge for me being a crap mother, a rubbish mum who failed every time despite trying everything to help: cuddles, long walks, colic drops and rubbing his tummy; even baby paracetamol when no one was looking – checking the instructions time and again – feeling desperate to do something but swamped with guilt.

'Thank God you're home, Miles! He's cried constantly for the last two hours,' I'd say at the front door at seven thirty, thrusting Joe into his father's arms. Then our son would stop bawling and I'd glance at Miles's frown and know what he was thinking: *Ali's making a fuss, she's being neurotic, perhaps she has post-natal depression or even worse.*

But I was simply a new mum whose close network of friends were all at work. I had a million aunties in Sheffield, but no relatives close by to help. No one to make me a cuppa or a sandwich, to entertain Joe for a few minutes so I could shower, brush my teeth, even pee. Or just sit down for five minutes and breathe. There was Madeleine, of course, but I wasn't that desperate.

I dragged myself back to the stuffy Friday afternoon. My mother was visiting tomorrow. As a helper, not a guest. But Mum was dead. She died on her way to the hairdresser's, not back; she was dead without *respectable* hair. Would someone comb it for her? Someone tender and kind?

It still didn't feel real.

'My mother is dead,' I tried aloud to the leaf-printed wallpaper. But I heard the words as Miles might; they sounded melodramatic and foolish, perhaps a little crazy.

I tried again with sleeping Joe: 'Grandma has died, Joe.'

That hit the mark. I felt the prickle of tears behind my eyes, the burn at the top of my nose. Not for my mother's death – that still hadn't sunk in – but for Joe's loss, the deprivation of his warm and loving maternal grandma.

Which left my poor boy with only Madeleine.

I abruptly remembered the ice cream. It had been an achievement of sorts; selecting half a trolly of food items without my pelvic floor collapsing. Did I bring in the shopping from the car? No, the hanging baskets had caught my eye. 'Water me, water me,' they'd said, and for the first time in five weeks, I'd noticed their beauty. It had felt like a good omen.

Hefting bags an effort too far, I laid on the floor and stared at a stripe of sunshine on the ceiling. Mum had died at three minutes past one. What, exactly, had I been doing then? Should I have felt something momentous? And should I call Miles? Would it be odd not to? He'd come home when the cat died, straight away. But he'd been in chambers that day, this Wednesday, two days ago. Charlie had been missing for a week and when she finally appeared, her eyes were filmy with blindness. Skinny and scraggy, she'd padded around my ankles in confused circles.

It had been the logistics, I remembered; the practicality of carrying a large moggy in her basket in one hand, a baby in his car seat in the other. My Charlie had to be put down, that I knew, so I'd scooped up my mobile to call Miles without thinking. 'Miles, you need to take the cat to the vet as soon as you can. She's in pain, she's suffering; she needs someone to hold her when she… goes.'

Like Mum, my mum, grasping that collar. Did someone cradle her as she died? Had they styled her hair and made her respectable?

I sighed. Calling Miles was the thing. He'd come home for Charlie, no questions asked. But then again, he'd loved that cat.

Chapter Three

'Ali? Wake up Ali. The front door was ajar. Why didn't you call me?'

It took a few moments to stir and sit up, more to focus on my husband's frown. His blue eyes were puffy, the tip of his nose pink. I immediately thought of the cat, quickly followed by Joe. Then I followed his gaze down to my damp shirt. As ever, my breasts were heavy, hot and tight, but today the milk had seeped through both the cotton pads and my bra. Great. So much to give, yet I still struggled with feeding. It was only maternal guilt that stopped me reaching for the box of formula always waiting, ready-made and inviting, in the fridge.

'I fell asleep.' I snapped my head to the empty car seat. 'Oh, God. Where's Joe?'

'He's fine. I've just sorted his nappy.'

My baby was on the changing mat, kicking his legs. The moment his eyes caught mine, he bleated.

'I needed to lie down,' I continued. 'I'd been shopping and my pelvic floor really ached...'

As though I needed justification today of all days. But I'd heard Miles talking to Madeleine on his mobile, despite his low, secretive tone. Last night, most nights. Discussing me as usual, my husband, her spy.

Struggling. Tired. Tearful. Coping? I really don't know... Yes, of course I will, Mum, but I have to work...

'It's fine, Ali. It's fine. I'll get Joe.'

Our son's whimpering became louder, stopping as Miles passed him to me. Unzipping my feeding bra, I took a deep breath, tensing as always. Would this feed be a fight?

Despite five weeks of practice, it still felt as though my baby had fangs, his latching on akin to 'stamping on broken glass', as I'd described it to Mum. Oh God, Mum. Wincing at the sudden flash of red on a shattered windscreen behind my eyes, I replaced it with the smiling perfect-toothed mother feeding her dolly baby on a poster at the antenatal clinic. Why wasn't anyone honest? Why didn't they say that motherhood had its challenges, that it wouldn't be plain sailing? Even a bloody *struggle* at times? But perhaps it was just me. There were real mums I knew with perfect babies and smiling teeth.

It was my own fault really; I'd set myself up to be a successful mother, just like I had been a successful law student, a successful pupil, then barrister-at-law. I hadn't expected failure; I hadn't anticipated being crap at pregnancy, even worse at giving birth. But then again, I hadn't foreseen my mum dying, when somehow I should have *known*.

'You could always use formula, Ali.'

Miles's comment broke my thoughts. He'd said it before, many times. And even though I hated those tempting words, I got where he was coming from: he needed a break from the stress as much as I did. But if I couldn't feed my own child, then what was I good for? *Breast was best*; it was hammered in by the midwives, the books, the smiling poster women with those damned smiling teeth. Besides, I'd feel even worse if I gave in and exposed my baby to increased risks of heart disease, obesity, diabetes, stunted growth, low IQ or whatever the current research implied. A load of middle-class propaganda, probably; I had survived with good health until now; trends changed all the time. Had Mum breast-fed me? Was I dragged out by forceps? Two things I hadn't asked her. Too late to enquire now.

'Why didn't you ring me?' Miles asked again.

'How did you find out?'

'Laura called me,' he muttered eventually. 'She thought you seemed strange on the phone. She's worried about you, Ali. Quite rightly. Eve's dead. It's horrendous, unbelievable. Of course I came home immediately.'

I glanced at my husband then. His blond hair was dishevelled; he looked boyish and vulnerable and dazed. He'd got on nicely with my mum, always said that if that's how I'd look in thirty years, he'd done pretty well. And the shock was understandable. Both his parents were fit and healthy, his mother Madeleine especially, very much alive on the telephone and colluding about me every night.

'What did Laura say?' I asked, not really wanting to know, but wondering if she'd told Miles something she hadn't mentioned to me. She'd said I seemed 'strange'. An echo of my bloody mother-in-law. Wasn't I entitled to be *strange* today? Odd, peculiar, downright insane if I wanted? Even on a good day, I didn't have Laura's talent for letting out emotion, for 'working problems through' and exorcising them. That just wasn't me. Of all people, my sister knew that, didn't she?

Miles didn't reply. The silence felt uncomfortable, so I filled it in.

'Has she spread the word, from the chief executive to the toilet attendant? Tweeted the news and updated LinkedIn? Condolences will be flowing even as we speak...'

I didn't add that it was a relief she lived so far away; I didn't want her telling the postman or the newsagent or the whole bloody street about my bereavement when I still hadn't grasped it myself.

I was being harsh, of course. Communication was Laura's way of coping. Mine was the opposite. I'd been loath to share the dreadful news with my husband, for God's sake. How could two siblings be so different?

Closing my eyes, I sighed. Would she phone me back or should I call her? We spoke rarely and only for a purpose, Laura's purpose: 'What have you bought Mum for Christmas? We don't want to duplicate. I'm at Mum's for a week. Will I see you?' And men – weirdly, she seemed to want to talk to me about men. If a new boyfriend was on the horizon she'd call, even asking my opinion: 'He's Jewish, he's a ginger, he's black; he earns less than me, he's married. Does that matter?'

An honest answer wasn't required.

Sometimes I wished she would ask about my world, about Joe or even Miles. Yet part of me understood. What interest did a baby hold for Laura, or our strait-laced legal lives, for that matter? She'd stomped off to Canada at eighteen to nanny some spoilt rich kids and had ended up at the top. An executive in a pharmaceuticals company, no less. I admired her tenacity, her efficiency, her lack of sentimentality. But occasionally a little attention, even praise, would have been nice.

How I had adored my big sister as a child. Yet still she'd left me. I sniffed at the thought. Our lives had changed today. Perhaps this would make us; give us a new reason to keep in touch.

Or maybe it would finally break us.

Chapter Four

Miles brought up brandies to our bedroom at nine.

He glanced at Joe, asleep in the carrycot by the side of our bed. 'A thimbleful won't hurt,' he said with a small smile. He took an unsteady breath. 'I need one too. A pretty large one, if I'm honest.'

I took the tumbler but didn't drink. Instead, I inhaled the warm zest and asked my burning question: 'Have you told Madeleine about Mum?'

He seemed surprised at the query. 'No, not yet. There hasn't been time to—'

'Could we leave it for a while? I'm still getting used to it.'

'Sure, but we do need to tell her soon, Ali. She'll be devastated for you. You know how much she cares about you.'

His guileless face was a picture. 'I know,' I replied. 'But there's no need to spoil her and Henry's holiday. Not yet. OK?'

An old image of Madeleine fired in, her brown irises loaded with concern. Not for her son, who'd just been admitted to hospital after crashing his car, but for me. An ironic recollection, considering today. It was swiftly followed by another more recent snapshot, but this time she was pitching and reeling, her hand to her cheek, those beautiful eyes stunned.

Pushing the uncomfortable memory away, I glanced at Miles. 'Helplessness, terror. You know how that feels,' I said. His expression was perplexed. 'That's what you said after you wrote off the Stag.' I was saying the words but still couldn't absorb them. 'The hopeless, sliding moment before impact, then the terrifying collision itself. The sickening sound of crushing metal. Remember? That's how you described it to me back then.' I smiled thinly. 'You walked out almost scot-free; I'll never know how you managed it.'

He nodded apologetically. Then he pulled me into his arms and held me tightly. 'I know; I was incredibly lucky. I'm so sorry about Eve.'

I almost cried then. It was lovely; the closest we'd been for weeks. The smell of his aftershave, the silkiness of his hair, the softness of his skin. Those old tender kisses. I missed all that.

The peal of my mobile broke the moment. It was Laura.

'Oh God, what about Mum's house?' she asked, to the point as usual. 'Is it secure? An empty building is a magnet for squatters.'

She catalogued her other concerns. The sudden thought of my mum's absence made my heart thrash, yet my sister was thinking about practicalities: someone needed to turn off the water and the heating, make sure the windows were locked, throw out perishables, deal with the bins. I half listened and drifted, trying to breathe through the surge of anxiety.

'The Lodge' had been our childhood holiday home, a pretty, white-rendered bungalow in a small village called Horning on the River Bure. After five years of idyllic summers we'd abruptly stopped going and it was let out to holidaymakers. But when I was eighteen and left home for the University of Manchester, Mum suddenly decided to move from her beloved Sheffield to Norfolk, lock, stock and barrel.

I never got to the bottom of why she upped sticks and left all her siblings behind. She'd never settled in Horning during the Easter or summer vacations. She'd complained that the bungalow and its contents were old-fashioned and dank, the locals over inquisitive and she'd never got rid of the 'damned smell'. But that autumn, she called my hall of residence telephone to tell me her plans.

'Do you mind, love?' she asked. 'I know how attached you are to your bedroom and all your things, but I'll rehouse them at The Lodge, I promise, and the journey isn't too bad when you travel by train…'

A Liverpudlian boy – who wrote me exquisite poems – was waiting in my single bed, so I didn't really absorb the shock of her words. 'Not at all. Sounds brilliant. Go for it!'

By the time I'd reached my room, I found I was crying. I managed to hold back the deluge until my beau left, but in the following days I was inconsolable. My flat mates thought I was crazy. Why cry over the sale of a house? It was only bricks and mortar after all, and maybe I would get some of the dosh. What they didn't understand, because I hadn't told them, was that it felt like the final goodbye to my dad. My brilliant, smiley, long-lost, handsome dad.

I tuned back into what Laura was saying and the penny finally dropped: I was the UK-based daughter; that's why she'd called with her to-do list. Though Miles was watching, I couldn't hold back my agitation. 'I've just had a baby, Laura! I can't simply drop everything and drive to Norfolk to sort out bloody bins. I'm still feeling...'

Did I really want to confess how bloody difficult I was finding motherhood? Not only to my businesslike sister, but to Madeleine, via her unwitting son-spy? I took a deep breath to settle the quaver in my voice, but Laura spoke first, her concerned tone catching me short.

'I know it's hard for you, Ali. It's hard for us both. But we can't just bury our heads. You see that, don't you?'

I detected a sniff down the line.

'But we have the Hagues to help us out, so there's no need to dash down there. They're desperate to do anything they can, but haven't called you because they don't want to—'

There it was again, like bloody Madeleine. *Is Alison coping? Are you sure, darling? Ali's not herself just now. You can see that, surely, Miles?*

'They don't want to what?' I demanded, a little too shrilly.

'God, I don't know, Ali. I have no idea, but people say that having a baby is really tough in the first few weeks. Tom and Joan never had kids either, so what do they know, but I think they're just trying to be thoughtful by holding off.'

Embarrassed by my outburst, I said goodnight to Laura and ended the call. Tom and Joan Hague were an elderly couple who sounded out of place in Norfolk with their distinct Yorkshire accents. I didn't know chapter and verse, but they'd both lived in Sheffield back in the day. Dad had been Tom's accountant and they'd become good friends over the years. When Tom retired, he and Joan had moved to Horning, and it was they who'd told Dad about The Lodge when it came up for sale. The two oldies were part of my rose-tinted summers: helping Mr Hague clean his boat on the sparkling river cut; baking swollen fruit cake and scones with his straight-talking wife at their riverside thatched cottage.

'Call me Auntie Joan,' she'd said every holiday, but it had never felt right, so with a deep breath, I steeled myself to call 'Mrs Hague' and discuss water, refuse, perishables and heating.

It was answered after two rings. 'Bureside 6275.'

It was Tom. I'd seen him at Mum's in more recent times, but my mental image was how he'd appeared twenty-five years ago. Slim, handsome and dapper, he'd have been in his early fifties, but to me he'd seemed quite old, his teeth too white, his gaze resting on me for a beat too long for comfort. Touching my cheek, I remembered the soft tickle of his moustache. It had taken some time for me to warm to him and Joan, but then again, I'd been wary of everyone in those days.

'Hello. It's Ali.' I swallowed. 'Eve's Ali. Could I speak to Mrs Hague please?'

'Hello Alice, love. Will I do? Joan's upstairs. She's too upset to talk at the moment,' he replied.

'Yes, of course you'll do.'

I was thrown from my questions about day-to-day mechanics. Mr Hague had always mistakenly called me Alice instead of Alison, but that wasn't why I tensed. The old feeling of danger was growing, reinforced by his heavy sigh. I was going to be told things I didn't want to hear.

There was a catch in his voice. 'This is a terrible business, a terrible business. Your beautiful mum, our Eve. Far too young.' He cleared this throat. 'I'm still reeling if truth be told, so goodness knows how you're feeling, but I thought it might help if I was your – well, sort of liaison officer, if you like. Save you from the upset of having to do it yourself. It certainly doesn't hurt to be an ex-copper at times like this. What do you think, love? Save you that worry?'

Emotion burned behind my eyes. He'd always been kind, and his suggestion was exactly what I needed right now – someone to look after me. 'Yes please. That would be great.'

'Well, I'll give you the bare bones, then you'll know everything I do and that can be the end of it.' He paused to blow his nose. 'The other driver was a youth. Off for a day out to Great Yarmouth with his pals. The funfair's my bet. Driving too fast, showing off… But here's the thing, love. From the tyre marks and suchlike, it's clear your mum came out of a side road into the path of his car. He tried to take evasive action, but he couldn't help clipping her little Mini, which then went into a spin, so it's doubtful the police will charge him. But that's probably for the best, eh? I don't need to tell you about the trauma of raking over things in court. The lads were shaken, none hurt. But the worst of it is…'

He took an audibly shaky breath. What could be worse than spinning in a car, waiting, petrified, for the final outcome? I was tempted to pass the phone to Miles, still by my side and silently listening. Even better, end the call. I'd done it at ten years of age, but covering my ears and refusing to listen wasn't something I should do as a professional woman in my mid-thirties.

Mr Hague continued. 'Well, while they were waiting for the police, recovery and so on, they sat on the grassy bank beneath the cherry trees, stretched out their legs and drank cans of beer. Seems they'd had them stashed in the boot for their day out. It may have been hot, but whatever happened to respect?'

I blew out the trapped air from my lungs. The triviality of someone else's devastation. While Mum was clutching that damned brace and bleeding out, a group of young men were laughing and joking a stone's throw away. And presumably there'd been a witness standing by, mentally recording each detail and gawping, perhaps even a little excited at the drama. That's how life went. Like the mum who'd shaken the life from her baby. Another person's tragedy, not mine.

I brought Tom back to the mundane. 'So The Lodge; Laura and I—'

'No need to worry about that, love. My legs aren't what they used to be, but we're only down the road and there's also your mum's cleaning girl and the gardener. They live in the village and both have keys. They'll make sure everything's sorted, look after the moggies and feed them. Look, I'll let you go now, love. You'll have the littl'un to see to.'

'Thank you for everything. Bye.'

Turning away from Miles, I hitched down the bed and pulled the duvet over me. Though I was unbearably tired, my breath was shallow, my heart pounding again. God, Mum's cats; I had completely forgotten about them. It was just one of the myriad of details I'd have to focus on. Of course they could live with us, but when I'd have the energy to drive over two hundred miles to collect them, I simply had no idea.

The next thing I heard was Joe grumbling in the dark. Shaking myself awake, I lifted him out of his carrycot. He abruptly stopped whinging and gazed at me expectantly. The surge of love was there, thank God.

I looked at the bedside clock. 1.03 am. Mum had been dead for twelve hours.

Chapter Five

The weekend passed, still and surreal; my mother was dead, but everything else stayed the same: Miles spent an inordinate time on his mobile; people smiled; children laughed; the neighbour said his cheery hello; the sun lit up the dust on every surface; the bathroom sink was smeared with toothpaste; the whole house needed a good hoovering and the huge tower of ironing seemed to glare.

When Monday arrived, Miles offered to stay home, but I knew he had commitments he couldn't just ignore: court hearings, paperwork and conferences. He was finally at the point in his career where instructions from solicitors rolled in for him personally, so it was important to be consistent and reliable. And anyway, what difference would it make where he was? I was in the limbo between death and burial. Nothing felt solid or real. Perhaps if I'd seen Mum every day, or even every week, it might have been different. Like Charlie cat. I still peered through the kitchen window to see if she was hidden in the cat-mint, or opened the back door out of habit, almost calling her name. I still felt the slight breeze at the lounge or the kitchen entrance, expecting her to slink in. But I'd forget Mum was gone until a small Joe development reminded me: a smile that seemed to be more than just wind, the letter about immunisations. *I must ask Mum… I wonder if*

Mum knows... I must tell Mum when she calls... Mum would find this funny...

That was when self-recrimination fired in. I'd cut her short the last time we talked. I'd ignored her other attempts to speak to me. She'd been due to visit on the Saturday; what on earth had been so important she'd needed to say it sooner?

–

Still in no man's land on Tuesday, I met up with two mums I'd befriended on the maternity ward. Our friendship was in its infancy, and I suspected our tiny babies were all we had in common, but I enjoyed their company and chatter. I didn't mention Mum. I knew it was probably irrational but I couldn't face that old fear they'd judge me if I cried and think me unstable. Or, even worse, ostracise me.

We met in the Marie Louise gardens for a picnic. Karen struggled with a messy nappy, and as I passed her a wipe from my changing bag, I wondered if I looked or seemed any different. Could she tell that something terrible and irrevocable had happened in my life? Thank God I didn't have to share my bereavement, not like at ten, when the teacher made an announcement to the whole form that 'Alison Baker's daddy has sadly died'. Perhaps she'd tried to be kind by her instruction to the children to 'please be caring and sensitive to your little classmate'. But with me sat at my desk in the room? All eyes turned and ogling at me? Really? What had the woman been thinking?

Of course kids were just kids. Not knowing what to say, let alone how to be 'caring and sensitive', they'd abandoned me instead. Only as an adult did I understand that my pals' distance had been from ignorance and fear. At the time, the loneliness and isolation had been unbearably hurtful, pain on top of the deepest pain; my daddy had died and my closest friends shunned me. I'd turned to Laura for love and support, but she'd emotionally disappeared, then after four years, she physically vanished too.

Laura. We'd spoken every day since *that* call on Friday, but the conversations were brief, as though she was checking off the 'Ali' box before moving on to the next thing on her agenda. She'd vaguely said she'd talk to Tom about the 'next steps' but I hadn't asked her to elaborate. I wanted her to offer the information without me having to beg like when we were kids: *Why are you going out again, Laura? I'm so sad, can't you stay at home with me? I need you here! Can I have a hug? Please?* My questions didn't feel so very different today: *Are you coming home, Laura? When? Will you be here for the funeral? I really need you to be there. Why haven't you bloody said?!*

Though I wasn't sure, Miles was certain she'd fly over soon. His blue eyes loaded with intrigue, he'd speculated on how she might appear this time. We'd holidayed in Canada a couple of years ago, travelling miles out of our way to see her in Vancouver, but when we arrived at her glassy offices, the nasal male receptionist denied all knowledge of our visit, despite the appointment I'd made. When she finally emerged from the lift, I didn't recognise her at first glance. Her blonde hair had been replaced by an auburn business-like bob, and she was wearing dark tortoiseshell glasses and a wide-legged trouser suit. Though I chuckled with pride and pleasure, it was a little surreal too; instead of the Anglo-American drawl I'd expected, she'd cultivated an extremely clipped British accent without even a hint of Yorkshire vowels. And she was surrounded by simpering and sycophantic men.

Miles had laughed from the corner of his mouth. 'They're all hoping for a good spanking.'

I thought that rich coming from a spoon-fed Alexander-Jones. But of course I was an Alexander-Jones too, by marriage at least, still enthralled to Madeleine, charming Madeleine, being moulded by her and becoming the identikit daughter she'd never had.

Chapter Six

Wednesday was roasting. Absently making a tuna sandwich, I stared at the garden through the smeary windowpane, searching for movement. The plants and the grass looked arid, the heatwave still in full swing. I hadn't watched the news for weeks but, his finger almost wagging, Miles had warned me about the hosepipe ban. It had made my lips twitch. Did my law-abiding husband really think I would be sprinkling the garden when no one was looking? Still, I'd wanted to water the hanging baskets on Friday; perhaps whisking out the hosepipe would be further progress away from my giving-birth-daze. Or maybe Miles surmised I'd be unbalanced enough to do the heinous crime, something to report to his mother. Had he told her about Mum yet? From her lack of contact, I assumed not. But I didn't want to think of her now; Madeleine in all forms was too overwhelming.

Planning to escape from the house, I took a small bag of peas from the freezer, put Joe in his bouncy chair and carried him to the loo. His face had the same incredulous look as Miles's when he'd caught me doing the same, but it was a question of needs must: my episiotomy scar still stung when I peed. I wasn't sure whether the home-made anaesthetic really helped, but I was clutching at straws, willing the bloody thing to heal. Though I hated going to the doctor's at the best of times, I'd been through the additional humiliation of showing a young medic my downstairs bits. 'Hmm,' he'd said, looking pretty appalled. 'Let's see how it goes, but it might need re-stitching.'

I'd had enough poking and prodding over the last few months to last a lifetime; no one would be slicing me open and sewing me up again, that was for sure. Besides, who cared that I now widdled slightly off-centre? I doubted I'd ever have sex with my husband again, let alone anyone else.

It was Mum who'd suggested the frozen peas. Cabbage leaves too, for my sore, engorged breasts. My resourceful mother who had a practical remedy for everything. My mother, who was apparently dead. A notion struck. Oh God, had she had some sort of premonition about the car crash? Was that why she'd tried to speak to me? As though hearing that thought, my mobile rang.

It was Laura, her tone brusque. 'So I gave Tom carte blanche with the burial arrangements, service and so on. He has a funeral director pal in Sheffield. Thought that would be for the best.'

'Oh, right.' Then, 'What about our aunties? Maybe Peggy or Brenda? They're local, too. Won't they be offended if we don't ask them to get involved?'

'Ali, what planet are you on? Mum hadn't spoken to Brenda for a good decade. Probably longer.'

'Really?' During my childhood, Mum had telephoned at least one of her five sisters every day, even though most of them lived within a mile, but when she moved to Norfolk, relations seemed to cool. Or at least she didn't talk about them as much. But a rift with Brenda was certainly news. 'Why didn't I know that?'

'You probably weren't listening.'

The usual swipe. And rich, coming from Laura. 'But Brenda was at my wedding. I didn't notice a thing.'

'Hmm. Maybe your *wedding planner* didn't allow you to mix with the proletariat.'

'What did they fall out about?'

'God only knows. Anyway, next Wednesday.'

'What's next Wednesday...?'

'Ali! Just focus, won't you? The funeral. At the old church at noon.'

Oh God, just a week away. It felt far too soon. I quickly checked the date of Madeleine and Henry's return from their Caribbean sojourn. Yes, Wednesday too. But the flight was long haul; they'd never make noon. Thank God for that.

'Ali, are you there? You can let the rellies know.' A pause and then, 'You can manage that, can't you?'

Mum was one of eight; six girls and two boys. My uncles weren't a problem; taciturn Yorkshire men, they'd have nodded sadly into their pints of pale ale when they heard the news. But my aunties would've made up for their reticence. I could visualise their faces, shocked but animated: '*Who would have thought it? In her brand new Mini, too? She wouldn't have known those country roads like she had here. Upping sticks and moving to her holiday home, eh? Goes to show that acting above your station always ends in tears.*'

Of course they wouldn't say it, but that's what they'd think.

The notion of them plus a funeral made me breathless. Couldn't Laura and I take Mum's ashes to the Bole Hills and let the breeze scatter them? The Sheffield moorland had been her and Dad's special place. We could climb the thirsty banks, just the two of us, collect bilberries on the way, gaze down at the mottled green Rivelin Valley and picture them courting. Fanciful, I knew, but so much less painful than the public display I dreaded.

Bloody hell. I hadn't really focused on the wake; that drifting in limbo, I suppose. The last one I went to was Dad's. That bewildering nightmare was twenty-five years ago, but could have been yesterday. Like a film trailer, the memories were there in crisp clips, the star of the show a clingy ten-year-old who hated being watched. It had felt as though every pair of eyes were on me as I'd walked into the church; some indulgent and some furtive, some caring, some tearful; some downright rude.

It was an unbearably sad day, not just because I had lost my precious daddy, but the shock of seeing Laura's tears from beginning to end. I hadn't expected that. Nor had I imagined the vicar would stand and welcome the congregation to *celebrate* Dad's life. When I looked at the prayer sheet, the word was there too. A celebration was a happy and joyful party, wasn't it? Like a birthday or an engagement? I couldn't get past that word; the adults had got it so wrong.

Mum had asked if I really wanted to go. She said no one would mind if I said goodbye to Daddy in my own special way. But even at ten, I was conscious of what the aunties would make of it. There'd be gossip and frowns, judgmental comments, sour lips and sucked-in cheeks. The same faces, only older now, as there would be at Mum's.

I dragged myself back to the present. Laura was still talking. 'Tom's made the arrangements to transfer her from Norfolk.'

Her voice was surprisingly thoughtful. I pictured her doing that thing she used to do with her hair. Twisting the silky blonde strands around her forefinger until it was so tightly bound that it knotted like a ring and wouldn't unravel. Occasionally Mum had to snip the braid with scissors, which hadn't gone down well. '*You'll ruin my hair…*'

'*Well, if you didn't mess with it in the first place…*'

'And her… body,' Laura now said. 'We're allowed to see her if we want.'

White, dead flesh; a rotting corpse. The smell of blood and the hum of flies… Shuddering, I tried to block the old nightmare from my mind, but Laura continued in a wry tone: 'Though sadly we don't have a front parlour handy for the rellies to inspect her.'

That made me smile. She was referring to Mum's anecdotes from her childhood: wizened dead great aunties and uncles in their coffins, duly dressed for church, but with sunken cheeks and no teeth.

'Now, that would make her *turn in her grave*,' I replied, using Mum's expression. The exchange cheered me; it showed that despite our physical – and emotional – distance, we spoke in a language we both understood.

Though we fell silent, I knew Laura was still there. Wearing those dark tortoiseshell glasses and flicking through paperwork, was my guess. I swallowed; she hadn't yet said what I most needed to hear, so I muttered. 'So, the old church. Not that it looks so old since its renovation…'

With its black bent spire, dull stained-glass windows and weathered stone elevations, the church had seemed ancient to us as kids. In my ideal world, Miles and I would have married there; I'd have walked up the aisle on my lovely dad's arm, happy to hear the aunties' commentary. But the wedding was arranged by Madeleine; I was under her spell then.

When I last visited the church to tend Dad's grave, I'd guiltily stared at the overgrown patchwork of weeds and grass. Only the top of the marble headstone had peeped out. Drowning, not waving, it seemed to say. I had knelt, taken out my trowel and set to work, as ever wondering why the nettles and sharp thistles grew so easily and in such abundance, when the pink and purple perennials I'd planted were long gone.

It hadn't struck me at first, but when I scrubbed my soiled nails at the outside tap afterwards, I realised the stone elevations were different. Like an ageing actress, they'd had a facelift, blasted from dirty black to a sandy grey. When I stepped back, I saw the spire had been renovated and the coloured glass in the arched windows sparkled.

Tears had welled then. I needed the old church to reappear; I longed for the atmosphere, the stillness and peace, the fearful childhood thrill that a spirit might be lurking, a tombstone might creek open, the eyes of Christ on the cross might flicker.

I wanted my safe, infant life. I wanted to be ten again.

And now we would be burying Mum in that same black hole as Dad, when everything changed.

I cleared my throat; I just needed to ask. 'And will you fly over for the funeral?'

'Ali, what the hell?' Laura hotly replied. 'Of course I'm bloody well coming.'

Chapter Seven

Laura had planned to stay with us in Manchester on the Tuesday evening, but her flight times were altered, so she texted to say she'd make her own way to the church and meet us there. The change threw me; I had wanted to see her first, to settle back in with the adult sister I barely knew, to have her by my side when we arrived at the old-but-new church.

Chattering to fill the silence, Miles negotiated the Snake Pass to Sheffield on Wednesday morning. I still felt slightly spaced out, but anxiety set in when we approached the Rivelin Valley.

'Not past the house, not today,' I snapped, when we started our ascent up one of Sheffield's seven hills. 'There's a different route to the church. I'll show you...'

'Sure,' he said, but he glanced at me with a frown.

'*Ali's not Ali,*' thumped in my head. Perhaps I was being irrational, but I couldn't bear the thought of seeing my childhood home. Nor could I climb out of the stuffy car when we arrived. Instead, I sat stubbornly and watched mourners pass by, their black attire incongruous in the bright sunshine.

Smoothing his hair, Miles shuffled in his seat. 'Come on, Ali, we have to go in. We look weird just sitting here. Besides, Joe's getting tetchy in this heat,' he eventually said.

He was right, but it was difficult to function, to breathe. I was stuck in my ten-year-old head with no one to chivvy me. Groping for an excuse, I inhaled, but to my surprise, the passenger door was flung open.

'For God's sake, Ali, get out. People are staring.'

Long blonde hair. And obligatory Ray-Bans. Laura, thank God.

She looked me up and down when I finally tumbled from the car. 'Haven't you brought sunglasses?' she demanded. But before I could answer, she delved into her handbag. 'As I suspected.' She thrust a cellophane-wrapped pair into my hand. 'I bought them on the plane. For moral support. I have no intention of blabbing like the last time and neither should you.' She held out her elbow. 'Are you ready?'

'Not really.'

'Then tough. Come on, onwards.'

I duly took my sister's arm. Like a bride and groom, we made our way through the wooden archway, past the mossy gravestones and along the patchwork path. Without stopping at the doors, she continued to propel me down the aisle like a very keen Mr Rochester. The bridesmaids – Miles and the pram – struggled to catch up, but we finally reached the front row, taking seats at the far side like we had as girls before shuffling back to the centre. We were, after all, today's star attraction.

Inclining my head, I tried to shape a suitable expression for the solemnity of the occasion, but in truth, I wanted to roar with laughter. I was so pleased to see Laura, and the familiar twitch around her lips showed she was desperate to chortle too. We were both wearing ridiculous sunglasses and the congregation was ogling, for once not at me, but at Laura's huge chest. Her new boobs were bigger than mine, and I had an excuse. Miles's eyes were popping; even Joe was looking expectantly towards them.

The hilarity finally broke at the sound of a throat clearing. His stockinged feet protruding from tan sandals beneath his cassock, a vicar was standing in front of the altar. A simple pine wooden box topped with lilies was stationed to his side. Mum was already there.

Overwhelmed by a sense of detachment, I stared. I hadn't shed a tear as yet; it still felt unreal. If the clergyman tripped and knocked over the casket, I was sure an impostor would tumble out and surprise everyone but me.

Tom Hague had telephoned yesterday to excuse himself and Joan from attending.

'I hope you don't mind our absence, love. It's a long journey and Joan isn't so good this week. We've already said our goodbyes. Will you see her yourself?'

He'd meant seeing my dead mother at the undertakers. 'No, neither Laura nor I want to,' I'd replied.

The image of a lifeless body had made me shudder, but perhaps I should have said yes; it might have linked this coffin with Mum and made it more tangible. But Tom had been kind.

'To be honest, love, I think you made the right call. She doesn't look like your mum. She had such a beautiful crowning glory with her hair and they'd got it all wrong…'

Oh God; her aborted trip to the hairdressers. 'But was it *respectable*?' I'd asked in a croak.

If he'd thought the question odd, his voice didn't show it. 'Yes, very respectable, love.'

A sharp nudge from Laura brought me back. The organist was lifting his arms; the mourners were standing.

The day Thou gavest, Lord, has ended…

It was a lovely hymn, one my sister and I had sung here and at Sunday school. I belatedly stood and took her hand. It was a strange feeling, her slim palm in mine. The only other one I ever held was my husband's. Intermittently these days; reserved, it seemed, just for birth and death.

I glanced at his handsome face. To my surprise, he was crying.

Chapter Eight

Little Joe did so well throughout the twenty-minute service, but once it was over and we'd led the congregation outside, he began to get tetchy. I didn't blame him; the heat and bright sunshine were quite shocking after the coolness of the nave. Then there were my aunties and the other older ladies of the parish who immediately swooped on him like a volt of buzzards after carrion.

Though I scooped him out of his pram and tried to reassure the poor little man, he wasn't for settling, so I made my excuses and ambled to the rear of the church, sat on a bench in the shade and fed him breast milk from a bottle. Like an amateur milkmaid, I'd managed to express a pathetic amount last night. I'd earmarked it for later to save me from the trauma of breastfeeding in public, but the lowering of the coffin was the aspect of the funeral I had particularly dreaded, so at least Joe's demands allowed me to escape graveside duties and observe the goings-on from a distance.

Trying to analyse why this part spooked me so much, I hung back in the shadows and watched the mourners quietly stroll towards the gaping hole that would become my mother's final bed. Was it a worry that my dad's coffin would be exposed? Or that old fear of teeming flies? Absurd, I knew, and I did have a handle on my brimming pteronarcophobia these days. The efficient blowflies were just nature going about its business. As a prosecuting barrister who read pathology reports and studied photographs of corpses as part of the job, I understood this as much as anyone.

A sudden tussle at the graveside lightened my morbid thoughts. The seven siblings and their spouses were jostling for position. Whether to watch the casket being lowered, or to inspect Laura's boobs at close quarters, I wasn't sure. But it was a relief to be on the periphery and stifle a laugh; another funny story I made a note to tell Mum.

Laura eventually sauntered over, holding onto Miles's sleeve. Both with glowing complexions, blond and attractive, they looked like brother and sister.

'Chuffing hell, I was nearly shoved in,' she chuckled, sounding more Yorkshire than I'd heard her for years. She glanced at Joe, now asleep in his pram. 'There were mutterings about the village hall, Ali. Please tell me I misheard. The Sportsman is grotty, but even that would be an improvement on nylon and formica.'

I laughed. 'You vowed never to set foot in The Sportsman again.'

'I might be more forgiving after twenty-something years, Ali.'

'But the landlord's wife might not be...'

Miles was looking on, his eyes wide with interest. 'Go on, Laura, spill the beans,' he said. 'What happened with whom in The Sportsman?'

'I suppose one would call him a paedo these days, but I thought he was drop-dead gorgeous. Dave the landlord. I'd had a crush on him for yonks before the fateful night when we—'

'Medallion man *gorgeous*? You're joking,' I cut in.

'So?' Miles prompted.

'I developed early, you might say.' Laura shrugged. 'Fourteen going on eighteen. Fake tan badly applied and pencil-thin eyebrows. Clothes that were way too tight. I drove Mum nuts. He was probably only our age, you know.' She paused for a moment as though envisioning the scene. 'He had a dark hairy chest that tapered all the way down to where the sun doesn't shine. As for the clinch itself… well, all I can remember is the stench of beer in that cellar.' She flashed Miles a smile. 'I was desperate to shake off the burden of maidenhood. I'm sure you know what I mean.' She came back to me, changing the subject as only Laura could. 'But the village hall for Mum's wake, Ali. Really?'

I was gazing at my husband and his enthusiastic nod. He was clearly still on Laura's 'burden of maidenhood' comment. As ever the polar opposite to my sister, I'd been fussy when it came to romance and sex. My ideal man was a thoughtful, chiselled and poetic type who'd fall in love with me despite himself. Boyishly handsome, easy-going and posh, Miles didn't fit that brief, but from his tears since Mum's death, more emotional than I'd supposed.

'Ali, are you with us?'

'Yup.' I dragged my thoughts back to the issue at hand. 'Not guilty on the venue for the wake, but from my spy seat just now, I gathered Tom – or his funeral director – consulted with…' I nodded meaningfully at Auntie Kathleen, bustling away with my uncle.

Laura dramatically covered her mouth. 'Noo…'

I laughed. Kathleen lived in the village, and was probably on some relevant committee, but she was an in-law and not an actual sister.

'But what about—?'

'I know!'

When Mum had lived in our house down the road, there'd been a pecking order of siblings – albeit an unspoken one – with Peggy and Brenda generally vying for top slot. Which was why it was still a shock that Mum and Brenda had fallen out. Still, I only had Laura to deal with, and that was a challenge, so perhaps I shouldn't have been surprised.

I glanced at the two woman now, still by the mound of soil. Dabbing their eyes with handkerchiefs, their arms were tightly linked. I'd always liked them both, but Brenda, a former teacher, was the more no-nonsense and straight-talking auntie. With her strident 'home truths' type of style, she'd always scared me a little, if I was honest.

'Kathleen, eh?' Laura said. 'Mum *will* turn in her grave.' She lowered her shades and looked at me pointedly. 'See, I was listening.'

'Touché…' I began, but the distinct aroma of J'adore Infinissime perfume, followed by an accent out of place, interrupted me.

'Alison! There you are, darling girl.'

Bloody hell; Madeleine. I didn't bother glancing at Miles; I was certain his cheeks would be flushed with culpability.

Her arms outstretched, she strode forward. 'Darling girl. I couldn't not come. We managed an earlier flight.' Looking both exquisite and soulful beneath her black hat, she placed a hand either side of my shoulders. 'I'm so, so sorry. Little Joe causing trouble with his colic and then this. Our beautiful Eve. How are you coping?'

Without waiting for an answer, she pulled back and smiled at Laura. 'And Laura, hello.' She kissed both her cheeks. 'How wonderful to see you. Such tragic circumstances, but how nice for Alison to have you around. It's nothing to worry about, but Ali hasn't quite been Ali of late.' She rubbed my arm and peered at me with loaded sympathy. 'You've been a bit out of sorts one way or another, haven't you?' With an elegant hand, she gestured to our surroundings. 'Such a lovely place to rest. So, where do we go now? Come on then darling, let's walk together and you can tell me all your news—'

But Laura had already linked arms with me. She nodded at the pram. 'You're in charge of thingy, Miles. We're going on the swings.'

Chapter Nine

We strolled along the cracked path to the far end of the graveyard. Most of the weathered dedications were familiar from childhood: Elsie and Elizabeth, George and Harold, Mabel and Frederick, born centuries before. Few were new graves; there wasn't enough space. We were lucky that Dad had bagged a place for Mum.

When we reached the low wall, Laura removed her jacket. Her sleeveless shift dress emphasised her slim arms. 'Weren't there some steps here? Oh well; there aren't any now.' She slipped off her high heels, rucked up her skirt and jumped down to the grass below. Then she held out a hand to help me. 'I believe you had an episiotomy. Mum said. And that it got infected or something. Sounds pretty revolting.'

Her flippant comment chafed. Childbirth was hard, wonky stitching even worse. Sure, I was slightly neurotic about my privacy, but I was still peeved that they'd been talking about me like that. With an inward sigh, I pictured the aunties getting merry on plonk in the village hall. God, I hoped Mum's indiscretion had stopped at my sister.

'Seems you're the expert at stitches,' I replied. 'I assume a boob job involves them, not keyhole or whatever.'

Laura didn't appear to notice my sour tone. 'You mean the latest in power dressing?' she replied easily. 'The op took about as long as choosing a dress, actually.' She raked back her Ray-Bans. 'Oh don't look so disapproving, Ali. You were the rebel, remember? Sticking that needle in your ear lobe for hours until it finally pushed through to the other side.'

I laughed. There it was again, common language. 'Yeah, and when I finally wanted to wear a *pair* of earrings, I had to pierce the other and they didn't match.'

'So you're not quite as perfect as I'd thought. Let's have a gander...' She peered at me intently for a beat, then tugged me into a hug. Eventually she pulled away with a sniff. 'Sometimes I miss you, you know.'

'Sometimes?' I replied, my throat clotted with emotion. 'I am honoured.'

'So you should be,' she replied, hurtling to the swings in bare feet.

Held back by the dull ache in my pelvis, I didn't belt after her as I would once have. Instead, I ambled to the refurbished play area, perched on a swing and pictured a scene from our childhood. Me and a pal on the see-saw, Laura chatting to boys with a hand on her hip. Was it a memory or a photograph? My heart sank at the thought of the task ahead. Mum had so many belongings, made all the worse by her tendency to hoard. She'd kept everything, from our school reports, toys and books, to our artwork, craft and sewing. How lovely it would be to go through it all with Laura and speak our common language. But I knew it would be asking the impossible.

I turned to her now. 'I miss you too,' I said. 'Not so much when you've gone, but when you're here, if that makes sense.'

'It makes perfect sense,' she replied, stretching out her tanned legs from the swing. 'That's why I didn't come home very often. The more I was here, the harder it was to go back. And if I'm not careful I might feel guilty,' she added, pulling a wry face. 'I hadn't even spoken to Mum for two or three weeks.'

I thought of the missed calls. What had Mum wanted to tell me? Her tone on the Monday had seemed... yes, worried. 'Don't feel bad about it,' I said. 'About anything. It's the last thing she would have wanted.'

Feeling guilty myself, I eyed my sister. Fair, classical and beautiful, she was a younger version of Mum. She didn't need to dye her hair nor enhance her boobs to look stunning. But then again, I was more my natural self than I had ever been. I'd gone for an 'alternative' look growing up. 'Alternative to what?' Mum had asked, but in truth the spiky pink hair, torn clothes and dark make-up was *alternative* to my big sister. There was no point emulating her; I'd never be as popular, as blonde or as pretty, so I chose the opposite.

'Ali's attention-seeking as usual,' Laura had always commented. It had never felt that way to me – more a question of hiding. I'd spent so many years as an ugly duckling that I never noticed I was growing into something else, not a swan exactly, but attractive enough.

I must have been staring, as Laura abruptly snorted. 'Yup, botox around the eyes and on my forehead.' She smoothed her flat belly. 'And I only eat one meal a day.'

'Bloody hell, Laura! Don't you get hungry?'

'Yes,' she replied, opening her handbag and plucking out a packet of Marlboro. 'Which is why I still indulge in too many of these.'

I frowned. Mum had recently made a point of telling me Laura had given up cigarettes. It made me feel uneasy, that who-said-what-to-whom discomfort I didn't like. I was relieved we were outside and away from Joe; he already had a mum who apparently 'wasn't herself', so I didn't want him passively smoking. Laura must have followed my thoughts as she said, 'Little thingy is cute. Still ugly, but cute.'

I lifted my eyebrows. 'I hope that's a joke. It's common knowledge that all newborn babies – and brides – are beautiful.'

'Hmm, if you say so, but I'll still opt out of cuddling.'

'No cuddles? Mum says it's the nicest part of being a grandma.' With a jolt of emotion, I corrected myself. 'Said. Getting all the best bits, then giving the baby back.'

Taking a deep drag, Laura looked away. 'It might make me broody.'

'Would that be such a bad thing?' I asked. 'Not that I recommend the delights of pregnancy and birth, but the ugly prize at the end is quite nice,' I said, trying for humour.

'Not when you've been sterilised,' she replied flatly. She glanced at me and shrugged. 'It seemed a good idea at the time. I put on weight with the pill, the coil gave me excruciating periods, and I wasn't about to rely on rubbers.'

I reeled. Bloody hell. *Sterilisation?* Yet was it a complete surprise? 'I'll never get married or have children,' she'd frequently say to Mum. 'So I'm saving you money. Can I have a car instead?'

But Mum would look a little sad and shake her head. 'One day you will, Laura. One day, your own baby will be the most important thing in your life. You'll hold that newborn in your arms and feel a surge of love you can't imagine.'

I now took a deep breath. Laura had always been wilful, doing pretty much everything in the face of sound advice to the contrary. Yet still I was shocked, not only at her deciding to do something so huge and final, but that she'd found a doctor who'd condoned it when she was so young.

'Could it be reversed? If you change your mind?' I asked. 'Surely they can do all sorts of things these days if you have a womb.'

Laura guffawed. 'Do you remember how we hated that word as kids? Womb! Vagina too. And vulva…'

She had changed the subject. As smoothly and expertly as ever.

'Discharge, menstruation and puss…' I added, knowing the conversation was over. Suddenly aware of my full breasts, I looked at my watch. 'Time to face the music?'

She crinkled her nose. 'If we must. Talking of which: your wedding planner…'

I sighed. Madeleine, of course. Like a dolly, I'd complied with her every command: hair by Peter; make-up by Paul. A bespoke ivory silk wedding dress with a train, satin shoes and a floor-length veil; a cake with five tiers and the reception in a fourteenth-century castle. All done with the greatest of taste, as one would expect of my mother-in-law.

Laura was mimicking her enunciation. '*Such a lovely place to rest*. Yeah, in the middle of rickety gravestones, ancient monuments and thistles.' She cocked her head. 'So what was that all about earlier? You being out of sorts?'

I paused before answering. I didn't want to talk about it, even to Laura. Was I unhinged? Maybe. Paranoid? Perhaps. 'Nothing. Just Madeleine being—'

'A psychiatrist?'

'A *retired* psychiatrist.'

'On a busman's holiday?'

That snapshot of Madeleine fired in. Her eyes astonished, her hand to her cheek as she pitched and reeled. Then me, staring at my stinging palm.

'Ali? What's up?'

'Nothing.' I smiled wryly. 'We'd better get back to the *party*. Rein the aunties in.'

Laura stood and lowered her sunglasses. 'Has my mascara smudged?'

Wondering when the tears had come, I nodded.

'Then a trip to the ladies' room is in order, my dear,' she said in her best Mary Poppins voice. 'Let's hope that frightful place has toilets.'

Chapter Ten

We walked down the concrete steps to the village hall. Their edges were still rough like a tooth. I could clearly remember tripping on them and badly grazing my shins. The blood had sparkled and stung and I had wanted to cry, but other school children were behind me and I couldn't bear to hear their laugher.

I nodded to The Sportsman across the road. 'Do you still fancy going in?' I asked Laura with a grin.

'Bloody hell, can you imagine?' She looked pensive as she stared at the sixties-build pub. 'Mum sent Dad to "have words" with Dave. Not that they knew anything specific… But I was so angry at their interference, I refused to speak to either of them. So bloody humiliated; I couldn't get over it for weeks. Then Dad died. It felt as though the two things were linked, that I'd somehow accelerated…' She shook her head. 'A lifetime ago, eh?'

Surprised at her revelation, and the guilt she had clearly felt, I took a breath to comfort her, to say that a rapid-spreading cancer wasn't anyone's fault, but she'd lifted her chin and stepped into the foyer.

At the double doors she turned and raised her eyebrows. 'So what do we think? Unchanged is my bet. Curtains matching the brickwork. And those formica tables. Shades of orange! God help us…'

The room was warm, a glut of people milling in the large, rectangular space. The church hadn't felt empty, but I'd been too preoccupied keeping my gaze fixed on my feet to take in the numbers.

'Perhaps it's the bingo crowd come early for a free glass of sherry,' Laura whispered as we edged past the egg and cress sandwiches towards the toilets.

'Or more likely our cousins and their kids. Any idea how many rellies at the last count?'

'Nope.'

Finally in the ladies', Laura took off her sunglasses and peered at herself in the mirror. 'Good God, I look like a Goth.' She glanced at my handbag. 'What have you got in that bloody satchel to fix the damage?'

I unzipped my old Mulberry. It was large in comparison to her slim clutch, for sure, but not a patch on the sack of baby essentials I usually lugged with me. 'Cheeky mare. Baby wipe or baby wipe?' I replied, offering her the small packet. 'Is it me or is there an aroma of prunes in here?'

'You and your smell obsession. It stinks of shit, Ali. Fruity shit, I grant you. I bet they haven't refurbished these loos for years. They are pretty disgusting.'

I opened a cubicle door and peered in. 'No chains anymore.' I chuckled. 'Maybe we should have sampled the ones at the park—'

'Oh my God. They *were* revolting. Metal panels instead of mirrors; graffiti and faeces on the walls. And tracing-paper loo roll.' She snorted. 'You wouldn't believe the number of boys I snogged in there, though. Mum always seemed to know. "*Girls who get pregnant out of wedlock ruin their lives, Laura.*" Said conversationally as she prepared tea, as though she wasn't being completely obvious.'

'Maybe the smell of poo on your clothes was a clue. Not to mention the love bites.'

'True. But it *was* only snogging—'

'And biting...'

'Bet you've never had a love bite. Have you, Ali?' Laura asked, plucking out an expensive-looking mascara from her purse. 'The good golden girl.'

I self-consciously touched my long ponytail. Over the years I'd tried every feasible shade of hair dye, but I never went blonde. As for length, I eventually grew it for Miles. He liked my hair the Madeleine way: dark, thick and way past my shoulders. People used to say that we looked like sisters, which of course she adored.

'You had the blonde curls; the *real* golden girl,' I commented.

Laura spent a few moments applying lipstick, then replaced the lid with a sharp click. 'Was I really?' Seeming to shake her thoughts away, she straightened her back. 'Sergeant majors are awaiting. Are you ready for the inspection parade?'

–

With admiration – and love – I watched Laura mingle with the mourners. It was how it should be: all eyes were on her – not just her new figure, but her glowing face, her bearing. The aunties and cousins hadn't seen her for some time, so appraisal was inevitable, but she was indeed soldier-like, erect, regular, symmetrical and neat, but with a genial smile like a starlet opening a local fete. Although their colouring was different, she reminded me of Madeleine. Acting, I supposed. Of course I'd been theatrical when needed in court, but on a personal level I'd never been able to pretend. Hiding or avoiding was more my thing. But today I felt surprisingly fine, as though I was in the 'damned village hall' for an auntie's sixtieth birthday celebration or a cousin's wedding reception, rather than the wake of my mother.

In the spirit of positivity, I looked around for Mum's favourite pair of sisters to say hello and give them a tight hug. They had, after all, been genuinely heartbroken at the graveside, and I wanted to thank them for their love. Clocking them at a table, I shuffled past cousins and their noisy offspring queuing for food, but when I was almost by their seats, I could see the two women were in deep conversation. Hovering behind them, I tried not to eavesdrop.

'I just wish I'd picked up that phone.' Oh God, Brenda was crying. And if her slurred voice was anything to go by, a little drunk too. 'I intended to. If I'd known that Eve… I can't believe I let seventeen years fly by without shaking some sense into her.'

I frowned. Seventeen years? She and Mum hadn't spoken for that length of time? Part of me knew I should stop listening, but I was glued to the spot.

'You wouldn't have changed her mind, love,' Peggy was saying. 'We all made her a promise and you broke ranks.'

'But—'

'I know you thought it would be for the best, but it was Eve's call, not yours. She thought you hadn't respected her firm wishes.'

'Of course I had. I wasn't about to say anything; it wasn't my place to. I just thought it was the right time to be truthful and said as much to Eve. Even you must have thought her response was a huge overreaction.'

'In all honesty I did; we all did, but after everything with Doug… Well, perhaps there was more going on than we all…'

As though suddenly sensing my presence, Peggy spun around.

'Oh Alison, love, there you are.'

Though I knew I was blushing, I stepped back and gestured to the food table. 'Just having a nosey at what's on offer.' Then, moving forward for a hug, 'How are you both?'

Peggy patted my back. 'I'm so sorry about your mum, love. She was besotted with little Joe; so pleased he was a boy.'

'Thank you.'

To hide the prickling behind my eyes, I looked at the floor. It was strange; my own loss wasn't tangible but I felt Joe's acutely. He'd settled peacefully in Mum's arms when she'd visited immediately after his birth. He'd never actually remember her, and any feeling of knowing her would be from photographs, but there'd be a void in his life nonetheless, that undefined feeling of something being missing we all suffered with from time to time.

Brenda loudly blew her nose, then clutched me tightly. When she pulled away, she studied me so intently that I froze with alarm. What on earth was she going to say? Then she spoke. 'Is that a little someone I can hear?'

I pricked my ears. Yes, a baby was crying, but it took a few moments to realise it was mine. Feeling a rush in my boobs, I looked down at my shirt. I'd forgotten about Joe, but they clearly hadn't, and they'd missed out on a 'feed'. God, I hoped the breast pads would do their job today.

His skin pink and hair dishevelled from anxious smoothing, Miles appeared through the bodies.

'Where have you been?' he hissed, knitting his pale brow. 'Joe has been passed from pillar to post. I have no idea who half these bloody people are but they seem to know all about me. He was nearly dropped three times. No wonder the poor little sod is crying…'

As he handed Joe over, I noticed Madeleine talking to a man wearing an apron. Quietly but firmly interfering with the catering, in all likelihood. As I watched, she sidled up to my youngest auntie and took her hand. I inwardly sighed. Sucking in poor Patricia with those eyes, no doubt. I turned away then; I didn't want to witness my relatives fawning. I preferred them to be true to themselves – a little barbed or gossipy at times, but good, solid folk who'd go the length to help out.

I glanced back at Brenda. At least that's what I'd always thought. She'd apparently *broken ranks*. What the hell did that mean?

Chapter Eleven

Knowing there was no way I'd breastfeed in public – even discreetly – with Madeleine in the vicinity, I headed for the ladies' again. There wasn't a chair, so the loo seat would have to do. The smell of sour fruit mixed with hairspray and soap was unsettling, but not as much as the thoughts bouncing around in my head.

I tried to replay Brenda and Peggy's exchange word for word, but the cubicle handle was tried every other minute.

'It's only Alison trying to feed Joe!' I called. 'I'll be out in a tick…'

It was a fib and I knew it; with his colicky tummy, it took Joe at least twenty minutes to settle, sometimes longer. But right now I was glad of the excuse to hide. What the hell did that conversation mean? They hadn't specified who 'she' was, but Brenda had mentioned seventeen years… Why was that significant? Laura would have been twenty-two then, whereas I… Oh God. I would have been eighteen, an adult. They had to be talking about me.

I kissed Joe's downy hair and blew the old panic away. I wasn't baby Ali anymore. I was a professional woman, a grown-up, a mother. It was time I got a handle on the stupid fear of hearing something I didn't want to know. Dad had been dead for twenty-five years. It was time I just faced the trauma. And yet part of me still wanted to shrink back into that ten-year-old body.

I sighed. A *promise* to Mum... Clearly a secret the whole family had kept. And 'after everything with Doug'... It was obviously something about Dad. His cancer? But would one express it like that? '*Everything*' with Doug? And '*more going on*'? Bloody hell. Did I want to know? Not really. And yet...

As though she'd heard my internal wrangling, Laura's voice echoed through. 'Open up, Ali. It's me.' She peered through the crack. 'Everything OK? You can cry if you want to. The sunglasses were just...'

So Peggy had sensed my tears earlier. And inevitably sent Laura to investigate. I detached Joe and stepped out of my feeding box. 'I know. I'm fine, actually.'

Laura was still gazing. 'Hmm, strangely so.' She put a hand on her slim hip. 'It didn't occur to me until Peggy came running that I'm in charge of you now.'

'I'm not a bloody dog, Laura.'

'As the head of the Baker family, I'm your next of kin or whatever.'

'No you're not. I'm married to Miles, remember.'

'A fake posh Alexander-Whatever? Hardly; you kept your name. And though Miles is pretty, he *is* completely hopeless—'

'I'm not twelve and I don't need you or anyone else to be *in charge* of me,' I snapped.

Was that true, though? My ridiculous attachment to Dad, then Madeleine... And yes, in a way, Laura too. But right now, that made her comment even worse. She'd always stamped her authority on me, but had never been there when I'd needed her, which just hadn't been fair. Feeling the old disappointment, I rose to the bait.

'You seem to think that because I've had a baby, I've become frail or needy,' I fired out. 'It's just challenging at times, that's all. But it's also the best thing ever, actually. If you hadn't been so stubborn and single-minded as to—'

She dropped her clutch bag on the side and stared at me coldly. 'You need to fix your face.'

'Just like you do? Revealing nothing?' I replied. I put Joe in her arms. 'Here, you can have *thingy* for a while. He's called Joe. I'm sure you'll remember if you practise hard enough.'

Despite my annoyance, her startled expression made my lips twitch. I threw a muslin cloth over her shoulder. 'In case he pukes,' I added, enjoying the moment.

Once she'd left, I spent a little while playing with Laura's few key pieces of posh make-up, painting my face tastefully as Madeleine had taught me. When I finally emerged, the room was half empty. I wryly laughed to myself. I was probably the only daughter in the world to spend her mother's wake on a swing or a loo seat. But then again, I'd had a peculiar sensation alone at the mirror I couldn't quite describe. It had felt like a cushion of comfort surrounding me, nothing visible, but most definitely there.

–

Laura and I returned to the grave before we left. The death notice in the newspaper had asked for a donation to charity instead of flowers, but there were several bouquets laid over the loose, drying soil. Crouching each side, we leaned forward to read the messages.

'Oh bugger it,' I said, sitting on a mound of bleached grass.

'Dodgy fanny, I suppose,' Laura commented. Scraping her hair back with her sunglasses, she read out loud. '"Do not stand at my grave and weep; I am not there. I do not sleep." From Tom and Joan Hague. Who would've thought they'd be so creative?'

'They didn't spend hours at Bureside writing it, Laura. It's a well known bereavement poem.' The attachment I'd had for them at seven or eight abruptly swelled in my chest. 'I'm surprised they didn't travel up today. I wish they had.'

'What?' Laura snorted. 'For one of Tom's dodgy cuddles?'

'He was just being affectionate. Don't be rotten.'

'Rich coming from you. You hated poor Joan and her earrings. Ran away and hid under that ugly black piece of furniture in the hall. What did Mum call it? That's right, the *chiffonier*.'

'Only at first.' I smiled wryly. 'I pretty much disliked any strangers. I was convinced they brought on the spooky dreams.'

'Those bloody nightmares. I wasn't keen on them either. Having you climbing in my cosy bed and—'

'Breathing! "*Stop breathing, Ali, or you can sleep on your own…*"'

Laura laughed. 'Poor you; I guess that was a tall order.' Her eyes glazing, she looked into the distance. 'I finally got my own bedroom that last summer…' She sighed deeply. 'They should have told us about Dad's cancer. Mum should've told me. Why didn't she? Even now I don't get it.' She frowned. 'Maybe that's why she was so ratty with me, with us all. Do you remember? She pretty much stayed in The Lodge the whole holiday and refused to go anywhere with us. If I had known, I'd have been around more, made an effort. But she didn't say a word. It still makes me feel…' Her voice trailed off.

Filling the silence, I went back to the poem.

'I wonder who wrote it. "I am not dead". But that's how it feels, don't you think?' I asked.

Feeling a ripple of movement, I glanced over my shoulder. No one was there. Mum's 'presence' would be a crazy thing to mention, but despite the usual exhaustion creeping in, there was definitely a sense of calm and comfort enveloping me. I wondered if Laura felt the same, but she shrugged.

'You and your notions, Ali. Sometimes you sound like Dad and his poems were rubbish.'

She didn't say it kindly and it smarted. It wasn't just her ability to put me down with a few choice words, but how she spoke about Dad.

'I don't recognise half of these names, do you?' she asked eventually, and when I didn't reply: 'Her art class, do you think? Maybe they were childhood friends, or Dad's old clients.' She tossed a tiny pebble into my lap, hunched her shoulders and squinted one eye. 'Or maybe the half breeds from Norfolk?'

'Not nice,' I said, relenting. 'They all seem to be from men. "Here's to the good times we had" from Clive. And from Oliver: "I'm glad we met again". And this one is from Ted: "To the Sunniest Girl in the office".'

'Maybe they were all Mum's lovers…' Laura replied, teasingly. 'Especially if *Oliver* was Oliver Tobias with his come-to-bed-with-me eyes. She must have watched *The Stud* twenty times.'

I gave my sister a hard stare. I didn't want to be reminded of my rude behaviour whenever I'd been introduced to one of Mum's 'new friends'. Laura had been bad, but egged on by her, I was far worse. Yet in some ways it had been a good time; Laura and I absolutely on side.

Laura snorted. 'I know; all those creepy *uncles* who appeared out of the woodwork. I don't think she liked them any more than we did. The name Ted sounds familiar, though. I think she worked with him before she got married. Clive, too.'

'When she was a *civil servant*, don't you know!'

'That's because she was the only girl in the family who went to *grammar school*.'

'Married an accountant and had a cleaning lady.'

'And a new car every September...'

'A holiday home too...'

I frowned; I'd never thought of the money angle before. 'How on earth did Dad afford it all? A pretty meteoric rise from his tiny office in Walkley.'

'Not that Mum ever mentioned *Walkley* at the golf club...'

We smiled. Evelyn Baker could be such a snob, but she was *our* snob. We stared at the mound for a moment longer, then Laura stood up and held out her hand. 'A quick peek at *Kellogg's*?' she asked, using the nickname for our old family home. 'Then I think we're done.'

–

Once Joe was settled in, Miles drove the short journey to our childhood house. Dad had commissioned the new build in the late seventies, and someone had famously described it as looking like a 'cereal box', so the joke had stuck. I knew what they meant – long and symmetrical with large plain windows, it looked unimaginative from the outside, but inside it was more interesting with its central split-level design, 'sunken' lounge and three sets of stairs.

A memory flew back at me as I gazed: Laura, leaning over the top landing to see how far down my spiral Slinky toy extended. I was whinging, of course. '*You'll break it, you'll stretch the spring!*' And Mum, her face astonishingly bleached with anger. '*Stop it, Laura. Just stop it. Never do that again. Do you hear me?*'

Reaching for a fonder memory, I looked to the side garden. Though partially hidden by trees, the rusty double swing was still there, *our* double swing. Wondering if she'd registered it, I glanced at Laura, but her Ray-Bans were back on. She was tired, so was I, astonishingly so.

I once read that bereavement was like a large black hole that got smaller with time. For me, the gaping abyss seemed to grow when my dad died. Consumed by grief, the darkness followed me everywhere: I breathed it, smelled it, touched it and ate it, even during rest, when sleep terrors plagued me. Eventually, a night came when I didn't dream at all. The void had closed a tiny fraction and continued to contract as each year went by. But it wasn't until the house was sold that I was able to say, 'My father died when I was ten years old,' without crying.

I'd always supposed Mum somehow knew I needed that closure; that she'd needed it too, but had waited until I was at university, had accommodation and was settled before moving away. But Brenda's words were echoing in my head: *the right time to be truthful...* About what? And: *Eve's response was a huge overreaction...* What was the 'huge overreaction'? Was it selling the Kellogg's box and transferring her whole life to Norfolk? If so, what on earth was Mum running from?

Chapter Twelve

Laura stayed with us for the rest of the week. We considered a quick trip to Horning, but, to my relief, she was shattered and couldn't face the prospect of the five-hour journey before an even longer flight home. Any free time she had was usually consumed by wining and dining business people, or catching up with paperwork she didn't have a chance to read at work, so she fancied a few days to chill out. I understood completely, but it was funny to hear the words roll off my sister's tongue. The Laura who left home at eighteen had flunked her A levels and spent most of her life on the Parker Knoll sofa in our cornflake-box lounge, only becoming animated when she was going out; how times had changed.

Though I still struggled with peeing, my pelvic floor and soothing Joe's tetchiness, it was lovely to have Laura around. She didn't venture outside, not even for a smoke. Finally discarding the sunglasses, she donned a T-shirt and jogging bottoms, curled up on the sofa and didn't move.

'Ditch your bloody mobile, Miles. You're on catering duty,' she directed on Friday morning. 'Your wife has presented you with a son and heir and I'm on holiday. Bring anything that's bad for us. Things I can't buy at home.'

Raking fingers through his hair, Miles was genuinely perturbed. 'Oh, God. Like what? Do you mean a take-out? And what type? Or I'll go to the supermarket if you want, but I'll really need a written—'

'Mashed potato and mushy peas; apple crumble with custard; eggy bread with ketchup; minced beef and onion pie with… God, yes, Henderson's Relish…'

Laura's list surprised me; it was all the winter stodge we'd either hated or taken for granted as kids. She scrunched her face. 'I know! A pork bread-cake dipped in the dripping, with crackling and apple sauce! Wouldn't that be good, Ali?'

'Bread-cake? What's that then?' Miles asked and we laughed. But at the end of the day Laura's culinary desires needed to be home-cooked by our mum. I could have attempted the mashed potatoes or even the eggy bread, but how to bake the meat pie or make custard from scratch was a mystery to us both.

We settled on a fish and chips lunch. Miles dutifully delivered it before leaving again to catch up at work, saying he'd be back when he was back and to have fun without him. Though still glued to his phone, he'd been away from chambers since the funeral, so I understood the need to get on top of his paperwork, but I suspected Laura's menu had freaked him, especially the crackling.

'Working-class food!' as his mother would say. I could visualise her uttering it with the slightest wrinkle in her otherwise perfect nose. She hadn't been in touch, but that wasn't surprising. Neither she nor Laura had said anything, but I'd always sensed a stand-off on the rare occasions they'd met. Perhaps my sister had had the measure of Madeleine long before I did.

–

That evening I succumbed to a glass of chilled prosecco. I felt faintly guilty about drinking alcohol, and Joe even paused his colicky grumbling to give me a curious peep, but I'd done everything by the book throughout pregnancy and birth, and look where that had got me. It was nice to savour the cold warmth in my throat and after a second glass I felt just a little bit pissed, good company for Laura, who was well on her way.

'Why have you hidden that photo of Mum and Dad?' she asked suddenly, mid conversation about a new house she fancied on a Sheffield-like hill in Delta.

'What photo?' I said, though I knew perfectly well.

Laura teetered to the bookcase and pulled out the framed Baker family portrait. 'Hmm. Hidden between *Wuthering Heights* and *Jane Eyre*. Is that significant?'

I snorted to cover my embarrassment. 'Probably more noteworthy that you were eyeing up a Brontë novel to read. You must be missing Yorkshire.'

She studied the smiling image of the four of us, then turned it to me. 'Ali the pixie. How old were you here?'

Dad was in it, so I was younger than ten. But as though Laura had had the same thought, she looked rueful and slipped it back where she'd found it.

I took a sharp breath. I'd wanted to discuss my eavesdropped conversation with Laura since Wednesday, but I hadn't quite decided how to put it. What did I want to say or to know? But the moment my question popped out, I knew Dad was the crux. Somewhere along the line, Mum hadn't told us everything about him.

'Do you know something about Dad that I don't?'

Her response was clear surprise. 'Dad? Like what, for example?'

I stroked Joe's hair. 'I don't know.' *After everything with Doug…* Peggy had said.

I sighed. 'I was ten, and I guess not the easiest of kids to talk to. Maybe you were told more than me about what was going on.'

'I wasn't. Like I said the other day, neither of them told me about Dad's illness. I didn't understand why at the time and I still don't now. It really pisses me off when I think about it.'

So Laura didn't know anything more than me. It was a relief, if I was honest. 'Maybe they were protecting us?' I suggested. 'Giving us one last carefree summer?'

'Perhaps.' Laura didn't sound convinced. 'But Mum was definitely off with me.' She smiled thinly. 'Even more so than usual.'

'What do you remember about Dad?'

She shrugged. 'The usual – indulging you mostly.' She frowned. 'But he stayed for the whole six week holiday, so that was different.'

I nodded; I remembered that too.

'And frequent outings in Tom Hague's Rolls-Royce…' She raised her eyebrows. 'Maybe hospital appointments?' She glanced at the bookcase. 'Why are you asking now?'

I couldn't quite shape an answer to that one. Instead, I kissed Joe's lolling head. 'Bedtime for this one,' I said. 'I'll take him up for his last feed.'

'Can I come too?' she asked.

I'd got used to my sister's inspection of my fumbling breastfeeding technique and sharp intake of breath when Joe clamped on. 'Of course.'

She followed me to Joe's nursery, sat on the small sofa and watched silently as I fed him.

'Oh God, Ali. I wish I wasn't so impetuous at times,' she eventually whispered, putting her hands to her face.

I waited for her to say more.

'I've met someone. Someone really nice. He's not said it exactly but he's hinting about us settling down and having kids…'

Ah, the house on a hill. 'And you haven't told him about…?'

Laura shook her head. My heart went out to her. She could share the most intimate details of her life to a stranger, yet couldn't confide in a person she really loved. For fear of losing him, I supposed. So much in life came to that.

'Oh Laura.' I took her hand. 'You have to tell him, surely? If he is worth loving, and if he really loves you, then he'll understand.'

She nodded, but stayed silent. My sister didn't like being given advice, even if it was sound. Well, who did? It reminded me of Madeleine, whose words of wisdom had become uncomfortable and intrusive eventually. No wonder I'd hidden that family photograph.

Back in the lounge, I curled up on the sofa and took a deep breath. 'So tell me about your man,' I said, peering out of the window. 'I'd love to hear everything about him…'

Taking in a gorgeous band of peachy-orange sky, I steadied myself for the rebuff I'd become accustomed to as a child, when a four-year age gap made all the difference: *Are you still a virgin, Laura? Do you have a boyfriend? Have you ever taken drugs? Who were you kissing at the park? What exactly is masturbation?*

'*Shut up and get lost!*' had been the usual sharp retort. It had worked every time; I'd clam up and sulk for days, trying to work out why Laura spoke to everyone about everything, but didn't talk to me.

An instinctive sunny smile was today's immediate response. 'He's called Brian, of all names. But he's from Birmingham, so I call him Shelby. I finally find a man I like and he's bloody English.' She turned her glass, watching the bubbles. 'He's thirty-nine, divorced, nice-looking and incredible in the sack.'

I chuckled. 'Is that in any particular order of importance?'

'No… but good in bed is pretty vital, don't you think?'

I laughed again and took a sip of my wine. I wasn't about to discuss my sex life, nor the larger-than-salad-sized forceps which had been used to drag out poor Joe, but Laura didn't seem to notice my reticence.

'Mostly, I've found sex disappointing over the years,' she said thoughtfully. 'Even after I got the hang of doing it for me and not for them. I can't recall a single one-night stand when I actually came.'

'So all that practice didn't make perfect?' I asked with raised eyebrows.

She gave me a soft thump on the arm. 'Oh come on, Ali. Even you must have really fancied someone and been desperate to shag the arse off him. Surely you've had… what do they call them? Beer goggles or something like that. When a bloke seems so attractive and funny when you've had a bottle of wine, then in the cruel light of day…'

I smiled politely, but in truth, I'd never been like that. I had a couple of clinches in my teens, but didn't lose my virginity until my long-term Scouser boyfriend, Sidney, who was still a friend to this day. I fancied Miles of course, but that had been a gradual thing. On the rare occasions I had the stirrings of attraction for somebody, I had an irrational desire to escape. Fear of abandonment, I supposed, taking steps to preempt the inevitable. It was only because I was at uni with Sidney and worked with Miles that I wasn't able to do just that. Then there were a couple of incidents in between, sexual disasters I had kept to myself.

I laughed at the sudden impulse to share.

'What?' Laura asked.

'Do you remember I went on holiday to Tel Aviv with Mum after bar school? I met a man in the hotel reception and he asked me out for a drink. I've no idea why I said yes, but the next thing I knew I was in his car being driven miles away in the black night to his flat. He was an Israeli soldier with a very small penis. Does that count?'

Laura's mouth dropped open. 'Ali! That's scary. You might've been raped and murdered.'

'I know! No mobile phone either. I wasn't drunk; I didn't fancy him at all. I don't know why I did it.'

I hadn't thought of this memory for years. The soldier had stood me naked in front of a full-length mirror. 'Look,' he'd said. 'Just look how beautiful you are.'

I'd had intercourse with him even though I hadn't particularly wanted to, but the fact he'd thought me beautiful was a complete revelation.

'Did you ever tell Mum?'

'God, no. "*Be careful, don't jump in, think of the consequences first…*"'

'And annoyingly right most of the time.'

I was thoughtful for a beat. 'Maybe I'm too like her. Doing things by the book. Nothing impulsive in case I end up with egg on my face. Fear of humiliation, I suppose.'

'Though possible rape and murder didn't bother you in Israel...'

'I know! Isn't that strange?'

'But you're happy now. Caution has made you happy, hasn't it? With Miles?' Laura asked, peering at me.

I nodded, deeply wanting the same for her. 'You know you have to keep in touch far more often now you're "in charge" of me, don't you?' I said.

'Absolutely.' She pulled me against her shoulder. Then she laughed. 'Orphans, eh? Who'd have bloody thought.'

Chapter Thirteen

Sunday came around far too soon.

I felt soulful and lost as I watched Laura pack her small suitcase. She had promised to visit more often, but the closeness I'd felt over the last few days suddenly seemed nebulous. Mum was the glue that had held us together, those daughter-to-mother-to-daughter conversations I had always mistrusted had gone. Save for dead parents, we had nothing in common any more. Would I have chosen Laura as a friend if she wasn't my sister? Would she have picked me? Probably not, if I was honest.

The unrelenting sunshine on our backs, we climbed in my car in heavy silence. I sat on one buttock, carefully slipped on my seatbelt and glanced at Laura's to be sure she'd done the same.

'Do you really need to sit like that?' she asked eventually. Her voice was clipped and the Ray-Bans were back in place.

I tried not to bristle. 'Dodgy fanny, remember?'

I didn't mention that the episiotomy cut was after a failed ventouse delivery. '*Did you know they use something resembling a toilet plunger and put on Wellington boots and a plastic mac like Paddington Bear?*' I thought of quipping. But that would have been insensitive and unkind – Laura wouldn't be having a baby any time soon. Yesterday I had asked if she'd consider adoption or even surrogacy if IVF wasn't an option, but she'd just frowned, so her reticence now made the subject taboo.

But today the direct-talking big sister was back. 'Weeks have passed since the birth, Ali. I'm sure it's just habit now. Besides, it looks weird.'

Weird, odd. Tired, tearful. Ali not bloody Ali.

Irked at her comment, I glanced at her dark shades. 'Why do you wear those bloody things all the time?' I asked.

'So the world doesn't know what I'm thinking.'

I snorted. 'But you always tell everyone what's on your mind.'

'I share what I want them to know,' she replied, turning to the passenger window.

I set off for the airport. Perhaps I wasn't entirely surprised at her answer. She certainly gave the impression of being open, telling people all manner of things I considered to be very personal. But humans were paradoxes: I'd been the secretive and private child, yet found it difficult to hide my feelings. Try as I might, my face gave me away. I suppose that's why I'd retreated if I was emotional; I hid so no one would know what was going on inside. There was a thought: maybe the painted features, bizarre clothes and dyed hair had been the equivalent of my sister's sunglasses.

'What were you contemplating when you looked at our old house, then?' I asked eventually.

Slipping down her Ray-Bans, she studied me. 'Do you really want to know?'

'Yes. That's why I've asked, Laura.'

'Nothing,' she replied. 'I thought of nothing at all.'

I turned to her quizzically but she laughed, dryly.

'Look, that's good, Ali. I paid a lot of money to get there...'

'What? You mean you've had therapy or counselling?' I asked, trying to keep my eyes focused on the busy motorway despite my buzzing mind.

'Yup.'

It was silly to be shocked, but I was. Laura had always been so confident and certain, so completely together. 'But why?' I corrected my knee-jerk response. 'Sorry; it's none of my business; I'm just surprised.'

Laura sighed. 'You always did squeeze your eyes so tightly shut...' She took a shuddery breath. 'Why do you think I went halfway across the world when I was just eighteen? Why do you think I escaped as soon as I could?'

I shook my head; I didn't know. I was fourteen when Laura left for Canada; we had no mutual interests. I was a nuisance; we barely spoke.

'I was unhappy, of course! I never felt loved, even when I was small. Well, perhaps by Dad sometimes. But Mum; she just didn't—'

'How can you say that?' I hotly interrupted. 'Of course she loved you dearly. She was horrendously upset when you left. She missed you constantly; she couldn't hide her delight when a postcard arrived. She watched the flaming telephone, willing it to ring. "*It's lunchtime now in Canada. Perhaps Laura will call today*". She was always the first to the post, snatching it up with bated breath.'

'It worked two ways, Ali. And I was still the child, she the adult. Why didn't she call me?'

'I don't know, she never said. But I guess it was because she thought that you were having fun, that you had better things to do than be bothered by your mother! She was old-fashioned; it was rude if people called when we were

73

eating dinner or after ten o'clock at night, remember? She wouldn't want to intrude in your life or the family you lived with. Before you left, you'd disappeared every evening to your friend's house or the pub. Why would it be any different in Canada?'

'I scarpered because I couldn't stand all the constant criticism from her. I don't know what she wanted or expected from her first child but I wasn't it. For as long as I can remember it was as though I'd let her down. I never felt good enough. I really did try, Ali, to be clever and polite, speak when I was spoken to, say please and thank you, behave impeccably in public and all those other bloody rules she had. You know what it was like; she didn't need to say anything, she'd just have that sharp look if we fell out of line, if *I* fell out of line...' She blew out. 'I guess I thought I might as well be that bad person, the "difficult teenager" she projected onto me. Sex with older men, dressing provocatively, smoking, a few drugs, skiving school, doing no homework, flunking exams...'

We fell quiet then. I felt the tension radiate from Laura's being. She was waiting for my response, but I didn't know what to say. Mum did have those outdated ways, but they weren't prescriptive; she never smacked us or was cruel. They were just a generational thing and it was easy to comply.

I thought back to Mum. '*Laziness, Laura. And ingratitude. What a dreadful waste of school fees. Cash doesn't grow on trees. Dad made sacrifices for your education. And so did I,*' she'd say crisply. But she'd always worried about finances and was careful with money. True, she had sometimes been critical of Laura's appearance, but I had never realised it was so bad, nor that it had cut Laura so deeply.

God, perhaps I had been blind. Laura's defiance, the '*I hate you!*', the frequent stomping and slamming had been part of my childhood; I'd assumed it was simply a rebellious daughter thing.

My skin tingled as I drove. *Eyes so tightly shut…* Was this the only thing I hadn't 'seen'?

'Did you ever tell Mum how you felt?' I asked eventually.

Laura took a while to reply. 'No. The therapist thought it might give me closure if I did and I was full of resolve to tackle it when I next visited her. But when we got together it was so lovely to see her and I didn't want to spoil the nice time we were having.'

As the airport came in sight, I considered what to say, but Laura spoke again. 'Looking back, I think she would have given me a truthful reply if I'd asked. We had become more like friends, I suppose, more open and honest. I think we were better suited as adults, if you know what I mean.'

I nodded. I'd once read an article about different mother-types. There were five sorts, apparently: perfectionist, unpredictable, best friend, me-first and complete. Madeleine was 'me-first', undoubtedly; perhaps Mum was a 'perfectionist'. But after only a few weeks, I understood motherhood wasn't plain sailing. One could only do one's best. I so wanted to do that for Joe, yet what sort of mother would I be?

We were approaching the car park entrance. It was time to say goodbye to my sister.

'If you pull up I'll get out here and save you the cost of parking,' she said. She laughed. 'See? I am my mother's daughter after all.'

We hugged tightly. When Laura moved away, she stroked back a loose strand of my hair and smiled thinly. 'I don't know anything more than you about Dad, but don't go chasing shadows, Ali. If Mum had wanted you to know something, she'd have told you.'

Wiping the tears from my eyes, I watched her elegantly stride to the terminal. Then worry took over my sadness. There *had* been something Mum wanted to tell me. What the hell was it?

Chapter Fourteen

July morphed into August and the solid heat soldiered on, but my grief wasn't remotely comparable to the collapse of my world at age ten. Indeed, it was so vague that I had to remind myself not to call Mum for a chat, or mentally store the day-to-day mundanity we usually discussed – the death of a film star she particularly liked, the yo-yo price of milk, a new TV drama, the fewer incidences of Joe's mad colic moments.

When Joe napped I tried to focus on her death, but my thoughts were shallow and painless, that strange blanket of comfort still there. But I did cry easily. Little things got me down – Miles's white work shirts tinged green from just one cheap flannel in the washer, the inevitable demise of the petunia in my hanging baskets, a broken best plate. Big things too, like my lack of energy, which was exacerbated by a heavy cold and an intensely sore throat that wouldn't shift.

Although the breastfeeding had become easier and Joe's colicky bouts less frequent, I found myself lying awake when I should be sleeping, obsessing about his next cry and my tiredness. I became swamped by the responsibility of providing milk for him myself and not giving in to the box of formula in the fridge. The 'perfectionist' mother was usurping me when I so wanted to be 'complete' and give Joe the best of all types. Then there was Norfolk, bloody Norfolk, calling me. At night, my mind tried to grasp all the threads of *something* and piece them together, but I was so very weary. I would go there soon; I just needed to get better first.

I had no doubt that Madeleine continued her subterfuge with Miles, but she called me most days too, asking if I was in for 'a little visit'. The thought of her looking into my soul with those searching eyes felt overwhelming, so each time I reached for a chirpy voice and said I was out and about with Joe, and that we'd pop in to hers on Saturday. When the weekend came, I couldn't bear the inevitable analysis, so I sent Miles with Joe alone.

On the fifth evening of my painful throat, I rummaged through the bathroom cabinet in desperation. I stared at an old blister packet of codeine, then pushed two out and threw them back with a slurp of water from the tap. Convinced they'd rush immediately from my oesophagus to my mammary glands, I laid my head on the pillow, ready for guilt. Instead, blissful unconsciousness was almost immediate.

Moments later I jerked awake with a thunderous jolt. My nose and my throat were clogged, my heart speeding and thundering. Oh God; my lungs were solid, my chest exploding. I couldn't breathe, I couldn't gasp, I couldn't even scream.

A cardiac arrest for certain; if I didn't do something I'd die.

I groped for Miles but his side of the bed was empty. Propelled by the horrendous thought of leaving Joe motherless, I forced myself up and leaned forward, battling to suck in air, fighting the faint as the walls caved in.

It took only seconds, yet the awareness I wasn't dying but having a panic attack was excruciatingly slow. By the time Miles sauntered into the room with a sleepy yawn, I was sitting cross-legged on our bed. Cold droplets of sweat dripped down my spine and I was shivering.

'Ali?' He did a double-take. 'What's wrong? What's happened?'

'I woke up and couldn't breathe. An anxiety attack, I think...' Tears fell from my eyes. 'But I was so scared, Miles. It was horrible; I truly thought I was dying...'

His concerned expression fell away, shortly followed by resignation, a 'what the fuck next?' type of look. He'd clearly never had a panic attack. Until then neither had I, and it was difficult to explain how it had felt, the metallic taste in my mouth, the sharp pains in my chest, the sheer terror, even when reason kicked in.

He grudgingly asked if I was OK, climbed into bed and turned away, his breathing soon rhythmic and heavy. Pushing away the ragged fear of it happening again, I focused on the comforting sound and his presence, closed my eyes and willed sleep to come.

The hairs abruptly erect on my arms, my body real-ised sooner than me that someone else was in the room. Without looking I knew – a figure by the door, inching towards me, its bleached hand held high, a glint of metal catching the light. Was this real? Yes, God yes. I could clearly hear the low hum of busy insects, I could *smell* the stale blood. Realisation dawning, I stared at Joe's cot; oh my God, the malevolent presence wasn't coming for me, but for him.

Bursting from the nightmare, I sat up and muttered under my breath to reason with myself. Everything was fine. It was simply a bad dream. It was not a hallucination, a vision or premonition. I flicked my head to Miles's pillow. He hadn't woken, thank God. The panic attack was one thing, but I knew better than to even hint about this to him.

–

Miles left a Post-it by the bed the next day: *Hope your cold is much better this morning. Please make an appointment for your throat xxxx P.S. Still OK for tonight?*

The anxiety episode wasn't mentioned in the note, nor when he telephoned and suggested I have a chat with his mum, but the unspoken words were there: *You're not normal, you need help.*

Part of me understood his irritation and reticence. Last night had been embarrassing. Hell, *I* was embarrassed. I'd shown weakness and vulnerability, and he wasn't cut out for the role of supporter or carer. He wanted life to be smooth and stable and easy. Clearly Ali wasn't being Ali again. She was slightly crazy for having such a wacky incident. Or even worse, making it up.

I did as I was told. Facing the doctor was preferable to Madeleine, but I drew the short straw at the emergency surgery. The list was running late and the look on the GP's face was not dissimilar to Miles's when I tried to explain just how raw my throat felt. I embellished by describing the knock-on effect of lack of sleep, but the doctor's eye contact was with the computer screen and not with me.

'Ah, a few blips along the way with baby,' she commented. The inevitable questions followed: How was I coping? Had the health visitor stopped coming? Had I had my postnatal check? Was I getting out of the house? Did I feel listless and low? Any feelings of guilt, hopelessness and self-blame?

I saw where this was going. Give the 'sore throat' a name, prescribe anti-depressants, tick the box, job done. It felt like a conspiracy. But perhaps that was just paranoia.

Laura would've been proud. In a suitably clipped tone, I said the check-up had been fine, feeding a breeze, motherhood hunky dory... and would she just examine my bloody throat.

The mask didn't last long. By the time I arrived home I was blubbering into Joe's blue blanket, wondering what had happened to the woman who'd stood in court and ruthlessly cross-examined witnesses until she prevailed. The GP had taken a cursory look in my mouth and declared it a virus that would go eventually, I just had to be patient. The old me would have argued until she wrote a damned prescription, but the current me was a wreck without balls.

No antibiotics, no miracle cure, I thought as I saturated Joe's bedding. Miles would not be happy.

Chapter Fifteen

I was wrong; Miles was on cloud nine when he arrived home, momentarily at least.

He'd had a drink; I could tell from his sing-song voice. 'Ali, darling? We're here! Where's my beautiful boy?' I heard him call from the front door.

I was feeding Joe upstairs, willing him to sleep. '*We?*' I mused, followed seconds later with a jolt of realisation. Oh God, was it really tonight? Miles had written it on the calendar last week. And, fuck, he'd even mentioned it on this morning's Post-it. It was only a quick visit from a couple of barristers, but still…

How had Miles put it? '*It's no big deal, Ali. They'll drop their bags, meet my son and heir. We'll have a snifter or two before going on to the function…*'

Bloody hell; bloody hell!

'Down in five,' I called back, popping my wide-eyed boy in his cot.

I dashed to the bathroom and studied the damage in the mirror. My hair was in a limp ponytail, my dark eyes still stinging from excessive self-pity and my top was blotted with baby puke. I scrubbed my face vigorously, changed my T-shirt for a blouse and sprayed perfume to cover the likely pong. But I hadn't cleaned the house, so the state of downstairs was out of my hands. My only hope was that Miles's 'heir' would be a distraction.

Following the sound of laughter, I carried Joe through the lounge, trying to rise above the scattered cushions and toys, the empty crisp packet and half eaten sandwich, the abandoned mugs of congealing milky drinks. Stopping at the kitchen door, I took a deep breath. Oh God; the basket of damp washing, the tower of dirty dishes, the heap of nappy bags I hadn't yet taken outside... Miles would be angry. He was proud of his house; he'd want it to be gleaming.

I shook my head. He'd want me to be shiny too, but the sparkle had all gone, replaced by this frail and needy person. The thought burned my nose, but I puffed it away; I had to get a bloody grip.

I pushed down the door handle. 'Hello everyone! Here's baby Joe to say hi...'

Though I said it brightly, the conversation abruptly stopped. Four sets of eyes stared at me: one cold and annoyed, two polite and attentive. And the fourth? Well, that pair was female and loaded with fake sympathy.

'Ali, you poor thing! Miles said you were under the weather. I guess caring for a baby must be harder than it looks. How's it all going?'

Julia bloody Lambert, of course. Had Miles mentioned she'd be one of the visitors? More likely than not she'd got wind of the plan and tagged along with her turned-up nose, polished accent and glossy cheeks.

True to form, her attention for another woman lasted all of two seconds. She'd already turned to Miles, now holding Joe, and was positively cooing. 'Hello little boy! Golly, he's so like you Milo! Mini-Milo, that's what I'll call him. He's just gorgeous, isn't he?'

Fixing a smile on my face, I turned to the two men. Both fairly new recruits to chambers, I had met them before but couldn't remember their names. 'Has Miles offered you a drink? Sorry about the mess. I had completely…' I crouched down to the wine rack. Hoping the dust wasn't as obvious to them as it suddenly struck me, I plucked out a bottle. 'This Amarone looks a nice one. We do have white, but it hasn't been chilled. Sorry, I should have—'

'It needs to breathe, Ali, you know that,' Miles interrupted, his voice almost staccato. 'We have gin, don't we? And tonic in the garage? Surely we can manage that for our guests?'

The tears pricked my eyes. 'Of course, I'll just check. Back in a—'

'And food, Ali? *Nibbles*, remember?' Stepping closer, he glared, his jaw tight. 'We've all been at work, we're hungry,' he hissed in a low voice. 'No one was expecting a three-course meal, but there's an M&S Simply Food in the village, for God's sake.' His face was ruddy with irritation. 'Ready-made canapés, spring rolls, sausages, even bloody crisps.'

Joe started to bawl behind me. Ignoring it, I scooped up my car keys. 'They'll still be open. I'll go now.' I smiled at the young men. 'I'm just popping out for a few snacks. It'll literally take me two minutes…'

Pink with embarrassment, they shook their heads, murmuring that it was fine, they weren't hungry, just a drink would be nice.

'OK; great. I'll just grab the…' Praying for tonic water, I headed for the garage.

Julia's eloquent tones followed in my wake. 'For God's sake let's just go,' she said. 'This kitchen stinks of baby shit and Ali looks bloody dreadful. We've only an hour to kill.

Let's go to the pub.' Then her high-pitched tinkle, 'Oh come on Milo, cheer up. I'm sure they'll do *nibbles*.'

–

Though dropping with fatigue, I made myself stay awake for Miles's return in the early hours. I needn't have worried about missing it. Sleeping through the hum of the taxi and loud conversation with the driver, let alone the slamming front door and thundering footfall up the stairs, wouldn't have been easy.

'Miles, I'm so sorry about earlier,' I began when he finally reached the bedroom. 'It's just that—'

'Don't start,' he interrupted, lifting a hand. His hair was dishevelled, his blue eyes charged. 'I have an important trial coming up, Ali. I know the last few weeks have been hard, but I need some normality too. A regular wife, a stable home, food on the table, bloody sleep. I'm unbelievably stressed. Can't you, just for once, stop being so bloody self-obsessed and think about me?'

It felt like a sharp, unwarranted slap, but I took a deep breath. He was stressed, that was all. The high profile case was listed for several weeks in London. The other parties were represented by Queen's Counsel, so he'd been lucky to get the brief. He'd always worried about work, and being the only junior barrister on the case was scary, so I suspected imposter syndrome was elbowing in. 'Nibbles' and house-cleaning apart, I had neglected him too. He wasn't used to that: Madeleine had flitted in and out of a hands-on mother role, but he'd had nannies or au pairs in between. He'd always been cosseted and loved; he wasn't emotionally equipped for the roles to be reversed.

His speech petulant and slurred, he eventually came to the point. 'Look at the house! Look at you! You're a mess, a bloody embarrassment. Mum wants to help. I don't understand why you won't let her. Don't understand you. You're a stranger. Going to bed now. In there. Don't wake me.'

Without even taking a pee, he shuffled to the spare room and banged the door behind him. Trying to rein in the hurt and overwhelming sense of loss, I pulled up the duvet. Did I really smell a woman's perfume in his wake? Was my marriage imploding? Would Miles leave me? I had a tiny baby; how on earth would I cope if he did?

Chapter Sixteen

Though over a week passed, Miles didn't come back to our bedroom. He worked long hours in chambers, and in the evenings he barely spoke. Only Joe bridged the void between us. '*I need you, Miles*,' I wanted to say, but did that sound *self-obsessed*? Knocked by the panic attack and the old nightmare, my confidence was so low that I wasn't sure of anything anymore. But I had to do something to break the stalemate, so I dragged myself up at six on Friday morning to make him his favourite breakfast. The effort of pulling out the griddle pan felt huge, but I persevered with hash browns, black pudding, crispy bacon and scrambled eggs.

I couldn't face eating any myself, but after he'd finished, I put my hand on his. 'I miss you, Miles. Don't let's drift apart.'

His replete expression turned into a scowl. 'Why do you always bring these things up when I'm on my way to work?' he muttered. 'What am I supposed to do when you push me away?'

I looked at him questioningly. He was still in his dressing gown, so hardly en route. And how on earth had I 'pushed him away'? I'd had the baby we both wanted. It had been tough, that was true, but it wasn't my fault and I was trying my best. There was Mum, but I had barely mentioned her death. And it wasn't me who'd moved into the spare bloody bedroom.

But Miles shook his head and scraped back his chair. 'You always were a cold fish, Ali,' he said over his shoulder before leaving the room.

His description stayed with me throughout the morning. While Joe napped, I tried to focus on chores – the dusty surfaces, the grimy bathroom, the flaming ironing pile which seemed to grow faster than knotweed – but listless thoughts consumed me. Perhaps he was right. Maybe I was cold. Unloveable, too. But capable of deep love, surely? I'd instinctively held back any unguarded devotion after Dad died, but as his own mother had said to me, 'But darling, who wouldn't?'

And what about my mum? Had I 'pushed her away' by not taking those calls and cutting off her need to say something? Oh God, probably. And now I'd never know what it was…

The sound of the knocker interrupted my contemplation. The condolence cards and flowers had petered out, but I hoped it was the DPD guy with a parcel for Joe. Still dressed in my pyjamas, I cracked open the door. Bloody hell; Madeleine. I'd just thought of the devil and now here she was, carrying her white Bichon Frise. Before I'd had chance to take stock, she'd swept into the house.

'Hello darling. I was just passing,' she said, as though that would wash.

Her eyes huge and soft, she studied me for longer than was comfortable. Then she put down the dog, sighed deeply and took my face between gentle palms. 'Oh, look at you, my poor darling. You're so busy looking after our dear little man, you've forgotten to look after yourself.'

My head wanted to protest, but my heart immediately contracted. The words were said sweetly and the angle of her eyebrows was kind. When she held out her arms, it was too much to bear and the tears hurtled out. Drawing me to her, she rocked me like a child.

'I've a whole host of cleaning products in the car, but let's start with you,' she said, finally pulling away. 'Have you eaten today, any breakfast?' She took a handful of my hair. 'Oh, Alison. When did you last have a shower? Food first, then I'll wash it.'

Too weak to resist, I stepped aside. Eventually following her to the kitchen, I stood against the jamb and observed her open cupboards and the fridge, shake her head and quietly sigh. Finally, she turned with a beam.

'Hallelujah, we have muesli! The oats will give you energy. Sit down, darling.'

She poured cereal, added honey and a scoop of Greek yoghurt, then she sat across the table and watched each spoonful go down. Finally satisfied I'd left a clean bowl, she led me up the stairs to the bathroom, whisked off my dirty top, knelt me down by the bath and washed my tresses over the side, her fingers brisk on my scalp.

She seemed so elated and full of energy, she made me feel tired. 'I love this part at the hairdresser's, don't you? A good old massage, shampoo twice, then conditioner? Leaves you feeling super clean.'

Hanging back after she'd finished, I wrapped my hair in a turban and covered my modesty with a towel. When I stepped onto the landing, Madeleine was at my bedroom door, her hand on her tiny waist, scanning the room. 'Oh, Alison!' she tutted. 'I won't ask when the bedding was last changed. Be a darling and crack a window, would you?'

Conscious of the stain on the front, I slipped on my dressing gown and observed her strip the bed, collect a selection of dirty tumblers, then open my wardrobe door. Like an infant, I dumbly watched her move along the hangers, throw several items in the direction of the laundry basket, others in the bin and a selection to me, which I meekly put on.

'Right, let's look at you,' she said, when her mission was complete. She tilted her head and squinted at me. 'Perhaps a touch of blusher on those pale cheeks?' Lifting her palm, she stilled and listened. Her eyes widened with pleasure. 'Oh how lovely! I think our little man has woken. Shall I do the honours? You go to the lounge and get comfortable for his feed. I'll have a little cuddle, then bring Joseph down.'

For a moment the name threw me. '*You can't just call him Joe,*' she'd stated at the hospital shortly after his birth. '*Shorten it if you wish, Alison, but give the poor chap a few choices.*'

'*It's going to be just Joe. Miles and I have agreed,*' I answered firmly, the Ali-before-pregnancy-and-birth still there, albeit deeply hidden.

But Madeleine had tagged along with Miles to register Joe's birth. Joseph Charles Henry Alexander-Jones, they'd named him. How I'd loathed her interference, but even that didn't rile me just now. There was no energy, no fight; it was so much easier to simply comply.

Listening to Madeleine's humming and the clack of her heels on the tiled kitchen floor, I fed my hungry son. I absently wondered what she was doing or throwing out, but I didn't care. Like falling off the waggon I knew she was bad for me, but it was such a relief for someone to help, to take over responsibility, just for a little while.

With her usual efficiency, Madeleine strapped Joe in the back seat of her Range Rover and slung the pram in the boot. Chattering all the way, she headed for the motorway, driving smoothly and fast for several miles before taking the exit. Sitting next to Joe, I gazed through the window at the pretty tree-lined country road and sparkling canal beyond. I knew we were headed for a village called Lymm. We'd been there before; it had always been Madeleine's first choice for 'a small expedition' as she called it. In recent times I'd given an involuntary shudder whenever the Cheshire village was mentioned, but today I barely noticed the road signs. Like Laura, I thought of nothing; no pressure, no stress, no decisions. No bloody panic, Mum, Norfolk or *cold fish*. I just took in the passing cottages and greenery, the sunshine and feeling of space.

Madeleine eventually parked up and turned. 'Here we are, darlings.' She beamed. 'My two favourite people in all the world! Let's spend some of Henry's dosh.'

We spent an hour in her regular haunt, a minimalist citrus-smelling boutique that sold ridiculously expensive clothes. The assistants fawned over Joe as we drank cappuccino and nibbled Biscotti di Prato. Madeleine bought herself several 'mix and match' items for autumn, finally persuading me to try on a pair of tight jeans, which surprisingly fitted. Then we ate a late lunch in the French Bistro, Madeleine ordering a glass of champagne for me, but sparkling water for herself. There wasn't a gap in her light-hearted patter until she slipped Joe from his pram and proudly presented 'her gorgeous grandson' to the chef and the kitchen staff.

It was a lovely afternoon – heartwarming, in fact. Charming, funny and generous, I had forgotten what easy company my mother-in-law was.

–

We eventually arrived home and greeted the dog. Still feeling calm, relaxed and hopeful, somehow, I carried my sleeping son into the lounge.

'Thank you, Madeleine.' I nodded to Joe's contented expression. 'That was just what we both needed.'

I couldn't help yawning. I was replete with delicious food and the alcohol had made me sleepy.

'Why don't you lie on the sofa and close your eyes, darling? I'll slip Joe in his cot and programme one more wash. Then I'll love you and leave you.'

'Thank you. If you don't—'

'When have I ever minded? It's a pleasure.'

Sleep must have been almost instant and deep, as I only became aware of the conversation when I heard Madeleine's eloquent tones drift in from the hallway. Wondering who she was speaking to, I pulled myself upright and absently listened.

'Yes, she's in a bad way I'm afraid,' I heard. 'Looks truly dreadful. Miles is worried, of course, but there's only so much he can do when he's so dreadfully busy. We can only hope that she's looking after little Joseph properly. But I'm here now to keep an eye on everything, and if I have the slightest concern, then of course I know the right people to bring in. Do you know the Priory? They offer inpatient mental health services in a safe and supportive environment. A beautiful setting, and just down the road. A couple of weeks in there is sometimes all it takes and I'll gladly have Joseph. In fact it would be a delight, he's such a lovely little man and some one-to-one bonding would be a treat…'

My heart thrashing, I stood, my ears pricked. What the hell? What the bloody hell…?

'Glad to hear the pussies are well,' she was now saying. 'I don't think she'll be collecting them in the near future, perhaps not for months. She's really not up to anything, I'm afraid. Could this George fellow take them on full time? To be honest, Joan, I think we might just have to sell the property. Get a price for the contents, of course. These clearance people are very efficient. Yes, of course, dear, I'll pass on the message.'

My whole body icy, I looked at my watch. It wasn't just the alarming conversation and the appalling suggestion she separate me from my child that bothered me, it was my mother-in-law's enunciation. No one else might have noticed, but I knew. We'd only been home for twenty minutes. In the days before she went 'dry', Madeleine could drink for hours before that telltale slur appeared. I had absolutely no doubt she'd driven me – and more importantly, her grandson – along a bustling motorway and back, topped up with God knows how much vodka.

I didn't slap her cheek today. Instead I kissed her goodbye, thanked her for her help and for an enjoyable afternoon. I don't know how my face appeared; I couldn't have hidden my sheer anger or determination if I'd tried. But the gratitude was genuine and I hoped that was what she'd see. She'd forced my hand, unwittingly goaded me into action; she'd injected me with a surge of strength and energy I hadn't known I possessed.

No more prevarication or excuses; Joe and I would drive down to Horning. We'd live at The Lodge for the duration of Miles's trial. It would give me time to sort out Mum's affairs, then return with the cats. If Miles wanted to see his son over the next couple of weeks, it would be easier for him to travel from London to Norfolk at the weekends.

I nodded. *If* he wanted to save his marriage. That part was up to him.

Part Two

Chapter Seventeen

Monday

The journey from Sheffield to Norfolk had always been tortuous. I had no idea what route Dad took, but it was four hours on a good day, much longer on a bad. Laura and I had sat in the back of his Jaguar, each of us with a comic and a bag of sweets which were to last the whole trip. Mixed with the odour of leather seats, the smell of confectionary soon made me nauseous. I never actually vomited, but part of me wished I had; it would have stopped my churning stomach and proved to my sister that I wasn't making it up.

Today Joe was in her place, snug in his car seat, and I smiled wryly at the memory. 'Don't start moaning, Ali. Nobody believes you,' Laura would say, turning away to the window.

How I hated being in her bad books. I'd hand over my Refreshers or Love Hearts and try to talk her round by asking things that, looking back, weren't wise – about the mascara she wasn't allowed to wear, the secretly bought bra she didn't yet need, the spotty boy who'd slipped her a note at Sunday school. And when those queries were ignored, I posed the usual all-embracing question: 'Did I do something wrong, Laura?'

Why she complained long and loud about our stays in Horning, I never knew. She had such glorious fun once we were there. Unlike me, she made friends easily wherever she went and the small boating village was no different. As ever, her entourage comprised mostly boys. With their soft broken accents, bobbing Adam's apples and acne, they'd seemed so mature and knowing to me then. Would Kelvin and Ivan still live on the estate behind the narrow high street? Maybe they now had kids of their own who stole their granny's homemade elderberry wine and shared it with the tourists. I was only offered it once, but the sweet and sharp tang had never left me.

Despite the persistent drizzle, I felt lighthearted and positive as I drove. For the first time since Joe's birth it was comfortable to drive on both buttocks, and it was rewarding to have made a firm decision, to take some control of my life after the haze of the past few months. I had no idea what to expect when I arrived, but that was fine. Tom and Joan knew I was on my way and so did Miles.

It had felt stilted and strange dropping him off at the railway station yesterday, but his face had flooded with colour when I asked if we'd be seeing him at the weekend. 'Of course I want to see you both,' he'd said, as though life had been hunky-dory at home for the past couple of weeks. 'I've already checked, and the trains go from King's Cross to Norwich.' Then after a beat, 'Why on earth would you think otherwise?'

Was he deluded or was I? And why was there a shiftiness behind his eyes? But it made no odds; I was on a mission, not only to sort my mother's belongings, but to unravel the secret about Dad. Because surely that was what

Mum had wanted to discuss with me? The reason for the calls I'd ignored.

Unless Miles had come too, I'd travelled to Mum's by rail over the past few years, so I enlisted the assistance of the SatNav to keep me on track. Would it give a fond nod to the medieval town my dad used stop at halfway? I wasn't sure where it was, but he'd park outside a church with turrets and we'd use the public toilets nearby.

My questions and goodies were always gone by then, but I'd beg Laura to wait outside the cubicle for me. When I emerged and looked to the sinks, there'd be a moment's panic at her absence, but she'd be outside the block, her slim arms folded, her foot propped against the wall.

Twenty-five plus years ago. How time had flown: some things were so clear in my mind, yet others hazy. As I headed east, I squeezed out the memories. I was ten, Laura fourteen that last summer. Apart from Dad being there for the whole time, was there anything different about it?

I sighed and shook my head. Nope, I couldn't remember anything odd, even in retrospect. It was a wonderful holiday. The sun shone with little rain. Laura won the beauty pageant at the fete on the village green. She snogged Kelvin *and* Ivan. She gained yet more followers, bribed me with coins not to be seen anywhere near her crowd. In truth, she was hardly there.

But that didn't matter one jot. I was in heaven with my grinning, fun Dad, busily doing the things I loved, but for weeks instead of days: inhaling the sugary smell of summer; plucking chubby green apples, firm cherries and plums from the trees in our garden; picking bucket after bucket of melting strawberries at a farm. The wind blowing my hair and the sun singeing my arms, we trundled along the dappled river in our motor boat and hunted for brown, sausage-headed river reeds. We moored at Black Horse Broad, swam in its dark water and ate thick-crusted sandwiches at a riverside pub. My orange lifejacket swamping my skinny chest, I'd climbed into the canoe and learned how to sweep through the water.

'Oh Ali,' Mum would say when we finally came home. 'Look at you. You tan like a berry!'

The memories rushed as I drove. That summer we borrowed Tom Hague's cruiser and motored further down the River Bure than ever before, past the cottages and windmills, the broads and tall grasses, eventually reaching an intersection with the River Ant and staying on the boat overnight in the market town of Stalham. Dad won a bid on an antique writing box for Mum at the auction. We climbed up the thin steps of the dank church spire. When I reached the top and strode onto the balcony, I discovered a thrilling and terrifying fear of heights.

Perhaps I was cramming five years of memories into one, but it felt as though it had all happened during that perfect two months. If my fair-haired, handsome Dad was ailing or ill, I didn't notice. He was funny and generous and kind.

And Mum? What of Mum? I could only remember the day we came home to the aroma of strawberries, rushing into the kitchen to peep at the glossy red jam bubbling in tureens on the stove.

'You've arrived just in time, love. Pop down to Evans's to buy me more jars. I've used every one.'

But even the local hardware shop had run out, so Dad and I drove to Wroxham for more. Longing for edible candy pebbles or a dummy or hearts, I hovered at the confectioner's window, but Dad laughed. 'Bad for your teeth, love.' Instead he bought me a quarter of coconut mushrooms, and though I didn't really like them that much, I gobbled them up so Laura wouldn't know.

Digging deep in my memory, I tried to picture Mum. With Laura out and about all hours with her village friends and me monopolising Dad, did she feel abandoned that summer? But she had her artwork, of course, that exquisite eye for remembered detail that neither Laura nor I had inherited.

An image of her face floated back. Perhaps she had been tense or preoccupied as Laura had said. But she liked to be alone when she painted. The delicate flowers, the reeds, the river birds; the swan-like sailing boats at the regattas. And me and Laura, pencil drawings of us as babies and happy fat toddlers. We'd argue which one was who, but Mum always shrugged and said she couldn't remember, that we were both beautiful girls. Only as an adult did I twig that she was being kind. Laura was the fair, pretty baby with those curls and a smile; I was solemn with a shock of dark hair. Tiny tots had all looked similar to me then, but now I had mine, I knew each newborn was distinctive and different.

A recollection suddenly struck me at the traffic lights, a picture-perfect image of Mum and Dad at the stove when we'd returned with the jars. His arms around her waist and her reluctant laughter. 'You and those strawberries, Doug. What are we going to do with all this damned jam?'

'Eat it until Christmas,' he'd replied.

But of course, by then he was dead.

Chapter Eighteen

Taking in the yellow scene, I trundled through a large expanse of bright rapeseed and waited for the long canopy of trees. I'd know then I was nearing the home stretch and a tiny bakery where Dad used to pull up for fresh bread. After chatting with the old couple who owned it, he'd return with miniature loaves, piping hot from the oven. Neither I nor Laura liked the raspy feel of the crust, so Mum would wrap them in a tissue and we'd devour the warm dough knowing we'd soon be in Horning. But today I didn't stop. Miles hadn't either when he was at the wheel. He'd preferred to get there as soon as he could, driving too fast, which was always a worry.

'Always in a hurry, my boy,' as Madeleine had put it when we announced our engagement. 'You were the only thing he had to wait for, darling girl.'

Miles had fitted that awful cliché of 'everything a woman could want', or so my friends said. It was probably more a case of everything a mother would want for her daughter: he was reasonably tall, blond and handsome; personable, clever and athletic. He came from a wealthy family, had a good job, owned his own home and drove a sports car. But he wasn't my romantic hero. Devoid of passionate angst or poetic tendencies, he didn't have a creative or artistic bone in his body. He didn't particularly enjoy listening to music, either. He was more your straightforward, dependable type of guy.

Now catching sight of my pallid face in the wing mirror, I sighed. At least that's what I'd thought. His complete devotion to me, too. Perhaps it was the chase he'd found so appealing. Back in the day, he'd asked me out so many times it became a chambers joke. 'You'll give in sooner or later,' friends and colleagues said. 'No I won't,' I'd replied. And I'd meant it, I really had.

Why had I changed my mind? Was it really because his old flame reappeared on the scene and made me feel jealous? Or was it his mother? That weird attraction we'd had for each other. And what had *her* devotion been all about? A desire to control me? Or was it to mend me? And my need to be... *repaired*? Discomfort spreading, I threw the thought out. I didn't need to go there; I didn't need to dwell on the bloody woman or why I'd found myself slapping her; for now I'd escaped.

As though he'd spotted the wooden signpost for Horning, Joe woke and moaned sleepily.

'Hello gorgeous,' I said over my shoulder. 'We're nearly at—'

Only then did I realise I must have driven right past the spot where Mum had crashed, the ambulance-and-collar, the youths-drinking-beer scene a witness had seen fit to report and pass on. Guilt and culpability flared again. The guilt for still not having *felt* the loss; culpability for not having *known* when she'd passed. They were feelings I couldn't explain, like that frequent sensation she hadn't left at all. Should I turn back, find the junction and make some sort of homage? But I wasn't completely sure where it was. My 'liaison officer' Tom Hague had dealt with the police collision investigation and forensics, the outcome and communications, as well as any press or social media releases. True to his word, he hadn't bothered me with any of it. He was a good man; a loyal friend to both my parents. I looked forward to thanking him in the next day or so.

Entering the medieval village was strange. I'd been here at Christmas, but it felt as though I was seeing everything through new eyes. As an orphan, I supposed. I had Joe now and I was immensely grateful, but had his birth unbalanced the cosmic scales? One person in and one out?

Passing the Swan Inn and the Sailing Club, I was soon in the centre of the village. The smart new-builds made the white-painted old properties look shabby. The thought made me feel disloyal; how I'd loved the few endearing outlets there'd been as a child – the tiny post office where I'd spent hours choosing comics or peering at the saucy postcards; the gift shop where I'd longed to touch the ornaments and windmills, and especially its perfume section where I'd inhaled the distinctive sweet aroma of lilac or lavender, which took me back even now.

The village green looked much the same, a large square of manicured grass gazing out to the river. Laura had hung out with a mix of locals and holidaymakers at a greasy cafe on the corner. The Baker family had neither been natives nor tourists and I'd always felt it. But that wasn't anything new to me; I'd fallen between two stools most of my childhood and in a strange way I'd liked the discomfort. Or perhaps I had just been contrary: yearning to be noticed, yet deliberately staying on the periphery; struggling with shyness but enjoying the knowledge I was clever. That contradiction had continued into adulthood too, in the way that I'd had no time for Miles when he'd pursued me, yet had wanted him badly when his attention was diverted.

The river looked dull from a distance, the grey sky reflected on its smooth surface. But as ever, the mishmash of moored boats gave the scene colour. Did the fish and chip boat still berth at a weekend, I wondered. A memory winged back and I smiled. There it was: Laura's exhilarated expression when she burst into the kitchen one balmy evening. 'Oh my God, you've got to come! There's a fight on the green; everyone's joined in. The chippy's on fire. Come on!' Her excitement was so contagious, even Mum dropped what she was doing and we went as a foursome to investigate, Laura so enthused she held my hand.

With a jolt, I realised that my dad must have had cancer that day. He'd kept it a secret – for our continued happiness, I was sure – but was that the only one?

I came back to my mission. Now past the shops, I was almost at The Lodge. At the peak of the hill, I took a deep breath and drove through the entrance. Though a lane circled the large plot of land, I took the 'shortcut', a pebbly driveway that had been slashed through the grassy mound to provide direct access to the bungalow.

The crunch beneath the wheels sounded loud in the silence. So did my racing heart. But Mum's sprawling home was no different from the last time I was here: white rendered walls with charming lattices which matched the panelled windows and doors. It was as picture-book pretty as ever. Still in the car, I glanced around. Enveloped by a semi-circle of tall poplar trees at the front, the grass was neatly manicured, the rectangular flower beds newly turned, the roses in full bloom. Mum would have been so pleased and proud. Ironic really; she used to complain that the lawns, the sunken garden and back yard were too much to maintain; that the interior was faded, dated and fusty. Yet she'd still moved her whole life here…

Frowning, I thought back to December. I had playfully challenged her about it then. The rousing sound of *Carols from Kings* in the background, I'd inhaled the exquisite aroma of Christmas cake, mince pies, pine tree, and chuckled. 'No "damned smell" these days, Mum. You couldn't wait to get back to Sheffield to escape it after our summers. What on earth changed your mind?'

Did she blush or her eyes flicker? No. She'd just shrugged and said, 'People change. Sometimes one needs to move on, adapt; have a new mindset.' And when I'd looked sceptical she'd laughed and added, 'Even you, Ali. You changed your mind about Miles and look at you now, you'll be a new mum in five months.'

And now my boy was here. One in and one out.

With a sigh, I climbed from the car and opened the rear door to fetch Joe. He gazed for a beat before smiling bashfully, his little face guileless and doting. No wonder mothers fell in love with their sons. Such a similar expression to Miles's after his car crash; I had decided I could love him then.

Did I still?

Chapter Nineteen

Holding Joe close, I fingered the house keys in my pocket. When we'd opened up as kids, the cold and musty feel of an unused property had wafted back. Complaining already, Mum would stomp around, opening every door and window, which made it even chillier. But Dad collected logs from the back yard, dutifully cut, piled and protected by our gardener, then made up the fire so the charcoal aroma would sweep through the rooms, making it feel lived in.

A thought suddenly hit me. It would be like that again. Not the cosy, warm home I had visited at Christmas. I'd be completely isolated with no neighbours to turn to. Suppose I had a panic attack or one of those 'dreams'? And how would I feel being there without Mum? My heart thrashed. Bloody hell; why had I'd been so hasty? I should have waited for Miles to come with me when he had the time.

Determined to gather my self control, I inhaled deep in my abdomen. Everything was fine. I had Joe and Miles; I was lucky, very lucky. Though our marriage was going through a sticky patch, it wasn't unheard of with work stresses and the challenges of a new baby. Both of those could be fixed, given time, and of course I loved Miles. I wasn't alone really. He hadn't died. Not like Dad. And that was part of the reason I was here, after all.

Sounds abruptly filtering through, I stilled and listened. Ah yes, I remembered them now – the mournful yet comforting calls of the cuckoos, the popping and rustling from the trees. The aroma on the breeze felt companionable too, a sweet fragrance of wild flowers and the nutty tang from the woods at the rear of the bungalow.

Recalling Laura's comment from the last time we were both here, I looked at the thistly expanse of flattened land adjoining Mum's plot. 'Dogging,' she'd said. 'I've just remembered. It used to be woodland too. Ivan and Kelvin said the doggers were pissed off when the trees were felled.'

'At least they still have the coppice behind here,' Mum had said, interrupting our banter. 'I could do with some light evening entertainment. Maybe I should get out the binoculars.'

Laura had laughed. 'Mother, behave! You're not supposed to know what that is, let alone join in.'

The memory of the happy exchange spurring me on, I stepped to the glass door, unlocked it and walked in. I turned full circle in the large reception foyer. Had anything changed? Nope; the black mahogany chiffonier with a large mirror above it was on the right, the brick archway and open lounge the other side. Even the bible given to me by the Hagues when I was eight or nine was in its place next to the telephone on the Queen Anne table.

My heels echoing on the polished parquet, I showed Joe around. Goosebumps spread as I peered at the sofa and armchairs. Though Mum was a tidy person, it was so neat and untouched that I was certain the house was not as she'd left it when heading out for the hairdresser's. And there was the sharp smell of wax and disinfectant and bleach. Someone had cleaned it, emphasising the feeling of emptiness. Joan Hague, perhaps, knowing I was due? Or maybe preparing it for viewers at bloody Madelene's behest.

Taking a deep breath, I headed along the back hallway to the bedrooms. Like tearing off a plaster, I tackled Mum's first. At the front of the bungalow, it had double French windows and looked out to the flower beds and poplar trees. As expected, the bed was made, the room spruced and tidy. I idly picked up a paperback from the bedside table – *The Tenant of Wildfell Hall* – and two bookmarks fell out. It was the one Brontë novel I hadn't read, but the folded note appeared to be Mum's jottings about the story, presumably to discuss with her book club: *What do the pictures mean? The trinkets too? They must have been stolen. And the lock on the door?* The second was a birthday card from Laura, postmarked from when she first went to Canada. The sight burned my nose. It was sent twenty-one years ago; Mum had clearly been looking at it whenever she'd opened the page. I hadn't told Laura I was coming here in case I chickened out, but I'd phone her tonight. 'See, Mum did love you,' I'd say.

Sniffing the air, I hovered for a while. Daft though it was, I wanted to suck in a trace of my mother, her soft soapy smell, her Chanel perfume, even the lavender from the pomanders in her wardrobe and drawers. The sun was trying to smile through the windows, but it felt weak and half-hearted. I put my face to Joe's feathery hair and breathed back the tears. I'd felt her with me back home; I had expected her to be here.

The door to the large bedroom at the end of the walkway was closed. It had originally contained three single beds covered in candlewick bedspreads, lined up like a dormitory, for family and guests. But Laura had complained, demanding to have it as her own. She was the eldest, she'd said, she needed her privacy. What was the point of having an empty room?

She and Mum had argued about it, of course: Mum felt it was far too large for one person; if visitors came, Laura would only have to move out; she should be pleased to share with her little sister; sometimes Ali was still afraid of the dark.

Laura hadn't been in the least 'pleased' to share with me, and she'd finally had her way that last summer. She'd chosen the bed next to the window and there it was now, neatly covered with a broderie anglaise throw and adorned with her teddies and pyjama case just as though she was there, still a child of fourteen.

Sighing at the memories, I skimmed my fingers over the ornaments proudly displayed on the bookcase – a polished brass horse, delicate china ballerinas, a Flamenco doll in a splendid scarlet silk dress, a jewellery box made of tortoise and tusk – all the items I had touched and coveted back then. *Grown-up* presents for Laura, childish ones for me.

The white drawers and bedside table had been so fashionable when we left, but now they looked dated and tired. It made me feel sad. Why had Laura felt so unloved? Why hadn't the connection with Mum been there? And what about me, the girl who squeezed her eyes shut? How curious that I hadn't seen it.

Moving onto my bedroom, I inhaled sharply and pulled back the sliding door. My heart thumping, I took in the array of gifts covering my pink duvet. Laying Joe on the carpet, I knelt down for a closer look. Like a stall at a craft fair, Mum had displayed baby toys, trinkets and outfits prepared, presumably, for this very moment. Strange she didn't pack them, ready to transport to Manchester for her week's stay in July. I shivered at my old thought of her having a premonition. Shaking the silliness away, I picked up an antique box engraved with the letter 'J'. It was heavy, so solid silver and worth a fair sum, presumably. I examined the other items. A set of old-fashioned building blocks, a pristine jester Jack-in-the-Box and a vintage train set. Not terribly practical, but I could picture her busy enthusiasm in charity and bric-à-brac shops, as ever keeping an eye on the price.

Emotional and anxious, I covered my face. What the hell was I doing? These items were only a small fraction of the enormous chore ahead. The house was stuffed with furniture, books, ornaments, plants, mementoes – let alone childhood belongings and paperwork. Where would I even start? The task felt impossible. I still had little energy; my hands were trembling right now.

A tiny part of my mind flitted to Madeleine's conversation with Joan. Perhaps I wasn't up to it; maybe a house clearance and sale was the only way forward. But it was only a moment before determination set in. I was famished, that was all. I needed to eat properly; my food was Joe's, and though he seemed to want feeding all the time again, I'd been advised by the health visitor to hold off with solids for a few more weeks. I was still trying to be one of the smiling mums from the posters, and doing things by the book, so I intended to comply.

It wasn't until I opened the fridge and found it impeccably clean but empty that it occurred to me I needed to feed Joe, then dash to the local shops to buy in fresh food. Unless things had changed dramatically, there was no late opening in this village. If you didn't make a purchase by tea time, you either went hungry or ate at a pub.

Chapter Twenty

Though cloudy, it was warm outside. I was still shaky but the clean air and crisp aromas seemed to settle my racing heart. With Joe in his papoose, I crunched down the driveway to the bottom gate. As I turned right into Lower Street, the sun peeped out, lighting the unkempt grassy bank. The wild shrubs had found a soft breeze and seemed to wave a 'welcome back' greeting. Foxglove, dog rose and oxtongue. And cow parsley, of course. Thinking the intricate white-headed flowers quite beautiful and something she might like to paint, I had once picked a handful for my mum.

'Oh, Mother's Death,' she'd laughed not unkindly when I presented them with a flourish. 'They're meant to be bad luck if you bring them into the house.'

But when she'd seen my fallen face, she'd explained it was just an old wives' tale and wouldn't let me throw them away. 'Do you know, I've never looked at it properly before. Some call it Queen Anne's lace, and they're right,' she'd said, arranging them in a jar on the kitchen shelf.

'You do know that if Mum dies, it'll all be your fault,' Laura had inevitably said when she saw them at tea time.

Now picturing a smashed windscreen, I shivered. The only 'fault' had been Mum's own, a moment's inattention or hesitation, resulting in such devastation. And why the hell hadn't she been wearing her seatbelt?

Now at the delicatessen we'd called 'the dairy', I came back to the expedition at hand. There was a Mace at the far end of the village but this was nearer. Mum used to complain about the extortionate prices, so had more or less boycotted us using it, but Dad would still send me for a slice of pork pie or a Cornish pasty for himself and a sausage roll for me 'while Mum isn't looking'. With a conspiratorial wink to Laura and me, it wasn't unusual for him to fib about prices in general to keep the peace.

The thought of his easy deception caught me short. Sure, that was only a white lie over something and nothing, but could there have been more serious deceit? Maybe another woman or a past affair? Nope; one thing I was absolutely sure of was Dad's devotion to Mum; if anything, she'd been the one to slightly hold back.

Joe nestled against me, I pushed at the door and stepped in. The old bell still rang and it was little changed inside: the curved glass display housed savoury pastries, pies and cold meats at one end, a selection of whole cheeses the other. And standing next to the electronic weighing machine were the yellow enamel scales I remembered. How I had longed to slip around the counter and slice glossy ham with the sharp rasping slicer, then feel the cylindrical weights in my hands, placing them on one side, the slivers of meat on the other.

I'd once heard Joan Hague tell Mum that the plump-faced owner slid a small weight beneath the meat to make it heavier, so on Dad's secret missions I'd watch for a magician-like sleight of her hand, both excited and panicked about what I should do if I witnessed duplicity with my very own eyes. Disappointingly, I never did.

As I waited in the line I mentally saluted Dad. Bugger the prices, I'd buy everything I needed from here. The fat sausages and artisan cheeses, the breaded ham and pink beef looked divine. Finally my turn, I took a breath to make my order, but I was cut short by a tap on the arm.

'You're Eve's daughter, aren't you? We've been expecting you and the baby.'

I turned. An extremely wrinkled lady with a disappearing mouth was peering at me with clear, shrewd eyes. On hearing her pronouncement, the other shoppers and staff looked my way with open curiosity. I had no idea who she was, but my instinct was to take her by the shoulders and manoeuvre her outside before she said anything further. How Laura would laugh at my discomfort. But this village was small; I'd have to wear sunglasses permanently if I was to stand a chance of any anonymity.

Hoping the woman would do likewise, I stepped away from the queue, but she firmly pushed me back. 'Stock's getting low, lovey. You don't want to lose your place.' She nodded to the customer behind me. 'This is Eve's daughter. You know, the nice lady at The Lodge who was killed by those lads?'

Though there were only six or so people in the shop, all of them women, it felt like a huge crowd. Nodding and looming, they patted my shoulders or hands and murmured condolences with mournful eyes. *Dreadful, disgraceful, shocking, poor lamb.* My need to disappear became overwhelming. Joe must have felt it too as he suddenly bawled. My pulse throbbing with alarm, I looked down at the papoose, but before I'd worked out how to disentangled myself, bony hands had scooped him out.

The soft, curly dialect was back. 'It's all right, lovey. You go ahead. I'll take him while you make your order.

Oh, look at all this gorgeous hair. I'll bet you had heartburn when you were in the family way...'

It took the best part of an hour to recover my child
and escape from that shop with two carrier bags of delicacies and a complimentary slice of vinegar cake. It turned
out my new friend was called Nancy. Jiggling Joe with
expertise, she explained she'd been Mum's cleaner before
'her Denise' took over, but she'd continued to visit Eve
for 'a cuppa, sit down and a chat'. She had recognised
me from my previous visits – and photographs – and
promised to call with some 'goodies' very soon. I had
started to wonder whether she was keeping Joe until then,
but she eventually relinquished him with a dry kiss on his
forehead. Not that he minded; the little traitor had fallen
asleep in her arms.

–

The hallway telephone was ringing on my return and I
fumbled with the keys to catch it in time.

'Ali! Thank God, I've been worried. Where have you
been?' Miles demanded.

'I've been out to buy some food and I met—'

'Why don't you take your bloody mobile with you?'

I fell silent. I'd almost felt content on my way back from
the deli – whether due to my escape from the coven or
their warm, straightforward friendliness, I wasn't sure. But
my husband's tone brought me short with a thump. Until
falling pregnant with Joe, I'd been so sure of his love. But
these days he seemed angry and irritated all the time.

And he'd tarred me with that 'cold fish' brush.

'Ali, are you still there? Look, I'm sorry; I don't mean
to snap. I've phoned about ten times today and I was

worried. It's a long journey there. What if something had happened? Like your mum? I couldn't bear to lose you and Joe. I'm missing you both already. I love you Ali, I really do…'

Although my throat clogged with emotion, I managed to croak. 'You're right, sorry; we're missing you too.'

His words were just what I had needed to hear. And I did understand the agony of waiting for a call. I'd experienced the very same thing with him.

As it happened, Laura and I were in Norfolk for Christmas when I finally agreed to go on a date with Miles nine years ago. Though I hadn't realised Laura was listening, her eyebrows were raised when I put down the phone.

'You're meant to be pleased when someone begs you to go out, Ali, not give them a hard time. You don't sound very keen. Is he your type?' she asked. Then for good measure, shaking her head: 'A *test date*. Really? You are weird, Ali. You do know that, don't you?'

Her comments had irked me, mainly because she was right. I was already regretting saying yes. I didn't want to go on a bloody assignation with Miles Alexander-Jones. The prospect of him kissing me wasn't appealing, never mind what might follow. It was only the thought of his old flame that stopped me from cancelling. She'd dated Miles at university and was clearly gunning for him again. In fairness, she was the type of glossy, polished girl one would expect him to marry, but I was jealous of their easy banter – green with it, in fact. I'd become used to Miles's attention and flattery, addicted to his projected image of me, one I certainly couldn't see in the mirror. So I agreed to a secret one-off. I had no idea what the 'test' was, but if he passed it, I'd become his girlfriend. If he failed, he promised not to pester me again.

When the day finally arrived, I chose my most bizarre outfit, one I hadn't dared sport for years, and applied heavy black eyeliner and dark lipstick. In truth, I looked ridiculous, but perhaps that was the point. Almost yawning with disinterest, I tapped my nails on the kitchen table for an hour before finally twigging he wasn't coming. For the next half hour I cried, exacerbating the goth look, then I guzzled a bottle of cheap wine. I felt much better after that, and by the time the intercom buzzed, I was ready for fisticuffs.

The words, '*You've failed big-style, mate! If you can't turn up on time, don't turn up at all!*' died on my lips as I opened the door. Not to Miles, but to a pallid, dark-haired and beautiful woman I just knew was his mum.

Naturally I assumed a mother's presence at my digs meant bad news – death or at least a coma – and I'm ashamed to say that for a moment, I was relieved. As it happened, Miles wasn't deceased or even seriously injured. Though he'd written off his Triumph Stag on the way to collect me, he'd miraculously escaped with only whiplash and a broken ankle.

Perhaps I should have learned something from that night. Would any other mother have turned up unannounced in those circumstances? Her doe-eyed attention was embarrassing, let alone strange and surreal. Wouldn't a telephone call have sufficed? But her charm and intimacy trapped me in a way I hadn't anticipated; I got caught in her web.

'Come on darling,' she said, studying me closely. She tucked my hair behind my ears and swept a finger across my cheek. 'You're just perfect. The loo and a coat, then we'll get you to the Alex.'

I did what I was told: like an obedient child I went to the toilet, donned my jacket and climbed into her car.

We must have looked odd, the two of us gliding into the private hospital reception, arm in arm. Waiting for an operation to pin his fibula, Miles was sitting up in bed, and there was a look between mother and son, an unspoken communication which seemed to say: '*Here you are, my darling boy; this is what you wanted, so I've brought her to you…*'

Though we hadn't even hugged, it felt as though we were betrothed. It was peculiar, ridiculous, but also compulsive. Madeleine hovered, but she eventually left the room with a gracious smile. I almost laughed when Miles tugged me towards him and put his lips to mine. The alcohol had taken the edge off my embarrassment, but the relief was still there. The kiss was nice, very nice, thank God.

After half an hour Madeleine escorted me to her car. I had expected her to drop me home, but instead she drove to her sprawling Cheshire house where I was introduced to Henry. I must have looked a state by then, a combination of messy make-up, excess alcohol and heavy snogging, but he showed no surprise. He was so like Miles I was embarrassed, as though I had been kissing the father, not the son.

Sliding her arm into mine, Madeleine guided me up a sweeping staircase to the guest room. She laid out a silk nightie and smiled. 'Slip in and go to sleep, darling. I'll wake you in the morning.' It was so surreal, so fairytale, so addictive. But now it felt as though it had happened to someone other than me.

'Ali? Are you still there?'

The sound of my husband's voice jolted me back to the call. 'Sorry, Miles, yes I am. I was just thinking about—'

A deep sigh. 'You're supposed to say you love me too.'

'Of course, yes I—'

'It's fine, Ali. Forget it. I'll speak to you tomorrow.'

Chapter Twenty-One

I couldn't settle in the evening. Sitting in Mum's armchair, I flicked through the channels on the ancient television, but even with the curtains drawn, the lounge felt too large and breezy for cosiness or comfort. I stood up to call Laura, then realised it would be the middle of the afternoon in Canada. She'd be busy at work, and trying to express my emotions wasn't something I could wrap up in two minutes. Not that I really knew how I felt. A strange combination of listlessness and anxiety; I was jumpy yet weary; I couldn't concentrate on anything for long.

Between tending to Joe, I tried re-reading *Villette*, leafed through the pages of an art magazine and sampled the vinegar cake. It had looked so appealing four hours ago, but tasted of nothing behind the metallic tang of panic which was threatening to appear. Moving to the sofa, I curled up my legs and stared at the walnut sideboard, knowing some of its treasures, but too agitated to open its doors and explore.

The near silence was oppressive. In my Manchester suburb I was used to a blend of generic noise through the open windows at night: the thud of car doors, a neighbour's late conversation, the low thrum of traffic, the mating screech of urban foxes. But here it was as though the popping pines slept at night, so when the quietness was punctured, the sound was loud and specific. Each hoot of an owl, every turn of a pebble brought me out in icy goosebumps. And was there a sound of soft wheezing behind me? Well, that was silly mind games. Yet I could still hear something, even when I held my breath.

Feeling a sudden breeze, I snapped my head around. No one and nothing except the black chiffonier. I shook the shiver away. It was an old, creaking property, that was all. Mum had considered adding doors between the lofty foyer and the lounge, but the archway was huge and it would have involved closing it in, which she thought was a shame. She'd spoken about it only at Christmas, when she'd said she had grown to love the feeling of space, that she was used to it these days.

The memory carried me to thoughts of her now, within the small confines of a coffin. Good God, my mother was dead. And yet it still didn't feel true, I still couldn't feel it. Rubbing my cold arms, I stepped over to the assortment of framed photos on the mantelpiece. One had fallen down, so I propped it back up and peered at the smiley photograph of two couples. The Bakers and the Hagues, the men sporting long collars, Joan a turtle neck and Mum a stylish jumpsuit. They all looked so young, especially my parents. I guessed it had been taken in the late seventies or early eighties. Goodness, they'd known each other for a very long time; no wonder they'd remained such close friends. The next was the same family portrait as the one I'd hidden in my bookcase, so I quickly moved on to a group photo of Mum's siblings and their spouses from my wedding. I focused on Auntie Brenda, at the very far end. What on earth had she and Mum argued about? Mum had lived here for seventeen years. How had she felt without her sisters or even immediate neighbours? Yet she'd been deprived of Dad for much longer than that.

The loneliness she must have felt struck me for the first time ever. I'd never thought to ask her about it, not even as an adult.

'Selfish, spoiled, Ali,' I could hear Laura say.

It was probably true. Though children were programmed to think only of themselves, childhood was long ago. When Dad died, Laura and I were both vehemently against another man in Mum's life. It was understandable for a while, but now, doing the maths, I realised with a shock that Mum was only forty when she was widowed. Both attractive and wealthy, no wonder there'd been all those damned 'uncles'.

I groaned at the recollection. Some of the regular visitors had been people we knew – Dad's clients or friends who paid their respects a little too often. Avuncular with us, solicitous and tactile with her, we hated them even more than the newbies and didn't hide our disgust. Maybe that was why Mum never encouraged them. Were we responsible? Did Laura and I exacerbate her solitary life?

My stomach rumbled, reminding me to eat, so I slipped on my mules and lifted my chin. Onward to the kitchen, woman; there was nothing to frighten me here; the front and back entrances were locked, every door was shut.

Flicking on lights as I went, I padded down the hallway. At the dining entrance I stopped. Mum had used it as her studio. Should I peep in to see if her canvases and artwork were there? Perhaps sense her warm presence? I debated for a moment, but the child in me won, my old fear of the room making the decision for me. I'd once found a pigeon in the grate. Concerned it was still breathing, I'd stepped closer to look, only to discover the movement was tiny maggots. Convinced the grubs would burst into flies before my very eyes, I had screamed the house down. Dad had rushed in and scooped me up, then he'd taken me to a mirror. 'See, Ali? No insects, just a very pretty frightened girl!'

He'd been right, of course, but the episode had reinforced my certainty that the dining room was haunted: it was colder and danker than any other area of the bungalow and had a dark stain on the parquet that was almost certainly ancient blood. To add to the chills, Laura told me the bird was a sacrifice. I had no idea what that meant, but her wide, spooky eyes told me it was bad.

Bloody Laura! No wonder I'd had nightmares. Laughing to myself, I let out my trapped breath and turned away. White-faced phantoms didn't exist, but I'd still wait until daylight before venturing into there.

–

As the night drew in, Joe seemed to sense my unease. I'd put him in his travel cot at the usual bedtime, but after an hour or two he woke up and wouldn't calm. The health visitor had advised a little grumbling wouldn't hurt, saying that in the long run it was better for babies to settle by themselves, but I couldn't bear the sound of his unhappiness. So each time he called, I picked him out for a cuddle. But he nuzzled against my breast, asking for milk.

By midnight, it felt as though I had fed him for hours. Thirsty for water, I carried him to the kitchen, slugged down a glassful, then sat at the table and cried. I was shaking with fatigue, but Joe was completely awake, gazing at me with big, luminous eyes.

'Go to sleep, Joe. Please go to sleep,' I pleaded between sobs. Then, louder, 'I can't do this any longer. For God's sake, just bloody well sleep!'

Alarm spread through my body. What the hell was I doing? Swearing, almost shouting at my vulnerable son. Picturing that ashen-faced mother in court, the terror burned in my chest. People harmed their babies all the time; I could hurt mine. After all, I had slapped Madeleine hard that day. It had been on impulse, but I'd lost control so easily; did that make me capable of anything?

Keep an eye on Alison; Ali's not Ali.

The panic overwhelming, I lowered my head. That was what she was suggesting, wasn't it? I wasn't normal; I was a liability, even dangerous. And a psychiatrist would know.

As I struggled to breathe, my heart thrashed. Oh God. What if I shook Joe, if I hurled him to the ground? I could visualise myself doing it, catapulting him from my arms, watching his head smash against the hard floor, then crack like an egg into a hundred tiny fragments.

But I held onto him gently, knowing I wouldn't hurt him, *hoping* I wouldn't hurt him, scaring myself. 'I'm just tired,' I repeated. 'I'll be fine in the morning.'

Eventually crouching to the floor, I managed to slip Joe into his bouncy chair. He was safe, I wouldn't drop him, so that was good. I just needed to inhale deeply from my diaphragm, then everything would be—

My ears pricked at a sound; my hairs stood erect. What the hell was that? Stilling, I listened. Oh my God, definite rustling, movement. This wasn't my imagination; someone or something was directly behind me…

My heart in my mouth, I snapped around and stared. Empty. A silent room. The black night through the window. A dripping tap. Nothing and no one was there. No phantom, no burglar. I was being ridiculous; I had to get a grip.

Trying to control the absurd fear, I picked up my tumbler and made for the sink, but a dark shape in my peripheral vision made me freeze. I could hear scraping noises too. My pulse thumping loud in my ears, I forced myself to look. Not just sound, but there was – there really was a silhouette beyond the panelled side door. And… Oh my God, fingers scratching at the glass and a distorted face peering in.

My scream pierced the quietness, startling poor Joe who started to wail. Though my instinct was to grab his chair and hide or even run, I was frozen to the spot and couldn't move. But after a second or two had passed, I realised the shadow was tapping at the door. What the…? Who the hell would be here at this time?

My voice quavery, I shouted, 'It's late. Whoever you are, go away.'

A muffled reply filtered through. 'It's George. The gardener.'

'Go away,' I tried again, but I was struggling to suck in any air. Joe was still bawling but my heart was racing so badly, I couldn't trust myself to pick him up.

'It's Ali, isn't it?' The voice persisted. 'Can I come in and explain?'

At that moment I would have let in Jack the Ripper for medical assistance. My tongue felt thick, my legs feeble and my lungs filled with sand. I tried to move forward, but my sight was narrowing, becoming darker and darker, then suddenly the world was black.

–

'You're all right. Inhale slowly and deeply. Everything is fine.'

Sound returned before vision. The man's deep enunciation seemed out of place. I tried to focus: the *gardener*? Really? Mum's old gardener had been local, but this person had a strong northern accent.

My head between my knees, I was now sitting on the floor. When I finally lifted my chin, I saw a huge man crouched in front of me, my son cradled in the crook of his elbow. I wanted to pull Joe to safety, but I knew my limbs weren't safe; my whole body felt so heavy I could barely move. A wave of self-pity overwhelmed me. There was my baby, sleepy and content in yet another stranger's arms. What the hell was wrong with me?

I tried to stand.

'You've had a shock. Maybe give it a minute,' the man said.

A flaming *shock*? He'd bloody petrified me. Swallowing, I found my voice. 'I need to put Joe...'

'Put him in his cot?' He stood up. 'Is it in your bedroom?'

'Yes. It's the one...'

But he'd already disappeared. Tears threatening, I pulled up my knees and tried to steady my thrashing heart. He returned shortly afterwards. 'He's sleeping now,' he said. 'You should be, too.'

'Right. I'll go in a bit. I'm fine now, so if you could...'

But instead of taking the hint, he hauled me to my feet. Though deeply embarrassed, my legs were jelly-like, so instead of protesting, I went with the moment, allowing him to half carry me to my door.

Perching on my bed, I took a shuddery breath to say something. I should have asked who he really was and what the hell he was doing here at midnight, but I was too winded – and exhausted – to shape words.

As though reading my mind, he nodded. 'Night, then,' he said, before striding off.

Anticipating an avalanche of introspection, self-recrimination and guilt for my inadequacies as usual, I pulled back the duvet and flopped down onto the cold mattress. Moments later, I was asleep.

Chapter Twenty-Two

Tuesday

The bright August sunshine beyond the curtains awoke me. Confused by my surroundings, it took me a few moments to work out where I was, more to realise I hadn't woken in the early hours to feed Joe. Oh God, was he OK? Stumbling from the bed, I lurched to his cot and stared, disbelieving. He wasn't there. I frantically lifted his bedding. What the hell? What the bloody hell…? It was empty; he'd gone. I tried to focus through the dizziness and need to vomit my panic induced. This couldn't be happening. Then the memory of last night came roaring back. Oh my God, what a stupid, irresponsible woman. I had let a total stranger into the house.

My soles slapping the parquet, I hurtled to the kitchen and looked in. No one was there; *Joe* wasn't there. My stomach churning, I lowered my head and willed the nausea to pass. Terrifying images swamped my mind, so graphic I could *feel* them. My son was hidden beneath a coat. He was whimpering with fear. He knew the person carrying him wasn't his mummy. He'd been stolen by the man in the night, I was sure of it. What now? I had to calm down and concentrate, search for my boy. No, time was of the essence, a call to the police should come first. Oh

God, what to say? Could I even describe the kidnapper? Tall and dark with a northern accent was as far as it went.

A thin breeze on my cheeks pierced the panic. The side door was open a crack, gently tapping against the jamb. Rushing forward, I shoved it open and gaped out. A man was strolling around the sunken garden. Not a man, but *the* man who'd said he was the gardener. Holding Joe in one arm, he was talking. Whether to my son or to himself, I couldn't tell, but he looked up as I approached, then passed Joe to me.

Both anger and relief screamed to burst out, but my throat was too constricted to speak, let alone shout. Taking a gulp of morning air, I prepared to challenge him: '*Who the hell do you think you are? Coming into the house – not just the house but my* bedroom, *then taking my baby? You can't just do that! I'll report you to the police, I'll—*'

But he didn't give me a chance. 'I'll be off then,' he said, already turning away.

Stunned and shaky, I watched him stride off, stop at a rose bed and blithely pluck out a clump of weeds. Stupidly wondering what he'd do with the bloody things, I gazed until he'd disappeared beyond the poplars.

The sheer alleviation was such that sudden mirth popped out. I peered at my son. 'What the hell, Joe?' I asked. 'Another character from an old British horror movie or what?'

But when I looked at my bare feet, it was me who appeared demented. My hair knotted with sweat and wearing the long nightdress I had found in Mum's drawer, I looked like Bertha Rochester escaped from her attic. Not sure whether to laugh or to cry, I buried my face in Joe's hair. He replied with a whimper.

I glanced at my watch. Poor baby! No wonder he was starving. I hurried to the lounge, sat in the armchair and Joe latched on immediately. As my eyes swept the room, I noticed the sofa. The cushions were no longer in the neat and ordered state I'd left them; they were disturbed and dented. Clearly someone had slept there last night. Bloody hell, what the…?

With a frown, I replayed what had happened at midnight. I couldn't say for certain, but I was pretty sure I'd blacked out before reaching the side door. Which meant that *someone* also had keys.

–

Prompted by my mother-in-law's interference, I had travelled to Norfolk with the vague notion of… what? Collecting paperwork for the probate, I supposed. But beyond that I had no real plan of what to do about mum's belongings, or indeed the house itself. Although Laura was usually so pragmatic, our conversations since the funeral had revolved around her not-so-subtle questions about my wellbeing: 'Everything OK, Ali? Is Thingy behaving himself now? Have you had lunch? What did you eat? What about all those check-ups you're meant to attend to make sure you're not cracking up?'

'Stop it, Laura. You sound like bloody Madeleine.'

'That's cruel, Ali.' Then, 'You two were besties. Why did you fall out? Did she stumble off the pedestal?'

'Very droll. How's sweet, savage love with Shelby going?'

I hadn't wanted to think about Madeleine, let alone talk about her. The trick with Laura was to change the subject, so I had. It had been lovely to listen to her unguarded prattle – what she and Shelby had done over the weekend, what she'd made him for dinner, the small but thoughtful gifts he'd regularly bought her. She hadn't mentioned the baby issue, so neither had I. But we hadn't discussed Mum's will and estate, or what to do about her reams of stuff or the bungalow's future either. Was the plan to pack everything up with a view to selling The Lodge, or would we keep it on and rent it out? Was it mortgaged to the hilt or were the title deeds somewhere in the house? The contents were immense, each pristine piece either nostalgic or antique, so I didn't want to sell items lovingly kept or sourced by my mum, but Miles and I only had so much spare room in our home. There were her siblings, of course, but how would I allot the trinkets and ornaments, lamps and books? And what about the larger items of furniture? The sofa suite, wardrobes, drawers and beds…

Perhaps Mum's friends would want a keepsake too. I gave a small smile at the thought of her horror film 'staff' and made a note to tell Laura about the addition of a giant, no less. But another thought occurred. The gardener and the cleaner were obviously still coming. Was anybody paying them? The house was running as though someone lived here. What about bills? The gas, council tax, water rates, a window cleaner? My chest felt tight with worry, but as I showered and dressed there was some wry relief that at least my legs were working this morning. I'd use them to visit Tom and Joan Hague and sound out things with them. Not only about finances, but the new bloody gardener who seemed to think it was OK to frequent my mum's house. Then there was the secret about Dad. That was still something I wanted to unearth.

Chapter Twenty-Three

When I finally emerged outside, a gentle wind broke the humidity. Hoping I looked saner than I had two hours previously, I put Joe in his pram and strolled the longer but smooth-surfaced route to the main road. Turning left, I retraced the steps I'd so often taken as a child. Times had changed, of course, but Mum and Dad had thought nothing of letting me amble down this tree-lined hill to Bureside, the riverside property owned by Tom and Joan.

Though I must have met them from time to time before I was five, my clear recollection of them started when Dad bought The Lodge. At that age, I was suspicious of everyone, so it was no surprise I hadn't liked them at first. Silly things bothered me – Joan's sixties-style spectacles and swinging earrings, Tom's over-friendliness and too-red lips. But after visiting Bureside with Mum on a few occasions, my adoration of their fairytale thatched cottage overcame my prejudice. Set in manicured gardens on the River Bure, it had its own lagoon complete with a white picket bridge, stunning weeping willows and a spread of pink water lilies. The inside was wonderful too, a dark Aladdin's cave, chock-a-block with exquisite classical furniture and antique books. Mum had never been into old things in Sheffield; mega modern had been her preference back then, so her friendship with Joan must have converted her. And on some level me, too. How many times did I paw the huge gilt-edged Holy Bible before Tom persuaded Joan to give it to me with an indulgent smile? The pleasure of lugging it home had been immeasurable, but Mum's sharp nose had shown her disapproval.

'Joan really gave you that? A valuable antique isn't something to play with, Ali. We'll put it away until you're older,' she'd said, taking it from me.

'Oh come on, Eve,' Dad had replied. 'It's a beautiful gift. Let's leave it out as a reminder of Tom's generosity.'

'Really? Such a dusty old thing?'

'Yes.' He'd circled her waist, deflecting her annoyance as only he could. 'The Queen Anne table will be an ideal place for it. Though not quite as perfect, it has long, slim and shapely legs like yours.'

A lovely memory, but the clutch of anxiety was there. The bible was another charming and delicate item to be moved and rehoused.

Waving away a plump bee, I waited for the road to clear and looked at Bureside's large driveway. Tom's Rolls-Royce Silver Shadow wasn't there as usual. It was probably thirty years old now, but it must have cost him a fair sum back in the day. Pretty impressive for an ex policeman. 'Bobby on the beat turned entrepreneur,' he once said when Laura asked what his job was. He'd winked at me. 'With a huge dose of help from your very clever accountant daddy.'

I pushed the pram into the shade of a canopy above the front door, lifted the brass knocker and waited for a while. Only then did it occur to me that I should have telephoned first. I wasn't a little girl strolling down to bother poor 'Mrs Hague' because I knew she'd be here and everyone else was busy. I was an adult now and I hadn't seen her in the flesh for years. Though older than the woman in the photo above the hearth, she'd still been a tall, square-faced and handsome lady back then. Her grey hair in a bun, she'd always worn those dangly pearl earrings. And of course the cat's-eye-shaped spectacles. Would she look the same today? I didn't find out as the door was answered by Tom. I'd seen him more recently at Mum's, so he was as I had expected – silver-haired these days, but still dapper with his neatly trimmed moustache. And those same lips and too-perfect teeth.

'Alice! Hello, love,' he said, obviously surprised. 'We didn't know you were here yet.' He clearly hadn't been to the deli or spoken to Mum's staff. The thought of the gardener made me hot with embarrassment. Since discovering the dented cushions, I'd been infused with indignation. What the hell had he been doing stalking the house at flaming midnight, let alone helping himself to the sofa? I'd managed to overlook what a hysterical idiot I'd been, but it was suddenly there, lit by spotlights. Screaming and bloody fainting, then rushing out this morning like Cathy on the moors. Still, if I was the subject of gossip, it hadn't yet spread this far out of the village.

Reverting to Tom, I stiffly waited for his greeting. Even a social embrace wasn't my thing, but he'd always been tactile with easy hugs and kisses, and I had welcomed them once the childhood attachment had set in. But today his pale eyes welled and he simply took my hand. 'Oh love, I can't tell you how sorry I am about your mum. How we miss her.' He blew his nose loudly and focused on Joe. 'Come on in then, and let's see your little smasher. Eve was so thrilled.'

Wondering how old Tom was these days, I passed my son into his steady hands. Mid to late seventies was my guess. Though wearing wire-framed glasses today, he still looked fit and held himself erect like a soldier. He'd probably been quite a catch in his youth.

Lifting Joe up high, he laughed. 'Aye, he'll do.' He kissed him on both cheeks and passed him back. 'Cup of strong brew coming up.' He smiled his white smile. 'It's the one thing I miss about Sheffield – not the tea, but the water; even when it's boiled, it doesn't taste right down here. Mind you, I get my Yorkshire puds every Sunday come rain or shine. I'm a lucky fella – my Joan's are still the best in the world. Take a seat and make yourself comfortable, love. I'll just be two minutes.'

He headed up the stairs, so I stepped into the oak-beamed lounge, propped Joe on my knee and glanced around. From the brown Chesterfield settee to the well-stocked teak bar, nothing had changed.

Hurtled back in time, I turned to the French doors behind me and pictured my parents drinking cocktails on the lawn. I smiled at the image. Sitting in stripy deck chairs, Mum was wearing a headscarf and swatting midges, Dad was popping the cherry from his glass into my mouth. The memory was so vivid, I almost felt the fruity crunch, the sweet and sour zip as it slipped down my throat.

Was the hammock still in the garden? I had preferred to gently swing beneath its shaded hood but Laura would stretch out on the grass in her tasselled denim shorts, desperate for her pale legs to catch the sun. Her shins were singed that last summer, hot and bright pink for days. 'Why do I always burn Mum? *She* doesn't. It's so bloody unfair!'

Coming back to the room, I put my hand to my chest in surprise. A row of eyes were watching me from the console table. I had completely forgotten about the 'sleepy-eyed' porcelain dolls. With their mop of human-like hair, creamy china skin and staring eyes, they were actually quite spooky, but as a child I was more intrigued than alarmed by them. I knew Joan's seven 'German Bisque' babies were very valuable and not to touch them, but I was fascinated by their exquisite Victorian outfits. I'd peer at their delicate eyelashes or peep into their pink mouths and spy tiny teeth. I'd longed to cradle 'Lucy', 'William' or 'Beth' to see what they felt like, but I always sensed I was being observed – by Mum with bated breath in case I dropped one, most probably.

I automatically began to count them, from the first auburn-haired boy to the last dark-haired girl, but a loud bang from somewhere made me look up. Was it Tom? Had he fallen?

'Alice.'

I jumped. Carrying a tray, he was right beside me. I rubbed my goosebumped arms. 'Oh sorry, I was miles away…'

Seeming to study me carefully, he put down the steaming drinks. 'One mug of best tea,' he said. 'Don't tell Joan I haven't used a cup and saucer or I'll be in trouble. Neither use nor ornament in my humble opinion.'

'She isn't here?' I smiled. 'Don't tell me she's swanning around in the Roller.'

'No, Joan doesn't drive. Not these days, at least.'

We fell silent for a while. I groped for what I wanted to ask about Dad. But where would I start? As lovely as Tom was, I didn't know him that well. I could hardly just say: 'Mum wanted to tell me something about Dad before she died. I was too absorbed in my own worries to listen. Do you know what it was?' And if it was something bad about my dad, did I really want to know? Tom was still intently gazing. Bloody hell, it felt as though he was reading my mind. And no, right now I wasn't ready to discover an Auntie Brenda 'home truth'.

I swallowed. 'How's *Sylvette*?' I quickly asked instead.

Sylvette was their spectacular ten-berth cruiser. She'd been integral to my rose-tinted summers, especially the outings on the Bure with Tom and Dad. Sleeping overnight in my very own cabin. Helping myself to fruity drinks from the bar. Eating fried breakfast on the decking. Feeling important at the helm of such a fine boat.

'Do you and Joan still go for river trips?' I added.

'Aye, we do, just the two of us escaping. Romantic as we like. Ask Joan and she'll tell you she's happiest there. "Free as one of those swans", she'll say.' He sat next to me and peered closely. 'The important question is how our Alice is today. You've got something on your mind. How can I help you, love?'

Taking a wobbly breath, I tried to explain the issues which were worrying me most, but it was hard to keep focus. I was still so exhausted; I could have fallen asleep there and then. But it was a relief to talk to him, to spill out my pathetic concerns. At that moment he was the closest thing I had to a father and he was patient, measured and kind.

'Let matters ride for now, love,' he advised. 'See how you and Laura feel about things in the weeks and the months to come. What's the hurry? Have a little holiday while you're here.'

Reaching an arm around my shoulder, he pulled me close and pecked the top of my hair. 'It's lovely to have young'uns around.' Then, with a twinkle in his eye: 'And no fretting about cleaners and gardeners and bills. We might be a little behind the times in these parts, but even we've heard of online banking, direct debits and standing orders.'

Feeling much brighter, I laughed and took a breath. 'Actually, talking about the gardener...'

'Aye?'

'He said he's called George, but Mum's old gardener happened to be called George too. I'm pretty sure they aren't one and the same.'

He smiled. 'Well, that's a relief. Old George died at least a year back.'

'Right.' I frowned. Why had Mum never mentioned employing a new one? 'He seems to have house keys...'

'Aye, he does.'

I inhaled to consider how best to approach last night's bizarre episode and the bloody man's clear familiarity with my mother's home. But Tom continued to speak before I had chance. 'Don't let that worry you, love; what with the holidaymakers down here, it isn't unusual.' He cocked his head. 'Besides, Eve trusted George with them. She very much liked him too.'

Chapter Twenty-Four

I left Bureside with mixed feelings. Tom's sorrow and concern were touching, and his advice helpful and sound, but I was cross with myself for wimping out of my questions about Dad. As Laura had recalled, he'd gone off with Tom in the Roller most weeks during that last summer. Perhaps it was the memory of Mum's tight face and her short temper, but those trips, looking back, seemed furtive.

'Where are you going, Dad?' Laura had demanded at some point. 'Why can't we come?'

'You don't want to travel to boring old Norwich,' Tom had replied, slipping us both a five-pound note. 'Save all your pennies for Great Yarmouth, eh?'

I frowned. After Mum's funeral, Laura had speculated they were hospital visits for check-ups or treatment. Perhaps chemotherapy. But that meant the Hagues must have known about Dad's illness…

The usual anxieties about who-knew-what made me unsettled. Sighing, I wondered what I'd do in the same position. Allow my daughters to have one last blissful holiday or prepare them for the horrific shock only weeks later? Laura was in the latter camp, I knew. She and Mum had row after row after Dad's death: she was nearly fifteen; Mum should have told her. Mum knew she could be trusted to keep secrets, didn't she? But I was in the former;

covering my ears and blocking out life's horrible truths was far preferable.

I inwardly groaned. Perhaps that was why I hadn't registered Madeleine's drinking for so long; maybe I had chosen to turn a blind eye.

The sun hot on my cheeks, I trudged up the leafy road. Stopping at the gates, I glanced up to The Lodge. Did I have the energy to slog around the perimeter road? Nope, it would be far quicker to take the shortcut.

A stupid idea. After only a few seconds of pushing against the stones, it became clear this route hadn't been designed with a pram in mind. Winded and dizzy, I soon gave up, sat on the grassy bank and lowered my head. Though truly pathetic, the thought of a battle with pebbles made me want to weep. Far easier to take Joe out and collect the buggy later. A plan, a good plan. But before I'd even got to my feet, strong arms had scooped both up.

Pink-faced and undignified, I scrambled after them, mortified to be such a pitiful figure yet again. I longed to explain that I was once an assertive, professional woman in complete control of my life, but knew I couldn't squeeze out the words without crying.

At the front door I fumbled for my keys.

'Have you eaten today?' the giant asked. But he didn't say it accusingly, as Miles might have done; it was just a question.

I shook my head. 'Joe needs feeding,' I replied. It felt like my mantra; life revolved around providing for my son, it was the only thing that kept me going.

He nodded. 'I'll make a sandwich then,' he said. 'The side entrance is open.'

Fearful the gardener might walk in with his offering any moment, I hid in my bedroom. Part of me knew I should be freaked out by this giant's constant presence, that I should confront him about sleeping on the sofa and even ask for the keys back, but now I had spoken to Tom and received Mum's blessing via him, I felt – even more weirdly – protected, of sorts. And even in my agitated state, I saw there was some humour in my situation. This man had all but carried me to bed last night and he was now making me lunch. It was bizarre and a little romantic. From what I had glimpsed so far, he was probably older than me, but definitely much younger and bigger than the old – dead – George. Though his face was half hidden by a shock of dark hair, this version was broad-shouldered and sinewy.

Picturing Laura's raised eyebrows, I smiled. 'Oh very Lady Chatterley,' she'd laugh.

But the smirk disappeared, replaced by a sudden notion. I wasn't Lady Chatterley; I was her daughter. This man had known where my bedroom was last night; he was obviously familiar with the lounge, the kitchen, the cupboards. He had a bloody key! And what had Tom said? That Mum 'very much' liked him. Oh God; perhaps he wasn't just *staff*.

Carefully laying Joe in his cot, I caught my face in the wardrobe glass. Though I had avoided mirrors over the past few weeks, I'd seen my reflection in windows, and in Madeleine's gaze, and I hadn't liked what I saw. Today was no different. The dark circles beneath my eyes were tinged almost purple; accentuated by my tight ponytail, my face was pallid and thin.

I snorted. My hair was hardly Madeleine-like at that moment. I pictured her look of determination as she'd washed and combed it last week. I'd felt so frail, I'd let her treat me like a dolly, but if I'd had a pair of sharp scissors right now, I would slice it all off.

'*You're an ugly pixie, found under a gooseberry bush, whereas I am a princess.*' Remembering Laura's regular childhood taunt, I glanced over to where her old bed had been. 'Yes,' I said aloud. 'Cut it off like a pixie's.'

I came back to the mirror and pinched my cheeks for a touch of colour. Ridiculous, for sure, but I had been a good looking woman once; it seemed important this new George should know I wasn't as weak and wan as I appeared.

Taking a steadying breath, I strode into the kitchen. Accompanied by a tall glass of milk, my sandwich was waiting. My first random thought was about the clump of weeds from this morning. Had he washed his hands? The second was irritation. Milk; really? Milk was for babies; milk was for *weak and wan* infants.

Conforming to type, I lifted a corner of the granary bread and peered inside. Ham, tomato and lettuce with far too much butter. But what the hell, I was hungry.

My mind did the maths as I ate. The man was at ease in the kitchen; that much was obvious. Mum had been in her sixties; old but not that old. Attractive, too. The gardener was... what? Early forties or so. Still, there had to be at least a twenty-something-year age gap. Could it really be possible they were in some sort of a relationship? If I was honest, the idea was uncomfortable. Would I even raise it with Laura? We'd been on the same page about the 'uncles' as kids, but I had no doubt of her response now:

'*Mum probably liked sex just as much as we do, Ali. A younger lover, eh? Good on her.*'

Furtively peering from the side door, I watched the 'younger lover' methodically turn dry clods of earth in the vegetable patch. Wasn't that peculiar? Tending the soil of a dead woman? Did he work at other people's homes or just spend his time here, visiting the house at midnight, used to being invited in?

The forthright Ali of old flooded back, so I marched across the grass and stood over his crouched body. 'Could I have a word, please?'

He continued his chore, shaking the soil from a bunch of bright carrots as though I wasn't there.

'Hello? Could I have a word?' I asked again.

He looked up at me then, squinting against the bright sunshine. Close up, his dishevelled mop was streaked with fine strands of grey. Yes, he was older than me, but much younger than Mum. Certainly too much for comfort. His eyes pierced blue beneath his dark frown, and with his sculpted nose, he resembled a cruel master, out of place in a garden. Then he spoke, his accent northern and deep.

'What can I do for you?'

Putting the veg to one side, he moved on, grasping the next cluster of leaves with long fingers and gently tugging. He'd made it clear I was disturbing his work. He was obviously an arrogant sod, usually a good excuse for my incisive tongue. But now I was here, I didn't know what to ask or where to start. *Why were you here in the middle of the night? Why did you sleep on my mother's sofa? Why are you still tending her garden? Were you fucking her?*

Instead I said, 'Would you like a coffee or something? With a biscuit?' Oh God, my voice had emerged imperiously: to my consternation, I'd sounded exactly like Mum.

'I usually get my own, thanks,' he replied.

I folded my arms. Should I point out that things had changed, that I might not be comfortable with a stranger coming into the house whenever it took his fancy? But a wave of loneliness struck, so I began to walk away.

'The cats are at my cottage, if you're wondering,' he called after me.

Oh God, I had forgotten about the cats; they'd completely slipped my mind. He must have seen my dismay, as his expression seemed to soften. He stood up and wiped his hands on his shorts.

'It's not something you need to worry about right now. I just thought I'd let you know.' He observed me for a few moments, his gaze thoughtful. 'If Joe's asleep, why don't you get some rest yourself?'

Shrugging, I walked away. Why did everyone treat me like an invalid or a child? I'd had a double whammy, that was all. A birth and a death. One in and one out. I would get better; I just needed time.

I looked in on Joe, then stepped across to Mum's bedroom. The sun glowing in, it smelled of perfume as though she'd just left. Running a hand over the silky throw, a memory hit me of a happy day I had almost forgotten. It had been the start of spring, our first visit at Easter, and Mum woke us up early. 'Come on girls. Quickly! Come and look at something special.'

It was April the first, sure to be a practical joke. But when she'd insisted, we'd shuffled to her room. The patio doors were open wide, and immediately ahead was a muster of blue peacocks, their exquisite feathers fanned out. We'd slipped between our parents and the four of us had laughed and laughed; it had been so unusual, so exciting, so far from our humdrum life in Sheffield.

I was six, Laura ten and that moment was perfect. We just hadn't known it then.

Chapter Twenty-Five

I woke in Mum's bed to the hum of the vacuum cleaner somewhere in the house. Nancy's daughter Denise, I assumed. If she was anything like her mum, I needed to be on my best form for inspection, so I decided to hide here instead and do something constructive. Opening the door a crack to listen out for Joe, I glanced around the bedroom, wondering where to start.

The large wardrobe seemed the obvious place, so I opened its solid mahogany doors, unsurprised to see the dresses, skirts and blouses were arranged neatly in sections, just like mine at home. Staring blankly for several moments, I pictured myself as Madeleine, throwing each item into a good, bad or ugly pile. But nothing of Mum's was bad or ugly, somewhat dated perhaps, but always best quality from Sheffield's Schofields or Cole Brothers. Few items were new, but they were immaculate and choreographed in colour and design, as were her old handbags and shoes.

Deferring the daunting task, I didn't rake through the hangers, but went straight to the coat section, pulling out two furs that were hidden there, unused for years. Like a husband and wife, I laid them side by side on the bed. The mink jacket for me, the ocelot for Laura, Mum had always said.

I hesitantly touched the soft ocelot. The thought of wearing animal skin revolted me, but these were a family heirloom, to be looked at occasionally, then stashed away. Opening the boxy pale mink by its invisible hook, I peered at the satin lining. Back in the day, Dad had it made especially for Mum, so her initials were embroidered there. She'd wear it with a floor-length dress to his charity dinners. 'Doesn't Mum look a million dollars?' he'd say.

I slipped the jacket back on its padded hanger. How much had this cost? A small fortune in all probability; Dad clearly had money to burn. Though earmarked for me, Laura could have it if she wanted. I pictured her laughing and saying, 'I'll wear real fur and be damned!' But I didn't really know if she would; my childhood memories of my sister and the real one had merged; without seeing her in the flesh, it was hard to judge which was which. Like Miles. We had only been apart for two days, but already he felt insubstantial, like someone remembered from my past.

With a sigh, I returned the contraband to the wardrobe and sat on the bed with Mum's jewellery box. Antique, of course. She'd spotted it in a dusty shop window recently, thrilled to discover it matched the writing box Dad had found at Stalham auction all those years ago.

The haughty glance of the gardener rushed back. Was he really Mum's lover? And how long for? Did she still think fondly of Dad, or had the feeling of intimacy gone, replaced by the presence of a younger man in her bed? The thought wasn't just embarrassing and uncomfortable, it was mixed with other emotions I couldn't quite describe.

Going back to my chore, I opened the lid and peered at the treasure trove. The gemstone and design of every sparkling ring, heavy necklace, bracelet and brooch were so familiar. One or two simple pieces had belonged to my grandparents, but the rest were gifts from Dad. I knew where each exquisite item had been bought and the occasion – Mum's birthday or Christmas, a short business trip or anniversary. Or just because he loved her. Money again; how he'd showered his wife with tokens of love.

I smiled wistfully at the memory of us girls pawing the sparkling jewels, wearing them, examining them and choosing who should have which. We'd argued and traded and then changed our minds. But I didn't want Mum's trinkets or clothes, her house or her money. I wanted *her* back, to feel her soft cheek comfort mine, to ask what she'd wanted to tell me about.

The strange feeling of lethargy mixed with impatience swamped me again. Another hour had gone by and I hadn't achieved anything. Taking a brisk breath, I stepped over to the dressing table and opened the drawer. Three ribbon-tied stacks of envelopes caught my gaze, but as I reached to pluck one out, a soft flurry of air swept my shoulders, stopping me short. Certain my wish had been answered and Mum was behind me, I scrunched my eyes and swallowed. She was my dearest mother, but I couldn't shake off the terror of what she might look like after several weeks in the ground. Still classically beautiful or invaded by maggots?

My heart thrashing, I slowly turned. Nothing was there; just bright sunshine through the windows and the mild aroma of her particular scent.

Shaking my foolishness away, I went back to the drawer, took out the letter bundles, then padded from the room to check on my son. His cot was empty, but I wasn't surprised, just irritated that the gardener felt entitled to elbow into my life.

Leaving my find on the spindled chair by my bed, I went to the loo, realising for the first time that my body was invisibly repairing itself. I could wee without peas or pain; I no longer felt the drag of my pelvic floor. I dared my eyes to the mirror. Hmm, if only my face showed it; if only my mind would obey too. But I lifted my chin. The Ali before pregnancy and birth was still there; I just needed to find her.

Resolved to assert my authority, I marched to the kitchen, but instead of finding the giant, I discovered Joe in his bouncy chair, clearly spellbound by Nancy. Or perhaps it was the bubbles spilling over the washing-up bowl.

'Hello, lovey. Just giving my Denise a hand,' she said, placing a soapy palm on her hip. She nodded to the table. 'Home-made preserve. Scones were baked this morning and tea's in the pot. He's been a happy little soul since he woke up, haven't you, love?'

Her near-toothless grin would have frightened me as a child, but Joe didn't seem to mind. He responded with one of his own.

Shamefaced at my irritation, I sat at the table. The baking was still warm and the butter she'd brought was the yellowest I'd ever seen. Glancing at the stove, I breathed through the image the jam conjured up. After Mum's funeral, I found an old jar of strawberry in the cupboard at home and I'd longed to taste it, to see if it was as delicious as I recalled, but its lid was stuck fast. I tried denting it to break the vacuum, donning rubber gloves, immersing it in boiling water, but nothing worked. When Miles finally arrived home, I had no interest in why he was so late, but begged him to open the pot, which he achieved with one turn. But the zingy smell of alcohol immediately biffed me; the fruit had frothed. The taste was not completely unpleasant, but it was certainly not the flavour of sweet sunshine I remembered.

The memory highlighted the sad passage of childhood, the fermenting of it, I supposed.

I didn't realise I was crying until Nancy appeared by my side and enveloped me in her arms. She wiped my cheeks with thick-knuckled fingers. 'There, there lovey,' she said. 'It's better to let it all out, you know. You'll weep until you think you can't weep any more. Then you'll weep again, but not so often.' She looked soulful, but only for a beat. 'I still cry for my mother from time to time, but I haven't set eyes on her for over fifty years. And look at me! I'm still here and still smiling.'

'Thank you,' I said stiffly, not used to such close proximity to anyone these days. Even Miles's hugs felt static; we didn't fold into each other as we had once. But I understood it was difficult for him; until recently my breasts hurt if he hugged me too tightly and I guessed he didn't want to imply anything sexual by holding me too intimately. I hadn't been ready for that and I was relieved he understood.

Nancy buttered a scone and covered it liberally in jam. 'There we are, love, that'll bring a smile to your bonny face!'

Now that did make my lips twitch; where I came from 'bonny' meant fat, and I was no longer rotund, my post-pregnancy layer a thing of the past.

A red-haired lady appeared with the Hoover. Nancy's Denise, I assumed. Her pretty face looked familiar; maybe I had met her before. I felt guilty again; these people had been Mum's friends and neighbours for years and I had taken no notice of them on my visits. I had wafted in and out carrying my sense of self-importance with me. It was having a child that made the difference, I thought. And a dead mother.

Tucking her hair behind her ears, Denise manhandled her chest until she seemed satisfied with her cleavage, then she slicked her mouth with lip balm. 'I'll just take a cuppa out to George. He'll be parched.'

'Denise doesn't half fancy him,' her mum commented when she'd gone.

'I thought he got his own drinks,' I muttered, but Nancy was still talking.

'Mind, all the ladies round here have a soft spot for him, me included. He came down a year or so ago and he wears a wedding band, but no one has ever seen a wife. We think she must have passed away. Why wear a ring otherwise?'

To keep the likes of Denise at bay, I imagined. But still, it was interesting. 'Where does he come from?' I asked.

'Up north. That's all we know. He doesn't say much, but he's a handsome man. A good listener too, and you know how us ladies like to be listened to!' She peered at me. 'Nothing wrong with that.'

I focused on her then. Her shrewd eyes looked knowing. Oh God, I was right; something had gone on between him and Mum.

Denise returned through the side door and gave a little sniff. 'I can't find him anywhere, but he's left his tools so he can't be far.'

He's probably hiding, I thought, as Joe began to cry.

Chapter Twenty-Six

They were both truly lovely, but I was glad when Nancy and Denise finally left. I wasn't used to such intrusion in my life and I wanted to make a start on another assignment, get busy and do something practical to stop me feeling sorry for myself.

Padding to the lounge, I stared at the walnut sideboard. As the keeper of photographs, correspondence and documents, school reports, bills, certificates, and everything in between, it seemed to breathe and bulge. But I nodded firmly nonetheless. I'd start from the left; anything financial would be there.

What would a solicitor need? Though I had some knowledge about probate and trusts, my area of the law was crime. I had worked on the defendant side when I first qualified. Initially, my clients had been straightforward car thieves and burglars, but when I moved on to rapists and murderers, I became frayed and demoralised, so I switched from the dark side to prosecuting.

Joe watching from his chair, I kneeled and dragged open the large bottom drawer. Pulling out a chunky folder, I sat back and flicked through it with a frown. It looked as though two separate files had become mingled, one relating to domestic finances – bills, bank statements, tax certificates, savings accounts, cheque stubs and the like; the other more legal – old-fashioned writs and statutory demands, company accounts and official receiver correspondence, even crispy copies of the *London Gazette*. I peered at the date on the newspaper. It was aeons ago, before Dad died; it was clearly a case he'd worked on for a client. Why Mum had held on to it, I had no idea, but I put it to one side and delved in again.

Sighing at my mother's inability to throw anything out, I found household instructions, pamphlets, receipts, guarantees and so on, but no house deeds, recent bank or building society statements, so I shoved everything back. I opened the next drawer, but despite my good intentions, I closed it again. It could wait, surely? As Tom Hague had pointed out, all was in hand bill and staff-wise. I could leave the probate documents until the weekend; perhaps Miles would help me then.

As though reading my mind, the telephone rang. At seven o'clock, I knew it would be my hubby and it was. 'Miles! I was just—'

'Is that my stunningly gorgeous wife?' It was what he always said after a few glasses of wine. 'How are things going?'

Pleasure spread in my chest; it was so nice to hear his voice. Taking a breath, I considered where to start. Perhaps my fright from last night; maybe the visit to Bureside and the flood of childhood memories. Or the huge volume of paperwork and the need for his input on Saturday. But the sound of music and laughter filtered through. He was clearly in a pub or restaurant, and my hesitation was enough for him to launch into an account of who he'd bumped into since Sunday, soon followed by a blow-by-blow description of his day in court. His trial was going well, he'd scored major points cross-examining a key witness who'd made admissions; the judge had asked pertinent questions – she was so very perceptive and had once been in their chambers – and things were looking pretty damned good.

I was pleased for Miles, but saddened too. Between our two worlds, the crater was still there. Like my childhood and the jam, it felt as though our relationship was slowly decaying. Did we have anything in common any more?

The call soon ended. 'Someone wants me, I'd better go. Take care, gorgeous. I'll call you tomorrow.'

And he hadn't even asked after Joe.

Going back to the lounge, I opened the cupboard on the right. As expected, the photographs were there, the packets labelled and neatly stacked. I reached for my parents' ivory wedding album. Laura and I had pawed it so many times, it was a wonder the silver tassel had any silky strands left. 'Dad! Dad! Come and look at your dimple!' we'd shout.

How handsome we thought he was, in accord for once. Robert Redford in *The Great Gatsby*, we agreed, but as I studied his image now, he didn't look like the dad I recalled. Though Mum was laughing, he looked tense. This wasn't the smiling man I remembered.

Sighing, I closed him away. How well did children know their parents? Would Joe study our wedding portrait and wonder who we were? I'd wanted a winter wedding like Mum and Dad, but Miles and I wed in spring because Madeleine told me to.

I groaned at the thought. So seduced by her, I became a different person. I stopped being alternative or individual; I grew my hair long, wore expensive, stylish suits and towering heels. A mini-Madeleine, in fact. But in fairness, she boosted my confidence; the ugly duckling had finally become a swan.

So who was the real Alison Baker? The shy difficult child, the punky teenager or the professional and confident barrister? I was none of them now. It seemed I'd transformed yet again, a fractured self. New mother, bereaved daughter, disgruntled wife. Maybe I wasn't grown-up after all; perhaps I was still evolving, still developing, trying to unearth the authentic me.

A chilly draught wafted by and I shivered. The dusk was finally engulfing the poplars outside, but I could still see the gardener with his tools in the distance. So isolated and lonely at that moment, I could have flung open the door and asked him to come in, begged him to hold me in his arms and warm me. As I watched him don his jacket and stride away, I wondered if that was how Mum had felt too.

Chapter Twenty-Seven

Wednesday

I slept solidly all night until Joe woke me at five. Although he nodded off after feeding, I was awake and surprisingly refreshed, so I stretched out in the warm bed and listened to the chattering birds. The toasted nut aroma of the woods filtered through the open window like air freshener.

Turning to my chair, I peered at the letters I'd left there yesterday. They had clearly been sorted into separate bundles and tied by differently coloured ribbon. I'd been nominated pink. There hadn't been much need for correspondence between Mum and me, but she must have kept every postcard, invitation and birthday greeting I'd ever sent. They'd been neatly opened with the bronze letter opener she kept next to the bible. I pictured her doing it, studying the writing for a second, then announcing who it was from with a delighted smile before slicing it open with one sweep.

The image felt both mellow and sad; the world was now so electronic. It wasn't just emails and texts; many of last year's Christmas cards had been online greetings. Would Joe ever be given a handwritten missive? Blowing him a kiss, I resolved to do it, to chapter his life. Then I thought of the bursting lounge drawers, let alone the whole house and its contents. Perhaps paperless brevity was a good thing. The fact Mum had kept these letters was lovely, but what would I do with them now?

I pulled out one envelope, my tidy longhand not so very different to how it was now. Each word was written in differently coloured ink.

> *To Mummy, happy birthday, lots and lots of love*
> *from Ali xxxxxxx PS I love you soooo much!*

It was twenty-six years ago now, but I still remembered the moment. Dad had taken Laura and me to the funfair at Great Yarmouth. Laura was in the front seat, so she was the first to spot the sea, but I didn't let that spoil my day. We ate clouds of pink candy floss, screamed on the rollercoaster and the teacup ride; we spent half an hour selecting a gift for Mum and I won a prize on the hoopla.

My eyes had devoured the huge furry tigers and elephants and cheetahs prominently displayed on the stall. Hopping from foot to foot, I couldn't wait to be rewarded with something so luxurious and indulgent, and tears pricked when I was handed a biro, a boring flipping biro! But when I studied it in the car, I discovered it had six different ink tubes inside: pink, blue, green, orange and purple. It even had yellow. Laura had won a spiral-bound writing pad and she gave it to me 'for my biro'. I hadn't known which to treasure the most, the memory of such a wonderful day or the present my big sister had given me without expecting anything in return.

Flicking through the postcards, I was reminded of the places Sidney and I had visited as students. We'd had a tight budget, but still managed to zig-zag the country with our tent. Then there were the more exotic holidays with

Miles, stunning locations in the Far East and Caribbean, as well as long weekends in Europe.

The memories made me smile. I'd gone to bed feeling disgruntled with Miles, but as I read through the scrawl and remembered the fun, the closeness and love, I felt more charitable towards him. He had a challenging job; I knew as much as anyone how stressful, yet exhilarating, the law could be. He had to absorb and understand every page of the experts' reports and voluminous trial bundles; he was the one who stood or fell before the judge and the person paying his fee. Someone had to lose, and the client's livelihood could be lost or his business destroyed on the barrister's performance, a misplaced document, an unreliable witness – even the whim of the judge.

'It's only money,' as Dad used to say. 'If I make a mistake, an insurer steps in. But if I were a doctor…'

Yet money was important; it still made the world go round. I was pleased Miles was on a high, that things were going well for him. Perhaps he lacked a little empathy at times, but it was easy for me. I *had* been in a courtroom. He couldn't give birth; he'd never suffered a close bereavement. I needed to build bridges and be more understanding.

Pleased at my own positivity, I reached for the next bunch of letters. Save for one, each pale blue envelope matched in size and was written in Mum or Dad's neat handwriting.

With a frown, I carefully untied the white ribbon to find at least thirty missives, written forty-four years ago. Why on earth had my parents corresponded so prolifically? They'd both lived in Sheffield, met regularly and courted on the Bole Hills…

Taking a nervy breath, I opened the first and slipped out the paper.

Ward 10 Men's Sanatorium it began.

What?

> *Hello beautiful! How are you this sunny morning?*
> *Lily, aged 103, has just finished cleaning the ward. Every time she bends down nature takes its course…*

Checking the postcode, I sat back in astonishment. My dad had clearly been in a Sheffield hospital. But why? I opened the next – this one in Mum's handwriting:

> *I've been trying all day to find time to write to you a) because I want you to get this tomorrow (my birthday) and b) because of your red nose and purple wrists sticking out of that too-tight pullover yesterday.*

Red nose and purple wrists?

I selected another from Dad:

> *I had my TB resistance test measured this morning. It measured 10 x 10 mm which the Sister said was very good (I deserve a kiss for that!) I was weighed too today – the same as last time (I deserve a further kiss for that!) Thank your ma for the chocolate biscuits and thank yourself for everything (you deserve a kiss for that – from me!)*

Bloody hell; though Dad's humour and love shone through his words, he'd had tuberculosis, another discovery I doubted even Laura knew about.

Leaning back against the pillow, I mulled over the news. It was shocking but interesting too. I'd been immunised at school, the round dent still obvious on my upper arm. Though rare in the UK now, people used to die of it, from Emily Bronte to George Orwell, John Keats to Chopin. How worried must Mum have been? And why hadn't she ever mentioned it?

Joe's shuffling brought me back to the time. Knowing he'd wake very soon, I pulled out the last, larger envelope. There was no address nor postmark on this one, but it was in Dad's handwriting again, inscribed '*To Evelyn*'. Inside the envelope was a single, undated sheet of white paper and just fourteen words.

> *Darling Eve. I'm so sorry. Please find it in your heart to forgive me.*

Chapter Twenty-Eight

The intermittent early sunshine glinting through the side door, Joe watched me eat breakfast from his bouncy chair.

'How about a walk along the riverside?' I asked him. 'There'll be ducks and swans, and if we're lucky, a shoal of slithery eels.'

As if understanding every word, he smiled in reply. Older and wiser about pram transport, I decided to try him in the new front-and-back carrier. It took a while to work out the straps and buckles, but I finally slipped him in and grinned proudly at his solid chubbiness. He hadn't been weighed for a while, yet he was getting heavier each day, something I had achieved all by myself.

I chuckled inwardly. Hark at me, I'd become one of those smiling mums in the smiley posters if I wasn't very careful.

Though the sky was still partially cloudy, I donned sunglasses and strolled down the hill. Would the coven still recognise me as I passed? The glasses reminded me to call Laura, to let her know I was here and that I could piss without peas. I'd mention her stack of letters too. Her yellow bow remained intact; it hadn't seemed proper to read her personal correspondence and there was that inherent worry I might learn something I didn't want to know. It was childish, of course, but I hadn't realised her unhappiness until she'd confessed on the way to the airport. She'd pointed the finger at Mum, but I felt culpable too.

Then there was Dad. I'd invaded his privacy. What on earth had he done to beg Mum's forgiveness like that?

Though tempted by the lavender breathing out of the gift shop, I turned left and ambled down to the Bure. Its ripples were winking and flashing. The river's 'unknown' had always fascinated me, an enthralling combination of excitement and danger – the dark depths which needed to be avoided, yet which called to be explored at the same time. I had felt it most on the trips with Dad and Tom to Black Horse Broad. The lagoon was clear near the bank but became darker and deeper the further out we swam. Safe in my orange lifejacket, it was fun to feel the cool water through my fingers, to doggy splash or play catch with a ball, but there was a dread of touching something with my toes I couldn't identify. An almost sexual feeling, the thrill so intense it made me want to wee.

Making my way to the water's edge, I pulled a crust from the pocket of my shorts and lobbed a few pieces in. A family of coots dutifully crossed, barely making a wrinkle.

'Look, Joe. Ducks.'

As he kicked his legs in reply, I spotted two herons, one amongst the reeds, another high up in its tree-top nest. 'A big bird!' I said, pointing. 'The daddy heron is looking for food to take back to the babies in the nest.'

Maybe it was the other way around, perhaps the mummy was fishing, but it was a nice thought. Miles was working hard for me and Joe. It was what my dad had done, what good daddies should do.

Inhaling the aroma of fried bread and bacon, I moved on and gazed at the boats, drinking in the bright colours and shapes, the anchors and ropes, the masts and vibrant tyre fenders like I used to. Some were modern and shiny, others looked fit to sink. I nodded greetings to the early risers on their decks; it was stirring to see folk starting a new day, opening their cabin curtains, preparing food in small galley kitchens or arranging deck cushions like I once had on *Sylvette*.

I turned to the village green. Save for a lush patch around the water tap, it was cracked and parched, somewhat incongruously, given its position beside a river. Though there was only a single dog-walker now, I wondered if the likes of Ivan and Kelvin still came here, whether I'd know them if I saw them, if I'd experience that flash of recognition that hits then dissolves, leaving you uncertain. I'd felt similar when I first looked at Mum's gardener properly. I'd probably seen him before at Christmas, but as ever, I'd been blind to… blind to the fact he was her lover? Bloody hell; was that what she'd wanted to talk to me about?

Strolling on a little further, I stopped at a bench outside the Tudor-style inn. The pub was true to its 'Swan' name, so I sat for a while, watching the graceful birds glide over the glassy surface. They looked cool, sophisticated and detached, not unlike my big sister.

Suddenly twigging the time, I rummaged in my pockets, hoping for more than breadcrumbs to buy a bunch of bananas and a newspaper on the way home. Joe had fallen asleep, but he'd be due a feed soon.

A fat moggy wound its way around my ankles. Reaching out to stroke its black silky fur, it took me a few moments to recognise the red collar. Oh God; this wasn't just any cat, it was one of Mum's. Sensing I was being watched, I glanced at the row of tiny cottages a stone's throw from the pub. Dark eyes stared back. Standing at the furthest, George's large frame filled his open front door.

'You've come for the cats, then?' he called.

The embarrassment was immediate. He'd mentioned them before, but I'd completely forgotten. Again.

'No!' I blurted, stumbling towards him. I held out my pound coin. 'I was just checking if I could afford some fruit on the way home...'

Oh God. Now it sounded as though I was asking for a loan. I tried for a smile. 'We've been aimlessly walking. Ducks and herons and boats. Turns out you find them on the Broads.' I stopped babbling and nodded to the quaint picket fence. 'Gardeners too, apparently. I didn't know you – and the cats – lived here...'

Did I detect the hint of a smile? 'Come on in,' he said, turning. 'I'll make us a drink.'

My impulse to politely refuse was too late. He'd already ducked and disappeared, so I followed him in. I took off my shades and glanced around. Though there were only two adults and the modest add-on of Joe, the old-fashioned parlour felt crowded. Was it owned or rented? Did the man watching me share it with somebody else? A patchwork knitted throw was draped over the sofa, the round coffee table was covered by embroidered linen and the vase of flowers on the mantelpiece were still in bud. It wasn't what I'd expect of a man in his early forties.

Leaving the room, he spoke over his shoulder. 'Take a seat. The kettle's on.'

Joe stirred and grumbled at the prospect. It was time to feed him; I needed to get home. 'Actually,' I called stiffly, the words coming out Sheffield-posh. 'I won't bother, thank you.'

After a beat he returned, carrying a china teapot. 'What did you say?' he asked, seeming to appraise me beneath his dark eyebrows.

Though I tried, I couldn't quite meet his steady gaze. 'I just realised the time, so—'

'He needs feeding, does he? Is he on solids?'

I shook my head. How could I put it without embarrassing us both?

'Feed him here then.' He shrugged. 'It's fine, I'll make myself scarce.'

Feeling the roughness of the old piping on the back of my legs, I perched on the sofa and gave an involuntary little sniff. Why I was suddenly so picky, I didn't know. It certainly beat those funeral toilets.

Already unsettled and tetchy, Joe protested even louder as I tried to pull him out of his cocoon. After a second or two, George deposited the teapot, pulled me up and turned me round with firm hands. 'Looks like he's stuck. Best take it off first.'

He didn't say it irritability, but somewhere close. Realising I needed to pee, I bit my lip. 'Sorry, could I—'

'Top of the stairs,' he answered, taking Joe to the window.

The bathroom was minuscule. Surprisingly, there was no shower, just a basin and small bath. Despite my agitation, I couldn't help visualising the moody man downstairs crammed in it like a scene from Gulliver's Travels. The humour fell away as I glanced around. No flaming toilet paper. Then I spotted a woollen cosy on the window ledge and I peeped underneath. All was not lost after all.

As I washed my hands, I searched for a mirror. None on the walls, but next to an electric shaver I found an old-fashioned tortoiseshell grooming set. Picking up the hairbrush, I rubbed a finger along the smooth handle thoughtfully. There were no hairs between its bristles; it was there for decoration. I held the matching mirror by its long elegant grip. The glass was corroded at the edges and my image distorted – a reflection of how I felt – but my cheeks were pink, and despite the dark smudges beneath them, my eyes were bright. I looked better than I had for weeks, but the hairs on my arms were erect.

The brush and the mirror: Mum used to have an identical pair.

Chapter Twenty-Nine

Feeling febrile and exposed, I unzipped my nursing bra in readiness for the feed, then made my way down the narrow staircase on shaky legs. The idea that the gardener was Mum's lover had been idle speculation, but his bathroom told me otherwise. And now I looked again, the mantelpiece carriage clock was familiar too. I could picture her flashing her friendly smile: '*Take this, love. It's really quite old. It would look nice in your cottage.*' Or perhaps Mum, like Denise, had a crush on him and had given him regular presents. Why that felt even worse, I couldn't say.

Fearful he'd say something, I avoided eye contact, but he passed Joe to me without comment and busied himself in the kitchen while I sorted out Joe beneath my baggy T-shirt.

After ten minutes he returned, placed a cup of tea and a plate of buttered granary on the table beside me, then settled down in the armchair.

Folding his arms, he finally broke the silence. 'Call me George, everyone else does.'

It seemed an odd comment; he'd already told me his name. But I nodded and self-consciously ate the bread. For a while he seemed to watch every bite, but his attention suddenly shifted and he stood. Moving to the window, he put a hand to his eyes and shook his head.

What the hell? Dumbstruck, I stared at his broad back. The man's whole being had darkened; he looked broken, his grief almost tangible. Oh God; so he was more than just Mum's casual fling… There'd been questions I'd wanted to ask him yesterday, but now the reality was here, I wasn't sure how I'd cope with the answers.

'Do you have children?' I asked when the stillness became oppressive. He'd handled Joe with such ease, it seemed like a safe question. But he turned, his face visibly clouding again.

'A son,' he replied.

The two words were clearly the end of our conversation. Cringing, I willed Joe to hurry, then blew out my relief when George left the room. But he returned moments later and topped up my cup. Though he took the armchair again, he didn't relax. Instead, he leaned forward with the deepest of frowns.

'He died,' he said in a flat voice. 'My son died, so you'll understand why I don't speak about him.'

The shock of his blunt words hit the back of my eyes. Losing a mother was horrible, but it was nothing compared to the death of a child.

'I'm so sorry,' I whispered.

His steady gaze didn't flicker, but his burning pain seared the air. In that instant I knew he hadn't been Mum's lover, that he wasn't anyone's. He was living with his personal, wretched black hole. I understood from experience that heartache wasn't good company and it made sense of Miles's 'cold fish' comment. This man was one too. That's why I'd felt drawn, sensed something I recognised, something in common. It was grief.

Focusing on the worn carpet, I fought back the tears. This man had just said he didn't want to talk, but the words came instinctively. 'How old was he?' I asked.

'Nine years old.' He cleared his throat and sat back. 'Benjamin. Ben. He was born with a heart condition, but it wasn't serious. He had a small operation when he was a baby and after that he just had to take pills. It didn't affect his life. He played sport; he was full of energy, a bright, happy lad. We just turned up to see the consultant every year for a check-up.'

He stood and stared at the neatly piled coal in the hearth. Then he took a deep breath and continued to speak doggedly, as though it was a speech he'd rehearsed many times.

'Ben was doing so well, the consultant suggested another minor procedure. Then he could live an independent life without worrying about taking pills. I wanted that for him; I didn't want him to be the boy reliant on medicine. I wanted him to live life to the full. That's what he wanted too. But my wife wasn't so sure. She was worried about the operation.'

He looked at me then, his face ashen behind his tanned skin. 'I was concerned as well. There's always a danger with anaesthetic, isn't there? But the consultant was confident. Just routine, he said. So I persuaded Emma and she agreed to the operation.'

As though speaking was an effort, he cleared his throat again. 'The hospital told us he might be a bit dopey after the operation. But when we visited him he was alert and bright. We were as proud as punch. It had all gone as planned and after a day, we took him home. I'd redecorated his bedroom, finally got rid of the babyish wallpaper. New bedding, new colours, new furniture, the lot. He went to bed that night, a beautiful happy lad. Then a week or so later, when Emma went to wake him, he was dead. We'd let him die all alone.'

I didn't have adequate words of comfort. My living son had finished his feed and was gazing with a shy, satisfied smile. I gently laid him on the sofa and straightened myself out.

When I turned back, George was still staring with unfocused eyes.

'I'm so very sorry.' Despite my best efforts, the tears had come. My throat felt scratchy and sore too. 'What had happened?'

As though the answer didn't matter, he seemed to shrug himself back. 'We'd stopped giving him the pills. He should have been weaned off them. No one told us.' He looked at his watch. 'I'd better get over to Mrs Willis now.'

Nodding, I wiped my face with a tissue. His brow was knitted; he probably regretted telling me already.

We stepped out to the dissonant sunshine. George helped with the sling, then held out a fiver. 'Hope that covers the fruit,' he said.

I took a breath to say something, to thank him or just say goodbye, but he'd already set off, pacing with long strides up the hill.

–

I was thoughtful as I ambled back home. Tears were just beneath the surface and I was embarrassed about weeping in the cottage. George's loss was so much worse than mine. Such a devastating story, told in his plain way. It was sad to lose your parents, tragic when they were taken early, but at least it was the natural order of things. He hadn't mentioned how much time had passed since his son's death, but the grief was clearly still raw and deep.

I didn't want him to think my snivelling self-indulgent, but in truth it was. He was a good person, far better than I. There must have been times he couldn't bear to see kids playing, laughing, running, skipping, yet he'd been kind to Joe, held him gently and soothed him.

Would I be so generous in the same situation? I doubted it, if I was honest.

After Dad died, I'd felt horribly rejected by my friends. But part of me was relieved to be shunned; it meant I didn't have to see Sally's dad arrive home from work, hang his jacket on the bannister, then greet her with a hug or a kiss. Or wait with Isabelle outside the school gates for a free ninety-nine cornet from her dad's ice cream van. Hear Ruth's dad call 'all right?' over the sound of the television in her smoky sitting room. They all had a father and I didn't. The jealousy was wedged so fiercely in my chest that at times I'd wished someone in their family would die, so they'd *know* how it felt.

A terrible, terrible wish. I was only a child, but still. Trying to distract my dismal thoughts, I entered the post office and peered at the newspapers, but the memory of Johnny Baker prodded. I'd always sat next to him in class because we had the same surname. A stream of green snot ran from his nose to his mouth and he smelt of old socks. During that time he was the only kid who still treated me as though I was normal. But one day he regarded me with his soft brown gaze and offered to share his dad if I liked. In retrospect, I saw his kindness and his logic; we had the same name, and though he was mixed race, people thought we were cousins. But I was furious and never spoke to him again; did he really think my daddy could be replaced?

I deeply sighed. My dad who'd needed forgiveness; who'd been '*so sorry*'. What dreadful thing had he done?

Chapter Thirty

The Lodge felt empty and soulful when I returned. It was hard to shake off thoughts of George and his boy. I'd put my hand on his arm when he opened the cottage door. Just a touch of understanding or reassurance, I suppose, but he'd flinched from it like I had flinched from little Johnny Baker's offer – perhaps I was now a reminder of his loss. I hoped not; I didn't want to scare him away. Even in the distance, he'd made me feel safe.

I called Laura's mobile, leaving a message that I was now at The Lodge, then read the local headlines and ate soup to finish my lunch. Joe was napping, so what chore next? The sun had moved and was lighting the shrubs and glistening the pond in the sunken garden, so it'd be shining through the dining room windows and warming it up. As Laura had always said, only cold rooms were haunted.

Steeling myself, I opened the door to Mum's studio. I'd anticipated the smell of cleaning products again, but a tang of varnish and turps seemed to hover like a cloud and I instinctively knew it was exactly as she'd left it. A small painting was propped on the portable easel, a watercolour of the swaying, reedy riverside, and a new stretched canvas on another. The tubes of oils had their lids tightly screwed on, but they bore the dents of fingertips and three or four squirts of thick paint sat intact on the palate, as though awaiting her return.

My throat dry and burning, I stared at Mum's chair. The velvet cushion was hollowed as though she'd just stood up. Had she stared at that blank cloth with any inkling her life would end only hours later? Any feelings, foreboding? Bloody hell; why hadn't she just worn the damned seat belt?

I turned to the fireplace. If there were any dead birds these days they were rotting on the board blocking the flue. A wicker basket of dried flowers decorated the grate and the room was warm and balmy. No pigeons, no flies; no phantoms nor ghosts today. No Mum, either.

Feeling the tension ease from my chest, I moved to the paintings stacked against the wall. She didn't hang her own art and gave most of her pieces away, but a few she kept: a watercolour of our old house, an oil painting of my grandpa that only we would recognise, the portraits she attempted of me and Laura as little girls, and of course the pencil drawings of us as tiny babies, a couple of which she'd framed. To my surprise, the one of me was at the front, as though she'd recently pulled it out. I traced the newborn's cheeks and smiled at its 'heartburn' dark hair. My smile fell. Perhaps she'd intended to bring it with her to Manchester. Another thing I'd never know.

I idly flicked through the rest. There were no portraits of Dad, but she'd never managed to persuade him to sit down long enough to get a likeness. Needing an errand or a plan, he never stopped moving, not even that last summer.

'*You're driving me mad, Doug. Can't you sit down for two minutes?*'

The roll of his smiling blue eyes. '*A minute, just for you, dearest Eve.*'

A minute, just a minute. How we'd all longed for that minute once he'd gone.

—

My dining room mission accomplished, and easily too, I decided to tackle the next hurdle. Mum's handbag had been recovered from the car wreck and was now sitting on the sideboard next to the silver tea service. Not quite ready to open it, I stared at the soft leather, wondering how it had come out of the accident unscathed, whereas Mum hadn't.

Inevitably remembering her medical collar, I put my hand to my neck and swallowed. My throat was definitely a little raw. Not another cold, surely? I didn't want to think about what had happened the last time, nor the fearful nights which had followed.

The peal of the telephone made me jump.

'Hello?'

'I told Shelby about the kids thing last night. He's only just left for work so I couldn't call before now. He was shocked, but he wasn't angry. You were right, Ali. We talked about it for hours. I'm so bloody relieved…'

It was Laura, of course, her voice excited and clear, as though she was in the next room. My heart soared from her happiness and positive news. I felt I'd helped in some small way and it lifted my spirits.

'Fantastic! I'm so pleased. So what now?' I asked.

A pause, then a sigh. 'He thinks we should look into adoption; he likes the idea of giving an unwanted child a home, but I don't know…'

I sensed her reluctance; before she'd shut down the subject completely in Manchester, we'd talked briefly about the options if she didn't go for medical intervention or if that didn't work. She'd admitted it wasn't a nice thing to say, but pointed out that adoption could go wrong, that some kids were badly damaged or challenging, and she wouldn't be the right person to help. But then again, she'd worried that surrogacy might be even worse; the minefield of choosing the ideal candidate to carry a child.

'It's an option to think about, isn't it?' I now asked.

'Maybe...'

Sensing she didn't want to talk more about it, I didn't push my luck. Instead, I filled her in about the funny aspects of Mum's horror film staff, Joe's treachery and my visit to Bureside.

'You and Bureside. And that bloody boat. What's it called?'

'*Sylvette.*'

'That's right. How was Joan? Still got her beehive?'

'She wasn't there. Or at least she didn't come downstairs if she was. A bit odd, really.'

Laura snorted. 'I expect Tom wanted you all to himself. Did he give you a humbug and a tickle?'

'Er, no!'

'You used to let him.'

'I didn't!'

'You did. "Oh here comes Little Miss Tickly Ribs." I was almost jealous.' She laughed. 'Only *almost*, though...'

'What? The too-perfect teeth?'

'They're false, Ali. Don't you remember Mum always told me off, "Don't be unkind; he lost his in the course of doing his duty. It doesn't come more honourable than that."'

I didn't remember; I couldn't recall the tickling either, but it wouldn't be the first time Laura had wound me up.

A tad uncomfortable, I looked for a change of subject. Should I mention my discovery about Dad's TB? His apology? Nope, I didn't know the full story yet.

'I've found a bundle of your letters and cards to Mum. Shall I send them to you?'

'No thanks,' she replied. 'They'll be filled with a load of affectionate tosh. I didn't keep any of hers. Bin them. Sentiment just clutters your life, Ali. Take what you want from the house and get rid of the rest.'

Both a burden and a relief, it was what I had expected from Laura. On the one hand, I didn't have to worry about chucking out the wrong things, but on the other, the overwhelming decisions were entirely mine.

'Don't you want anything? Jewellery, clothes, paintings, antiques? And how about The Lodge itself? I think you should visit first, have a look before making any rash decisions. If you did decide to have kids, you might want to pass things down the line…'

'Oh give it a rest, Ali.' She paused and I thought she'd gone. Then she laughed. 'The mink. You can save the mink jacket for me.'

When I'd finished the call, I scooped up Mum's handbag and emptied it out. Laura's comments about sentimental stuff had given me courage; they were only possessions, after all.

I went through the contents: a silk headscarf, of course; Mum never went anywhere without one. A mirror, lipstick, face compact, a handkerchief, her diary and her purse. And a hairbrush containing a few thick blonde strands. The thought of her *impossible* hair brought a small smile, but it was soon replaced with another thought: the grooming set at George's this morning. Though I'd only known him a short while, my feelings had gone through a confused spectrum of real terror, followed by irritation and dislike, jealousy and dependency. Now there was admiration, and if I was honest, a strange attraction.

I picked up Mum's diary, but put it down again. I had no inclination, or right for that matter, to look at it. Instead I opened her purse. It was as I remembered from childhood – at the doctor's or the dentist she'd let us go through it to alleviate the boredom of waiting – a few coins, notes, loyalty and credit cards. Her miscellaneous section was still there too: the one school portrait of Laura and me together in Juniors, Dad's old business card and the tiny perished baby's wristband Laura and I had always argued about. Joe's was in a box at home, along with other mementoes of his birth, ready to be glued into a scrapbook when I had the energy and time.

Suddenly yearning for Miles, I glanced at my watch. Unless the judge was allowing it to run over, the trial would be winding up for the day. He always complained I didn't telephone him when he was working away. 'Out of sight, out of mind,' he once said. 'If I didn't call you, you'd forget I existed.'

An exaggeration, of course, but I knew what he meant. Connected to that *cold fish* business, I supposed. But it was easier to hold people at arm's length; one's heart wouldn't get broken that way.

I searched for my mobile and fired it up. Though I had some missed calls and texts, they weren't urgent or important; anyone who mattered had the number for The Lodge. Inevitably, most were from Madeleine. Ironic, really, I hadn't been a 'cold fish' with her, not at first, anyway. I pushed the thought away, deleted the history and turned it off.

I called Miles from the landline instead. His mobile rang out for some time, but just as I decided to give up, it was answered.

'Hello? Can I help?'

A woman's voice. I was momentarily thrown. 'Sorry. Have I got the right number?' I asked. 'Is this Miles's phone?'

'Hi Ali. It's me. We're just in the robing room before eating. Milo's nipped to the lav. Do you want to hold on?'

I felt my stomach tighten. Miss Julia Lambert, his bloody ex-girlfriend, who'd never quite gone away. How perfectly nice. Miles hadn't thought to mention she'd be in London at the same time as him.

'No, it's fine Julia,' I replied. 'Nothing important. I'll speak to him later. Enjoy your evening.'

Chapter Thirty-One

The return call from Miles came pretty damned quickly. Hot and irritated, I ignored it. The telephone continued to ring intermittently through the early evening, but I made myself a radish and beetroot salad from a soily selection of produce I found by the back door. Then I played with Joe, showing him the tatty boxes of board games from my bedroom cupboard and demonstrating Laura's old Spirograph set, pressing far harder with the coloured biros than was necessary.

I wasn't in the mood to talk to Miles. If he wanted to shag Julia Lambert all night, that was fine by me. In truth I didn't think he really was, but why the hell hadn't he told me she'd be there? I gave Joe a final feed and put him to bed. The phone stopped ringing then. No doubt Miles was too busy at some expensive London dinner: Julia gossiping and tittering and twirling her hair.

Secrets and lies, how I hated them. Or even sleight of hand. Though did I really want people to be honest? Like Madeleine had been? I calmed myself; it was just an omission, anything else in my head was insecurity and paranoia. It was better not to mull, to escape the next peal of the telephone.

Closing the door to the kitchen, I eased my painful throat with icy water, flung open the side door and breathed in the warm night.

'Everything all right?' a voice asked from the dusk. George was perched on the sunken garden wall, smoking a cigarette.

'Oh, you're a smoker,' I commented, the childish response popping out.

'I am,' he replied coolly. 'It's not completely illegal yet, is it?'

'No it isn't.'

'Well then.'

His tone was offhand. He had shared something so intimate that morning, but the connection seemed lost. 'Why are you here?' I asked bluntly.

He shrugged and took a drag. 'You owe me five pounds.'

I pictured 'Milo' enjoying caviar and lobster with Julia Lambert, his charm, her shrill laughter. I doubted they were limiting their beverages to coffee or tea. The thought made me brave.

'My purse is inside,' I said. 'Are you coming in for a drink?'

Bracing myself for rejection, I headed to the kitchen, but George stubbed out his cigarette and followed me in.

'Best close the door or the moths will get in.'

Feeling his gaze on my back, I felt myself blushing. Perhaps my hormones were raging, or maybe it was my annoyance with Miles, but I couldn't help entertaining the romantic notion of being enveloped in his strong arms. Only God knew why. The comment about insects was hardly a come-on; he'd not given me an ounce of encouragement, the very opposite, in fact. But when I turned, his dark eyes were watchful, they seemed to speak far more than he.

'About today,' he said into the silence. 'I'm sorry I walked away. I dumped a load of information on you. Perhaps you needed to...'

Oh hell, the weeping, my attempt to touch him. I wanted to explain that I was flattered he'd confided in me, that the tears were for him as well as me. That I'd felt a shiver of connection in the small cottage room. But it sounded ridiculous, even in my head. He'd been talking about the death of his child, for Christ's sake.

My embarrassment was saved by a shrill cry from Joe. I gave a weary smile; it felt as though I was feeding him more than ever.

George stepped over to the kettle. 'I'll get this, you sort Joe.'

The curtains still open, I settled myself in the armchair. Hearing the crunch of tyres on the pebbles, I stretched to look out at the shortcut. No car appeared, but headlights lit the glass from the other side. I strained to see, but the heavy drape blocked my view.

'Everything OK?'

I came back to my visitor. 'Yeah, I think so. Just heard a car...'

Lifting a large hand to his forehead, he peered out of the window. 'Gone now. Probably a wrong turn.'

Who would make a wrong turn into a private plot? I took a breath to ask if it happened often, but George stood over me, observing for a moment. 'Have you thought about weaning him?' he asked.

Feeling judged, I immediately bristled: it wasn't for want of desire. I was fed up with the constant feeding, but I was trying to raise my son by the bloody book. My expression must have shown my reply as he continued to speak. 'Him waking so often… And life's tough when you're not getting enough shut-eye. Give yourself a break.'

Emotion stung my nose. He had no idea how I'd agonised over solids. Over bloody everything. He made it sound so easy. And his comment about lack of sleep smarted; I thought I appeared much better today, pretty even.

Putting down the mugs, he crouched and met my gaze. 'Look I'm sorry if I've… But you're being too hard on yourself. Joe's a big baby. You won't kill him by introducing a tiny amount of baby rice.'

His face clouding, he stood abruptly and moved to the sofa. Then the telephone rang, piercing the silence.

'Shall I get that for you?' he asked.

It would have been rather poetical to have George answer it, but I shook my head and smiled thinly. 'No, it's only my husband and I'm ignoring him.'

George's lips twitched too, in a surprising, warm smile. Catching the glint of his wedding band, I thought of his wife. Emma, he'd said.

'What was his crime?' he asked, raising his dark eyebrows.

'Oh just the usual,' I answered evasively.

Miles wasn't sleeping with Julia or anyone else. Court robing-room banter and barristers dining together wasn't unusual; I'd done it often enough myself. I just wished he'd been straight with me.

I laughed. 'I expect I'll get over it…'

George nodded, accepting my reply. 'I'll get off then,' he said, finishing his drink. 'I'll buy a box of baby rice on my way in tomorrow. Then it'll be in the cupboard for when you need it.'

'OK. Thanks.'

He left me feeding Joe. I was being managed in some way, I knew, but it was fine. In truth, it was exactly what I needed.

Chapter Thirty-Two

Thursday

I stirred to a new day thinking about Madeleine. Perhaps I'd been dreaming about her, but despite waking from time to time to sip water for my throat, my sleep had been thick and gluey. Though the morning was bright beyond the curtains, I had difficulty rousing myself. When I finally sat up, there was my perfect son, looking at me expectantly from his cot.

Feeding Joe, I drifted, Madeleine and the way she'd psychoanalysed me swamping my thoughts.

Didn't every daughter fall in love with her dad? Not in an inappropriate way, of course, but that blind adoration I'd had. It turned out that some did and most didn't; a few hated their fathers, others were indifferent, but the majority I'd spoken to over the years simply loved them.

Perhaps Dad's death wouldn't have hurt so deeply if I'd just 'loved' him too. After it, I put up a guard, was careful with people, pals and eventually men. Not that I didn't make friends; I was just very cautious about getting too attached. There was Sidney through university, and I still loved him fondly, the brother I'd never had, but I hadn't seen Madeleine coming. Because she wasn't a love interest or a friend in the conventional sense, I hadn't prepared myself and I fell for her completely, a school girl's crush.

She was the epitome of womanhood; beautiful, sophistic-ated, intelligent and witty. So accomplished there wasn't anything she couldn't do, from baking to badminton and backgammon. A dark-haired version of Laura, I suppose. But this replication was nice; she had time for me, she was interested; she seemed to adore me in return.

How I must have bored Mum on the phone. 'Well, according to Madeleine...' 'Madeleine says...' 'Guess what Madeleine has bought me...' 'You should see Madeleine's...'

Like Midas, everything she touched turned to gold in my eyes. Her rays and energy were focused on me; I was special and unique. Who wouldn't be seduced?

For a while it was like an intense affair; I spent my free time with her, which suited Miles. What better than being doted on by your wife and your mother? But I abruptly fell out of love. I discovered Madeleine wasn't what I thought she was. She didn't do anything terrible, a deliberate lie, but it had felt like betrayal, even death.

Sighing the memory away, I came back to my warm Norfolk bedroom. Sleep was threatening to pull me in again, so I put Joe in his cot, got dressed, then sat cross-legged on my bed, intending to carry on with the letters. Though they'd been written long ago, I was intrigued – and unsettled – by Dad's last missive. What had it meant? Was it a clue about whatever my two aunties had hinted at?

Noises in the house interrupted my thoughts. Nancy or Denise and not a flaming burglar, I hoped. I supposed I should have been shocked that they'd used keys and come in without knocking first, but I was getting used to this surreal new world where strangers were trusted. Though perhaps that was the point – they weren't strangers but people I felt I already knew. I padded towards the sound of the kettle. The kitchen was empty but the side door was ajar, a chilly breeze filtering through. The pot was on the side so I poured in the steaming water and set the cosy on top. It made me smile; I'd never owned a teapot, let alone a cover. It felt quaint and old-fashioned. I liked it.

With a small jolt of surprise, I realised it was the first time I'd thought of my Manchester home since I arrived. Lost in contemplation, I gazed out at the woods beyond the back fence. It was so different here, almost like being abroad. The friendly folk, balmy weather, the tangy, sweet smells. And despite the creaking pines and the birds, it was so very quiet.

Sound and movement behind my shoulder brought me back. Expecting to see Mum, I turned. For those few moments I had forgotten she was dead. But nothing was there; it was just an empty room, still and silent.

Goosebumps tingling my arms, I thought of the missed calls and Mum's attempts to talk, to say *something* which had clearly been important to her. Shaking the shiver away, I stepped to the door and looked out. George was pulling clumps of grass from the vegetable patch, but after a moment he lifted his head.

He came towards me and leaned against the wall. 'You look as though you've seen a ghost,' he commented. His muscled arms glistened with dirt, and sweat had soaked through to his T-shirt. I wondered what he'd been doing to get so hot when I felt so cold.

'Not seen one, but felt one…' I replied vaguely. 'The kettle popped so I… Do you mind if we go inside for your drink? I'm freezing.'

Though the creeping discomfort still lingered, I picked up the teapot and tried for humour. 'Tea?' I asked, noticing a box of baby rice in the cupboard above. 'You all but made it yourself, so I think it's allowed...'

With the hint of a smile, he walked past me. I wasn't wearing shoes, nothing to give me extra height, but still, I hadn't realised quite how huge he was. Miles was six foot, but this man was inches taller. Bringing the aroma of soap with him, he returned from the utility sink and sat opposite me.

I slid the baby rice towards him. 'You'd better tell me what to do, seeing as you are the fount of all knowledge,' I said.

For a moment he stared, the usual frown above his blue gaze, but eventually he laughed. It felt strange to see his grin; wide and wolfish, yet familiar and pleasant too.

'I've never been accused of that before.' He lifted the packet and read. 'You put a small amount in a clean bowl and mix it with milk, but not cow's milk,' he said evenly.

'God, I didn't think to bring my breast pump,' I blurted. After my pathetic efforts to squeeze out two inches for the funeral, it hadn't been high on my list of packing priorities.

'Apparently you can do it without a pump,' he said, straight-faced. 'Like milking a cow, I believe.' He paused for a beat. 'But if I were you, I'd use formula.'

He leaned over to the fridge and swung back with a small carton of ready-made baby milk. I suspected he was teasing me. I couldn't quite make him out, but the conversation felt warm and companionable.

Lifting it, I smiled. 'I have one of these at home too. Somehow, miraculously, I never used it.'

I hadn't panicked without it either, so perhaps I was making progress; maybe life was slowly inching towards the light. I met his gaze. 'Seriously, though, how come you know so much about babies?' I asked. 'I know you had Ben, but if Miles changes a nappy he expects a medal.'

Perhaps George slightly flinched at the mention of his son's name, but he answered easily. 'I worked at home, so I was a hands-on dad.'

'In the garden?' I asked.

'Sort of,' he said, looking down at his rough palms. 'But on paper. A landscape architect.'

Interesting, I thought, but his demeanour had clouded, so I remained silent and poured the strong tea.

'How are you feeling?' he asked after a moment.

I lifted my head in surprise. Had I been swallowing strangely or touching my troublesome throat?

'I meant about your mother. Yesterday, at the cottage, I was only thinking of myself. I should have asked then.'

Wanting to give an honest answer, I gathered my thoughts. 'I get upset when I least expect to,' I replied slowly. 'But the grief isn't as bad as I had anticipated. Sometimes it's as though...' Hmm, maybe not *that* honest. 'I guess it hasn't really hit me. Not like when my...'

'Your dad?' he asked, seeming to study me intently.

I nodded, a little stunned. Mum lived alone, but she might have been divorced. Then again, perhaps it was common knowledge. The Bakers had come here every holiday for five years; folk like the original George would have known why we'd abruptly stopped coming. Or maybe this George *was* a good listener as Nancy had said. Yes, I could picture Mum chatting, talking far more than him.

Oh God. What did he know about me and Laura? Like that mother-daughter exchange of information, the thought was uncomfortable.

'How long have you been down here?' I asked, changing the subject.

He spread his large hands. 'Twelve months or so. I needed to get away after Ben died.'

'And what about—' I started to ask. I was going to enquire about his landscape architect business.

'Emma?' he questioned, in a matter-of-fact way. 'We couldn't live together any more. It was too painful. We were both swamped with grief. And guilt.'

His features darkened again and I wanted to reach out, but I remembered how he'd pulled away from my touch yesterday. 'Why guilt?' I asked softly.

He sighed. 'Mine was straightforward. It was me who insisted on the operation. I should've let it go. But Emma's... Well, it was more complicated, still is.'

Assuming he'd stop there, I sipped my drink. But he continued with a nod of resolve. 'She didn't want children. I thought I was fine with that. You know – too many unhappy or unwanted kids in the world to add to their number. But she got pregnant unexpectedly and I wanted her to keep the child. Desperately.' He looked at the ceiling. 'I don't know why; the need to have a kid suddenly became overwhelming. My flesh and blood and all that. I persuaded Emma she'd love him when he was born. But it was a difficult birth, then she struggled to...'

He seemed to search for a word and I swallowed. Like me? I thought. A crap new mum?

'She didn't bond with him. There wasn't that instinctive connection most parents have. At times she couldn't cope with the demands, the responsibility; said she wished he hadn't been born.' He cleared his throat. 'But as he grew older, she loved him as a person. And when he died she blamed herself. She thought it was some sort of divine justice.' He shook his head. 'I couldn't handle that idea.'

Shocked at his candour, I said nothing. But it was tough being a parent. My fears had started even before I gave birth, followed by constant worry and those feelings of inadequacy, exacerbated by Madeleine's *Ali isn't Ali*. Then there were the thoughts of the woman in court: would I shake my baby? And only a few days ago; that dreadful impetus to throw Joe to the ground.

When I came back to George, he was looking at me quizzically. 'I'm talking too much and you're shivering,' he said. 'Maybe a jumper until you warm up?'

The thought that I might be coming down with another virus was too, too depressing, especially as I'd only just started to feel brighter. As I nodded and stood, the telephone rang. Could I ignore it? I didn't have the energy for an argument with Miles, but I was conscious of George's observant eyes, so I padded to the lounge to answer it.

Miles didn't bother with opening pleasantries. 'Why do you turn off your mobile, Ali? And why didn't you answer the bloody telephone last night? I rang a hundred times. I was worried about you.' He didn't stop for an answer. 'I'm working, Ali. I need to sleep properly. I shouldn't have to be calling you before going into fucking court in a morning to check you're not dead—'

Though my death overnight seemed a stretch, I felt chastened; it had been childish not to answer his calls. 'Of course I'm not dead. I'm fine and so is Joe. I'm sorry you were worried, but I told Julia it was nothing important.'

'I suppose this is about me having a drink with her.'

His defensiveness seemed odd; I'd tried to be nonchalant about the damned woman when she reappeared on the scene, but perhaps my face had betrayed me. 'No, not at—'

'You know full well that everyone stays at this hotel. She just happened to be here on a case herself.'

'It's fine,' I repeated. It was too much effort to point out he'd told me about every Tom, Dick and Harry he'd bumped into in London, but failed to mention her, let alone the bloody hotel coincidence. Yet, I felt shivery and cold, detached and far away. Whatever was going on in London, there was nothing I could do about it.

'How's my little man?' Miles asked after a few seconds. 'I keep scrolling through my photos to catch a glimpse of his cheeky little smile. Thank God it's Friday tomorrow. Will you kiss him for me until then?'

'Of course I will.'

I pinched my nose. Why it was far easier to cope with Miles's indifference to Joe than his love, I couldn't say, but I wished him well for the trial and promised to call later.

Chapter Thirty-Three

The side door closed, George had gone when I returned to the kitchen. To fend off the encroaching headache, I took two paracetamol and went to check on Joe. He was awake and sucking his fingers, so I scooped him out of the cot, sat him on my lap and went back to my parents' letters. There was something I was missing; something I'd subconsciously seen; what was it?

The first was from Mum: *I thought they'd got the wrong bloke until he said "he's sitting up in bed grinning all over his face like a Cheshire cat" then I knew there was no mistake*, she wrote.

That made me both sniff and smile. She had often teased Dad about being a 'smiling idiot' when they'd first met in a pub. Apparently he'd hung around and spoilt her chances with the 'hot guy with a Lamborghini'.

'That's me,' he'd always replied with the grin she'd described. Then, 'And you didn't do so badly, did you, love? Dashing good looks and everything you dreamed of?'

His humour and wit shone from each page. So did his clear adoration of Mum. His missives were warm, funny and loving, his neat script referring to her beauty and his desire for her kisses. In one he described her: *A pretty face set in… hair, wonderful nose, kissable – no, very kissable lips, inviting eyes, slim neck, unconventional blouse enhancing a curved bosom down to a narrowing waist.* It finished, *I'll now try and calm down – you excite me!*

In another he wrote, *I suppose you're as lovely as ever this morning. Don't let it go to your head. It's beautiful enough!*

And another, *I think I must be getting soft, for every day I seem to get fonder of you. I suppose it's similar to when I was ten – I had a goldfish and I grew fonder of it every day, although I didn't realise that fact until one morning I took it some ant eggs and found it floating. You're as pretty to me in this world as a goldfish must be to an ordinary fish in theirs.*

I paused for a while. There was no doubt that he loved her; indeed, it was something I was certain of myself. So what had he been apologising for?

Mum's letters were more circumspect and reserved, almost tetchy. She talked about the weather, work and clothes and signed most of her letters, 'Cheerio & love Evelyn.' Dad expressed his passion for her, yet she replied blandly with details of her mundane daily life, incidents at work, what she'd eaten for tea, when she went shopping and what she'd bought. Perhaps he loved her more, or maybe he was just better at expressing it. In one he wrote, *We've all just been having a discussion on "love at first sight". Bill insists his was. You know my thoughts on the subject – unfortunately I know yours.*

Feeling disappointed on his behalf, I slotted that one back in the pack. I wanted to rewrite her replies. But there was a fond wryness in his text and I could picture his smile as he caught Mum's waist, pulled her towards him and said, 'Ah, but who did she choose? Me or Mr Lamborghini? Mr Irresistible, that's who.'

I sighed. Mum wasn't a particularly demonstrative person with words, that was all. It didn't mean she wasn't capable of deep love. It was actions that counted, wasn't it? Too easy to say, 'I love you, Ali' but not see it through.

'Your turn now,' I said to Joe. Planting a kiss on his head, I opened a chunky picture book filled with bright images of animals and fruit. 'Dog! Cat! Apple!' I pointed. 'Mummy loves you so much,' I added.

It really wasn't hard. Perhaps I had to say the words whenever I felt them. Love letters survived but life was transient.

–

Mid-morning I searched for George through the windows, but there was no sign of him or his tools, so I ate a bowl of cereal and went back to the past. At some point during Dad's stay in the sanatorium, Mum travelled to Leeds for a week-long work course. Her early correspondence showed her reluctance to go, but the trip clearly wasn't as bad as she'd thought. Her letters described the boarding house and the other occupants with some humour. One letter read:

> *The owner is Mrs Dilworth. She seems quite nice but she's one of these know-alls. Your mother would get on with her just fine. There's a man from Newcastle. He's about 5 ft tall, weighs about 7st, has no hair, wears a flat cap and eats like a bird. Now I know where the expression 'seven-stone weakling' comes from – Newcastle! Then there's another man who's so old. He loves to talk about when he was on the stage. I rather think I'm expected to go out with him but I've managed to get out of it by washing my hair every evening. You should see it shine! He's quite harmless of course,*

but imagine going for a walk in Roundhay Park
with him. Then there's another bloke staying, a Mr
Lang. He's about thirty-five but very frightfully,
frightfully. He's very high up in the Post Office so
not very likely to take any notice of me.

She must have been missing Dad then as this letter was signed '*love and kisses, Eve.*'

I smiled at her sardonic wit; it was really so Mum. How she'd hated 'know-alls' and Dad's mother. Her own roots were fairly working class, but Dad's family came from the industrial side of Sheffield, so his were a rung lower in her view. She went to the grammar school; she worked for the civil service, don't you know! And how she loved Dad's success, the wealth that came with it. The exotic holidays, the jewellery, the new car every year and her 'daily'. Such a snob without realising it.

Later, when I was finally up and about and trying to programme the washing machine, I realised Dad hadn't just been in hospital for Mum's birthday, it'd been her twenty-first. I thought of her clear boredom and her insular or insensitive comments at times:

The queerest people come in to pay their telephone accounts
– a man today told me I had a lovely shaped nose.

Or: *If this weather keeps up and you're still in there I think*
I'll have to join something or other at work. Maybe swimming on
Thursday. Bert will look after me and keep me safe from Stan.
And: *I've got to do something and not just sit here waiting and*
looking miserable. And I do feel miserable – I've got the most
hateful tummy-ache.

What had I been doing on my twenty-first? I was with Sidney, but I was free from any grief save for getting essays in on time, and I didn't always manage that. Perhaps I was making excuses for my mum, but what must it have been like to have the responsibility of a boyfriend with a life-threatening illness? Frightening for sure, but her everyday life still went on.

At least their story had a happy ending. In Mum's final letter she wrote: *I feel wonderful tonight. We have so many things to plan. Dad has been asking about your intentions again. He thinks you look about eighteen especially when you grin. He says too that he's never known anybody grin as much as you do. Anyway, he won't have to worry once we tell them our news after your discharge on Saturday…*

Yes, a happy ending. I pictured Dad in his wedding portrait. Wasn't it?

Chapter Thirty-Four

The doorbell rang at three. It wouldn't be George; he had a key. But when I peered through the glass, it was a key-holder after all. Nancy was on the doorstep, a bright orange scarf tied charlady-style around her head. Hooked in one arm was a wicker basket, in the other Mrs Hague.

Though I couldn't say why, the unexpected sight of Joan made me gasp. It was quickly followed by pleasure. She was older, of course, but still fairly tall and otherwise much as I remembered. She was wearing those sixties-style spectacles but no dangling earrings today. A mark of respect was my guess; like her waiting politely at the front door with a bunch of pink tulips rather than striding in through the side door; like her sporting dark slacks and a cashmere twin-set to visit, despite the roasting heat.

She took my hand and squeezed tightly. Hers was trembling. 'Hello, love, how are you?' After a sniff, she turned her attention to Joe. 'Oh love, isn't he beautiful.' Her eyes turned rheumy and I thought she might cry, but Nancy stepped forward and briskly swapped her hamper for Joe.

'Come on then, little lovey. Let's introduce you to Joan. She's been longing to see you. Talked of nothing else since you were born.'

We made our way to the kitchen. Bustling like two noisy bees, the ladies set out a glossy fruit cake on a china stand and made tea; cooing and smiling, they tickled Joe's feet, delighted when he responded in kind.

'He does like an audience,' Joan said. 'Blue eyes, I see. Do you think they'll stay blue? And he's a blondie.'

'I think so.' I thought of Miles. 'He's like his dad all round,' I replied.

Not a cold fish like his mum. Though thinking of my own mum's letters, it wasn't exclusively me.

'Oh you're a bonny little lad,' Nancy said. 'Your grandma would have been so proud! She'd have loved having you here so much.'

'Aye, she wanted a boy.'

'And all those lovely clothes she bought him.'

'And the knick-knacks. Laid out on the bed like a picture...'

'We could've had a ladies' day out in your Roller. Eve would've enjoyed that.'

'Aye, she would.'

'Three women and a baby. Has your Tom got it fixed yet?'

'Let's hope he has by the time this littl'un's wanting to drive it.'

I glanced from one elderly woman to the other but I really didn't mind them talking about Mum. There was such a warm feeling in the room, I could almost pick out her Chanel perfume. She was with us, surely, and smiling.

At some point Nancy theatrically sniffed. 'If I'm not mistaken, someone's made a mess in his nappy.' Holding up a gnarled hand, she made for the door. 'You stay and chat, lovey, I'll change him.'

Joan suddenly leaned so close I could see where she'd missed her pale face powder. She peered intently. 'I just wanted to say that I'm so sorry about...'

Anticipating doleful condolences about Mum, I tensed. Maybe I wasn't so chilled after all.

'About those lads and the beer,' she continued. 'Drinking and laughing as though nothing was amiss. Whatever happened to respect?'

It was an echo of Tom's words. I took a breath to say something, but Joan spoke again.

'Young'uns think only of themselves. Think it's all right to just do as they like or take what isn't theirs. That's when they need to be brought to book.'

A shiver of discomfort rustled down my spine. It seemed an odd thing to say, but she'd been a copper's wife, so had probably come across many unsavoury *young'uns* over the years.

'I guess so,' I replied. Then wanting to be fair, 'But by all accounts it was Mum's fault, so...'

I expected Joan to protest, but she sat back and poured more tea. 'Aye, that's very true.' She nodded to the Dundee. 'Tempt you to another slice, love? When it's gone, it's gone forever.'

–

By the time Joan left, I'd got used to her straight-talking ways again. Seemed you could take the girl out of Yorkshire, but not the other way around. A spade was clearly still a spade in Norfolk. But I was used to that from my relatives, especially from Auntie Brenda. Seventeen years' worth, in fact.

Shelving that thought for now, I picked up the box of baby rice and read the instructions. Taking a nervy breath, I made up a small amount. Was I doing the right thing? But Joe must have known what was coming. Propped in his chair, he kicked his legs with excitement. I offered him a pea-sized amount at the end of a spoon. He hesitantly accepted it, rolled it around his tongue, then opened his mouth like a beak. Baby rice was clearly tastier than it looked.

I laughed through my taut emotion. My baby's first solid feed; Miles should have been there, but perhaps Mum was watching from somewhere. Making a note to record 'the first' in my diary, I frowned. Why would I do that? For me, for posterity and Joe too. One day I'd like him to read it and know my love and delight on this day.

Carrying his chair through to the lounge, I settled Joe down, flung open the sideboard door and stared at the shoe boxes marked 'Diaries' in marker pen. I took out the first and snapped the rubber band thoughtfully. Mum wouldn't have kept them if she hadn't intended them to be perused one day. But then again, when she'd left the oil paint on her palette, she hadn't known death was imminent.

I sighed. Was I being silly? I had read her love letters only this morning, was a diary any more private? I wouldn't mind Joe reading mine. In the past I had tried to write a proper journal. Not exactly Anthony Wedgwood Benn, but a thought or an event for each day. Now it was just a word or two about my son's progress: his long-gone colic, weight increase and height, his first windy smile. And now his first solid food.

I put the box back. The letters were enough for today, and in truth I didn't want to move on yet. Like finishing a good novel, I was still with the characters, the smiling handsome idiot and the woman who excited him. Except, astonishingly, these people weren't just a cast, they were my mum and dad.

Sitting back on my haunches, I thought of Laura. I'd definitely insist she read our parents' exchanges. We were our history; we were what they made us, not just through blood and genes, but nurture. Maybe if she understood Mum better, she might understand herself too.

Idly, I picked up a leather-bound pad and opened it. Mum's autograph book. From the date, she would've been about fourteen. I carefully flicked through the delicate pages. On one, her friends had described her in a few choice words:

Chasing boys, gossiping… Flicks, boys, gabbing… Boys, dancing, eating… Eating chocs, chasing boys, gossiping.

Then someone had written: *If courting was against the law and kissing was a crime, Eve the owner of this book would now be down the line…*

That made me smile; it sounded just like my big sister.

Chapter Thirty-Five

Though the weather was humid outside, the bungalow seemed chilly and hollow with just sleeping Joe for company in the evening. Headachy and anxious about my temperature swings, I now wished Nancy and Joan were still around, but Nancy had been under Tom Hague's 'strict instructions' to get his wife home by five. My neediness surprised me. Maybe I was softening, getting used to people dropping in without an invitation, even liking the claustrophobia of village life.

At the end of my pregnancy I'd spent hours on my own but I'd never felt as solitary as I did now. The stillness and silence of The Lodge had spooked me as a child, but I'd always been here with someone else; even Laura had resisted the temptation to sneak off when Mum and Dad went out. She'd been irritated, of course:

'If you weren't such a scaredy baby I could have met up with Ivan and Kelvin and had fun instead of being stuck inside with you, little weirdo.'

But she'd stayed nonetheless.

Once the sun disappeared, I became cold to the point of iciness, so I put on the central heating full blast, comforted by its familiar gulps and chugs. It was a crazy thing to do in the middle of a particularly hot summer, but the chill felt malevolent; I wanted it gone.

I was apprehensive and jumpy, but couldn't describe why. I wasn't a flipping kid anymore; a white-faced phantom wasn't loitering behind my closed eyes. Why the dreams had happened here at my happiest was a mystery. 'Mum,' I used to say, 'do ghosts exist?' and she'd reply firmly, 'Of course not.'

I'd be satisfied then. But after a moment she'd add, 'Even if they did, they wouldn't hurt a lovely girl like you.' And that would seed doubt in my mind: maybe the nightmares were real; a cold room, an old room, an unexplained breeze; the cat's bushy tail; the geranium-like smell of blood.

It had been ridiculous, of course, but still I sighed deeply. My febrile imagination hadn't just plagued my childhood, had it? Shaking my head, I pushed that distressing memory away. It was well in the past; no good would come of dwelling on it now.

Aware I was being irrational, but doing it anyway, I flicked on every light. Then I tightened my dressing gown and padded to Mum's bedroom, hoping I might feel her benign presence. I thought of lying on her bed and reading *Villette*, but I knew I'd only listen to the quietness, so I sat on the old piano stool and opened the dressing table drawer to examine her accessories as I had as a girl.

Scooping out an armful of gloves, I neatly paired them on the table top: pale brown kid leather; long satin in white, cream and black; delicate lace; a variety of suede, some with press studs and others with tiny round buttons. Had Mum worn them all? My small hands certainly had.

I dipped in again and found something solid. Ah, like a hidden jewel, it was a tarnished bottle of Chanel No. 5 with half an inch left. Not wanting to waste it, I didn't have a sniff, but placed it on the ledge like an ornament, then moved onto the handkerchiefs. All silk, differently coloured and patterned. There must have been fifty.

And there it was again, that sinking feeling in my stomach. Her treasured belongings were lovely, but what on earth would I do with them? There were two flat boxes of laced-edged hankies that hadn't even been opened. Mum had lovingly accumulated them all; I couldn't just throw them away.

The headscarves seemed stuck, so I gave a little tug and pulled out a scrolled document. Intrigued, I unfurled it, but it was only Mum's O level certificate. She had passed in eight subjects with excellent grades. Presumably she'd also taken A levels before joining the Civil Service. Yet she'd left a good job to become a full-time 'housewife', a docile – and yes, spoilt little wife.

Frowning thoughtfully, I remembered the thick wad of twenties Dad used to leave by the radio each week for Mum's 'housekeeping'. The image made me shudder; how I'd hate not to have my financial independence, the sense of self-worth working had given me. It felt as though my clever mother had sold out somehow. And yet, look at me. Right now I had no life outside this small village. My husband was in the hurly-burly capital, high with adrenaline and purpose, whereas I was alone, rattling around an old house, fearful that—

Keep an eye on Alison; Ali's not Ali.

I thrust *that* thought away again. Ali was perfectly fine. She was just feverish, that was all. Returning to the drawer, I made to replace all my finds, but a sheet of paper at the back caught my eye. Though not in an envelope, the blue notepaper was the same as the love letters, so I knew it'd be a missive between my parents. Separated from the others, it felt ominous. Would it be from Mum or Dad? Retreating to the bed, I took a breath and opened it.

Dad's handwriting:

> *Hello, my life's blood. For days now I've had an ache which reaches a climax in the evening and consists of bitterness, resentment, longing, high sensitivity, foul temper, jealousy, love and hate. I fight against this sickness which merely aggravates the blasted thing…*

Some of the pages were missing, but the fourth continued:

> *My uncle once told me that when he was in the 8th Army in the desert he liked his wife to have male 'company' at home. If that's normal then I'm very much abnormal. I know that I'm unnecessarily possessive and anti-social with things I love but I could never share you in any way, even if it means a broken heart. The trouble is that I love you so and I'm sorry I have to write this.*

Exhausted and perplexed, I folded the letter. What on earth did it mean? If it hadn't been for the familiar script, I wouldn't have recognised the tone as my grinning dad. He sounded so very sad… But sleep was tugging me, so I pulled back the bedding, climbed in and closed my eyes. This particular puzzle could wait until tomorrow.

–

A smashing sound jolted me to consciousness with a gasp. What the hell was that? I tried to listen through the thud of my pulse in my ears. It wasn't a nightmare. Someone was in the house; I could definitely hear them. The bedroom door was ajar, the rustling and movement coming towards me, unmistakable. This was not my imagination; this was real.

My mind thrashed. The car in the driveway last night… A burglar or even worse? Someone with ill intent. A person with a knife. Though my torso was scorching, shaking and damp, inside I was frozen with fear. I had to play dead; it was the only chance of survival I had.

–

Maybe I forced sleep, or perhaps I blacked out as the next thing I heard was a tap at the bedroom door.

My whole body was roasting. Hardly surprising; I was still wearing my robe and even my head was covered by the bedding. Peeling it away, the sudden chill hit my cheeks.

'Ali? Are you OK? Can I come in?'

Bloody hell; it was George's deep timbre. Though the curtains were closed, it felt like the middle of the night. Had something happened? 'Yes, sure,' I replied, struggling to hitch myself up.

I had no idea what to expect, but when he appeared, his eyebrows were knitted, his jaw tight.

'I've just turned off the central heating,' he said.

'Oh, right.' My head pulsed; I could barely move it. I was boiling and perspiring, but shivering too.

Clearly unimpressed, George's gaze swept over me and my dressing gown. 'No wonder you're burning up. The whole house is as hot as a furnace.'

Like a punch to the belly, I remembered my son. 'Oh God, Joe…' I said, a surge of dizziness hitting as I clambered upright.

'He kicked off his covers. He's asleep; he's fine.'

'Oh, thank goodness. I…' I glanced at the gardener's cloudy, tight face. 'You're cross with me,' I said, my thoughts blurting out. Pathetic though it was, I didn't want him to judge me; he'd seemed to accept the slightly crazy daughter of his employer so far, and I didn't want to spoil it.

He sighed. 'The cat had been missing all day. I came looking for her and every light was on. I was worried and rang the bell. No reply, so I thought I'd better check everything was…' He lifted his hands. 'It was a particularly warm night but you'd put on the heating, Ali. You have a baby in the next room…'

Maisie, Mum's tortoiseshell moggy, slunk in and brushed against his legs.

'I know, it was stupid of me but I was really cold,' I replied. 'Then I fell asleep and—' My God, how had I forgotten? The noises in the night, the break-in, the burglar; the certainty that someone was here to do me harm…

But doubt quickly rolled in. Perhaps I had dreamed it. Maybe Ali wasn't Ali after all. And Madeleine was right, wasn't she? I wasn't coping. I'd been totally irresponsible; I hadn't considered my son.

'I'm sorry,' I managed to croak. But I couldn't stem the deluge. The full-on tears I hadn't shed for the past two months seemed to hurtle out now. I was crying for Joe, for my dad, for my mum, for Miles and bloody Julia Lambert. I was snivelling for my pathetic, sorry self.

It felt as though George held back for an eternity before gathering me into his arms. Maybe it was only seconds, but I sensed his reluctance. He briefly held me in a tight, solid hug, before pulling away.

'Joe's fine. Really,' he said. 'I've opened his window. You're still feverish, though. Where's the paracetamol?'

'In the bathroom cabinet, but… Well, earlier I thought I heard…' My voice trailed away. Had it been real or in my imagination? I no longer knew.

With the hint of a smile George held out his palm. 'A burglar? I'll show you,' he said.

Safe behind his bulk, Maisie and I followed him to the kitchen.

'Careful where you walk,' he said, opening the door. Turning, he lifted his eyebrows. 'It's fine; you'll see.' But his tone was softer; the disapproval had gone.

Surrounded by a jigsaw of glass and pink tulips, what remained of the vase lay on the floor. My instinct was to step in and retrieve the pretty flowers, but George put out an arm. 'It's gone everywhere,' he said, nodding at my bare feet.

He scooped up the cat. 'Here's the offender,' he said, massaging beneath her chin with long fingers. 'She must have squeezed in through the open window.'

I tentatively stroked her particoloured fur. 'You've walked a long way,' I said. Was Maisie disappointed not to have found Mum? Probably not; this usually prickly, feisty moggy was gazing at George, her eyes half closed with pleasure.

He put her down, hopped across the floor, closed the top latch and ran the tap. Then, handing me a glass of water, 'It's late. You'd better get some shut-eye.'

I had no idea of the hour, just the black night through the window. 'What time is it?' I asked. He showed me his watch; an old Omega like my grandpa's. It was past two o'clock. 'Don't you ever sleep?' I asked.

'Not much.'

God knows how my face looked, but now I felt sane, I examined his. It was shadowy and drawn, his angular features emphasised by dark stubble. Determined never to cry in his presence again, I tried for humour. 'Maybe I'm not the only one who should be reprimanded about lack of *shut-eye*...'

'I don't have a baby to look after,' he replied, not taking the bait. 'Come on, he might sleep through tonight.'

I followed him to my bedroom, watched him expertly turn Joe and feel his back. Then he pulled up the thin blanket and tucked it in. 'He's cooled down now but I'd keep the window open,' he said.

'OK, thanks,' I replied, tugging back my pink duvet.

Replaced by obvious weariness, his friendliness had disappeared. 'Come on, Ali. You're still in damp clothes...'

That old hilarity bubbled back, but I managed to stifle the laughter. Poor man; he'd come to Norfolk to escape. Looking after a late widow's gardens by day and her hapless daughter by night wasn't what he'd planned, I was sure. I nodded, padded to my chest of drawers and he left.

As I dragged on a clean T-shirt, I listened to the sound of his footfall on the parquet. Turning off the lights, I supposed. I preferred to have them on, so I sat for a while, giving him enough time to leave. When the final beam was extinguished, I waited another minute, then hurried out to the hallway. Dizzy from the burst of energy, I lowered my head. When I looked up again, I saw George reclined in an armchair, his long legs stretched out on the pouffe.

He glanced over his shoulder.

'Oh, right,' I mumbled. He was apparently staying. 'There are plenty of beds if you—'

'I'm fine here,' he said. 'Makes no odds where I kip.'

'OK,' I said, retreating.

The deep blush burning my cheeks, I climbed into bed. What had Laura said about fancying someone, desperate to get them in the sack? For the first time I understood. It was probably my hormones, the fact George had zero interest in me, or maybe my generally unbalanced mental state, but as I stared into the dark night, that's exactly how I felt.

Chapter Thirty-Six

Friday

I heard my boy shuffling in his cot before he cried out. It was light and the birds were singing, but when I opened the curtains, the sun was pale and the clouds static as though still waking up. Joe had done well, though; he'd slept through the sweaty night, the cat burglar and my embarrassing torrent without the need for a feed.

My head rattled as though something had come loose and my raspy throat stung, but I felt positive and buoyed as I lifted him from his cot. He smiled and cocked his blond head as if to say: *'What's up, Mummy? You look happy today.'*

How would I reply if Laura asked the same question? That I'd fallen asleep thinking about a man's muscled arms, his sweat, his size and his smell? That I'd woken with a sense of excitement because I fancied someone? That despite my recent huge life events – a birth and a death – I felt I was getting back to normal? But it wasn't 'normal', was it? I didn't usually lust after anyone. And the subject of my affections was a guy maybe eight years my senior who hadn't shown the slightest bit of romantic interest in me. He'd been manly and strong, he'd been there when I'd needed him, but he'd positively flinched from my touch. He was sad, he was grieving. And more to the point, I was married. But that didn't come into my fantasy. Miles would be hurtling from King's Cross to Norwich to be with me this evening; it was just a bit of self-indulgent whimsy.

Joe finished his feed and his face filled with colour. Pinching my nose, I laughed. 'So this is what baby rice smells like! Nappy change needed PDQ.'

Heading to the bathroom for provisions, I stopped half way. Was George still here? Holding my breath, I crept across the parquet and peered through the arch. Covered by the throw from the sofa, he was where I'd left him last night. Still asleep, his head was to one side, his long fringe partially hiding his face. I gazed for a beat at his long, dark lashes and black stubble, which had grown thicker through the night. Goodness knows why, but that felt intimate.

As I turned away, his voice made me jump. 'What is it, Ali?'

Oh hell. Did he know I'd been staring? 'Nothing.' Why was I whispering? The sun was peeping in through the gap in the curtains. 'Go back to sleep. I just needed nappies…'

I changed Joe and sat on the bedroom carpet with him in my lap. We paired the wooden animals from Noah's Ark, built a brick tower, then opened a textured book with a soft mirror. Pressing his reflection with damp fingers, he smiled at his image. 'Yes! It's Joe. Pretty boy like Daddy! He's coming to see you later,' I said quietly.

The peal of the telephone sounded shrill in the silence. I dashed up to answer.

'Hello?'

'Ali, it's me.'

It was Joe's pretty daddy. Glancing at my watch, I was surprised to see it was a minute past nine.

A court tannoy was muffled in the background. 'You're there early,' I commented. 'Everything OK?'

Miles's voice was brisk. 'Not really. The shit's hit the fan. The other side's barrister tipped me off at breakfast. His client has found a box of documents we haven't seen before. I'm going to object, but it's a two-way thing. They might help as well as hinder, so I'll have to go through them after court tonight—'

'But you're coming here.'

'Well, not any more. And if there's anything significant, I'll need a conference with the client tomorrow.'

'It's Saturday tomorrow, Miles.'

'I know it is, Ali; you don't need to tell me.' Then a sigh. 'Look, I'm sorry. I'm as disappointed as you are, but you know what it's like.'

I did know, but I still felt a surge of despondency. I hadn't seen my husband for nearly a week and I'd looked forward to doing something other than fret about Mum's stuff or grasping at straws about a secret that probably didn't even exist. I'd intended to drive further than the village to select food for a slap-up dinner. Maybe even buy myself an outfit that actually fitted. The plan had given me some purpose.

'I'll have to see how it goes, but I'll do my best for Saturday evening or maybe just Sunday…' he continued. 'Look, the client's just arrived. Phone you later, yes?'

My desire to slam the phone down was stymied by etiquette. Holding the blanket in one hand and raking his fringe with the other, George was standing by his chair. He looked handsome and crumpled and embarrassed. He gestured to the front door. 'Sorry,' he said. 'I didn't have time to…' Wafting the throw, he spread it haphazardly on the back of the sofa. 'To disappear. I'll get off now and leave you to start your day.'

As he stepped out, the breeze rippled through and cooled my already flushed cheeks. I just had to be forthright and ask before he disappeared. Lifting my chin, I let the words fire out. 'Seems I've been dumped for a box of documents. I don't suppose you like fish?'

Chapter Thirty-Seven

With Joe in the back seat, I drove the seven miles to Wroxham. It was the closest town with a supermarket and a department store, which were housed in the same building. My memory was of a small centre, just trashy enough to appeal to a child with its toy shop, candy floss and coconut ice stalls. And, of course, a plethora of fish and chip outlets. When I finally opened the car door, I was pleased to discover some things didn't change. Though it had clearly had a facelift since last I visited, there was still the distinctive tang of frying oil in the air.

Still a little shaky from my high temperature and disturbed sleep, I studied my grocery list. The moment my rash dinner invitation was out of my mouth, I'd regretted it and prepared myself for rejection. George had rubbed his bristly chin, but I must have looked pathetic and needy in my bare feet and baggy T-shirt as he'd smiled eventually and said, 'Yup, I like fish.' But I was pleased he'd said yes, even if it was out of pity. It gave me a focus for the day, and despite rattling with paracetamol, I felt energetic.

First up was Wroxham Bridge. Holding Joe tightly, I lifted him from the pram and leaned against the railings. A smart white boat with blue fenders dutifully appeared from beneath us. 'Look Joe, a big boat!'

The day had clouded over and the water looked oily and green, but I smiled at the memory of a trip here with my daddy. We had travelled from Horning in our small motor boat, stopped for petrol and discovered it was regatta day on Wroxham Broad. Mooring the dinghy, we bought salty chips, then strolled to this bridge and watched the yachts dipping and gliding like huge stately swans. I had loved that sense of belonging, being a member of the boating community for those few hours. Dad must have sensed it as he'd pulled me to him and grinned. 'Just perfect, isn't it? And I know what you need. Don't move a muscle; I'll be back…' Then he strode to the gift shop on the quay, returning moments later with a sailor's cap – an expensive gift – just like that.

Sniffing back the emotion, I wondered what had become of it. Probably hidden somewhere so Mum wouldn't find out and think it frivolous and wasteful. I'd worn it on the way home, and when Dad turned the throttle to full speed, it had flown off my head, bouncing and skimming over the surface of the river. Making a huge ridge in the water, Dad had turned the boat and we'd chased the cap as it lapped away in the opposite direction. I remembered it clearly; torn between a need to whoop and laugh at the exhilaration of the chase, and cry because I hadn't wanted to lose such a precious possession.

I frowned. Did this happen during that last summer? And why had the younger version of that smiling man written such a doleful letter to Mum?

Slipping Joe back in his pram, I viewed the shops from the bridge. Had Roys of Wroxham always been so huge? Mum used to say it was known as the world's largest village store. Did it always have a DIY site, a food hall, a garden centre? Perhaps it had, but a child only sees what it wants to see: the toy and candy shops had been pretty much it.

There was inevitably a McDonalds these days. It made me feel hungry, reminding me of my errand, the hasty invitation I had made. The thought made my skin crawl. With embarrassment, mostly. God, what was wrong with me? George's face this morning revealed nothing other than a desire to get away. 'I'll be off then,' he'd said. To clean his teeth and shower, probably. To shave that dark stubble which had grown through the night.

Pushing a buggy around the department store felt weird. I hadn't done it before. In my old life I had paced past them, irritated with the space they took up and wondering why the mums didn't leave their babies behind. How little I knew.

I picked up one or two items of clothing and peered at the prices. Mum complained that Roys was expensive, but it seemed standard fare, catering for teenagers or grannies and not a lot in between. Meandering around the beauty hall, I studied the perfume selection and sprayed on a few. It seemed wrong to inhale a scent that wasn't lilac or lavender in this neck of the woods, but I felt almost human again. I hadn't ambled stress-free for a year; life had gone on hold the moment I became pregnant. I'd had to function at work as usual until my maternity leave started, but I'd rarely relaxed. One scare had merged with the next: from discovering my lack of rubella immunity to dodgy blood results, from high blood pressure to crap birth. Madeleine always observing, judging and knowing.

As Joe patiently watched, I examined sample lipsticks, winding them down to reveal the shade, then painting a line on my hand, aimlessly and gloriously time-wasting without an aching pelvic floor or leaky nipples. Though the most expensive, the gold casing was the final decider. I selected a nude colour; I hadn't worn any make-up for weeks and I didn't want to look too obvious for tonight's guest. Not that I had any romantic plans; I was a married woman.

The assistant pulled out a new one, inspected the tip, then read its name on the base. 'Seduce?' she asked, and I laughed.

Still chuckling to myself, I headed for the supermarket. It wasn't one I was familiar with, and despite my fish offer, I had no firm plan of what to cook, so I strolled up and down the aisles, hoping for inspiration. I wasn't exactly Nigella, but our dinner parties had always gone down well. The amount of alcohol consumed probably helped, though: fizz of some sort to greet the guests, liberal helpings of expensive vino to match the dish, followed by sweet dessert wine then spirits, the standard set by Miles's father.

I shook my head at the thought. Booze had been a huge part of our lives. Not just us, but our lawyer friends too. It was understandable; our jobs were stressful and alcohol was one way to unwind. Sometimes it worked a treat; Miles's easy-going personality would go up a notch with his embellished stories and mimicking, and he'd have everyone around the table laughing. But occasionally he became belligerent, argumentative and angry, a person I hardly recognised.

Like synchronicity, the 'Aqua' caught my eye. It wasn't Madeleine's main offence, but that's where it had started, when I'd snapped out of love. Protruding from her handbag like a fashion statement, her small bottle of Evian was a constant fixture. She'd take a swig every now and then, drinking steadily through the day.

'Aqua. Good for the digestive system, good for the skin, darling!' she'd laugh.

Like the sheep I'd been, I'd followed her example, but one morning I took a gulp of hers by mistake, stunned to discover it was vodka. When I told Miles, he'd shrugged. Her boozing bouts happened from time to time, and if it didn't affect her behaviour and she didn't drive, then it wasn't an issue. But it was; it was a huge, huge problem: I hadn't *known*, I'd been blindsided. I felt foolish, betrayed, belittled. Our trust had been broken. Even worse, I'd lost that person I'd placed so very high on the pedestal.

Unable to face my own devastation, I said nothing to Madeleine. Instead I cooled the relationship and distanced myself, blaming work commitments and the need to catch up with Mum and friends at the weekends. But she'd phone me each evening, 'For a chat, because I've missed you, darling'. God knows how much she'd drunk by then because it had shown. Her words garbled, she'd mutter with long pauses and weep: she had a rotten life, an awful husband, an ungrateful child; no one ever listened or really cared; she was completely alone.

I was selfish, undoubtedly, but I couldn't deal with this new person. The old one had gone, deserted me somehow. The calls abruptly stopped and after a few months of silence, Madeleine turned up with a bouquet of stunning flowers. 'Sorry, darling,' she said with those huge, sincere eyes. 'I've been out of sorts but I'm dry, on the wagon, abstaining. Even all three! I'm back now, sweetheart. How I've missed you and our chats.'

Her 'chats', of course, were the rub. Pushing that thought away, I tried to summon the anger I'd felt after the drink-driving trip to Lymm. It was no longer there, just relief I'd escaped. Maybe Norfolk had put it in perspective. Perhaps two hundred and fifty miles helped.

Going back to the busy supermarket, I moved down the drinks aisle, picking up a bottle each of red, rose and white to cover all bases. Then I thought of Miles's visit and added a brandy.

–

Exhausted and with a headache when we returned, I dumped the shopping in the hall and fed Joe. Though tiredness overwhelmed me, I remembered Mum's sweaty sheets and felt compelled to at least strip them. I dragged myself to her bedroom, but Denise had got there first. The bedding had been changed, the quilt turned down hotel-style. The thought of Denise in my space unsettled me. I was getting used to village life, and was a grown-up now, but I still didn't like the idea of being the subject of gossip. Paranoia, of course. What was it Mum used to say to me when she was chatting to the aunties? 'No, we're not talking about you, Ali. As lovely as you are, we've got better things to discuss!'

Flopping down on the mattress, I sighed at the memory. What a challenging child I'd been – part of me earwigging, the other covering my ears. 'Sorry, Mum,' I said aloud. 'I must have been a complete nightmare.'

Was I difficult all the time? God, I hoped not, though my big sister's constant moaning about me would suggest otherwise, especially here in Norfolk. Sighing, I shifted my mind to tonight. What planet was Ali Baker on? Preparing a meal for a man I barely knew, and a most reluctant dinner guest to boot. But it was kind of comical too, something I'd enjoy telling Laura about. But first, the blinking food needed unpacking, especially the chilled items. Food poisoning would not be a good start to my holiday romance. Lips twitching at the thought, I allowed myself another minute. The next moment, I was asleep.

–

Joe's grumbling roused me and I looked at my watch. Bloody hell, we'd both slept for three hours. Hitching myself up, I tried to snatch at a dream before it floated away. Mum? Yes, my beautiful younger mother, sipping coffee and blathering with her sisters. Me at the doorway, watching, listening. My nose burned at the blend of grief and pleasure; it brought back my loss, but it had been so lovely to see her.

As I plucked Joe from his cot, the doorbell rang. Looking distorted through the glass, it was Nancy. Perhaps she didn't have a key after all.

'We're not stopping,' she said, bustling in with a basket of something which smelled freshly baked. The 'we' stayed outside, a huge, ugly dog which wouldn't have been out of place on the lonely moorlands near Baskerville Hall.

'He's not mine. He's my son's and I've got to feed the damned thing for a week,' she explained. 'Flaming meat from the butcher's. It'll cost me a fortune.'

'What's wrong with tinned pet food?' I asked, chuckling at her sucked-in cheeks.

'Because it's his baby, believe it or not, so I'm not allowed. He's never been one for the ladies, but he's always had a dog. Out of my six I've only got two grandkids and they live in Norwich. Where did I go wrong? Still, I've been luckier than Joan.' As though the poor woman might be listening, she lowered her voice. 'Same as me. Six. Must have been a terrible thing.'

I frowned, perplexed.

'Miscarriages,' she hissed. 'Before she had the hyster-ectomy.' She tutted. 'Still in her thirties, but apparently Tom insisted.'

Shocked at the news, I simply gaped, but Nancy was lifting her eyebrows meaningfully. 'Those antique dollies. She must have been far on to know the baby's sex…'

I took a breath to mumble something – how I'd had no idea, how sad, how dreadful – but Nancy gave Joe a gummy smile. 'But here's our bonny little boy. I'll take him down in the pram, kill two birds as they say. Not that it's a very nice expression. We'll go and say hello to Auntie Joan, shall we? Give her something to smile about, eh?'

Making a raspberry noise, she took Joe from my arms. He chortled appreciatively.

'I bumped into George in the village,' she continued, deftly swaddling my son in his thin blanket. 'He almost had a twinkle in his eyes, which isn't like him. I spotted him coming out of Mace with a bottle. He sits in the Swan Inn of an evening, so it won't have been for himself. I wonder if he's got a fancy woman. I'd better not tell Denise, she'll be livid. She's been trying to get a bit of rumpy-pumpy out of him for months.'

She eventually drew breath, so I quickly slipped in a thank you for dropping round the baked treats.

'A pleasure,' she replied, eyeing me shrewdly. 'I'll let you get on with those bags. Looks like they need unpacking. We'll see you in a bit.'

Chapter Thirty-Eight

Like Nancy had earlier, George rang the doorbell at eight. It felt odd and formal and I was thrown by his attire. I hadn't expected him to don smart clothes; I didn't think he'd own any, especially not ones with branded logos. Purchased by Emma? But I liked this Emma, who had bought her husband nice outfits. Miles sourced his own; what I thought he liked and what he did like never quite married.

I stepped back to let him pass. Emphasising his tanned skin, the white shirt made him look more like a male model than a gardener. Or even a landscape architect. Didn't they wear flannel checked shirts and brown cords? Or was that secondary school maths teachers? Yup; I was prattling in my head to calm my ridiculous nerves. He offered me a bottle and the babble burst out.

'Ah, the famous purchase from Mace!' I tried to make contact with his questioning gaze. 'You were spotted by one of our local spooks…'

'Ah. You mentioned fish but the choice was pretty dire.' His lips twitched. 'It was the only one from a country I'd heard of. Shall I open it and see just how bad it is?'

'Yes. Good plan. This way to…'

He followed me to the kitchen, crouched down to say hello to Joe, then busied himself with a corkscrew while I hovered.

'Cheers.' He passed me a glass and looked at me evenly. 'Had a nap? You're looking a lot better.'

I felt myself flushing. The comment was just a statement; it wasn't meant to be a compliment, but the blush made it look as though I had taken it as one.

'As you can see, the little troublemaker's still awake,' I said, finding my voice. 'He hates to miss the action.' *Action Ali? Really?* 'Right…' I said, stifling my giddy nerves, 'I'd better get to it…'

I opened the oven door, an excuse for my red face. The rosemary potatoes and roast veg were already on their way, so I slipped in the herb-crusted cod fillets. Shoving everything in one place had seemed the safest bet. Mum's gas hob didn't like me, particularly when I heated milk, and it was a bugger to clean.

Rattling in cupboards, I spent a few minutes finding plates and my composure. When I turned back, both males were holding teaspoons. Joe was sitting on George's lap, his wide eyes watching George tap the back of a saucepan. He listened to the jangling sound for a beat, then rolled his head to study George's face. Would he work it out and do the same? I gazed with a smile, then remembered I was hosting. This very cute baby hadn't dropped off during his last feed, so at some point I'd have to patiently nurse him until his eyes drooped. And if I was too hasty putting him down, they'd open again and I'd have to wait even longer.

'You're meant to be persuading him to sleep, not getting him excited,' I said.

'I can do that too, can't I, Joe?'

My hand on my hip, I snorted. 'Go on then. I bet you a fiver you can't get him off in ten minutes.'

George laughed. 'Yes, but it would be my fiver I'd be winning back. Nonetheless, you're on.' He took a swig of wine and stood up. 'See you in the allotted time or less.' Cradling my son in one arm, he opened the side door and stepped into the sunlit evening. I watched for a while. How would he affect this miracle? I'd have cheated by putting Joe in my car and driving around for the 'allotted time'. But George the giant strolled beyond the flower beds and through the trees, slowly weaving in and out of the dappled shade and retreating sun.

Back in the kitchen, I sipped my drink and looked for something to do. I had been too efficient: the starter was already prepared, a wild rocket salad with walnuts and Roquefort. Blue cheese had been on the banned list throughout my pregnancy, so I had an irresistible urge for it. I allowed myself a small, guilty smile: funny how one's desire intensified when it wasn't allowed.

The ingredients I'd bought to make a challenging dessert were still in the fridge; Nancy's apple pie had looked so delicious I hadn't bothered. Mum would have frowned at the 'unnecessary calories' of a sugar-glazed pastry lid, but what the heck, I was in happy holiday mode. The tub of clotted cream I'd bought on a whim would be a perfect accompaniment; clearly I must have known.

The mellow wine embraced my throat and chest the same way as Kelvin's elderberry wine had all those years ago. Heady and warm, a pleasant tipsiness took hold.

It was curious how life was working out. At home I hadn't let Joe out of my sight, not even with a neighbour I knew well, but I was allowing a stranger to help here. I had an instinctive confidence in George, a connection, almost. Because Mum had trusted him, I supposed.

Humming to myself, I drifted to the lounge and looked for them through the small panes. Should I draw the curtains, or would that look odd? Would George mind being seen with a married woman? Not that anyone could peer in while passing. And he'd already slept here twice. Why would he worry when he had nothing to hide?

Stopping at the chiffonier mirror, I inspected myself, turning one way and back again. George was right; my appearance had improved. And tonight my hair was a dark cape around my shoulders without the usual bobble scraping it back. As I tucked it behind my ears, I caught George's reflection from behind me. It was strange to see him as he saw himself, different and yet familiar. Discomfort and delirium shot to my stomach. Or perhaps it was simply embarrassment; I'd been caught singing and admiring myself. Whichever it was, George had won his five pounds; Joe was asleep in his arms.

–

Once back in the kitchen, I presented the starters with a flourish and topped up our glasses. 'One of your fans was here today,' I said, sitting down. 'I considered passing her pie off as my own but I'm sure you'd have caught me out.'

I'd already mentioned the 'Mace' wine, but I had to start somewhere to fill the strained silence.

He smiled. 'Yes, I'm honoured to be a recipient of Nancy's delicacies from time to time.'

I lifted my eyebrows. 'Seems half the village are just waiting for the nod. Just think, if you gave them more encouragement, you'd have a lifetime's supply of home baking.'

He tucked into his food. 'Hmm, I think I'll pass, thanks.'

The expression 'rumpy-pumpy' popped into my head, but I held back from using it, thank God. 'The OAPs will be disappointed,' I said instead.

I was being clumsy and flirty, but I hadn't eaten dinner *à deux* with anyone other than Miles for years. We could've talked about our miserable lives, but I didn't want to dwell on death or tragedy or discordant relationships right then. And the wine was taking the edge off my natural reticence.

'I might be getting a few grey hairs but I'm not that old yet,' he replied.

'How old are you then?'

His eyes narrowed, but after a beat he answered. 'Forty-three in October.'

About what I had guessed, eight years older than me. I laughed. 'Sorry, that was a bit rude of—'

George spoke at the same time. 'You have a sister, don't you?'

'Yes, Laura. She lives in Canada. But I expect you know that…'

He frowned thoughtfully. 'Yes, your mother talked about you both.'

Ignoring the usual apprehension, I snorted. 'Nothing bad I hope.'

'Not at all.' He looked at me quizzically. 'She missed you both and was thrilled when Joe came along. She couldn't wait to tell us all the news.'

I nodded. On the way to Wroxham, I'd caught sight of a bunch of crispy, dried flowers at an intersection. Though I wasn't sure if it was *the* junction, I'd felt remarkably fine. Yet it was still difficult to group her and Joe together without a sharp stab of grief. Keeping my gaze averted, I cleared George's plate.

'Sorry,' he said. Then after a moment, his face all inno-cence: 'Something smells good.'

Oh shit, the grill. The potatoes had needed a little extra crisping, but I'd completely forgotten, despite the smoky aroma. Donning oven mitts, I pulled out the tray and presented it to him. The produce he'd nurtured was 'a bit on the brown side', as Mum would have put it. I decided I liked him then. There was something kind but humorous about his tact.

The tension broken, the chatter flowed after that. As we ate I told him about my boat trips with Dad as a child and it turned out he was a huge river fan too. Prompted by his own stories, memories of windmills, old churches and broads came flooding back.

'I wonder if the photographs are here,' I said eventu-ally. 'Let's take our drinks and look. I was only allowed a disposable camera back then. With just one button, not a lot could go wrong. However...' I chuckled at the memory. 'No Boots nor film services shop here in the village, so I'd send it off by post, wait for an aeon and then... Yup, only a handful were any good. Seems I was an expert...' I searched for the word. 'Guillotinist. I excelled at beheading people and steeples, vanes and turrets.' I thought of the trips on *Sylvette*. 'And even the good ones never quite caught the wonder and excitement of it all.'

George nodded. 'I get that.'

We ambled to the lounge. 'Nancy says you're a good listener,' I said over my shoulder. 'She's right.'

Madeleine's attentive expression appeared from nowhere. Unlike her son, she'd been a good listener too. Perhaps I'd been unfair; she'd been my confidante many times. But she'd dug too deep; she'd overstepped the mark.

Pushing that thought away, I knelt on the carpet and snapped open a pino noir. I hadn't counted how many glasses I'd had, but I felt lighthearted rather than drunk. George seemed at ease too, his face interested and affable without the frown. He had a warmth about him, a gentleness that belied his size. Relaxed in an armchair, he patiently watched as I rifled through packets of photographs from the sideboard. It took me an age to find the Norfolk ones because I was distracted by comical or nostalgic images of Laura and me as children, of Mum and Dad, the aunties and uncles at cousins' weddings. If he was bored as I showed him each one, he didn't show it. Helped by comparisons with actors, musicians or politicians, he had a good working knowledge of all my relatives by midnight. I loved his sharp wit, how easily we laughed.

Digging deeper in the cupboard, I found the wallet marked 'Laura misc', a selection that didn't fit in any other category, but my equivalent didn't seem to be there. Miles and I had gone through it only at Christmas, chuckling at the images of Alison Baker through the years – a dark-haired, solemn toddler; a skinny, bespectacled schoolgirl; almost smiling in a pink tutu for ballet; then finally a grin as I held the hundred metres swimming cup aloft. There'd been pictures of me during my 'alternative' days too, from mid-teens and through university, but by the time of my weekends and holidays with Miles, my transformation had begun, and was finally complete in our engagement day snap. But one 'post-punk' image had been misfiled in Laura's pack, that of a teenage girl with pink spiky hair, her brown eyes exotic, her lips vivid red. Wearing a torn netted vest top, leather jacket and zipped combats, she looked confident and sexy with heaps of attitude. 'Guess who this is?' I asked, passing it to George.

He peered at the photograph, then at me. 'Wow. Is this really you?' He laughed. 'A crucifix and rubber bracelets, no less...'

'Let me look again,' I said, kneeling in front of him. But he held it away so I couldn't reach.

'Mine now,' he laughed. 'You'll find it tomorrow morning in the post office window. "*Madonna tribute band for hire*".'

Reaching again for the snap, I found my lips next to his and on impulse, I leaned in for a kiss. For a moment he seemed to freeze, then he moved me away, his hands firm on my shoulders.

'No, Ali.'

I sat back on my haunches. 'Why not?' I asked, the words tumbling out before my pride could stop them. 'You like me, I know it.'

His face closed and cloudy, he shook his head. 'Sorry,' he said, standing. 'I'm not looking for this.'

'Don't you fancy me at all?'

I don't know why I asked. The humiliation was unbearable already. But I suppose I needed to know.

He made for the front door, opened it and looked out to the black night. 'You're a lovely woman,' he said, finally turning. 'But you're married, you're grieving and confused. You don't know what you want.'

I took a deep breath. Who knows what I might have said? That he was wrong, that I wasn't befuddled or crazy, that from the outset I'd felt an intense connection or attachment that wouldn't let go? But he lifted a palm to stop me.

'I'm not looking for anyone, Ali,' he said steadily. 'And even if I was, you're not for me.'

Chapter Thirty-Nine

The breeze cooling my cheeks, I watched George's retreat. When I could no longer hear the crackle of pebbles, I closed out the darkness and covered my eyes. How I dearly wished I could rewind the last five stupid, stupid minutes. What the hell was wrong with me? Was I crazy? Did I have no self-respect? But a flash through the window brought me back. Car headlights again. Alarm spreading, I stared through the glass, frozen to the spot as the bright beam came closer.

My heart thrashed. My thoughts weren't as hysterical as they had been last night, but suppose this visitor was sinister? What if someone threw a stone or tried the door handle? Or just mucked about outside for a lark? Who would I call? I had offended the only protector I had, and Miles could hardly come charging from London. But the vehicle was now turning beyond the vegetable patch and going back the way it had come. I shrugged off the alarm. It had simply lost its way. Like me. Or perhaps the driver was a 'dogger', heading for the woods. Though they needed someone to watch, didn't they?

Too agitated to even consider sleep, I yanked the curtains closed, then sat amidst the scattered mess. Feeling a dreadful sense of loss, I lifted the 'Norfolk' packet. So busy chattering and discussing the other photographs, I hadn't even got around to opening it. Why did bad things happen here? Or maybe more accurately, why such devastating lows following such brilliant highs: the last summer succeeded by Dad's death; nightmares after a blissful afternoon at Bureside; a dead, teeming pigeon in an otherwise perfect day. Then this evening, so comfortable, so content, so flaming alive one minute and then…

As the wooziness hit, I realised I was pissed after all. What a complete fool on all counts. It was so unlike me to go too far, to lose control, almost. For once I'd been like my sister, I'd thrown caution to the wind, and look where it had got me.

I scooped up an old snap of her. 'Still seeking your approval, wishing I was you,' I mumbled.

Memory flooding back, I studied it more closely. Yes, it was Laura's last school portrait before leaving for Canada, when the four years between us had seemed enormous. Though her fair hair was tied back and she was wearing little make-up, she looked confident in her own skin. I had too in the one I'd shown George, but that wasn't my skin nor my hair nor my smile.

'Time for sleep,' I muttered to the photograph. 'Keep me company tonight.'

Unsteady on my feet, I made it to my room, propped the snap of Laura on my bedside chair and sighed deeply. 'One day, big sis,' I said to her. 'One day I'll tell you about this evening and we'll laugh.'

Sleep immediately grasped me, but I couldn't quite sink deep enough to reach the next level. Though my muscles were relaxed, my mind ticked over, neither awake nor asleep, but drifting somewhere in between. It was nice at first, like I was floating in Black Horse Broad with the sun beaming down on my face. Eyes closed, I bumped along with the ripples, safe and secure in my lifejacket.

Then something below the surface brushed my leg. As I jerked away, I looked at my chest. No orange lifejacket. And I was no longer buoyant, but sinking like lead, down and further down to the river bed.

Oh God, I had to swim, get back to the surface. My limbs almost paralysed, I pushed through sludgy water until rays of sunshine seeped through and it began to clear. But when I reached the top, the surface was covered by images looking down at me. Desperately searching for oxygen, I moved from one to the next – Laura in school uniform, Mum's neat handwriting, a baby's name tag, Dad's purple wrists, Grandpa's Omega watch, my young mother yawning, a carriage clock, Dad's tense wedding face, the walnut drawers breathing, then Laura's face again, again and again.

Bursting awake with a huge gasp, I bolted upright. My pulse raced, my throat rasped, I could barely swallow. Tears of self-pity prodding, I lowered my head until the dizziness passed. It was fine; everything was fine. Exacerbated by the wine, I'd simply had another nightmare.

Dragging myself from the bed, I checked on my sleeping son, shuffled to the bathroom and gulped from the grubby toothbrush holder. Glass after glass of cloudy liquid.

Norfolk water, I thought, remembering Tom Hague's comment. Too soft or too hard, I didn't know, but I should have drunk it before sleep; it had been the saving grace after boozy nights out when I'd had to be at a court in Preston or Plymouth or Prestatyn the following morning by nine. But today the concern was my breast milk. How bloody irresponsible I'd been. Again. I could only pray the alcohol would be diluted by morning.

Depressed and guilty, I stared at my shadowy reflection. Could my self-esteem tumble any lower? I had humiliated myself and lost a person I valued as a friend, but even worse, I'd been a crap mother.

'*Be kind to yourself, love. No one is perfect. We all make mistakes. No one knows that better than me.*'

Mum's words. As though she'd said them now and was right behind me, I cautiously turned. Nothing and no one was there. Of course, there wasn't. But fragments of the dream were filtering back. Like falling snowflakes, I tried to snatch them before they dissolved.

Collecting my thoughts, I perched on the loo seat. Mum. Mistakes. Something she'd wanted to tell me. The aunties gossiping. The change in mood of the sanatorium letters. Dad's tense expression, his sincere apology…

Hurrying back to my bedroom, I grabbed the photograph of Laura and stared. Yes, shocking though it was, it all made sense now. I remembered Mum's old comment and groaned. '*No, we're not talking about you Ali. As lovely as you are, we've got better things to discuss.*' She was right, absolutely; this wasn't about me, but herself. Breathless from my discovery, I tried to steady my racing thoughts. Could it really be true? How could I be sure?

An idea forming, I slipped from the bed and padded to the lounge. The sideboard's doors and drawers were already gaping, so I sat cross-legged on the floor and removed the boxes of Mum's diaries. Mostly small and slim to fit in a handbag; I guessed there were at least fifty. Organised according to size rather than year, it took several minutes to order them on the parquet.

As my eyes quickly jumped from one decade to the next, I wondered if she'd kept them for this very day. 'The past is past,' Laura would say, but some history needed to be recorded in black and white. Yes, then acknowledged.

Finally finding the one I wanted, I traced the embossed gold date with trembling fingers. Such a slender journal for something so momentous. Was I right? Would the entries confirm it? Taking a deep breath, I opened it a crack at the silky page marker. A folded piece of paper fell out.

Chapter Forty

Saturday

The weak sunshine rousing me, I yawned and glanced at my watch. Too early to get up just yet. Then last night's shocking discovery hit like a slap. Mum's note, her shaky handwriting. The moment I'd read it, I'd known what to do as soon as Joe woke this morning. Then I'd slept peacefully, an astonishingly deep and dreamless sleep...

I nodded. Yes, it was a sign of approval, confirmation I should follow my instinct and see it through.

Although eager to leave the house, I felt strangely measured and calm as I dressed, ate breakfast and washed up the dinner pots. His timing impeccable, Joe woke as I slotted the final plate in the rack. The memory of how I'd made a pass at George was something I wanted to obliterate forever and perhaps one day I would, but for now it was as sore and tender as a gash.

In case the pram was spotted by the postman, the deli staff or the workers in the boatyard, I deciding on driving. My car was surprisingly chilly inside. A blanket for Joe was in order. Remembering the headlights from last night, I scooped him out rather than leave him, even for seconds. He was everything to me now; his loss would be simply unbearable.

I trundled down Lower Street, pulled up behind The Swan and climbed out. Carrying Joe in his seat, I made my way to George's picket fence and inhaled the crisp air. His tiny front garden was scented like the gift shop, a friendly aroma of sweet blossom, but I wasn't here to admire the wild flowers today. I had property in my possession which didn't belong to me. It felt hot in my hand; like Prometheus and his theft of fire, it had to be passed on.

Hoping I wouldn't wake the neighbours, I rapped lightly on the door. I didn't feel nervous, as much as anxious and determined to complete my mission. Chin lifted, I waited for a minute, maybe two. Eventually stepping back, I glanced up at the drawn curtains. Would George be deeply asleep after the late night and wine? I pushed that thought away; no good would come of contemplating my clumsy kiss, but it came back in Technicolour the instant he stood at his threshold. Wearing a T-shirt and boxers, he looked tired and ruffled and handsome, but most of all surprised. The situation was so absurd that part of me wanted to dryly laugh. But if he thought I was a bunny-boiler or that I'd finally lost the plot completely, he didn't show it. Instead he stood back and let me in without a word.

'Sorry for the early call, but I've come to give you this,' I said, holding out the diary. 'It's yours.'

He didn't reply. Instead, he took my offering and studied the cover. He was noting the year; he knew what it meant.

I turned to leave; I had done the necessary. Time to return to The Lodge and face the reality of clearing it out with a view to selling it PDQ.

'Ali.' George caught my forearm. 'Don't go,' he said. 'I'll put on the kettle.'

It was the first time he'd reached out to me and I almost smiled at the irony, but this wasn't a funny occasion. Instead I followed him into the cool cottage.

As though lost, he raked his hair, then put his treasure down on the cloth-covered table. 'Tea,' he said. 'I'll make tea.'

Scooping Joe from his seat, I perched on the sofa and listened to the loud tick of the carriage clock. George eventually returned with two mugs, sat in his chair and glowered at the journal as though it might burst into flames.

'How did you know?' he asked after some time.

Laura's comment from the funeral tumbled back: *you always did squeeze your eyes so tightly shut…* She was right; I had been almost wilfully blind about this. 'It's been in plain sight, staring me in the face since I met you. But it was a photograph of Laura that finally shook me to reality in the early hours of this morning.' I smiled thinly. 'I had bizarre dreams and then… Well, when I looked at her again, there *you* were. Same nose, same smile. Just different colouring.'

He glanced at me and sighed. 'I'm sorry. I should have said something that first night. Or at least the next day, but you were grieving for your mother, struggling with Joe. And besides, Eve had never told you or Laura; I didn't know whether she'd want me to.' He rubbed his chin thoughtfully. 'Eve and I had a long talk the first time we met, but after that, the subject wasn't broached again. I think once she had acknowledged me, she wanted us to carry on as though we were strangers, or at least house owner and gardener. We spent time chatting over a cuppa when I was there and she'd occasionally give me a gift, but no more than she did for Nancy or Denise.'

I nodded. My grandpa's watch; *his* grandpa's watch.

His expression clouding, he was silent for a while. Then he cleared his throat. 'I got the impression it was a painful memory for her, something she didn't want to talk about or to dwell on.' His jaw clenched. 'Perhaps I reminded her of him, my father. Have you read it?'

'No, I haven't, but…'

His haunted look said it all: the fear of the unknown; the terror of finding out something dreadful, yet needing to know too. Though I couldn't read his mind, the sensation was so familiar, I could almost taste it.

'But there's a letter inside. That's all I've read. It's none of my business, really. I brought it to you as soon as I could…'

I studied him as though for the first time. Tanned and angular, his features were classical, fine. Yes, a manly version of Laura in many ways, and Mum too, of course. This man was my brother. My half-brother, more accurately, yet still a blood relative. But now I was here, it didn't feel even remotely tangible or real. I sensed no sibling connection; there was no sudden revulsion; he was still the guy I had kissed yesterday, the person I'd really liked.

His whole demeanour was so troubled I wanted to comfort him somehow, but my touch had repelled him and now I knew why. Instead, I smoothed my son's hair and waited for him to speak.

'After Ben died, I needed to get away. Emma and I couldn't live together any more, so I decided to come down here. I didn't have any firm plans, I just thought I'd find a way to meet Eve and see what she was like. It was my mother's idea, actually. She thought it would give me some focus, help me to think about something other than Ben.'

He massaged his forehead. 'My parents, they're both great. I was adopted by good people. They were open and down to earth about it since we were toddlers. Both me and my sister. They even kept the names our birth mothers had given us.'

He paused. 'Eve asked if I minded being called by a different name down here. She suggested George – same as your old gardener, I believe. Perhaps it was an odd request, but it helped, in a way. Distanced us from, well, the truth.' He gave the slightest of smiles. 'My real name is Oliver. Oliver Newman.'

Of course; the '*glad we met again*' flowers on Mum's grave.

'As soon as I introduced myself, she knew. She studied me for some time, then said, "My Oliver?" and I said "yes"…'

He took a deep breath. 'So that first time we had a coffee and she talked about it a little, but only about how sorry she was, how much she'd loved me and how painful it had been to give up her baby and…' Something in his frown made me stiffen. 'She said she'd made a promise to your father…'

Nodding, I said nothing. I didn't like Dad being drawn into the story; I didn't want him to be the villain. Perhaps George understood, as we fell quiet for some time.

'Did you feel a… I don't know, an attachment or a spark when you first met… Eve?' I asked eventually.

'Not really, no. I was content with my life until Ben died. I had loving parents, a happy childhood, I didn't want for anything; I didn't particularly need to find my natural parents. But after Ben… once Mum suggested it, it felt the right thing to do.'

'And when you got to know her more…?' I pressed.

He spread his hands, his big, safe hands. I was glad he wasn't really called George, but I could never think of or call him Oliver. I'd shockingly discovered the man I had really fancied was my *brother*, and that was *his* name.

'When I got to know her better, I just thought that Eve was a nice lady who loved her two daughters and missed her husband. There was no sudden bonding, why should there be? It was a newborn she gave up, a baby she missed, not a grown stranger. We never went beyond civilities, never got too intimate. When she asked me about my family, I told her I had solid parents and a sister.' He paused. 'And a son who'd died. But that's as far as it went. I didn't go into detail about my life and neither did she.'

Rising abruptly, he stepped over to the window and looked out. 'This letter you've mentioned… Does it say who my father was?' He turned, the tension tight in his cheeks. 'Or how my conception happened?'

I shook my head. 'I don't think so, but you need to read it yourself. There isn't much to it, I'm afraid,' I said. I stood. 'Maybe the diary will tell you more. I'll leave you to it. Miles is coming this afternoon if he can get away.'

I left my brother scowling at our mother's secret life. Would he open the diary? Or would it remain on the table, burning a hole in it forever?

Chapter Forty-One

As I drove back through the village, Mum's missive rattled in my head. Though I'd only scanned it once and I felt awful for reading it, for invading her and George's privacy, I knew the heartbroken words would stay with me forever:

> I haven't written anything in my diary this year because there's nothing good to say. Except for you, my dear little boy, it has been the worst year of my life.
>
> I have spent the last two months in a boarding house in Leeds, a stone's throw from where it all began. But I've been content to spend time reading my books in the garden with you growing and thriving inside me.
>
> You were born an hour ago and they have let me keep you with me for just a while. You took such a long time to come into this world but the pain was bearable because I knew the longer it took, the longer you would be with me. And here you are, a perfect baby boy.
>
> My heart breaks to give you away but I have nothing to offer you but love. And if I'm honest, it takes more than just love. It takes a house and a home and clothes and the care of a good man. And that is what I have. I have a man who loves me

with all his heart but that love can't extend to you because you are not his and you'll be a constant reminder of a terrible error of judgement that I will always hold myself responsible for.

It wasn't until I was parked and unbelting Joe that I noticed Tom Hague, a forlorn figure amidst the rough wasteland beyond the sunken garden. He was looking towards the woods, the wind blowing his silver hair.

Why was he here, and so early in the morning? 'Hello,' I called. 'Lovely morning.'

He turned and put his hand to his ear, then he stepped over the thistles and clods of long grass. His eyes seemed watery, but perhaps it was the wind. 'Hello love. You're looking well.' He waved to Joe. 'And there's your hand-some little man.'

'Would you like to come in for a tea or coffee?' I asked. I didn't want company right now, but I sensed a sadness about him.

He straightened and gazed as though my offer hadn't registered. Then he gestured to the scrubland. 'Promised your mum I wouldn't sell it.'

That was a surprise; I hadn't known he owned it.

As though reading my mind, he nodded. 'Bought this whole plot at a snip,' he said. 'Thirty years ago now. The usual plan; get planning permission and build.'

'Oh right, so you're going to develop it? Residential housing, I assume?' I asked. I was being polite; it didn't really matter; I was moving on.

'No.' His expression was wistful. 'Money isn't everything, is it?' He stepped closer and for a second I froze, remembering Laura's comments about tickling and cuddles. But he simply patted the top of my arm. 'Of course I miss Eve very much and so wish I could turn back the clock, but I still pine for your dad, his friendship, his good company, by heck I do. He was like a breath of fresh air. No one else could make me laugh like he did. A long time ago, but sometimes it feels like yesterday.'

His croak was so loaded with emotion, I felt a sharp burn behind my own eyes. And Laura's sarcasm was wrong. When I'd been rifling through the photographs last night, I found a stray one of Tom and me dangling our legs over the bow of *Sylvette*. Wearing a stripy swimsuit and the sailor's cap, I was obviously giggling, but happy too. He'd been kind, a solid friend, and perhaps a father figure to Dad.

Could I ask about Dad's illness and the trips to Norwich in the Roller? I wasn't sure I was up to the answer right now, but I probably wouldn't get another chance. I took a quick breath. 'That final summer. I suppose you knew?'

'Aye and I did what I could. But he'd left it too late. If he'd not buried his head…' His speech strangled, he pulled me into a hug. 'Always smiling, your dad, but who knows what he felt inside.' His humbug breath brushed my neck, and for moments he held me. Just as I began to feel uncomfortable, he stepped back and stood erect. 'Yours and Laura's happiness was what mattered, Alice. Some things are best kept hidden for the greater good.' He gestured to Joe, watching from the car. 'You'll probably understand now you've got a littl'un. Kids' happiness and safety, that's what matters. Right, enough nostalgia for today; I'll get off.'

Suddenly remembering all the babies he'd lost, I searched for something comforting to say, but he'd already started his descent down the shortcut. 'How about that drink?' I called. 'I could rustle up a biscuit…'

He didn't look back, but his clotted voice carried on the breeze. 'Another time, love. I'd better get back to Joan. She isn't so good today.'

Tom's words stayed with me as I carried my chubby baby around the house. I breathed in Joe's smell, touched his soft skin and nuzzled him, finally knowing with certainty that I'd never hurt him. It was hard to focus on positives right now, but I knew I was lucky. The Hagues had never managed to bring a baby into the world, Mum had given away her firstborn and George had devastatingly lost his only child.

Mum's letter continued to prod my thoughts as I tidied. The fact she'd had an illegitimate son before Laura was finally hitting me. It was astonishing, unreal. Had I not seen it in black and white, I would not have believed it. Her words had been so searingly honest, too. George was the product of a 'terrible error of judgement'. How was he feeling about that? And what about her? How difficult had it been to give painful birth in a hospital, but leave her newborn behind? Had she felt desperate sorrow or relief it was over? She'd referred to 'a home and clothes and the care of a good man'. Would George condemn her for taking the easy option? I cuddled my son. On some level, did I?

The door to the dining room was ajar, a shaft of bright sunlight inviting me in. I spent a few moments skimming my fingers over the dusty surfaces, lost in thought. I didn't want to dwell on my younger parents, those two vibrant voices in the love letters, but they were inescapable. How painless had the 'easy' option been? Dad had clearly adored her, he'd been seriously ill in hospital, yet she'd been unfaithful; she'd slept with another man and made him a cuckold. He'd obviously forgiven her, but only on the basis that he didn't have to 'share'. What had his letter said? *I could never share you in any way, even if it means a broken heart...*

'In any way' clearly meant baby Oliver. And those dreadful terms made sense of his short note of apology: *Please find it in your heart to forgive me.* Had there been anger, recrimination and blame both ways? Did Dad condemn her for her infidelity; did she blame him for not accepting the child? Was Oliver always there, a silent torment between them, like a bruise? Or did they just forget him, move forward and put the past firmly behind them?

Lying Joe against a cushion, I stepped over to Mum's canvases, extracted the framed pencil drawing and placed it on the table. I must have looked at it a hundred times, but as I studied it now, I could see that this child with 'heartburn hair' wasn't me. Like the tiny, perished wristband she kept in her purse, it was a memory of her lost boy.

Chapter Forty-Two

Though I would have to pull everything out again soon, I'd just finished stacking packets and boxes in the sideboard when the steady crunch of pebbles broke the silence. My ears pricked at the sound. A car again. A little perturbed at another unexpected vehicle, even though it was daylight, I picked Joe up from his play mat and made my way to the window. A taxi appeared at the top of the drive, circled the flower beds and stopped at the door.

Putting Joe back down, I composed myself. 'Daddy's here,' I said to him, but he was too young to hear the lack of excitement in my voice. I felt flat, despondent and tired, but at least I could go to bed and catch up on some sleep; it was the only thing that seemed important just now.

I opened the front door and tried for a smile. 'Miles! What a lovely surprise.'

It didn't wash with him. 'You could at least look pleased to see me,' he said, stepping in. 'I caught the early train just for you, Ali. You've no idea how hard I had to work last night to get through the new disclosure.'

'I am pleased! Sorry, I'm just a bit zonked. I had a disturbed night…'

It was clearly not what my husband wanted to hear, but his frown was abruptly replaced by a grin. 'Look at you. I'd forgotten what a stunning wife I have! And you're tiny again.' His gaze took me in. 'But not everywhere…'

The weight hadn't disappeared in one week alone and the comment was crass, but it was a relief he still found me appealing. I looked down to my chest and chuckled. 'Yes, but sadly they are only temporary.'

'All the same…' he began. But his words were cut short as he peered over my shoulder. Sheer love and delight spread over his face. With a look of determination, Joe had spent the last half hour trying to roll-over and he was almost there. 'Hello, my little man! Haven't you grown in a week!'

Scooping him up, Miles laughed. He nuzzled Joe's neck and kissed his cheeks. The moment was so perfect I wanted to catch it on camera. But it made me sad, too. For George, for his loss. For what had turned out to be his double loss.

Miles pecked my lips. 'I'm desperate to get out, breathe some fresh air. How about a pub lunch?' Then turning to Joe, 'Look at the ducks, little man?'

I wasn't up to facing the village and certainly not the cottage at the end. 'The Ferry Inn would be good.'

'Which one is that?'

'Left at the gates. Past Bureside? It's a bit of a walk but it's fresh air as requested.'

'Sounds good, let's go.'

I eyed up my husband. In fairness, he was an attractive guy, similar in looks to the man from the wedding album in the cupboard. The word 'cuckold' jumped into my head again. Poor Dad; I had no idea what had happened forty-four years ago, but my guess was that through no fault of his own he'd neglected the young and bored woman in the love letters. I should be more careful with Miles. I'd smarten myself up, apply make-up and wear my new jeans. The thought reminded me of Madeleine; she'd probably messaged several times by now, but I wasn't even sure where I'd last seen my mobile.

'Give me two minutes. I just need to wee and...'

The two minutes was ten and by the time I emerged from the bathroom, Joe was already in his pram.

'Gorgeous, but about bloody time, we're hungry,' Miles said, manoeuvring it outside. 'See you at the bottom. Loser pays,' he said, making a head start.

I scrambled to find my handbag and lock up, but by the time I'd pelted down the shortcut and reached the road, he'd turned the wrong way and was half way to the deli.

He stopped. 'Catch up, woman!' he called with a smile, then he chatted animatedly about his trial, the new documents disclosed, the look of defeat on his opponent's face and his client's praise, as we continued down the slope.

I was interested and I wanted to listen, but my mind drifted as we headed further into the village. Distracted by Miles's arrival, I had temporarily shelved my staggering discovery, but now it was back. Haunted by a secret, I had travelled to Norfolk to sort out Mum's affairs and I'd found a brother. Bloody hell; how on earth would I explain it to Laura? Would she want a relationship with a new half-sibling? Should I even tell her? The past was the past, as she always said, she wasn't sentimental. But she'd been so heartrendingly eloquent about her childhood and how she'd felt unloved and inadequate. Now I knew why. Would it help her to know there was a reason for it? Or would the truth make it worse?

Agitated and hot, I tried not to brood on my behaviour last night. I had been blind to George's attempts to keep me at arm's length; I'd been heedless of his brotherly care all week. In short, I'd been a ridiculous fool. I was deeply embarrassed for him too. The poor bloody man had been kissed by his sister. That wasn't a comical situation I could laugh about with Laura now or ever. Part of me wanted to run to his cottage right this minute, bang on the door and apologise for putting him in such a dreadful position. But it was better to say nothing, to avoid him henceforth, to pretend it had never happened.

The sun beamed through the breeze and we strolled around the green, a happy little family at last. A flurry ruffled Joe's silky hair and he chortled. Who'd have thought I'd be a wife and a mother? Twenty-five years ago I'd been here on my lonesome as usual, sauntering around the fete stalls, eyeing up sweaty cupcakes and glossy candy floss, stopping to watch someone hook a duck, get caught on the buzz wire or splat the rat. And of course on the podium, there was my big sister, grinning inanely and proudly pointing to her sash.

I turned to Miles. 'Laura won the "village queen" contest just here,' I said. 'It was hosted by a minor television personality, so we were star-struck.' I shook my head. 'Pretty damned awful, looking back. Sexist, misogynistic... Not that Laura minded. She knew what she was doing, even then.'

I paused. Or that's what I had supposed. There'd been a tent that served drinks and hot dogs which turned into a disco at night. I was too young to go in, but I peeped through a gap and the celeb had been there, a man in his forties being over-familiar with her.

'Go Laura,' Miles replied, watching me with a soft frown. 'But you're the real beauty of the family.' He felt his pockets. 'Wait here, will you? I just need to grab something; I'll be back in a mo...'

Returning a few minutes later, he presented me with a gift bag. 'I do love you, you know,' he said.

'Gosh, thank you…' Even before I explored the tissue paper, I was touched by his thoughtfulness; the aroma of Norfolk had already escaped. I had told him the story of my childhood lavender fetish long ago, and he'd remembered it.

'I love you too,' I replied. And in my cold fish way, I did.

Linking my arm through his, I kissed his cheek and we headed for the Swan Inn. I sat with Joe at a weathered picnic table and waited for Miles to return with the drinks and a menu. Would a cat brush against my legs today? Maisie had stayed at The Lodge, but I assumed Mum's black moggy was still living with George. Would he want to keep them when I left? Indeed, would he stay? He'd come here to meet his birth mother, but perhaps he'd grown roots.

'Is it me or has it gone chilly?' Miles asked, interrupting my thoughts. He passed me a glass of wine. 'You seem pensive. What are you thinking about?'

'Mum's cats,' I replied, not a word of a lie, realising for the first time that I had almost been unfaithful to Miles without thinking about it that way. Because it had felt so easy, so natural with George? Some sort of narcissism because we were siblings? There was a syndrome or concept which covered it. What was it called?

The shame rising, I glanced at Miles. It would still have been betrayal. If the boot was on the other foot, I'd be devastated. Bloody hell; an affair like my mother, cuckolding a man. Goosebumps pricked my arms. 'Yes, it has gone cooler. Shall we go inside?'

The interior was dark, the walls covered in boating memorabilia, the furnishings elegant but faded and worn. Though I used to watch the high spirits on the river and village green from the pub's outdoor benches, I'd never been inside before, not even for the toilets. Always alone and on the periphery, nervously waiting for someone to move me on.

Joe soon fell asleep. Both gazing at his perfect face, his daddy and I chatted companionably about him. I told Miles about our week, the progress he'd made, his attempts to roll over, his love for Nancy and baby rice. Then we moved on to London, who Miles had bumped into, his couple of evenings hanging out with a school friend. I didn't mention the gardener; he didn't mention Julia.

I finished a goat's cheese salad, Miles a ploughman's. I stood. 'I'll just go to the loo before we leave,' I said.

He caught my hand. 'Everything back to normal?' he asked.

'I certainly hope so.'

I knew what he meant, and it was, I supposed. I'd abandoned the frozen peas, my 'undercarriage' was healed and the dull ache in my pelvis had long gone. It was just the natural healing process, of course, but it felt as though this small village had analeptic powers.

Until last night, when everything changed.

My heart lurched and I sharply inhaled. Oh God, the subject of my thoughts was right in front of me. Sitting alone at a table, George was nursing a pint. Though his shock of hair had fallen forward, what I could see of his face was tense. As if he knew I was gawping, he lifted his head. For a beat, his dark eyes met mine before looking away.

Genetic Sexual Attraction snapped into my head. God yes, that was what the syndrome was called.

I doggedly continued my path towards the ladies'. What had I thought about bruises between Eve and Doug only this morning? There was one deep in my chest, tender and painful.

Nothing was 'normal' at all.

Chapter Forty-Three

After a dreamless nap in the afternoon, I spent the rest of the day preparing dinner. I'd bought steak for Miles who liked it plain and rare, so there wasn't a lot of room for invention. Still, it was nice to smell the scented breeze through the open side door and potter around the house without worrying about Joe; he was having fun with his dad in the bath.

'I'll take you fishing when you're bigger!' I heard Miles say when I passed. It made me smile; we were here on the idyllic River Bure, but I had no doubt he was referring to the 'big fishing' in the Bahamas he did every year with his father.

As I struggled to stiffen egg whites with a hand whisk, I contemplated my life with Miles. Until the birth of Joe, it had been comfortable and in the main, carefree. We had money, a nice home, good friends, successful careers; we went on fabulous holidays. Was it only now that I had a sense of something missing, or had it always been there? Was Miles really my soulmate or had I gone for the easy option like Mum had? And yet I was lucky; I had a husband and a child, I was loved. I had no right to feel dissatisfied; I had to be sensible and appreciate the many blessings I'd been given.

Though Miles drank wine steadily throughout the meal, I stretched out my half glass and tried not to compare last night with this. *This* was fine, more than fine. Miles was a good guy, the father of my son; he was back to personable, affectionate and attentive now my neediness had passed. And however I felt about the shadowy man in the pub, he was completely unattainable on so many levels.

Miles made up for my lack of ready patter, filling me in on lawyer gossip and regaling me with a scandalous story he'd been told about our former head of chambers, now a judge.

He knocked back a large brandy after dessert. 'Lovely meal, thank you,' he said, offering me the bottle as he topped up his glass. 'Eton Mess hits the spot every time.'

I smiled. 'Glad you liked it, after my heroic efforts. I couldn't find an electric whisk, so the meringue took an age to get stiff.'

He laughed. 'Well, I can assure you that won't be a problem. In fact…' He scraped back his chair and held out a hand. 'The dishes can wait until morning but I can't…'

'OK.' Joe was asleep and my boobs were no longer sore. I was back to normal, apparently.

Once in Mum's bedroom, Miles held me tightly for a while. 'Oh God, I've missed you. You have no idea,' he said, his voice surprisingly raw with emotion. He gazed intently at me. 'Not just this week, but before. I'm so glad you're back, Ali.'

His kisses were warm and my body responded, but in a familiar and pleasant way rather than urgent lust. Had it ever been like that with Miles, though? The sizzling passion I'd imagined as a girl? But I had to stop analysing and engage in the moment.

With a smile, I sat up, slipped off my bra, then kissed my husband's chest and slowly inched towards his undies.

'Are you sure about the open curtains?' I asked him after a moment.

'Yes, don't stop.' His eyes were half shut; he was enjoying the build-up. Then, with a groan, 'Actually, maybe you should close them.'

Hopping to the window, I reached out an arm, but I immediately jumped back.

'Ali?' Miles asked.

'Someone's out there.'

'What? Who?'

'I don't know. Someone was on the terrace.'

He sat up. 'What did they look like?'

'I don't know. It was so quick. A white face at the glass and—'

'A white face… For fuck's sake, Ali.' Miles flopped back against the mattress. 'Tell me this isn't happening again.'

'What isn't…?'

'Phantoms, visions, bloody hallucinations. Or whatever else your crazy imagination came up with.'

I took a deep breath. 'There was someone out there, Miles. I saw them.'

'Like there was the last time? Only then they were *inside* the bedroom.'

'That was just work stress. I wasn't suited to representing and defending criminal clients, Miles. I let some of them get under my skin. You know this.'

'Stress, right.' He snorted. 'Waking the whole avenue with your screaming? Completely freaking me out with your jabbering? They don't put you on a psychiatric ward and dole out fucking anti-psychotics for *stress*, Ali.'

I tried to swallow the hurt. My psychotic break wasn't something to be mocked. I had put it behind me and Miles knew full well I hated talking about it.

'That was seven years ago,' I said steadily. 'It isn't something I'm proud of, but I did what you and Madeleine asked of me. I had a short stay in the Priory, took my pills, had my therapy and got better. It's in the past and has nothing to do with now.'

His jaw tight, he glared silently, but eventually his temper got the better of him. 'Well, maybe tonight's *someone's outside* was just another excuse to get out of sex, eh?' He stomped from the bed and turned at the door. 'I'll sleep with my son. What are you good for, Ali? Because, quite honestly, I can no longer remember.'

Chapter Forty-Four

Sunday

Miles looked like a guilty schoolboy when he finally stumbled into the kitchen.

'God, Ali, I'm so sorry about the time. I must have needed the sleep...' Then, lifting his arms hopelessly, 'And last night... I don't know what the hell got into me. All I've wanted for weeks is... you.'

I stiffly accepted his embrace. There was no point arguing. It wasn't the first time Miles had turned on a sixpence after having too much to drink. When love was young I'd gently put my palm over his tumbler to stop him having a last 'top-up' of brandy, but even then it hadn't gone down well. And in fairness, sometimes I'd joined him, welcoming the instant anaesthetic, the blocking out of my 'criminal' clients' faces. Of course they weren't all murdering, knife-welding psychopaths; some were even innocent, and I enjoyed getting justice for them, but it was a huge relief to switch from the dark side after my break. My *psychotic* break; bloody hell. Had that really been me? I shuddered. Was it still?

Miles continued to hold me. 'I don't know why I do it, why I push you away. I need you so much,' he muttered into my hair. 'And now I have to leave in an hour.' He looked at me pleadingly. 'Forgive me? Please?'

His words reminded me of Dad's one-line note. Perhaps it had been easier for him to write it rather than just ask her. *Please find it in your heart to forgive me.* I wondered if Mum ever had.

–

Sitting in the back seat of my car with Joe like royalty, I watched the arid Norfolk countryside fly by. Miles was silent as he drove, but from time to time I glimpsed his rigid expression in the wing mirror. Even before he'd made his apology, I'd taken pity on him and held back Joe's baby rice feed so he could have the pleasure. And it had been lovely, too. Though Miles hadn't needed to convince our son to open his little beak, he'd done all the 'Choo choo coming into the station' routine, making Joe chortle and even me laugh. But he'd now switched over from daddy to lawyer mode. He was thinking about work, the afternoon conference with the client and the intricacies of the case.

Though his '*what are you good for?*' words still hurt, I tried to look for the positives: he clearly loved his boy, he'd bought me the lavender water and it had been good of him to trek all the way here for a night when he was under so much pressure.

Reaching another set of traffic lights, Miles groaned again. 'Bloody hell, not more roadworks,' he muttered. He tapped his fingers on the steering wheel. 'The last flaming lot added ten minutes.'

There was nothing I could say. His face through the mirror was pale with anxiety. I could feel his sheer panic. At this rate he'd only catch his train by a whisker; he might even miss it.

Finally screeching to a halt in the car park, he grabbed his bag and bolted without even closing the door.

'Good luck with the trial,' I called after him, watching until he'd disappeared through the arches.

Sad that he'd gone, I didn't move for a while. Now there was nothing to distract me from the reason I was here. It was time to sort Mum's belongings, fish out the paperwork, instruct a solicitor and estate agent. I had to draw a firm line under Norfolk.

My son gazed at me with round blue eyes. 'What now, Joe?' I asked.

He didn't answer. I wasn't surprised, I didn't know either.

–

My jaw aching from resolve by the time I was back, I immediately strode to the phone and called Tom Hague.

'Sorry to bother you,' I began.

'You're never a bother. How can I help you, Alice?'

That was something I liked about Tom; he didn't prattle on but seemed to instinctively know when I needed something. I sniffed back the image of his teary face yesterday. My 'breath of fresh air' dad. Yes, they had that same kind intuition.

I yanked back my mind to the issue at hand. 'Could you recommend a local probate solicitor, please? I wouldn't know where to start.'

'Roger Bakewell,' he immediately answered. 'I've used him for my company and commercial needs for years. Norwich-based and senior partner these days, but he's your man. He'll sort you out.'

'Brilliant, thank you. I just need a pen. Could you—'

'No need, love. I'll ask him to call you.'

Before I had time to take stock, the solicitor himself was on the line. Probate was probably a comedown from his usual work, but his soft accent was warm. 'I was very sorry to hear about your loss. I met your father, of course, but never your mother. Leave everything with me. Tom Hague's an old friend. I'm always glad to do him a favour.'

'Thank you. That's so helpful. Remind me, what will you need?'

'Tom says he'll let me have what he's got—'

'Like what?'

Roger cleared his throat. 'Well, the death certificate for starters—'

'Sorry, yes, of course.'

'A will, if there is one. Then anything legal or financial. You know, official-looking paperwork. If in doubt, send it in.' His tone was a little patronising; I doubt he realised I was a lawyer. But then again, I had been a pathetic sap asking Tom to be my police 'liaison' and I was effectively passing the buck again now.

'Great. Thanks again.'

'Righto. You'll find all our contact details on the BRB Solicitors' website. Call anytime.'

Relieved Roger had given me the 'if in doubt, send it in' carte blanche, I put Joe on his mat, knelt at the sideboard and pulled out the right bottom drawer. The almond-like smell of parchment breathed back. Bingo. Various certificates for marriage, birth and death. Then underneath, a buff envelope labelled '*The Last Will and Testament of Evelyn Marie Baker*'. Holding my breath, I slipped it out and quickly scanned the two pages, but there were no surprises. Laura and I were executors, and after payment of funeral expenses, debts and so on, the residue of her estate was to be split equally between us.

A separate 'letter of wishes' listed particular items of jewellery she'd earmarked for her sisters, sisters-in-law and nieces, but there were no monetary bequests to her siblings as I'd expected. Frowning, I sat back. And nothing for baby Oliver. I sighed. She'd made no effort to contact him for nearly forty-three years, so perhaps it was not surprising. But shouldn't he inherit something? He was her flesh and blood; they'd become friendly over the past year. She was only sixty-five and had had no reason to believe she'd die. She'd given him the gold watch, she'd pulled out the baby drawing; perhaps she'd been planning to include provision for him. I shook my head. He was no longer my business – indeed, he never had been.

Leaving the certificates behind, I scooped out the remaining documents and briefly scanned jewellery valuations, the receipt for her fur coats and other miscellaneous insurance documents. Then I moved to the other drawer and pulled out the old client file of Dad's I'd already seen. Absently opening the cover, I thrummed my fingers in thought. To send it to Roger or not? I decided to bugger it – he already thought I was a weak and feeble woman, so there was no harm in including it. I picked up the padded envelope I'd bought at great expense on the way home, bundled everything in and sealed it with gaffer tape. I blew out the trapped air. Well, that had been easy. I'd find the solicitors' contact details on the internet, then a trip to the post office tomorrow and they'd be poor Roger's problem, not mine.

It took a while to locate Mums iPad and search for 'BRB Solicitors' online, but when I finally put a marker pen to the envelope, I paused. I hadn't been paying much attention to Dad's old file, but a letter at the start had been from a firm of solicitors called 'Bakewell, Roberts and Butcher'. Their offices had been on Meriden Way, same as Roger's. Were BRB Solicitors and Bakewell, Roberts and Butcher one and the same firm? With the same initials, it seemed likely. And Dad had been Tom's accountant, which meant all those dusty documents had related to Tom Hague's business dealings.

Remembering the contents of the old file, I frowned. Writs and statutory demands, company accounts and official receiver correspondence, the copies of the *London Gazette*... Goodness, that all added up to bankruptcy.

I stared at the envelope. Part of me was intrigued, but did I really want to know? I'd already unearthed one troubling secret this weekend. And besides, everything was signed, sealed and ready to be delivered to Meriden Way tomorrow. I could check that box as done and move on to the next chore. I nodded. Yes; I'd leave it there; it was one step closer to moving on.

Chapter Forty-Five

Once Joe was napping, I made myself a coffee, ambled back to the lounge and vacantly gazed through the window. The mottled, morose sky reflected my mood. Bloody hell, I'd cocked up. If only I had done things differently: if I hadn't been so damned impulsive I would still have George's friendship, that warm security of having him around, knowing he was near if I needed him.

With a groan, I pictured the flash at the glass I had seen last night. Someone had been on the terrace, I was sure of it. Wasn't I?

A cold flurry on my neck made me spin around with a jolt. Nothing was there, not even the cat, but when I automatically turned back to the flowerbeds for reassurance, I spotted George sitting on the bench in the shadow of the poplars. I squinted to catch his expression, but he was too far away. Tensing, I stared. Why was he here? God, to work presumably. He couldn't just stop, he had a living to earn. Intending to hide, I stepped back, but he abruptly stood.

Half hopeful and half fearful he'd stay, I moved away from the window and listened for the crunch of pebbles. As his footfall came closer, I expected him to head for the sunken garden as usual, but he tapped at the front door. A smile of relief replaced my rattling nerves. He was here, so that was good. We could forget Friday night and go back to how we'd been at the beginning of the week – distant but civilised.

Even as I opened the door, my heart sank. George looked exhausted, ill almost. Dark shadows smudged his eyes, his hair was unkempt, and he had the start of a beard. Though his expression was unreadable, he held out his palm and offered his key.

'Oh, so you're leaving, then?' I asked.

He shook his head. 'I don't know. Maybe.' Then he frowned. 'No, not yet. I thought you might want this back.'

'Well, I don't,' I blurted. I took a deep breath. 'Look, I know I've made things really awkward and I'm so sorry. But it has been great having you around to keep an eye on me and Joe.'

His face was so dismal, my impulse was to cry, but I scrabbled for humour. 'You know, making sure I don't overheat Joe or burn down the bungalow. I'll only be here for a few more days, so please don't desert us.'

His jaw was tight. My attempt at banter was having no effect; if anything, his frown deepened.

'I am truly sorry,' I said quietly. 'About everything. Please don't be angry with me.'

Raking a hand through his hair, he turned towards the rose beds. 'I'm not angry with you, Ali,' he said. 'But you now know that your mother... that she... I didn't think about it until last night, but those trips on the river you'd described; you were clearly very close to your dad, and she...'

'Betrayed him.' I sighed. 'I know, but—'

'Because a father is important. A huge part of anyone's life.'

'Yes, that's true.'

The conversation wasn't going as I had expected. What was he trying to say? I watched his long fingers curl around the key. Like a thunderbolt, it struck me. My thoughts about Mum's will and whether he should benefit had all been very charitable, but it went further than that. It was about identity. Recognition. Acceptance. Did he want to be known as Eve's son, meet Laura and the family? Go public, effectively? Perhaps he needed to be more than a dirty secret; maybe he wanted to be introduced to the world as my brother.

'Oh God,' I said, my thoughts firing out. 'I hadn't considered how you must feel about everything. Would you like to, well, come out? Tell everyone your birth mum was Eve? I can phone Laura and break the news to her.' My mind was in overdrive, thinking ahead. 'Then there's money, of course, your fair share of everything. I instructed a solicitor just this afternoon. I can ask him what to do about varying the will and—'

As though I'd slapped him, his head whipped back. 'For God's sake!' The force of his anger made me jump. He thumped his chest. 'You have no idea,' he said, turned on his heels and strode away.

–

The sky turned to slate grey at five, followed moments later by a heavy squall. The rain assailed the windows but its violence was comforting just then. Passing as quickly as it came, I felt a sense of relief. Fate and the weather were urging me on.

I stared at the heap of stuff I'd amassed. Did Laura and I really need to go through childhood artwork and craft, ballet, violin and piano grades, 'star of the week' certificates or even old school reports? I would keep the photographs for posterity, but otherwise black bin liners were the thing. A thought occurred and I smiled thinly. No wonder George had been so interested in the aunties and cousins. Like an idiot, I'd thought him attentively charming, but he had been studying his own family. I'd tried to say the right things about recognition and money, but the bloody man had shouted me down and stalked off. Too like my blinking husband. Though my emotions swung and fought, irritation was definitely among them.

Chatting to Joe as I worked, I added old playing cards, tattered board games and childhood annuals to the 'throw away' pile. As I stretched my stiff spine, the sound of footsteps filtered through. No guesses who it was; he'd rushed away with the key he'd been so keen to hand over. Opening the door before he knocked, I stepped onto the wet terrace and held out my palm. Clearly not registering my body language nor my frown, he stared at the sky.

He eventually met my gaze. 'I'm sorry for shouting,' he said. 'It was bang out of order.'

'It was.'

My arms folded, I waited. What now?

He took a shuddery breath. As though having terrible news to impart, his shoulders were tense, his expression bleak. 'Can I come in?'

Worry took over. 'Are you alright?' I asked, standing back. 'Has something happened?'

He smiled faintly and spread his arms. 'Apart from this?' He dropped them to his sides. 'It isn't my forte, but I need to talk, I suppose.'

'Of course…'

Scooping up Joe, I made my way to the kitchen and made tea, my mind buzzing. We hadn't broached the unmentionable yet. God, I hoped the kiss would be brushed under the carpet. And yet, and yet… the desire to reach out and comfort him was almost overwhelming.

His head down at the table, he didn't speak until I joined him. 'The letter. Eve's letter…' he started. 'I've read it fifty times and I can't get an idea out of my head.'

Unsure where he was going, I sat quietly opposite him and propped Joe on my lap.

'That he, that my real father…' Abruptly he stood and stared through the side door. 'This idea, this notion… It makes sense.' He turned back, his look haunted. 'I think I was the product of rape.'

I couldn't hide my surprise; that hadn't been my interpretation of the letter at all. 'I didn't think so. Why did you glean that?'

He clenched his hands into fists, then released them. 'There was something in me when Ben died. Anger, fury. Nothing resembling… nothing criminal. I didn't hurt anyone other than myself. But the rage was uncontrollable at times. It scared me. It frightened Emma too.' His eyes met mine. 'I think it has always been there, just below the surface. God knows, I'd never do anything like *that* but… Perhaps I'm my father's son.'

'No! I think you're wrong,' I replied impulsively. Then trying to focus on facts, 'Did the diary say anything? You know, nine months before your…'

He shook his head and sat down. 'There wasn't a great deal in it. Just the odd word or phrase. "Shopping." "Pictures with Peggy." Then "letter from Doug" most weeks. Was your dad working away?'

'No.' I smiled thinly. 'He spent some time in hospital, so they wrote to each other. I think she… got together…

with your father during that period. Maybe someone from work.'

'Sheffield then?'

'I guess so.' Scanning the letters in my mind, I tapped the table top. Work… The office colleagues she'd mentioned. A week away on a course. The boarding house she stayed at… God, that was right:

> Then there's another bloke staying, a Mr Lang. He's about thirty-five but very frightfully, frightfully. He's very high up in the Post Office so not very likely to take any notice of me.

'Did she mention someone called Mrs Dilworth in the diary?'

'I can't recall…'

'Or a work course in Leeds?'

'Just Leeds, I think.'

I passed over Joe, dashed to the bedroom and returned. Kicking his legs and smiling, Joe seemed to sense my excitement. I swapped him for the envelope. 'Open it,' I said. 'It's nothing bad and I could be wrong, but…'

I watched the emotions pass through George's face as he read our mother's letter. Yup, he could easily be the son of a 'frightfully, frightfully man' high up in the Post Office. Only Eve was beautiful and charming; Mr Lang clearly had more than just 'noticed' her.

'Mr Lang,' George said eventually. 'The dates add up. And Leeds, again…' He sighed deeply. 'But that doesn't mean he didn't…'

I looked into his dark, troubled eyes. 'I think you're too gallant. That letter's just one of many between my parents, and reading between the lines… Well, my dad wasn't around, Mum was just twenty-one and I think she was bored, lonely and longing for romance.' Not really wanting to dwell on the insular young Eve, I took a breath. 'She said *she* made a mistake. My guess is that she was up for it as much as Mr Lang. Even instigated it. Crazy though it might seem, it has been heard of...'

George gave a droll smile. 'I know. I'm not a caveman, Ali.'

I cringed; I was trying to lighten the atmosphere with my Laura-style quip, but it was too flaming close to the bone. I peered at Joe to hide my flushed cheeks.

'Do you think you might try to trace him? Mr Lang from the Post Office?'

He didn't reply.

'Have I helped at all?' I asked. I wanted him to smile; I longed to see some release in his features. But his head was down, his fingers absently rubbing the table top.

'There's something else bothering you. What is it?'

He sighed. 'I thought it was all over. After Ben. I thought it was over.'

'What was?'

He finally looked at me. His jaw was tight, his blue eyes burning. 'I don't know... Life. Living. The ability to laugh.' Seeming to study his wedding ring, he spread his hands. 'Feeling anything at all. Joy. Love. Happiness. Envy...'

He scraped back his fringe. 'When I saw you and Miles in the pub, I tasted that rage again. The spite of life. I was jealous, Ali.' He shook his head. 'It isn't supposed to be this way.'

Not sure what he meant, I stroked my son's feathery hair and searched for something to say. Then Joe broke the silence with a raspberry noise and I couldn't help laughing. That old levity was back: it was funny, it was nerves and Joe was bouncing with the pleasure of learning a new trick.

'Sorry,' I said. I glanced at George, who appeared more bemused than anything. 'I've no idea what to say. And I'm sorry to be so insensitive at a time like this, but I'm starving. I haven't eaten all day. Can we get something to eat?'

He pulled back his chair. Had I messed up again? But he nodded as though he'd made a decision. 'Food,' he replied. 'Yup, I can do that.'

Chapter Forty-Six

George asked if he could borrow my car. I anticipated fish and chips, but when he returned, I inhaled the undeniable smell of prawn crackers. A less overwhelming discovery than Friday, but a surprise nonetheless. The village had a Chinese take-out, apparently, hidden behind the primary school.

George lifted his eyebrows and nodded at my son. Joe's eyes were drooping but he'd protested each time I'd tried to put him in his cot. Maybe he'd got wind of the noodles. I'd had a taste of his bland baby rice, so I didn't blame him for making a last ditch effort to join us.

'He's on a dirty protest, so...' I started, but George held out his arms.

He opened the side door and stepped outside. 'No stealing all the spare ribs,' he called over his shoulder.

I snapped on the oven and slipped in the cartons. Rather than wine and the associations it evoked, I put a couple of beers on the table. I was a rattle-bag of nerves, but everything was fine. Joe's raspberry noise had helped George and me over an invisible hurdle and we were back to where we were before my indiscretion. Two people who got on. Friends. And maybe Mum had been pulling strings from above. But for my impetuous kiss and my subsequent realisation, George's true identity might never have come out. He wouldn't have been able to fill in some blanks about his conception, nor would he have faced his clearly agonising 'father' demons. Though I had no doubt the fears were still there, his whole being already seemed lighter. Maybe truth and honesty were the way after all. No good did ever come of secrets.

A breeze wafted in and I rubbed my arms. The shiver was from the cool night air, that was all, yet still the sudden peal of the telephone made me start. Though tempted not to answer, I made my way to the hall. Miles had been cross with me last time I'd ignored it, and rightly so.

'Hello?'

There was no reply for a moment, then a voice, as though surprised. 'Oh hello, Alice.'

'Tom? Is that you?' My stomach clenched. Though I couldn't say why, the unexpected call unsettled me.

'Yes, only me, love. I won't keep you. I was just checking in on you and the littl'un.'

We'd spoken earlier, so the question seemed odd. 'Yes we're fine, thanks. Is everything—'

'Good, very good. Then I'll bid you good night.'

Still perplexed by the brief conversation with Tom, I almost leapt from my skin when the phone rang again. I snatched it up. 'Hello?'

'Bloody hell, Ali, that was a bit quick. Are you on guard or something? It's me.'

'Me' was my big sister.

'No. I just had a weird call from Tom Hague.'

Laura snorted. 'Weird, hmm? No surprises there. How are things going with the rest of the Village of the Damned?'

I smiled; it was nice to be asked, even if it was a meek effort. Had Laura posed the same question three nights ago, I might have regaled her with a story about a tall, dark and handsome man I fancied. Thank God I hadn't. And today an answer wasn't required. Her quaver of excitement was palpable.

'So what's happened? Share with the class—'

'Shelby's proposed!'

'Oh, Laura, fantastic! When and where? Tell me everything.'

'I don't know yet… he's only just asked me and I wanted you to be the first to know…'

The surge of affection and joy was immense, not only at her news, but that she'd told me before anyone else. And I understood perfectly; she would have phoned Mum first and I was the next best thing.

'You said you'd never get married…' I said teasingly. 'Good job Mum didn't buy you that car.'

Laura laughed. 'I know. But I had to make an exception for Shelby. He's so lovely, Ali. You'll really like him. Did I tell you he has virtually no hair, but I love him anyway?'

'Perfect. Mum would be so happy for you—'

'And Dad.'

'Absolutely.'

The line fell silent.

'Laura? You still there?'

'I let him down, Ali. That stupid incident with Dave-the-paedo.' She sounded teary. 'I was barely on speaking terms with him after that. Then a few days before he died…'

I knew what she was referring to; I remembered the argument clearly. 'I wish you were both dead,' she'd yelled to both our parents before slamming out of the house.

'Don't go there, Laura. Dad was seriously ill, you couldn't have possibly known. And you were only a child.'

I thought of Madeleine and that slap. 'I've done far worse as an adult. We all have regrets…'

Be kind to yourself, love. No one is perfect. We all make mistakes. No one knows that better than me. Yes, Mum too; the words finally made sense.

A thought occurred. Should I tell Laura about my discovery right now? I took a breath, but she spoke again.

'So, I want you to meet Shelby. Or should I say *my fiancé*? We have to get together very soon. Is that Miles I can hear?'

George had walked past with Joe asleep in his arms. This was the perfect opportunity to say something, but where would I begin? And did I really want to? 'No, it's Mum's gardener, actually.'

'The *gardener*? What blinking time is it over there?' She guffawed and I knew what was coming. 'Shouldn't one resist and send Mellors back to his coop and pheasant chicks? Though if he's as sexy as Sean Bean…'

I brought the subject back to her own sexy man and chatted a while longer.

I found George in the dark, sitting next to Joe's cot. 'Ben?' I asked quietly.

The sunset through the window partially lit his face. 'Yes,' he replied. 'I haven't thought about him as much this week. I've been… busy.'

'Straying cats and hysterical women?'

'Something like that. A therapist would say it's a good sign. Focusing on other things. Moving on, as they say…'

'The bottomless black hole. After Dad, I thought it would never close, but it did.'

He nodded. 'Time heals, or so they say. But it's been painfully slow. Some days I make progress, then I see him in a crowded street or a busy park, on a bus or a boat passing by, and it devastates me again.' He stood and stretched. 'It's not as though he'd be here, anyway. He'd never been to Norfolk. Stupid, really.'

'It isn't at all.'

I turned to Mum's bedroom. Her spirit or her presence was only in my head, but the cushion of comfort had been there for me this time – and still was – buffeting me from grief, like those colourful fenders on the river boats.

–

When we were finally settled at the kitchen table, the conversation flowed as we ate. My fingers sticky with sauce, I asked George to talk me through his working week, the gardens he tendered, the routine repairs here and there.

'Bureside on a Wednesday,' he said.

'Not the manicured lawn?' I asked, smiling at the memory of Laura's pink shins.

'Yup. Painting the bridge and general handiwork.'

'Polishing the enamel on Tom's Roller?'

He laughed. 'Not yet. I saw it earlier, actually.'

'Oh right. Has it been repaired?'

'Only caught a glimpse. I was too busy bribing Joe to go to sleep with my last fiver. Some work on *Sylvette* – I enjoy doing that.'

The mention of the Hagues' boat brought on a warm spread of nostalgia. I hadn't noticed her along the river cut on Tuesday, but I remembered Tom's comment about Joan. Something about romance and freedom. 'Ah, *Sylvette*,' I replied. 'Tom said they still sail her.'

'Sometimes. He likes to keep her pristine inside and out.'

An old memory flashed. 'Are the benches and furniture still upholstered in cream leather? The chintz drapes matching the bedspread in the double berth? Do they still have the teak bar and soda fountain?'

He nodded. 'Pretty much. You remember it well.'

'I do and I don't. I guess memories are like that.' I shook an uncomfortable shiver away. 'So, who else might I know in the village? I need all the gossip so I'm prepared and don't gape, open-mouthed, when Nancy tells me.'

My request was met with an amused rise of the eyebrow, and the conversation was cordial until we'd finished the meal. All of a sudden it felt as though we hadn't jumped the hurdle as cleanly as I'd thought. Or at least I hadn't. *What now?* I wondered. Were we siblings or friends? What had he meant about feeling jealousy when he saw me and Miles in the pub? '*It isn't supposed to be this way,*' he'd said. And in truth, wholly inappropriate though it was, I'd found my mind wandering as we ate – what might his broad torso look like beneath his T-shirt?

As though reading my mind, he suddenly looked at his watch and stood. 'It's late, I'll get off,' he said.

It was a huge relief. Any lingering symptoms of the GSA syndrome had to be eradicated. Anchoring the sibling thing was the answer.

'That was Laura on the telephone earlier,' I said. 'Her boyfriend has proposed. He's called...' I couldn't remember his proper name. 'Shelby,' I added.

'That's great news.'

'It is. I'm really pleased.' My heartbeat clattered in my ears. I didn't want him to go, but I was afraid he might stay.

'Night then,' he said. He opened the side door and stepped out before turning. 'Tomorrow's my day off. Do you fancy an outing on the river? My small boat isn't quite up to the standards you're used to, but she's still pretty special.'

Another surprise; I didn't know he had one. 'Yes please,' I immediately answered. Then a little more measured, 'Thanks, that sounds lovely.'

He lifted his arm. 'Tomorrow then,' he said. 'I'll text.'

Chapter Forty-Seven

Monday

The wind whistling through the tall trees woke me before Joe did. It took a while to work out where my life was up to. Was something traumatic hanging over me today? Did I need to prepare myself? Because that's how each morning had felt for the past year. And, of course, during that period of high anxiety seven years ago when I'd 'taken a little break from reality for a while', as Madeleine had put it.

I sighed. In truth she'd been my rock, more *there* for me than my own mother because Mum had been here, many miles away from her real home. I never did get to the bottom of why she left Sheffield so abruptly. Was it connected to baby Oliver? Or something else?

Shelving that puzzle, I smiled. Today was a good day; after a twenty-five-year interlude, I'd been invited on a boat trip. Remembering George mentioning a text, I jumped from the bed and searched for my mobile. My lips twitched. The idea of an electronic communication felt a little comical; messaging by pigeon would've been less of a surprise. That was silly, of course, but everything in the village felt antiquated and this house was no exception. Like a time warp, the contents were pretty much the same as they had been when I was eight or nine, from the towels and bedding to the three-piece suite in the lounge, the pressure cooker and kitchen gadgets, the hostess trolley and electric typewriter. So state-of-the-art at the time and now so dated. But then again, they'd lasted, so perhaps Mum was right and 'quality' did count.

Feeling a little flustered, I waited for my mobile to load. The first message to appear was from George.

The boat trip, the text started. Oh hell; was he going to cancel? I'd gone to bed buzzing at the thought of a day on the broads.

> How do you feel about leaving Joe with Joan or Nancy for a couple of hours? Outside the Petersfield at 10?

Without thinking too deeply, I took a quick breath and typed:

> OK.

—

It was still only eight, so I put Joe in his carrier and headed for the village. Milk and fresh bread were on my list, so I didn't need to venture further than the deli.

'Morning!' I said brightly to the woman behind the counter.

I expected the usual friendly chat, but she eyed me and grunted something I didn't catch.

Heat swept my body. I'd agreed to meet George without the chaperone of Joe. Did she know something was going on? Not that it was. Not at all, on any level. Bloody hell, what was wrong with me? The poor woman was just tired or hungover. And even if there was tongue-wagging about the amount of time the gardener spent inside The Lodge, they couldn't possibly know we were related.

Trudging back up the hill, I gave myself a good talking to. Everything was fine. I wasn't doing anything bad, wrong or sordid. I was allowed a flaming day out, for God's sake. Not even a day, but a couple of hours.

The mastiff outside the front door was the first clue that Denise had made an early start, the second was the hum of the Hoover. Nancy was in her usual place at the sink.

She was giving the plastic cartons a good scrub, so sniffing the air theatrically wasn't necessary, but she did it anyway. 'Someone had a take-out last night,' she commented. 'Chinese, I'd say. Was it with your handsome chap? We saw you all in the village on Saturday.' She kissed Joe's head. 'I should've known your daddy was a blondie.'

Gossip, indeed! I had intended to ask her to mind Joe, but now decided against it. She already had the dog and she'd certainly ask questions about where I was going or simply just *know*. Instead, I found myself hiding in the guest bedroom to call Mrs Hague. Joan answered immediately, breathlessly thrilled at my request. 'Oh love, I can't think of a better way to spend the morning. I'm honoured you've asked. Give me half an hour and I'll be there.'

–

Nancy, dog and daughter departed moments before a tap on the side door came. I glanced through the glass. It was Joan Hague, with twin-set and perfect timing.

'Hello!' I said, letting her in. 'Thank you so much for helping out at such short notice. He's just been fed so…'

Her eyes glowing, she made a beeline for Joe. 'Look at you, all smart in your sailor suit. Your granny was clever to buy the perfect size. What a beautiful boy you are. The spit of your grandad, you are. I can see it, I can!'

'Isn't he just?' a voice said from outside.

I turned in surprise. Wearing a flat cap, Tom Hague was stepping in, his attention fixed on his wife. Gently pulling her back by the shoulders, he patted his own earlobe. 'You forgot the earrings, love. Can't be too careful.'

'Oh, so I have.' Pulling the clasps from her ears, Joan slid the dangly pearls into the pocket of her slacks.

'Littl'un might pull,' Tom explained with a shrug. He was smiling amiably but the image it conjured made me shudder. I could clearly picture Joe with one in his chubby fist, putting the shiny stones to his mouth. Oh God, was I doing the right thing? But I couldn't change my mind now and suddenly send them away; it would look odd and offend them.

'Yes, of course. Thank you. I'll only be gone a couple of hours but…' Trying to breathe through my anxiety, I gestured to the baby rice packet. 'I've just fed him now, so he'll be fine until his lunch. Two or three teaspoons mixed with the formula in the fridge should see him through until I'm back, but if he gets unsettled, there's a bottle and the rest of the box. Oh and everything you'll need to change him is right here in this bag…'

Seeming to read my mind, Tom patted my shoulder. His eyes twinkling, he lifted his iPhone. 'Don't worry yourself, Alice. There's two of us and this newfangled thing called a mobile phone. A few hours to yourself is allowed. Now off you go and have fun.'

Chapter Forty-Eight

As I marched down the shortcut, I felt ridiculously light without a papoose or a pram. Guilty and hyper too, like I was bunking off school. I was running a little late, and as I approached the leafy entrance to the Petersfield Hotel, I couldn't spot George. A blend of disappointment and relief clenched my chest. He'd stood me up or had second thoughts, and it was probably just as well. But after a moment he emerged from the shadows, nodded and crossed the street. My heart whipping, I followed, tapping down the wooden steps which led to a boardwalk tangled with knotweed and roots. After a few paces, he stopped and turned.

'Everything OK?'

'Just a bit anxious about Joe. He's with the Hagues.'

George raked his hair. 'We can go back for him if you like, but when I thought about it before bed... Well, he should really wear a lifejacket.'

Ah, so he'd suggested I come without Joe for his safely. The tinge of disappointment was replaced by the memory of Friday night's drowning dream. George was absolutely right. Though wearing mine had taken the shine off a river adventure, it had made me feel secure. Joe was far safer with Joan and Tom than with me on the water; I should have thought of that myself.

'You're right; thank you.'

'Watch where you're treading. It gets soggy further on.'

He held out a hand and I took it, his grasp firm as the aromas and the path became oozy, the wooden planks sunken. Dodging wispy grasses and bushes, we reached a small fishing boat. Something tugged at a memory and I finally looked up. Moored up at the Bureside jetty, *Sylvette* was in full view.

I found my voice. 'I know this place. I didn't realise until…' I nodded to the lush vegetation. 'It's so overgrown these days, I didn't recognise it. This was our cut. The one we used for our motorboat.'

'Makes sense. The land belongs to Tom Hague and he lets me use it…' He squinted. 'Everything OK?'

The shiver was there. *Incestuous*, I thought, entirely without irony. Perhaps village life wasn't so comfortable after all.

'Yeah, sure.'

'Catch,' he said, throwing over his rucksack. Leaning across the canvas hood of his boat, he dusted off leaves, then untied the ropes with practised fingers.

'Ready?' he asked.

'Yeah, sure,' I said again, stepping in.

George manoeuvred the vessel from its mooring, started the engine and turned left at the intersection. Though my vocabulary seemed stuck, memories flowed as I inhaled the old aromas: the zest of petrol, the tang of stagnant fish, the citrus perfume of water lilies.

He eventually spoke, the hint of a smile lighting his face. 'I thought we could try Ranworth. See if we can spot the ghost.'

I felt the tension ease from my shoulders. We had talked about Ranworth Broad during Friday's 'dinner date'. Focusing on the myth rather than that excruciating night, I smiled too. The mere was said to be haunted by a twelfth-century monk who rowed across the still water in the early morning mist. I'd been there with Dad several times, and though I remembered the imposing church, I had never climbed its tower.

I'd first read about the fable in a collection of stories called *Ghosts of the Broads.* Both fearful and thrilled, I'd spent hours pawing the book in the post office, gazing at the blurry photographic evidence and feeding my certainty that phantoms *did* exist. Laura bought me a copy that last summer and stashed it away for my birthday. It would have been the most thoughtful present ever, but Dad had died by then.

Focusing on the here and now, I took in my carriage. Though far from new, the boat was clean, had a wheel and a padded bench, so I sat back like royalty and absorbed the old landmarks as we chugged along – the Ferry Marina, the petrol station and windmill, the pretty thatched cottages and tall, swaying reeds. The river valley soon opened out to the lakes.

George eventually cut the engine and dropped anchor. 'I thought the outer broad to take in the scene. Is it as you remember?'

I glanced around. The visitor centre was already bustling in the distance, but we were surrounded by shades of dappled green. Save for a dull whistle through the trees, the air was silent, the water tranquil. 'Yes. Beautiful.'

'It really is,' he replied. He dug in his rucksack. 'Here you go,' he said, lobbing over a foil-wrapped item. 'Breakfast.'

'Thanks.' I had avoided looking at him until now. Without yesterday's beard, his skin looked smooth and tanned, his eyes sapphire blue. God, he really was an attractive man.

'Budge up then,' he said. 'I hope you like mustard.'

He was clearly at ease, so I relaxed too. 'I'll eat anything if someone else has prepared it,' I replied, hitching along the seat.

Expecting a wad of butter, I took a hungry bite. My eyes immediately stung and I sneezed. 'Ah, sorry,' he said with a smile. 'Too much of a good thing? That's the trouble with living alone; I think I've become desensitised. Must try harder.'

Maybe his 'must try harder' had a ring of permanence to it, but I suddenly felt both happy and shy. Accepting a piece of kitchen roll, I blew my nose, then went back to my sandwich.

'Sleep OK?' he asked.

I nodded. 'And you? Did you think about it?'

He turned and looked at me solidly. 'About?'

'Mr Lang from the Post Office, of course.'

Feeling hotter than the mustard, I turned to the mere, spotted a duck and tossed in a crust. A whole team darted from nowhere, buffeting the glassy water as they competed to reach it.

'You've gone and done it now,' he said, chucking in more bread. When the mallards had had their fill, he poured tea from a flask and passed me the cup.

Conscious of his long, muscled thigh next to mine, I inwardly groaned. I had to stop thoughts like that, stop the instinctive urges to stare at his chiselled face and lithe body. I had to bloody replace the word 'man' with 'brother'.

He laughed and I blew out the panic. It took two to tango and this weird GSA illness had clearly only infected me.

'Who'd have thought a Yorkshire lad would end up having a boat on the Norfolk broads?' he was saying. 'Especially one called *Ruby Jane*.'

His insouciance was contagious. I elbowed him. 'Ah, so little Ruby Jane was your first crush. Primary school, aged eleven?'

'Nope; that was Sara Dyson. *Ruby* was already named, but I like it.'

'Wonder how she gets on with the twelfth-century ghost?'

'*Frighteningly* well, apparently.' He motioned to the thatched visitor centre. 'Shall we swot up? Have you got time?'

I thought of the Hagues and their kind, eager faces. They probably wouldn't need to use the bottle, and even if they did, formula milk wouldn't be the end of the world. 'Don't rush back!' Tom had called after me. 'Having Joe to ourselves is a treat for us too.'

Contentment frothed in my chest. 'Yes, absolutely, let's do it.'

Chapter Forty-Nine

George moored in a space between two handsome boats. He took my hand to help me out, then tugged me towards the church. 'Cathedral of the Broads first?' he asked. 'Fourteenth-century, I believe. I haven't had the chance yet.'

'Yeah, sure.'

At the entrance I bent down to tie my trainer laces. When I caught him up, he was reading an old handwritten notice. 'Fancy a bit of exercise?' he asked. 'Eighty-nine uneven steps, two ladders and one trap door, apparently.'

Remembering my disorientation at the top of Stalham steeple, I swallowed. Would I still have a fear of heights? 'Surely the ancient books of psalms would be more fun?'

He laughed. 'Very droll. We can't come to Ranworth and not see the views from the tower. Are you up for it?'

'Yeah, sure.'

He dropped a ten-pound note in the donation box, then put his palm in the small of my back as I went ahead for our ascent. I was fine at first, but as we climbed higher, the enclosed spiral staircase began to feel claustrophobic. Too embarrassed to say anything, I hugged the rough wall and continued to lift my heavy feet, but my breathing became fast and shallow; my heart thrashed. When the old taste of panic seeped in, I tried to go on, but my limbs wouldn't let me, so I suddenly stopped. George collided into me, and we both wobbled, but he put an arm around my waist just in time to stop us tumbling back.

Leaning against the stone, he steadied us. 'Are you OK?' he asked.

'Sorry,' I said, lowering my head. 'Feel a bit… Just give me a minute.'

'OK.'

When the dizziness had passed and I'd straightened myself, he turned me towards him with firm hands. 'Better now?' His face was so close I could smell his shampoo. For a beat, then another, he didn't move. Then he blinked, stepped back and smiled. 'Maybe give the view a miss, eh? Can you make it down? I can offer a fireman's lift…'

I puffed out the trapped air and my tingling nerves. For those few seconds I'd thought he would kiss me. But the moment — and my panic — had passed, thank goodness.

'Hmm, how gallant,' I said. 'Not sure hanging me upside down would be a good move right now. You lead and I'll follow.'

Though he went in front for our descent, he held a hand above his shoulder. I took it and we eventually reached the bottom. We soon hit bright sunshine, but he didn't release his tight grip. Instead he led me to the staithe. 'Better keep an eye on the time,' he said.

–

Back on my bench seat, I watched the glinting ridges in the water as we headed for home. After a few minutes, I dared my eyes to George at the wheel. What was going through his mind? His profile was still and thoughtful, the wind blowing his hair.

He turned. 'Fancy a go?'

My mouth shaped the words I'd been saying all morning. 'Yeah, sure.'

In truth, I wasn't sure about anything.

He stood to one side. 'If we moor in the village, we could have a coffee at the cottage before you get back to Joe,' he said eventually, his gaze fixed ahead. 'What do you think?'

Keeping the wheel steady, I peered at the unfathomable, dark water. What, exactly, did he mean by 'coffee'? There had been a bolt of *something* between us in the tower, hadn't there? Did he feel the pull, the connection, the attraction too? Or was it my imagination? Did coffee simply mean coffee?

My throat dry, the inevitable words came out. 'Yeah, sure.'

The journey went too quickly and before I could even think, let alone take stock, we'd moored beyond the Swan Inn, tied up *Ruby Jane*, then taken the path through the yacht club. Our knuckles touched as we walked. When the cottage was in view, he stopped and turned to me.

'Look… Just a drink will be nice.' His eyes cloudy, he seemed to search for what he wanted to say. 'A chat, a few minutes of privacy. Just you and me.' Smiling thinly, he raked his hair. 'An odd thing to say when we've spent the last hour and a half together but—'

'It's fine,' I quickly interrupted. 'I'd like that too.'

But he spread his arms and peered at me intently. 'I've no idea what's happening here, but I don't feel like a bad person. The opposite, in fact. It's like I've woken up. I'm alive, exhilarated, complete, whole. And that's down to you, Ali.' His smile spread. 'You're a complete liability, of course, but you're charming and funny and complicated.

I really enjoy your company.' He gestured to his home. 'I'd like to stretch it out a bit longer, that's all. Hold your hand, hold you – is that wrong?'

I usually ran away from men and emotion, but the moment was so compelling, I couldn't have moved if I'd tried. 'No; I don't think so.'

'Good. Good.' His earnest gaze didn't falter. 'I don't know where we're going, but if you ever change your mind about anything, you must tell me. Promise?'

I kicked the dusty gravel. 'I promise, I will.' Then I laughed. 'I am thirsty, as it happens. Though if your mustard sandwiches are anything to go by...'

He grinned. 'Weak coffee it is.'

We ambled to the cottage, but at the gate he stopped abruptly. His front door was ajar. 'Oh,' he said with a puzzled frown. Pushing it wide, he called, 'Hello?'

A solid woman with cropped grey hair and glasses appeared. She dried her hands, threw the tea towel over her shoulder and nodded to me with a genial smile.

'I thought I saw you two by The Swan just now.'

Standing on tiptoes, she kissed George's cheek. 'Hello, you.' Then she tutted. 'You haven't been answering your mobile. Having too much fun on the river is my guess. Still, I've given the cottage a good clean.' Her eyes sparkling through the lenses, she turned to me. 'And who's this then?'

George didn't reply. He simply looked at me, bewildered, lost.

'Hi, I'm Ali,' I said to fill the silence.

The woman stared, briefly taking my outstretched hand before dropping it. Her warmth had set to steeliness. 'You must be Oliver's sister then,' she said.

I had no words. Her description chilled me, despite the hot sun. How did she know who I was? I was Ali, just Ali.

Realisation cracked like an egg. The person who'd persuaded George to find Eve. He'd have kept her updated. Finding his birth mother and her death, then meeting her daughter, Ali.

'And you must be Oliver's mother,' I replied.

Chapter Fifty

Like a film on pause, time stood still. Then someone pressed play and the characters moved. But the brightness had dimmed, irrevocably.

Seeming to shake himself awake, George spoke. 'I'll put the kettle on. Stay and have a cup of tea with us.'

Needing to bolt and desperate not to cry, I shook my head and stepped back. 'Thank you, but I've just noticed the time so...'

I had no idea how his mother knew about the sexual chemistry we'd felt in that tower, but she did.

George reached out. 'You don't need to go, Ali.' But he said it half-heartedly; his voice sounded as defeated as his expression.

'Thank you, but I need to get back to Joe. Thanks for a lovely trip,' I said.

Holding my head high, I managed to walk until I was out of sight. Then I ran, my trainers beating the dry pavement. The people I passed seemed to look at me coolly and I felt judged – for leaving my baby at home, for spending a morning delighting in the river. For whatever might have begun at the cottage.

By the time I reached The Lodge, my lungs were fit to burst, so I slowly strolled to the side door to catch my breath. Joan Hague was perched at the kitchen table, absorbed in a novel. She jumped when she noticed me.

'You're back! Did you have a nice time?' she asked, slipping the book into her shopper. Then after a beat, 'Is everything alright, love?'

Her voice sounded more northern than I remembered. Like a sparrow, she cocked her head, her eyes shiny and knowing behind her thick glasses. Her bun had slightly fallen to one side and with a jolt, I realised it wasn't real. Had it always been a hairpiece? And beneath her powdered cheeks, her skin was so pale. Right now she resembled one of her 'sleepy-eyed' antique dolls.

I wanted to slap my own head. She *was* old, of course, at least ten years older than Mum, and I'd left her in charge to have a date with my brother.

Reaching out a bony hand, she took mine with a surprisingly strong grip. 'Tom's still with Joe in his bedroom. Both of them fast asleep by now, I should think. They've had such a lovely morning – a long walk here and there, then building a tower with bricks, and a bungalow. Well, Tom would, wouldn't he? Little Joe's been very happy.' She nodded to the sink. 'We gave him few teaspoons of baby rice a while back, like you said.'

'Thank you.' Surprised Tom had been the main child-minder, I gave her a hug. I'd always thought of her as a big lady, and she was still large-boned, but she felt fragile too, the skin on her arms dry and speckled. Sniffing back the emotion, I held on for a moment longer; my own mother might have been like this one day, but she'd been taken away before her time. Finally stepping back, I registered why Joan's scent was so appealing. It was Chanel, the same as Mum's.

I felt breathless as reality smacked. I wasn't a teenager or living a fantasy. There were still a lifetime's belongings and this house to sort out. And George, his mother… Oh God. What on earth would happen now?

'Thank you, Joan,' I said again. 'And thank you for being just down the road. You and Tom are… well, the closest thing I have to relatives here.'

As though looking into my soul, she regarded me closely, but didn't say anything. Instead she collected her handbag and patted my shoulder.

Tom appeared, yawned and stretched. 'Littl'un's asleep; I'm nearly too.' He held out his arm to his wife. 'Come on then, my love. What did you say we were having for lunch? There's that nice beef gravy in the fridge from yesterday. What about your best Yorkshires to perk us up?'

Following them outside, I watched Joan shuffle away with small steps. They hadn't driven here as I'd supposed. I glanced at my car. Should I offer them a lift? No; Tom had said Joe was asleep and I'd have to wake him. And quite honestly, I needed ten minutes to gather my thoughts and work out what the hell had just happened.

–

Too agitated to do anything constructive, I sat in the lounge, listening out for Joe and waiting for George. My febrile mind kept me busy. What had gone on after I left the cottage? Did George and his mother have a frank exchange? What, exactly, had been discussed? Did he explain what he'd said to me? That he felt alive and exhilarated, not like a bad person? The permutations were tenfold, but I was certain about one thing – George would turn up here as soon as he could.

After an hour, Joe woke. As though he hadn't seen me for a week, he reached out his arms, all smiles.

'Oh Joe,' I said, holding him close. I was so lucky to have this gorgeous little boy, and yet I still wanted more. The situation was so complicated; I couldn't shape what that 'more' might be, but it felt as though George and I had jumped a different hurdle outside the Swan Inn. One of honesty. He hadn't declared love exactly, but he'd sincerely set out how he felt, despite the difficult circumstances and his obvious internal conflict. If we were frank with each other, surely we could find a way forward and work something out?

I gazed at my son. Oh God, what could that *something* be? I was married to this beautiful boy's father, a good man who I loved. What on earth was I hoping for? A clandestine relationship with my brother? An *affair*? The whole notion was preposterous and yet... George had wanted to hold me; I'd so wanted to be held. And if it had gone further, what then?

Noticing the dent in my duvet cover, I gave a little shudder. Joan had clearly been right about Tom's napping. But I had to be more charitable. He'd left a blue inhaler on the spindle chair; like his wife, he was elderly; it had been good of them both to come. They'd walked up the hill especially, for goodness' sake.

I returned to the lounge and played with Joe, biding my time. The afternoon dragged into evening, but the grounds remained silent. When I finally heard the doorbell from the kitchen sink, I had almost given up hope. But George was here, thank God. My instinct had been right.

I dried my hands, smoothed my hair, scooped Joe from his highchair and trotted to the front door. Before I reached it, my heart fell. The figure through the glass panes was no taller than me. Part of me wanted to hide, but Mum had brought me up well: the 'pleases and thank yous' were already under my breath.

'May I come in?' George's mother asked.

Although not his flesh and blood, on reflection I could tell they were related by her accent. 'Posh Leeds,' as Mum would've said. Not 'posh Sheffield', like us. Both were Yorkshire accents, but distinctive if you knew. Like St Agur and Danish blue, one was a little softer than the other.

Standing back, I let her in. Holding my son like a shield, I nodded to the lounge.

As grave as she'd been several hours ago, she sat in the armchair and I perched on the sofa.

'This won't take long,' she said.

George had told me she'd been a secondary school Headteacher. More homely than the suited, younger staff who'd taught at my school, she still had a shrewd, intelligent look behind her glasses. I couldn't imagine she'd taken any nonsense from pupils or their parents.

'I know what's been going on and it has to stop,' she said bluntly.

'Nothing has—' I began, but she lifted a plump hand to stop me.

'Oliver hasn't said anything to me. He's barely spoken since you left. But I'm not a fool. I saw you both from the cottage. Your body language, your expressions, your smiles. He's been my son since he was two days old, and I know him better than anyone ever will. For one glorious moment I thought he'd found somebody...'

The steeliness fell from her face and for a second I glimpsed a mother who loved her child, but the shutters soon closed again.

'Perhaps nothing has happened, as you say, but it's clear what might unless I intervene.' She cleared her throat. 'I believe you're a lawyer, so I'm sure I don't have to tell you that relations between siblings is wrong. Legally, ethically and morally. Incest isn't condoned by society and it won't be condoned by me.'

Flinching at the word, I hung my head. There was no point in protesting. I'd had lascivious thoughts; I suspected we both had. Part of me still wanted to argue, the barrister part, I suppose. To say something about deep connection and finding a soulmate, despite the short time we'd known each other, but the words would have sounded risible and besides I couldn't speak. Tears were rolling from my chin, splashing onto Joe's head.

I came back to her speech. Though only a touch, her tone had softened. 'And even if you were able to live with the condemnation of family and friends...' She paused and took a breath. 'You have to see it's not fair to Oliver, and if you really care for him...'

I looked at her then, wiping my cheeks with a trembling hand.

She gazed for a beat, then sighed and moved next to me on the sofa. 'When Ben died,' she continued softly, 'Oliver was beside himself with grief. He was so angry and bleak I thought he might harm himself. He left Emma and came to live with us and I was glad. I could watch him. A razor blade, the end of a rope, pills; I could see it coming.' Her pale, clear eyes were intent. 'I was certain that one day my son would go to bed and never wake up, just like Ben.'

She put a hand on my knee. 'Outwardly he's so much better, but I think he's still grieving. I don't think he's... *right* yet, and it's affected his emotions. Why else would he have got himself into this dreadful position? He's usually so

299

measured and controlled in everything he does. Even you must see that it's an almighty lapse in anyone's judgement to have romantic feelings for someone you are related to...'

An almighty lapse in judgment. Like Mum and Mr Lang. Her words hurt, but I knew from her solid gaze she was willing me to understand. She had given the lecture of condemnation and now was speaking to me as a mother who loved her son. As distressed as I was, I couldn't help but admire her.

Pulling away, she straightened her shoulders. 'If you persist in this stupidity – even friendship – you'll ruin his chances of moving on, finding someone suitable to love, and most importantly, having more children. Ben was the making of him. Oliver had a nice life with us and his sister, but Ben filled the missing piece, that of flesh and blood. Blind eyes and pretence might feel appealing, but a child of his own is something you can never, ever give him.'

She stood up and nodded at Joe. 'You have your lovely little boy, but Oliver lost his. He was a wonderful father and he will be again but you must free him. I don't care how you do it, but please do it now. Nip this foolishness in the bud. Not for me, but for him.'

Chapter Fifty-One

It didn't take long to pack up; I hadn't brought much with me, just Joe's things, mainly – his travel cot, changing mat, chair, carrier. And his clothes, which were suddenly too small. What took so much longer was the note I had agreed to write to George. Ironic, I thought, as I searched for writing paper. Letters. Who'd have thought they'd make such an impact on my life?

Sitting at the kitchen table, I doodled for some time. What to say? I barely knew him, yet it was as though he'd been part of my life for years.

I wanted to describe the 'magnetic' connection I felt for him. An old chestnut, for sure, but that's exactly how it was: compulsive, compelling and secure. I longed to add that I'd never forget my exhilaration as the river led us home. That walking away left me empty inside. '*It's all your mum's fault*,' I scribbled. '*If she hadn't been there at that moment…*' But I wouldn't say that because she was right. I had to kill any hope of an 'us', even friendship. Though I didn't want to be unkind, I had to be harsh to give him the impetus to move on from his grief – and from me. And yes, give him the chance of having another child. In the end the message was hurried and brief. It read:

Dear George,

On reflection it would have been a sordid mistake. I'm going back to Manchester tonight. I won't be coming back, so here are all the keys to The Lodge. It's yours to do with as you wish. I'll ask the solicitor to deal with the formalities.

Ali.

—

Careful not to wake Joe, I slipped him in his seat and fastened him in the back of my car. I climbed behind the wheel and handled the blue inhaler thoughtfully. Now I'd made all my decisions, I wanted to start the long journey home, but Tom might need his medicine, he may not have a spare, so with a sigh, I turned left at the gates. It was only a small detour; I'd post it in his letterbox.

The Rolls-Royce was parked in Bureside's driveway – not just parked, but pretty much pressed against the double garage. I pulled up behind it, grabbed the inhaler and hurried out, but as I passed the silver car, I noticed its bonnet. The night was dark, but from the beam of my car's headlights, it looked as though Tom had smashed it into the garage doors.

Concern set in. That was odd. I glanced at the inhaler. Was he OK? Should I knock, and wake the household up? I hovered, undecided. Nancy had mentioned the Roller being in for repairs; maybe it was the brakes which hadn't been properly fixed; or perhaps Tom had been drinking. Was that really my business? But something alerted me to movement, so I turned to the rippling, dark river. A figure was on *Sylvette*'s bow. I squinted through the gloom. It was Tom.

'Hello Alice,' he called. 'Thought I heard something.'

I moved forward. 'You left this at The Lodge. I thought you might need it.'

'That's kind of you, love. Joan'll appreciate it.' He looked up to his house. A light was on in an upstairs room. 'She'll be asleep by now.' He raised a tumbler. 'Join me for a nightcap? I'd appreciate the company for five minutes.'

'Joe's in the car...' I began, but Tom's eyes seemed rheumy, sad. The happy photograph of the two of us on that very spot flashed in. I inwardly sighed. 'But he's fast asleep, so a quick one will be fine. I'll just get him.'

By the time I was back, Tom was in the saloon, preparing drinks. I popped Joe's seat on the rug, sat and glanced around. Bloody hell; it *was* exactly as I remembered. Though the teak cabinets looked a little dated, the dark wooden flooring was polished, the leather sofas were still plush, cream and littered with cushions. And there was the well-stocked bar, the soda syphon still where I'd last used it.

Tears stung the back of my eyes. My life had gone so dreadfully wrong since then. Sure, there'd been wonderful parts in between, but one way or another, my father's death had tainted everything. Cancer, bloody cancer, such a brutal, insidious disease.

Looking concerned, Tom tilted his head. 'Thinking about your mum?' His expression a little strange, he glanced at the ceiling. 'Eve, oh Eve, why did you—'

'I know, the seatbelt.' I didn't want to open that can of worms, but the old question suddenly surfaced. 'When I was eighteen, she moved here. To Norfolk. Have you any idea why? I mean, why then?'

'I don't know, love, but I expect it was your and Laura's happiness which counted until then. You were at school, you had your friends, Sheffield was your home.

So she waited until Laura had gone and you were settled at university.'

I frowned. It had been Mum's home too. She'd loved everything about her birth town. And she'd left her sisters, who were also her best friends.

'Why leave even then?' I asked.

Tom shook his head. 'Bad memories.'

I frowned. Bad memories… Everyone was different, but I'd never associated the Kellogg's box with Dad's death as such. I was surprised Mum had; if anything, it would have been his final weeks here, wouldn't it?

'Lord, I miss him.' Tom's spluttered words made me jump. 'I tried to help. But it was too late. He'd buried his head…'

His comment was so similar to before, I wondered if he might have dementia.

He blew his nose but his eyes welled again. 'If he'd told me, it might have been different. But I was here and he was in Sheffield, so I didn't see him. If I'd seen his face, I'd have known something was wrong and got it out of him.' He sighed. 'He wanted to do it his own way. He didn't want your mum to know…'

'What?' I frowned, confused. 'Mum must have known. How could she not?'

'Not until later, when it was all too late.'

Gaping, I thought of Laura and her disappointment with Mum for not confiding in her as a daughter. Bloody hell, how must a *wife* have felt about being kept in the dark?

'Really? Are you sure? Mum must have been deeply offended. And horribly shocked.'

'Aye, she was. She took it pretty badly, if I'm honest. It doesn't have the, the… the shame it once had. But in truth, she was. She was ashamed of him. You know what your mum was like; a proud lady. She was humiliated by it; she was very angry.'

What the hell? Perplexed, I stared. But memories were tugging…

Tom groaned. 'If he'd just told me. Money wasn't a problem; he knew that. He was the son I'd never had; it was coming to him anyway. But he tried to handle it himself.' He cleared his throat. 'Then he got in deeper.'

The clamour of my heart was loud in my ears. At ten years of age, I had covered them with tight hands, but I'd still heard the quarrel:

'Come on, it's only money. I'll get back on track.'

'Everyone knows, Doug. I'm ashamed, humiliated. I can't bear to go out.'

'No one else cares, love. Come on, Eve, give me a smile. What do we always say? You can't take it with you.'

'This isn't a joke, Doug. I can't bear to look at you. Take Ali with you and get out of my sight.'

Realisation smacked. The court judgments and statutory demands, letters from the official receiver and *London Gazettes* in that old file. Tom hadn't been made bankrupt, Dad had. Could a bankrupt still work? Certainly not as a chartered accountant.

It all added up: Mum had hardly left The Lodge that last summer; she didn't join us on river trips, the village fete or the pub. She stubbornly stayed in the house. 'So Dad was here for the whole holiday because he couldn't work?'

'Aye. Pretty much.'

Mum had hidden from the shame in Norfolk. The ignominy must have been even worse in Sheffield with her well-to-do friends, let alone the smirking aunties. 'But we returned home in September...'

'Kids come first, like I said. You and Laura had school and your friends. You couldn't stay here forever.'

I breathed deeply. Oh God, how I'd longed to go back to that summer when life had been perfect. But it hadn't been perfect at all, had it?

Removing his glasses, Tom wiped his cheeks. 'His arrest...'

Arrest? I reeled at the new shock, but Tom was still speaking, his voice clotted with emotion.

'... wasn't fair, not one bit. They said it was theft, but it was just panic, knee-jerk panic. Juggling so many financial obligations. He'd buried his head, that was all.' Reaching for my hand, he squeezed it. 'He was never dishonest like they said, Alice. Never.' Then, as though to himself: 'That's when he stopped laughing. Aye, it was then.'

I closed my eyes. Pictured 'the smiling idiot', my lovely, lovely dad.

'The arrest,' I croaked eventually. My throat was so dry, it was an effort to speak. I knew I was clutching at straws, but I still had to ask. 'Didn't the police take into account his illness, his—?'

'There was no cancer, Alice. The police investigation, then the charges... well, they broke him. He wasn't in his right mind.'

That memory of my Slinky toy came hurtling back. I could picture it so clearly: Mum glancing to the upper landing, seeing it swinging, then her expression abruptly changing and yelling, '*Stop it, Laura. Just stop it. Never do that again. Do you hear me?*'

'He hanged himself. He hanged himself from our top bannister,' I stated.

Tom nodded. 'Aye, love, he did.'

Part Three

Chapter Fifty-Two

An embarrassing torrent of tears had come then. Not just tears but sputtered misery between my chest-jerking sobs. It was sheer, devastating grief for my mum and dad, but also for the loss of George. 'Why me? Why have I lost both my parents? Why do all the people I love get taken away? Make me feel safe and loved one minute, then they're gone. What have I done to deserve it?'

Joe had stirred and I'd stared, suddenly terrified I'd somehow be deprived of him too. 'Oh God, will my life always be like this? Devastation waiting around the corner?'

Hovering with concern, poor Tom had clearly not known what to do, but at that point he'd sat next to me and spoken firmly. 'Nothing bad will ever happen to the littl'un. Or you. Do you hear me, Alice? Nothing.'

It was said as though he'd had the power to ordain my life, so I'd pulled myself together then, taken the proffered orange juice and given Joe a quick feed. When I'd finally left *Sylvette* I'd given Tom a small, shaky smile, but I was now at the other side of the village. Pulling up outside George's cottage, I gazed for a minute. There were no lights on downstairs, but a dull beam glowed through the front bedroom window. George or his mum? I hadn't discovered where he slept and it was just as well.

I took a deep, shuddery breath. Good God; a married mother on the fringes of adultery and incest rolled into one; was it simply Genetic Sexual Attraction, another break from reality or genuine, adult love? I didn't know; I couldn't think about it right now. My whole being was numb. I'd been dealt a knockout blow, and in truth I wanted to stay in that state, unconscious, unfeeling and curled on the ground.

I posted my letter and shook myself down when I returned to the car. I had to concentrate on my son's safety, so I peered through the windscreen and negotiated the leafy lanes, sharp bends and nocturnal animals with care. Although a glint of moonlight pierced the clouds, the black night was dense and the trees seemed to glower, but at least the long empty passages hastened my journey home. As the roads became busier and wider, both my body and mind seemed to thaw and aching sorrow spread, so I tried to go through this evening's discoveries methodically, examine them, absorb them, acknowledge them, then hopefully file them away.

The dark secret I'd felt tugging at me was about Dad after all. Not just a secret, but secrets. He had got himself into debt, but instead of seeking help, he'd not only ignored it, but 'got in deeper' as Tom had put it. Robbed Peter to pay Paul? I'd seen that so many times; defendants furiously scrabbling to keep their heads above water by 'borrowing' funds from the till or a client, vowing to themselves that it would only be temporary, that they'd soon be in a position to pay it back, they just needed time.

And why had he got himself into that dire situation? Spending too much. The expensive holidays and gadgets and cars, sending us to private school, funding that lifestyle. And pleasing my mother. Yes, always that. Buying her love? Still trying to repay his side of the bargain? Furnishing her with those wads of cash and a comfortable life in exchange for giving up baby Oliver?

Remembering her letter, I swallowed. *It takes a house and a home and clothes and the care of a good man.* Yes, Dad had provided all that. And she'd enjoyed wealth and all its trappings to the full – the golf club, dining out, charity balls; the clothes, the jewellery, the bloody fur coats. The holiday home, for goodness' sake.

Then there was the bankruptcy and how my proud mum would have seen it: so public, so official, so inescapable; the golfing ladies, her siblings, the whole village gossiping about her humiliation. Going through the ignominy of the trustees' visits, the collection of assets for the creditors, the removal of Dad's valuable items, his Rolex, his gold cufflinks, his cameras, his car. Maybe even replacing jointly owned belongings with cheaper alternatives, reducing her plush possessions to 'basic domestic needs'. Then the worry about losing the house, our home. Perhaps she did a deal with the trustee about that, maybe the mortgage was so huge it wasn't worth them seizing, but the anxiety – and the effort of hiding it from me and Laura – must have been huge. Bloody hell, no wonder she'd been so snappy with Dad that last summer.

Pieces slotted into place as I drove. Mum's sudden frugality, her obsession with every penny we spent. Her lack of new clothes and household goods, her scouring the sales, charity or bric-à-brac shops for bargains. Then Dad's trips to Norwich – not to a hospital, but to consult Roger Bakewell in Meriden Way, of course.

I shivered. The police investigation, the arrest for theft and Dad's suicide… How low must he have felt to do *that*? With a frown, I strained to recall how things had been at home in the short period between returning from Norfolk and his death. More tense silent periods or arguments, more irritation from Mum? I couldn't recall; Laura and I were back at school, our priorities were our friends, having tea on the table, inanely watching TV. But how must Mum have reacted when the worst happened? She'd been spoilt, a snob, she'd been used to a lavish lifestyle, so she'd naturally been angry up to then, especially as Dad hadn't confessed the debts to her, but did she feel dreadful, terrible guilt for her lack of support? When she found him hanging in our home? When she read his suicide note, because surely that's what it had been? Not on blue paper and dated like the rest of the letters, but on a white sheet, written with a shaky, desperate hand:

> *Darling Eve. I'm so sorry. Please find it in your heart to forgive me.*

Chapter Fifty-Three

I pulled up on my Manchester driveway in the early hours. Exhausted and achy, I turned to Joe. 'We're home,' I whispered. He didn't reply. Nor did he stir as I unbelted his seat and carried him to the door. He was a contented baby these days.

When I stepped into my home, the absence of aromas struck me. The house hadn't been lived in for a while – no cooking, no laundry, no nappies – so perhaps it wasn't surprising, but I *noticed* it; I was aware of something that was no longer there. My senses had changed. So had I. Like Mum and 'that damned smell' she'd ended up embracing.

Detached and overwhelmingly weary, I put Joe in his cot. He stretched and shuffled, so I sat on the small sofa and closed my eyes, trying to float over my analysis in the car. My parents were dead, their pasts and their decisions were history; as much as I would love to rewrite it with a much happier ending, I couldn't, so I had to shelve it somehow. Then there was George. As my shoulders eased, I couldn't escape his look of defeat the last time I saw him. I knew the what-ifs and regrets would hound me, and that I'd have to find a way to explain everything to Laura – including my impetuous decision to give our brother Mum's home – but for now I had to look forward and search for positives. I had no alternative, after all. But a glimmer of *something* was already there. The Ali who had left this house nine days ago was different to the one now. And that was a good thing. It was just hard to *feel* it.

Though Joe continued to kick his covers, he didn't wake for a feed so I snoozed, but I eventually jerked to consciousness. Oh God, I hadn't told anyone my plans, least of all Miles. He might call The Lodge this morning and receive a scrambled message from Nancy or Denise that I'd left without warning. Was it too early to call him? I peered at my watch, surprised to see it was nearly seven. Miles would be awake, reading the headlines before his shower.

Widely yawning, I shuffled to my bedroom, pulled out my mobile and perched on the bed. A text was waiting from Madeleine.

> Hello darling. Hope you're coping with all the challenges in Norfolk. Would love to have a chat soon. Always remember I'm here if you need me.

Challenges indeed. Which one would I choose? My father's arrest and suicide? The discovery of a half-brother? Or my thwarted attraction to George? Well, the last was something I couldn't share with anyone, ever, particularly not her. Deeply sighing, I shifted my thoughts to Miles. What should I say about my sudden departure? *'I've handed over The Lodge and its contents to Mum's gardener'* wouldn't sound good, nor would *'I found myself falling in love with a man who turned out to be my brother'*. I rehearsed a few things in my head: Tom Hague had offered to clear out the contents; there was a problem with mice; the central heating was on the blink; the banks of the bloody River Bure had broken. But in truth it didn't really matter; Miles would be preoccupied with his trial, so I'd just mutter something about the paperwork being in the hands of solicitors if he asked.

I pressed the icon and waited. As it turned out, I didn't need excuses, because a female voice answered.

'Hello?'

Julia Lambert. It felt like déjà vu, but it wasn't the afternoon or evening now, it was three minutes past seven in the morning. How many times had she snatched up my husband's phone over the last week, hoping it would be me? An unsubtle way of dealing with things, but effective nonetheless. Like the impersonal letter I had written George. Brutal, unkind.

Seconds passed. My lips shaped a caustic comment: '*Remember this moment, Julia, because one day you'll be at this end of the telephone.*' But it wasn't all her fault: it took two, she wasn't married and part of me felt sorry for her. Who would want to force their lover's hand in this devious way? Besides, I didn't have the energy; I was too knackered and battered. So I gave her a message to pass on. That Joe and I were back in Manchester, so Miles would know where to call.

A dry tear piercing my paralysis, I fell back on the bed. I had once been so sure of his love. Too sure, I supposed; I'd taken it for granted. Or perhaps the needy tables had turned. He'd coped with my psychotic break because Madeleine had taken over, but I'd ditched her during my pregnancy, so I'd had to depend on him.

I wasn't entitled to wallow, though; I had fallen for somebody else too. Shit happened, as they said. It was just tragic my shit had no future.

The peal of my mobile jerked me back to consciousness. Miles Alexander-Jones.

'Ali, you called me! Julia popped in to see if I had a spare collar and my phone was ringing so...' he said in a high, breathy voice. 'She saw it was you and thought it might be important.'

The explanation was pretty poor, but I was too tired for sarcasm or arguments or even plain angst.

'That's OK. I'm dog-tired, so I'll speak to you later.'

I pulled a pillow beneath my head. Joe would wake soon, but that was fine. If I couldn't sleep now I'd do it later, ask one of my mum friends or my neighbour Melissa to mind Joe for an hour. Or catch up when he had his afternoon nap. I could do this.

I gave a nod to the chink of light. The secret about my dad had been far more devastating than I'd ever imagined and my heart was broken, but at least the 'crap mother' anxiety had gone.

–

I slept for an hour without dreaming, only waking at the sound of post firing through the front door. Sighing at the thought of my letter on George's doormat, I padded to the nursery and peered in. Occupied by the tinkle of ceiling chimes and the taste of his fingers, Joe was kicking contentedly in his cot.

The wave of grief was so sudden, I had to sit down. My halting steps into motherhood had finally become strides, but who would I share it with? My dead mum, my absent sister, my unfaithful husband? The one person I would choose was wholly and completely unavailable to me. Not just unavailable but taboo. It felt so very unfair. But I had to get a grip; I had to focus on the memory of his mother's face, the disgust and ultimately, the love.

Chapter Fifty-Four

The new normal was keeping busy and resolutely looking forward. Maybe taking modest steps for now, but moving onwards and not back. Back was the enemy; back was Dad and the black hole of my grief. It was Mum, sore boobs and sleepless nights, it was panic attacks and hopelessness. It was George. Handsome and kind and complicated George.

After Tuesday's brief call, Miles phoned regularly. 'Just to check in,' he said at the outset. But the conversations were strained, the 'I do love you, Ali. I really do,' at the end uncomfortable, so I didn't always respond with an automatic echo. I had no idea whether I loved him or not. Was my marriage over? Until I saw him in person, I just didn't know.

Trying to be positive, I jotted notes on a pad, to-do suggestions and activities for the week. My projections were short, like my breath, but I tried to put them into practice: I phoned friends to catch up. I offered to host the mum and toddler get-together on Friday and joined a new baby group at the church. I made a list of goodies to bake, and in Madeleine style, I went through cupboards and drawers, creating a towering pile of stuff for charity.

Over the next few days, I kept active. I popped over the road to deliver a parcel to Melissa and accepted her offer of a drink. The radio constant in the background, I tackled the ironing pile and the sticky kitchen units, the fridge and the oven. I took Joe for long walks, played with his toys and read him books. Trying to block out Norfolk, I chatted with my mum friends in the park, but sunny memories seeped through all the same – the dawn chorus and the acorn tang of the woods, the taste of warm scones and yellow butter, safe hands and safe arms.

Practicalities meant I had to look back too: calls to Roger Bakewell and the Hagues, for starters. I told Joan an emergency had brought me home and that George would be caretaking The Lodge, but the conversation with the solicitor was trickier. Perhaps my decision had been somewhat knee-jerk, but giving George the house – or at least my half share – still felt the right thing to do, not only because he was entitled to part of it, but in terms of finality and seeing the promise I'd made to his mother through. But how on earth would I broach it with Roger? In the end, I just had to say it. If he thought it was odd, he didn't mention it, but he carefully explained that nothing could be finalised until the probate was through. As Laura and I were both beneficiaries and executors, the decision had to be joint.

You're doing well, Ali, was my mantra each morning. But gulps of unhappiness still overcame me: how had George responded to my letter? Did he hate me? Was he living at The Lodge? Had he gone back north to look for his father? Then there was the constant worry, tight in my chest: Was George OK? Was he safe, not self-harming or hanging at the end of a rope? Like my father. Oh God.

My decision to shelve all thoughts of Dad and his final year was successful in the main, but when I least expected it, unanswered questions pestered me. Presumably his suicide was what Mum had been keen to discuss with me before her visit. But after a twenty-five year gap… why then? And if she'd decided to tell me, then why not inform Laura too? Maybe she'd remembered Laura's '*I wish you were both dead*' comment, but that didn't ring true. Laura was thirty-nine and the dispassionate, practical daughter, not the one who'd take it the hardest.

I squeezed my mind back to Brenda and Peggy's conversation at the funeral. The siblings had made Mum a promise and Brenda had 'broken ranks'. I could absolutely imagine my mother asking her family to keep Dad's 'shame', his arrest and suicide a secret, but Brenda had said Mum's response was a 'huge overreaction'. And there was no mistaking the fact that Brenda's challenge and Mum's departure to Norfolk coincided. Was Tom correct? Had Mum stayed in Sheffield until I was eighteen for my stability and happiness? Or was there more to it?

But I had to let those thoughts go. Of course, I could make a rare call to my aunties, open old wounds and demand the facts from them. But did I really want to be subjected to one of Brenda's 'home truths' lectures? Or even worse, her sorrow and guilty tears? No I didn't; I wouldn't do that. What remained of Mum's life would stay in the drawers and cupboards of The Lodge. I'd made a vow never to return and I intended to keep it.

—

I finally saw Miles in person on Friday evening. His jolly tone was forced. 'I'm home!' he said at the door. 'Ali? Where are you?'

'In here.'

Bounding into the kitchen, he took in the sparkling surfaces and clean cupboards. 'Wow, you've been busy.

Something smells delicious too. Don't tell me… Boeuf bourguignon, my favourite.' He pulled me into a hug. 'God, I'm glad to be home.'

It had been less than a week, but this suited man felt like a stranger. He disappeared upstairs to look in on Joe, but even when he returned with a fond smile and in weekend gear, the situation seemed staged.

'Are you hungry? I didn't know if you'd eat on the train,' I asked.

'Starving. Are those homemade…' He squinted. 'Got it. Bread-cakes! Fantastic, what a homecoming.'

We sat at the table, dipped the crusts in our casserole and drank wine.

It felt like a fifties drama. I was playing the dutiful wife in her pinny and Miles starred in the role of chirpy and appreciative husband. It was laughable, in truth. Would either of us mention the early phone call or Julia? Were we really going to pretend it hadn't happened?

Miles soon moved on from his polite questions about my week to himself, talking animatedly – and at length – about the trial, taking me through the 'inspired genius' of his cross-examination. He'd won on liability and wished I'd seen the sour look on Paul Jefferson QC's face. He'd be making submissions for damages on Wednesday but they were going to be 'fucking huge' after his 'bloody good win'. He'd be around until then, so we could have a lazy long weekend.

It wasn't as arrogant as it might have sounded to a stranger. We were, after all, husband and wife; we could be as egotistical and as candid as we liked.

But neither of us were being honest.

I analysed Miles as he spoke. He was amiable, attractive and undoubtedly good company. He had a moody side, but didn't we all. He was a good dad to Joe; he'd be thrilled to sire him a brother or sister. If I decided not to work, he'd gladly provide for me. We had a nice home and lovely friends. I just had to let it go; continue to be the girl with tightly closed eyes, or bluff like he did.

The words burst from my mouth. 'So, Julia and this thing you're having…'

'Sorry?' His expression was all innocence. 'There is no *thing*, Ali. I don't know what you mean.' Then as though the connection had suddenly landed, 'You can't mean Tuesday morning; I've already explained…'

Part of me wanted to guffaw. His acting was pretty impressive; had he practised on the train? 'Oh come on, Miles, I'm not that stupid.'

Perhaps it was my weary acceptance, maybe it was my lack of emotion, but the mask slid from his face, revealing the heightened features of a little boy who'd been rumbled.

'She's *nice* to me, Ali, which is more than you've been for months. She listens to me; she's interested. Ever since you got pregnant—'

I snorted. 'So that's when the affair started, is it?' I said the words idly, a throw-away comment I expected him to deny. But he didn't.

'You were totally self-obsessed, right from the start, Ali. You went completely over the top about the whole bloody thing. One crisis after another.' He glanced sullenly. 'You'd promised me all *that* was over. A one-off in the past, but I could see it coming back and it freaked me out. Things were tough for me too; I was lonely; I needed someone to talk to…'

I reeled from the shock. I *was* stupid after all. '*That*' was my mental health, a horrible and debilitating blip in my life he'd seen fit to discuss with bloody Julia. As if that wasn't bad enough, he'd been shagging her as Joe developed from a dot to a golf ball, from a soft ball to a football and finally a rugby ball in my womb. My chest smarted; he hadn't just betrayed me, but his son as well.

He topped up his glass and continued in a petulant tone. 'Look, I tried to end it after Joe was born but…'

Certain the rest would be along the lines of *'but your mother died and you neglected me again,'* I scraped back my chair and left through the back door.

Inhaling the cool night air, I paced around the dewy grass and tried to organise my thoughts. Though stunned and hurt, it was almost a relief to hear the truth. I'd been ignorant and blind, but not without culpability. Cold fish Ali had had it coming, hadn't she? She'd married a needy man; she knew this. She'd paid the price for taking her eyes off the prize.

Wiping a tear from my cheek, I sighed deeply. Miles and I had promised 'for better or for worse' when we married. Most couples would take a little neglect on the chin when the going got tough, rather than running to someone else, wouldn't they? But I had a better understanding of human frailty these days, not only my own, but my mother's. Like Miles, Mum hadn't coped with the loneliness and lack of attention; like Miles, she'd been unfaithful. She'd ultimately taken the easy option by staying with Dad, but it had been cemented by deep love, I knew that for certain.

I returned to the kitchen and took my seat. The pettishness had gone from Miles's face, replaced with charming apprehension, and I almost relented. But I took a deep breath of resolve. The *cement* had to be there.

'I'm sorry Miles, but this situation isn't something we can ignore or fix.'

As though I was joking, he stared, then his features crumpled. 'For God's sake Ali, it didn't mean anything. You're *sorry*… You don't mean you want to separate, do you? That's just ridiculous.' He knelt by my chair. 'Look, I was stupid and weak and… hurt, I suppose, but there's only ever been you. Julia knows this. I love you, Ali; I'll only ever be in love with one person and that's you.'

Sorrow burned in my throat. *In* love; that was the rub. I'd never been in love with this man. 'Oh Miles, I'm sorry, but I don't feel the same way. I love you too, but not like I should. I think you knew it sooner than I did.'

Tears falling, he nodded and turned away. He spent some time at the sink, looking out to the black night, but eventually he returned, poured more wine and talked quietly about this and that, the news and the weather. I liked and admired him more than I had for many weeks; he was being brave, far braver than he wanted to be.

Taking his hand, I smiled. 'You're an amazing guy, Miles, a really good catch. You'll have women queueing around the block… And you can do so much better than Julia bloody Lambert.'

His lips briefly twitched before the frown. The conversation had cut to the chase. 'What about you? Will you be looking for someone else? Another dad for Joe?'

'You're Joe's dad, Miles. He doesn't need another. And no, I'm not.'

For a moment I floated on *Ruby Jane*. Saw George's smile, his sincere look of love outside The Swan. Then I inwardly groaned. My brother; *our* brother. At some point soon, I'd have to tell Laura.

Chapter Fifty-Five

My husband and I spent a companionable long weekend concentrating on Joe. Miles slept in the spare room, but if anyone had watched us stroll with our son in his pram or feast on glossy pork pies and traditional lemonade at Tatton Park, they wouldn't have known anything was amiss. I hadn't changed my mind about us parting, but without a catalyst there was nothing to force it. From time to time I heard Miles on his mobile. Julia, I supposed, but his tone was hostile.

On Tuesday I drove him to Stockport station. We were silent on the journey, but when I pulled up at the cab rank, he didn't climb out. He turned with a breath. 'Look, Ali. I've been a complete buffoon, an incredibly stupid, selfish idiot and I'm so, so sorry. I promise it won't ever happen again. You and Joe are my world. Let's start afresh. Please. We can turn a clean page when I'm back from London…'

His handsome face was endearing. I was tempted, very tempted. Motherhood was so much easier – yesterday I'd attended my belated postnatal check-up and all was good 'down under', breastfeeding had become routine and Joe slept through much of the night. Hell, I even showered and applied a hint of make-up every day. Most importantly, Joe needed a dad, the stability of a full-time father who lived with us day in and day out. But that didn't mean it was the right thing to do. It had taken a trip on the River

Bure to discover that I'd never really fallen for Miles; the raw passion, that innate pull, had never been there. And what about the next time I took my eyes off the prize? If I went back to work, holidayed with friends, climbed a mountain in Tibet or had another child?

The long beep of an annoyed taxi driver roused me. Picturing George's mother, I focused on the cruel-to-be-kind certainty in her eyes. 'No, sorry Miles. I don't love you in the way you need me to. You deserve someone who does. Let's talk at the weekend and work everything out when we have proper time. You'll miss your train if—'

But he'd already scrambled out. 'Fine. Whatever. Your loss,' he muttered before slamming the door.

Breath caught in my chest as I watched him stalk to the terminal. He didn't wave or glance back; he hadn't even said goodbye to Joe. The reality of my situation punched me. What the hell had I just done? I'd always had that ridiculous fear of being abandoned, yet I was making it happen. I had no parents and I'd pushed away my flawed but loving husband. A shrill beep from behind came again. My feet finding the pedals, I put the car into gear and trundled down the hill on autopilot.

As I waited at the lights, a frost enveloped my whole being. Bloody hell; what was wrong with me? I was more alone, more an orphan now than after Mum died. But the word abruptly brought a smile. I had a sister; I still had my Laura. Though she'd messaged me with loads of photos, she wanted me to meet her fiancé in person, and there was nothing here to hold me back.

Swerving to the curb, I peered at the time. It was too early to call her, but I could start the ball rolling, so I pulled out my mobile and quickly composed a text:

> Tell me when Joe and I can inspect Shelby close up. The sooner the better!

Job done, I rejoined the carriageway and negotiated the lunchtime traffic towards home. The surge of adrenaline had buoyed me and I now had a plan. Or at least the start of one. I looked at my son through the mirror and smiled.

'Something to look forward to, Joe.'

Perhaps my life was on an upturn at last.

–

Finally by the Marie Louise Gardens, I waited for several cars to negotiate the road humps before turning into our avenue. I glanced at my house, then looked again. What the…? A car was parked outside – not just a car but a gleaming silver Rolls-Royce. As I drove alongside, I took in the dent at the front of the bonnet. It could only belong to one person. I dragged my eyes to the driver's seat and it was. Tom Hague was at the wheel.

My heart thumped. Oh God; George. Something dreadful had happened to him. My legs insubstantial, I climbed out of my car. Tom did the same, donning his jacket, then straightening his slacks.

'Hello, Alice, love,' he said when he finally looked up. 'Have you got five minutes for an old man?' he asked, as though a Manchester visit was perfectly normal. He smiled with those teeth. 'Shall I fetch the littl'un out?'

Too winded to answer, I peered at the Roller's tinted windows. Where was Joan?

He followed my gaze. 'She wanted to go home,' he said. 'She's asleep.'

Confused, I gaped. Bureside was two hundred and fifty miles away. 'Home?'

'Walkley, of course. Our Sheffield. That's really home. As much as we loved Horning, it always was.' He deftly unbuckled Joe's seat and followed me into the house. 'I drove over the picturesque way. Ladybower reservoir's low. If we're not careful we'll see the ruins and some think that's bad luck. They used to say you could still hear the church bell on a stormy night.'

As Mum would have said, I felt someone walk over my grave. I tried to smile away the shiver. The alarm too; but even Tom wouldn't be so chirpy if there was bad news to impart. 'That's just folklore, isn't it? Didn't the bell get rehoused in another church?'

He took off his cap. 'Aye, it did eventually. But they exhumed the graveyard when the village was flooded. I don't suppose those dead folk were happy being moved from their rest.'

Thankful it was bright daylight, I turned to close the door, but my neighbour was approaching. 'Hi, Melissa, how's it going?' I asked. 'Are you coming in for a coffee?'

She handed me an envelope. 'No thanks, I'm not stopping. Party invitation for you. Twenty-five years of hard labour! Silver, like your grandad's fab car.' She gazed at the polished vehicle and chuckled. 'Can you imagine if that turned up on my drive for our anniversary? Then I'd know he'd been up to no good for twenty-four years of them.' She lifted her hand as she walked away. 'September the thirtieth. Hope you and Miles can make it.'

Me and Miles, oh God. But here was Tom Hague, of all people. What on earth did he want? Willing my heartbeat to slow, I took a steadying breath and found him in the kitchen with Joe, looking out of the window. 'Cat,' he was saying, nuzzling his cheek. 'Say cat, Joe!'

Oh hell, Mum's moggies. Was someone looking after them? And when I looked to where Tom was pointing, there was no animal, just the patch of daisies which had grown over my Charlie's grave.

Taking Joe from Tom's arms, I shook away the disquiet. He was just a kindly old man, a friend of my parents'. 'Tea or coffee?' I asked brightly. 'No baking today, I'm afraid, but I have cake from the weekend or I can make you a sandwich.'

Still gazing through the glass, Tom didn't reply.

I slipped Joe into his high chair. 'The cat got dug up the night we buried it. A fox, I suppose,' I commented, though God knows why. 'Miles had to dig a much deeper hole.'

Tom turned then, and I noticed for the first time his papery skin, wrapped like a single white layer over his bony hands and face. Had he always been this thin? But his eyes were bright behind his spectacles. 'Aye. Your mum said that Charlie had died. She was sad that you were sad.' He seemed to shake himself. 'Yes, tea would be grand. See if your Lancashire water is up to the mark.'

Unsettled by that old feeling of who'd-said-what-to-whom, I busied myself with the drinks, finally offering him a mug. 'I can't vouch for the water, but it's Yorkshire tea, so...'

He removed his tweed jacket, put his cap on the table and pulled out a chair. 'We spoke every day, your mum and me. Either on the phone or she'd visit us, or we'd pop in on the way to the village. I do miss her very much.' Though the tea was piping hot, he slurped his. 'We'd been great friends for years, especially me and your dad.'

I nodded. Of course, I knew this already. Indeed he'd mentioned it to me very recently. Had he forgotten our chats? Or my deluge of tears on *Sylvette*?

As though imparting a secret, he leaned forward. 'I was a policeman, you know, a bobby.'

Yes, I was aware of that too. And could I detected the faint aroma of Chanel perfume? It was unsettling, though I couldn't say why.

'I liked the beat, the people, the community,' he continued. 'Not ambitious, not one bit. I didn't want to be pushing paper around a desk and telling folk what to do.' He leaned back and scratched his chin. 'But at some point I came into money, so I made an appointment to see your dad. His office was in Walkley back then. He'd set up on his own and there was just him and a typewriter in a tiny front room. Always smiling, he still looked like a teenager, but he'd married your mum and Laura was on the way. Long story short, he got me together with a local builder who needed investment. We entered what your dad called a "joint venture" and it came up trumps. Advised by your clever dad, I fell into the property business. We became firm friends, Doug and me.'

As though he wasn't used to talking for so long, his jaw began to click. I made to offer another drink, but he carried on without stopping. 'Your mum and him… Well, it was a difficult time. First bairns always are. You know that from having Joe, don't you, love? Challenging in all sorts of ways. But I was someone he could talk to, to get things off his chest. A father figure, I suppose, without the usual paternal judgments.'

He stopped then and peered at me, his eyes sharp through his lenses. 'Your mum's gardener, George…'

Oh God, here it was, the reason for his visit. He couldn't possibly know George was my brother, but he was well aware I was married. I thought back to those nighttime headlights through the windows at The Lodge. Had I caught a glimpse of silver as the car drove away? Could it have been Tom's Rolls-Royce? I'd done nothing wrong, but he didn't know that. Or could it be something worse? Had George done something stupid? My heart thrashing, I braced myself for something I didn't want to hear.

Tom cleared his throat. 'Your dad told me about the baby Eve had given away, love. That was the root of their unhappiness. I think they hoped little Laura would heal the wound, but she didn't. And when they tried again for another bairn, nothing happened, so your Mum had a lot of time on her hands to dwell...' He coughed. 'But I didn't twig, not until last week. Eve didn't say a word to me or Joan...' A spot of pink appeared on both his cheeks. 'Now, I know it's not ethical for a solicitor to breach client confidentiality and I'm sorry, but Roger was concerned you'd made an unusual request, asking him to transfer the legal title of The Lodge to a man called Oliver Newman, also known as George...'

My mobile beeped loudly and I jumped. But I was glad of the opportunity to let out the breath I'd been holding.

'Excuse me,' I said, scooping it up.

The message was from Laura:

Brilliant. Don't expect me to be around too much as I can't take time off work. Need to save it for our wedding! So whenever suits you.

It was followed by another.

> So excited for you to meet Shelby! He'll
> look after you both. Agreed; the sooner the
> better. There might be some standby
> flights. Talk later.

'Sorry,' I muttered, slipping it back in my pocket. 'It was from Laura.'

Feeling nauseous, I went back to the conversation at hand. What exactly was Tom trying to tell me? He knew Mum had given away baby Oliver; he'd worked out who it was. What else did he know? Steeling myself for a glare of disgust or condemnation, I dragged my gaze from the table top, but Tom had stood up and was feeling the pockets of his flannel trousers. Ready to leave, I assumed.

'These old bones,' he said, pulling out a handkerchief and polishing his glasses. Without them his eyes seemed lost in his face. 'Shall we have another cuppa and get more comfortable on the settee?' he asked, his voice emerging with a whistle. 'I've got a long story to tell you.'

Chapter Fifty-Six

A bad penny… Proper Mum and Dad… Lost without you… Beautiful girl… A baby needs her real mummy… The key wasn't under the mat… An unmistakable smell… Matted with congealed blood… Whimpering, struggling…

God knows how I managed to get Tom out of the house. Even before his words had sunk in, my body reacted with a will of its own and I had an overpowering need to vomit. When he'd finally gone, I returned to the sofa, curled up like a baby and tried to breathe through the sheer nausea, the disorientating images which were flashing in my head like strobe lights: the white face of a stranger, the glint of metal, my dad swinging at the end of a rope. Physical sensations too: the stench of geraniums, the busy hum of tiny insects, the marble feel of cold flesh. And hunger, darkness, claustrophobia, fear.

Desperate to block out the trauma, I must have fallen asleep, as I jerked back to consciousness after what seemed like moments. A searing pain gripped my chest and my heart was battering so badly I knew it would rupture any moment. When I tried to inhale, I couldn't suck in the air. I was having a heart attack. If I didn't do something, I would die.

Joe? Where was Joe? On the floor in his bouncy chair, thank God.

I was dying. Was I dying? A metallic taste in my mouth; my tongue thick… A crack of reason flitted in. It was deep, deep anxiety from shock, that was all. I had to stay calm.

Willing myself to inhale and exhale slowly, I focused on my son. But the old grief, that huge black hole was now surrounding me, and sucking me in. I couldn't do it alone this time; I needed help and there was only one person who could give it.

With shaking hands, I pulled out my mobile and scrolled for the number. It was answered after one ring.

'Madeleine,' I managed. 'I need you.'

–

Pacing the lounge, I looked down at my grumbling son in my arms. I shouldn't have taken him out of his chair. I should have left him on the floor where he was safe. But he'd started to cry and I'd instinctively done it. Should I put him back? Try to fumble with the clasps? Or sit down and feed him? I just didn't know; my mind wouldn't stop jumping and leaping from one thought to the next. All I knew for sure was that I had to keep moving; if I stopped, the utter panic would return and overwhelm me forever.

The doorbell finally rang, as Madeleine arrived.

'What's happened, Alison?' she asked.

Bewildered words trickled out. 'Everyone dies and leaves me alone.'

As though understanding my anguish, she nodded. 'I know, darling. But everything's fine, it really is. Let me have Joe, then we'll sit down and chat.'

I stared at those brown, inviting eyes. She couldn't possibly *know*, not really. And she'd wanted to take my baby not so long ago. Could I trust her?

Gently guiding me by the shoulders, she sat me down, rubbed my shaking arms and gazed intently at me. 'What happened today, Alison?' She glanced at the empty mugs. 'Has someone been here?'

My mind was too scrambled to explain about Tom's visit or his surreal and sickening tale. I was still tremulous from the terror of the panic attack, that certainty of heart failure and being unable to breathe.

'I'm so tired and Joe's hungry.'

She gently prised him from my arms and placed him on her lap. I had no energy to stop her.

'Well, neither are so bad. We can easily sort both, Alison.' She smiled. 'There's nothing to worry about; I'm here now.'

–

No dawn chorus, no birds, I woke on the sofa and hitched up. The curtains were drawn, my surroundings silent and black. It took a moment for the surge of dizziness to pass, another to focus.

Oh God, where was Joe? Joe and Madeleine, where were they? Jerking to my feet, I strode to the kitchen. The fridge buzzed, but the room was empty. I rushed to the stairs, climbed up on jelly legs and shoved open my bedroom door. It clattered against the wall. Vacant too.

Almost faint with terror, I turned to the nursery and stepped into the dark.

'He's been unsettled without his mummy so I stayed,' a voice whispered behind me. 'Let's go downstairs. I'll make us a drink.'

Relief sapped any strength I had left. Taking Madeleine's proffered arm, I returned to the lounge and sat in the armchair.

'Hot tea coming up,' she said, spreading her cardigan around my shoulders.

She handed over a cup and saucer I hadn't known I possessed. Bone china from a dusty wedding set, I guessed. She must have rummaged in the back of a cupboard to find it. 'Did you feed Joe before bed?' I asked.

'Yes.'

'The box of baby milk in the fridge?'

'Yes.'

It didn't matter; today teacups and formula really did not matter.

'Thank you. For coming so quickly too.'

Sitting in the chair opposite, my mother-in-law was in analyst mode, I knew, but that was fine as well.

'That's what I'm here for. What I've always been here for.'

I dropped my gaze. 'I'm sorry for slapping you. It was unforgivable. I don't know why I did it.'

I did, though. Denial, pure and simple denial.

'No it wasn't, Alison. I pushed you too far that day; it was a clumsy and unprofessional attempt to help you.' With a small smile, she flushed. 'And it's me who should apologise. The booze, the drink-driving to Lymm. That *was* wholly and utterly unforgivable. When I'm in that zone, I feel elated, invincible. I kid myself alcohol doesn't affect me like normal people. I can brilliantly function; I can drive safely. I can fly to the moon, give up the booze at the drop of a hat! Bipolar, of course.' She softly snorted. 'Physician heal thyself.' Leaning forward, she stared steadily. 'But of course none of us can, Ali. Everyone needs help sometimes.'

I nodded; we'd discussed it many times in the past. Most young children were attached to their parents, but

I'd been an introverted loner so my bond with Dad had been almost obsessive, the final separation creating high levels of anxiety and fear.

Although she'd never spelled it out, I knew Madeleine thought I'd got stuck in the denial stage of grief, that I'd never properly resolved it, so it harmed my other relationships – with Miles in particular. Being his mother, she'd had a conflict of interest, but I hadn't minded that. They'd only been friendly chats when we'd lunched or shopped and were helpful. And it had been fabulous to be the centre of someone's attention again, a parental figure who instinctively seemed to understand me. Then I'd discovered the Evian-vodka secret; the special bond and trust had been broken, the person I'd loved and admired was lost.

Madeleine was silently waiting. 'Why did you call me this afternoon?' she eventually asked.

Tom's story was too convoluted, too raw, too perturbing to express. I'd listened and nodded until he'd finished it, then I'd managed to say something about an appointment I'd forgotten about and bundled him out of the house before I puked.

'You were right about my dad,' I replied after a time. 'I found out today.' I shook my head. 'Or perhaps I should say that I finally listened, finally heard, finally saw.'

'Oh, Alison, I'm so sorry. I felt you already knew on some level. But I did it badly, clumsily, at the wrong time. Perhaps I was still disappointed you'd abandoned me, but I convinced myself it would assist and the opportunity presented itself. I thought it might help you to loosen the grip of grief, but it didn't, did it?'

Thinking back to the day I'd lost my temper, I didn't answer for a while. It had been the start of my pregnancy and Madeleine had rushed to the house loaded with gifts.

'I'm beside myself with excitement!' she'd declared, chatting about generations of the Armstrong-Jones family, whether it would be a boy or a girl and what he or she would look like. Her enthusiasm and excitement had been so genuine and contagious, I had almost forgiven the hidden drinking and warmed to her again. But she'd picked up the family portrait from the bookcase and traced my face with the tip of her finger.

'The whole gene pool is fascinating, isn't it?' she'd said. 'I wonder whether your exotic one will come out...'

'*Exotic?*'

The word had felt like a stab in my heart. When the young me had looked in the mirror, I'd only seen *ugly*, but deep down I must have known exactly what she meant. Different; darker; the subject of my aunties' whispering.

She'd gazed for a moment, then laughed. 'Oh, darling, look at the photograph. Blond-haired blue-eyed parents. You don't take after your pale mum, so your beautiful brown eyes and colouring must have come from somewhere. Not that it matters one bit.' She'd pulled a mock sad face. 'Poor daddies. They never really know, do they?'

I'd simply slapped her, the blow so hard it had stung my palm.

I came back to the present and her question today. There was so much to take in. 'I don't honestly know,' I replied. 'But when I called you earlier...' I tried to frame those paralysing sensations. The deep black abyss and sheer, hopeless agony. I nodded. 'My daddy. It felt as though he'd died yet again.'

Chapter Fifty-Seven

I didn't travel for a while. I wanted to take care with my packing, to make sure I had everything Joe might need for two weeks or a month. Perhaps even longer, who knew? I had to buy him clothes suitable for different weather. Much larger sizes, too. Funny how I hadn't anticipated my son would grow. I'd somehow thought our existence wouldn't change, that he'd stay a newborn forever. But life ebbed and flowed all the time. Mine had shifted unexpectedly, and part of me was still flailing and lost.

Talking to Madeleine helped. 'It's a shock, of course,' she said. 'I know you're reeling, but it doesn't actually change anything, not the security, the love nor the contentment of your early years. Everyone's past is set, don't try to pick it apart. You were happy, accept it, embrace it, move on.'

I knew she was right, but it didn't stop sensations of the ground moving under my feet. And it wasn't just my childhood; Miles's unfaithfulness had hit home too. He'd betrayed me for a year and I hadn't had an inkling. How blinkered had I been? Nothing felt certain anymore. Going forward, I needed safety, solid love and secure ground.

–

Summer had broken and moved on to early autumn. It had rained most of the night and I wore a cardigan to take the chill off the misty morning. I'd always liked my Manchester home and felt sad to leave it all alone again. But Miles would be back at some point fairly soon. Whether Julia would be in tow, I didn't know. Over the last two weekends, he'd stayed over with a friend in London 'to think things through'. I wasn't sure what that meant, but for me there was no going back to half a marriage. Did Madeleine realise the implications of her advice to move on? I wasn't sure, but she was right; I had to acknowledge the past and go forwards, this time, I hoped, with open eyes.

As I lugged my suitcase outside, I noticed purple and pink petunias had pushed through the damp soil in the hanging baskets. Looking for light, I supposed.

—

After an unbearably long journey, Joe and I finally arrived. It was a trip into the unknown and the sullen sky felt foreboding. Holding my chubby son in one arm and an umbrella in the other, I knocked on the door and waited for a while. No reply, but that wasn't surprising. Work, of course. Not everyone had this freedom I'd been given.

Strapping Joe back in the car, I retraced the route I had taken a month ago, but this time I didn't see the shops, the holiday flats, the boats or the river. Instead, I listened to the sudden squall battering the roof and looked doggedly ahead. I didn't know how this confrontation would go, but I was determined to see it through.

Throwing wet pebbles either side, my car lurched up the shortcut to The Lodge. I turned off the engine and sat for a while, studying the pretty façade through the sodden windscreen. The usual glow wasn't there; it looked empty, unwelcoming and dark. Taking a deep breath, I climbed out and trotted to the patio. For what purpose, I wasn't sure. I had no keys; I had given mine away.

The rain unrelenting, I peered through the small panes of the front door, then quickly followed the building around, squinting and tapping on the glass as I went. The hall, the lounge, the dining room, my heart falling a little further with every step.

Nothing had been touched. Everything was just as I'd left it.

I rushed back to the car, lifted Joe from his seat and sat him on my knee. Feeling impotent and rootless, I stared at the pinpricked puddles surrounding us. Then the windows fogged up, so I couldn't even do that. What next? To Bureside, I supposed, to beg a towel and a spare key.

Fighting the impulse to cry, I pressed the ignition and turned on the wipers. When the windscreen cleared, I glimpsed a figure by the sunken garden, unmoving, like a statue.

A jolt of alarm whipped my chest but I blew it away. Strangers and shadows weren't necessarily malevolent phantoms. I knew that now. I'd also learned that the living were far more dangerous than any spectre. But this effigy wasn't a stranger or a ghost. He'd be angry, for sure, and might not wish to speak to – or even greet – me, but I was here to try, to acknowledge the past and move on.

I quickly reached for something to keep my son dry. By the time I'd turned back, he'd gone.

Covering Joe with a coat, I scurried to the side door. It was open, thank goodness, so I stepped in and watched my brother rub his hair with a towel. Eventually he spoke without looking my way.

'So, you're back. To reclaim the house, I suppose.'

My heart thrashed; I'd almost forgotten his deep timbre. 'Not the house, no.'

He turned and raked his fringe from his forehead. His eyes were burning beneath his furrowed brow and a full beard emphasised the hollows of his face.

'What's this about, then? You don't need to worry; nothing's been touched or taken. I was still paid, so I just kept up the gardens.'

My cardigan was wet through and poor Joe was whimpering, stuck against it. Needing to peel it off, I passed him over.

'Do you really think that badly of me?' I asked. 'That I wouldn't trust you?'

He peered at Joe and his eyes seemed to relent a little before clouding again.

'You seem to change your mind very easily.'

He had a good point, and though I wanted to explain about his mother's visit, bringing her into it wasn't fair. She'd done the right thing after all, absolutely the right thing. We'd both been temporarily unhinged thinking any good would come of a sibling relationship.

I took a deep breath. 'Look, I'm freezing, so are you. Can we make up the fire? If you have enough time, I'd like to tell you a story.'

Chapter Fifty-Eight

We sat on the sofa and watched the flames dance.

'There once was a policeman,' I began, briefly looking at Oliver. I had decided that if this moment ever came, I would call him by his proper name; it only felt right.

I paused for a while. I hadn't shared the whole tale with Madeleine, and though I had practised it many times in my head, I wasn't sure how I'd feel about uttering it out loud.

Oliver hadn't said anything since the kitchen, but Joe was on his lap and his tense hostility seemed to have eased. His eyes were dark and watchful.

'It's a story, so the characters need names,' I said. I couldn't make this about me, not yet.

He nodded.

'So, this policeman, Frank... He was a bobby on the beat and he liked it that way. He was personable and good with people; no one kept tabs on him, he could turn up late, he was invisible at crime scenes. If he had more money than a constable should, nobody noticed because he stashed it away. Not that he'd ever take a bribe, but if a villain's cash was lying around, he might deduct a few quid for his troubles. Who didn't?'

That part was my interpretation; I was reading between the lines.

'Frank befriended a young accountant who'd recently set up on his own and this accountant – John – advised Frank where to invest his savings. The ventures came good, the two men became close friends and John confided in Frank, told him about his rocky marriage.' I glanced at Oliver again. 'Before they married, John's wife had become pregnant by another man. She'd given up the boy for adoption, and though they had a new child together, they struggled to get over the past.'

Oliver smoothed Joe's fluffy hair. I carried on. 'Frank had a good heart. For one reason or another, he and his wife hadn't been able to have kids, so he created his own family of sorts, keeping an eye on the needy, the old folk, the drunks and the druggies. He'd knock on doors to check they were well, have a chat over a cuppa and cake, or share a cigarette. If someone vulnerable disappeared for a while, he'd follow up, and if he had to, he'd let himself in with a key under a plant pot or a mat. Several times he carried out life-saving CPR, stemmed a razor blade cut or called an ambulance just in time.'

Frowning thoughtfully, Oliver nodded. 'You paint a good picture,' he said. 'Go on.'

I took a shuddery breath. 'Of course there was a beautiful girl. All fairy stories have them, don't they? Well, this young woman lived with her grandma. It wasn't easy having darker skin than everyone else on her street, but Frank had watched her grow up into a right little stunner.' I swallowed. 'He called her Ella because she could sing like a nightingale. When her grandma died, a bad penny moved in with her. This bad penny was in and out of trouble and didn't treat her well. He finally went off when she told him she was pregnant. She had the baby at home and became more or less reclusive – she'd had a horrible stint in a children's home before Granny stepped in – and her big fear was that the child would go into the care system like she had…'

Oliver pulled me towards him. Perhaps my voice had faltered, but I had to go on.

'Ella was a good mum; she tried, she really did, but she was young, didn't have much money and the bad penny turned up from time to time with his wares… Frank still visited and helped where he could, keeping an eye on her and the baby.

'"Why don't you take her, Frank?" Ella pleaded when she was low. "She'd have a good life with you and your missus. A proper mum and dad. That's what she needs."

'And he would reply, "A baby needs her real mummy. The little lass would be lost without you".'

Oliver left the room then, so I waited. He came back moments later with a toilet roll. 'No tissues,' he said. He put Joe on his play mat and pulled me back to his chest.

I wiped my cheeks and tried to focus on the tale as I'd heard it from Tom. 'Then one warm summer's evening, Frank was on his regular Wednesday round. He had half a beer and a slice of Victoria sponge with Mrs Bates at number ten before moving on to check on young Ella and her toddler. Ella didn't answer, and though that wasn't unusual, the key wasn't under the mat. But when he tried the front door, it was unlocked…' My breath was short, so I lowered my head. 'Even before he stepped in…'

I paused then. Had Tom told me this part? Or was it my memory?

'Even before he stepped in, the smell of blood was unmistakable. The only sign of movement was flies.'

'You don't need to go on,' Oliver whispered.

But I did. I had to go on.

'Clutched to her dead mother, the child's hair and clothes were matted with congealed blood. She'd been stabbed too, Frank assumed. He thought she was gone...' I gazed at the fire. 'What should we call her? This dead baby, this toddler?' I asked.

Oliver held me tightly.

'It's fine,' I said eventually. 'The story has a happy ending.'

Closing my eyes, I pictured Tom Hague's face. His pale gaze had been wet behind his lenses. He'd put his papery hand on mine. 'This is the good part, love,' he'd said. 'Pure madness, I'm afraid, but with a little godly intervention, perhaps.'

'The young mother and her dead child were a pitiful sight. It was a crime scene; the constable knew to leave it untouched. But on impulse, he peeled the baby away and put her inside his coat. Then he left the house, closing the door quietly behind him, and with a thrashing heart he walked the streets towards home.

'Perhaps he knew the child was still alive; maybe it wasn't a surprise when she whimpered against his chest. Perhaps he had in mind some grand plan to present his wife with the baby she'd never had. Maybe he thought of Ella's pleas. But as the little one warmed and struggled inside his jacket, he knew he and his missus were too long in the tooth to take on a tiny child. So the policeman turned around, panicking at what he'd done, not able to think clearly.

'Without any plan, he found himself outside the accountant's house. But it felt divine – here was someone to talk to, kind people who could clean, change and feed the child, help him work out what to do. His friend was visible through the bay window, eating his dinner alone.

When he tapped on the glass, the young man welcomed him in and poured him a large brandy. Sitting the baby on his knee, the accountant softly calmed her with weak juice from a plastic cup and fed her morsels of his own child's abandoned food. Nursing her until she slept, he listened to the policeman's jumbled worries without judgement, then disappeared with the child to find his wife.'

Stopping there, I turned to Oliver. This was something Tom hadn't fully explained, but I told it as he'd related it to me. 'Who knows what they discussed or why they did it, but John and his wife eventually returned to the room. "We'll take her," John said. He took his wife's hand. "We'll make her our own; we'll bring her up as our daughter, won't we, love?"'

The fire crackled and popped. Oliver spoke eventually. 'So we're not—'

'No.'

'How old was the baby?'

'Fifteen months.'

I wasn't sure who I was crying for, but the tears fell again and Oliver held me without speaking. Pulling away eventually, I laughed. 'There's so much to absorb and discuss, and I want to hear about you and how you've been, but right now I'm—'

'Hungry?'

'Bloody starving.'

He stood and grinned. 'I'm on it. Can I borrow your car?'

I watched Oliver through the window as he drove away, then I peered at the turning point, almost expecting the Rolls-Royce to appear. My feelings for Tom had gone through the gamut, but looking back at summer holidays, he'd always been around like my personal sentinel.

Even when I spent time baking with Joan in the Bureside kitchen or learning to crochet in the lounge, he'd been a watchful presence. Though I was still working out how I felt about my shocking adoption, I was grateful to him. Had he not checked on Ella that evening, I might have died of malnutrition. And if I had gone into care, would I have found such brilliant, loving parents? Or a beautiful big sister?

Oh Laura, my Laura. She'd been five when the interloper arrived, old enough to know I wasn't her real sister. The fact Dad had given me her juice and food wasn't lost on me. I'd elbowed into her family and demanded complete attention. How upset and rejected must she have been? But she'd kept the secret despite everything. That was love and loyalty at its very, very best.

Then there were Mum's siblings. She'd sworn them to secrecy too. They must have wondered why a straightforward adoption was shrouded in such mystery, but they'd kept their promise. Only Brenda had eventually 'broken ranks', resulting in Mum moving here. Mum's fear of the true – and unlawful – story coming out was understandable, but why had she decided to tell me just before her death? Because I was now certain that's what she'd been so keen to discuss with me. But perhaps that was a puzzle I wasn't supposed to solve.

Returning to Joe, I scooped him up for a cuddle. A living, breathing child beneath a coat… How had that felt? The sudden realisation and responsibility must have been overwhelming. There were so many questions I'd been too shocked and traumatised to ask Tom. A million more had thrashed through my head since. But would I enquire? I'd taken on Madeleine's advice that secrets and bottling up my feelings were bad for me, but did I really want to know it all? Tom had left me with Eve and Doug. What had happened after that? What arrangements were made, special handshakes or exchanges of money, to legally adopt me? It seemed too crass to ask. Tom was the man who'd plucked me from death. His flushed cheeks and pink smile had been radiant. He'd brought me into this world and his pride had been a picture.

I didn't need to dwell on the looming stranger, the glint of a knife, the flies and the smell. Or the warmth seeping away, leaving me cold and abandoned. I'd already lived it many times in my dreams. But there was some relief my psychotic episode hadn't come from nowhere. At the time I'd been representing a client who'd murdered both his wife and child by stabbing. The crime scene photographs must have subconsciously brought everything back. They weren't 'hallucinations' after all, but deeply buried memories.

Pushing those thoughts away, I stepped over to the mirror. I guess I'd always known my brown eyes didn't fit, but I hadn't wanted to confront it. In some subconscious way, I knew it involved my beloved daddy. I was so afraid of losing him. Then, of course, I did.

Chapter Fifty-Nine

Perhaps surprising in the context of our courtship, Oliver and I didn't sleep in the same bed that night. We didn't even cuddle or properly kiss. A coyness had developed between us. It might have been my brutal letter or the period we had spent apart, but I felt it was more a question of respect for the young mother who had died. Once Joe was asleep, we sat on each side of the sofa and softly chatted, the thoughts which had pestered me over the last few days emerging as words.

'Tom didn't mention Ella's ethnicity...'

'How would you feel about seeing a photograph of her?'

'I'm not sure. Muddled emotions, like everything else.'

Oliver nodded thoughtfully. 'There'd be ways of finding more information if you wanted to.' He raised his eyebrows. 'Like my Mr Lang.'

'Have you done anything to find him?' I asked. 'Or do you think you will?'

'No, I haven't.' He gazed at the fire. 'And I don't think I will. I don't need to. Not now.'

I looked at my hands. I hadn't really understood his fear about the circumstances of his conception, but I certainly did now. I'd only touched on it in my head because the idea terrified me, but I'd slapped Madeleine out of nowhere, I'd truly worried about harming Joe. Did my

352

real father murder my mum? Could evil be lurking in my genes?

As though reading my mind, Oliver pulled me into his arms. He kissed my forehead. 'Nurture and nature play a part, Ali, but at the end of the day we're just us. Human beings. Individual, unique. We have autonomy, we make choices, good or bad.'

Acknowledging the serendipity, I nodded; this man wasn't my brother, but we had so much in common; no wonder the bond had been there from the start. Deciding to shelve that particular worry for now, I leaned into him.

'Why do you think Tom decided to tell you the story now?' he asked after a while.

I'd thought about this too. 'I don't know why, but I had a feeling he knew about us. Maybe he noticed *Ruby Jane* had been out and put two and two together. Or saw you here.' I flushed. 'Then when I bolted and contacted the solicitor… I guess he wanted to put me straight. Perhaps do a bit of matchmaking.'

'Well, I'm glad he did.'

'Were you angry with me?'

'Yup. It was a tough three weeks.'

We fell silent for a while. 'I'm still astonished Mum and Dad took me in. The arrangement was clearly illegal, unofficial or however one would describe it, but they also took on the huge responsibility of a traumatised child. It couldn't have been easy.' I gave Oliver a peck. 'I think that was down to you.'

'Oh yeah?'

'Making a wrong right, filling a void, creating good out of bad.' I paused. 'Finally forgiving each other.'

He smiled. 'Very glad to oblige.'

I nodded to myself. I hadn't taken in Tom's words at the time, but later they'd filtered back: 'All a tad unconventional, I know, love,' he'd said. 'But I don't think Doug and Eve would have made it without you. You gave them a joint purpose, healed them and made them happy again. It was an absolute honour to watch.'

—

The September weather hadn't recovered by the time Joe and I surfaced in the morning. Apart from seeing my new housemate almost naked in the bathroom – and staring for longer than was proper – it was business as usual at The Lodge. As though a foghorn had announced my arrival, Nancy's arms were deep in soapy water, the vacuum cleaner hummed and cleaning products fragranced the air.

I found Oliver plumping the sofa cushions and I watched him for a while. Was he another attachment based on insecurity and need? Well, possibly, probably, but I sure did fancy him. 'Is the settee really that comfy?' I asked. I was still getting used to the beard, but on balance I liked it. 'We do have beds, you know…' Aware of my deep blush, I changed the subject by cupping my ear meaningfully. 'This must be the cleanest flipping house in the land…'

But Oliver was still clearly on the first topic. Pulling me to him, he smiled. 'Then I'll have to explore tonight. Which one do you suggest? A… comfy mattress was the first thing I thought of when I woke. Still thinking about it now…'

The sudden silence said it all, but if Denise was shocked I was canoodling with the gardener, she didn't say so. When the Hoover purred again, we laughed, deciding in

354

a hurried whisper that it would be simpler to maintain the status quo – for now, at least – and keep Denise as our cleaner, even though we didn't need one, Nancy as our babysitter, me as Eve's daughter and Oliver as George.

But of course there was Laura; I had to think about that.

–

Eleven o'clock chimed. Mum's best china on a silver tray was the first clue that gossip had reached Nancy's ears, the second was Nancy bringing a cup and saucer for herself. Like the queen at a tea party, she perched delicately on the armchair and glanced from me to Oliver, then Joe, with wide eyes.

That old hilarity was back. So was an impulse to seek this old lady's approval. But she'd put a selection of posh biscuits on a plate, so I guessed we already had that.

Seeming to realise an announcement wasn't imminent, Nancy lifted her little finger, slurped her brew and made one of her own. 'I'm worried about Joan. She's missed two Friday bingos now. There was no reply when I knocked for her at Bureside; the whole place looked empty.'

Oliver's cup looked lost in his hand. He put it down thoughtfully. 'I should've been there the last couple of Wednesdays, but Tom texted to say neither the garden nor *Sylvette* needed work.'

Picturing Tom's pink face, I felt a guilty jolt for not calling him yesterday. 'They were in Sheffield two weeks ago; maybe they're still there.'

Her hand on her hip, Denise joined the conversation. 'Nah, I saw the Roller driving through the village since then. Still had that big dent in the bonnet.'

Nancy frowned. 'I thought Tom had that fixed weeks ago. At the garage for repair, he said. His excuse for making poor Joan walk everywhere.'

'Well, he'd be wanting to don his cap and flash a grin to all and sundry, wouldn't he? Like he does on that posh boat. Men, women, kids and pets alike.' Denise glanced at Oliver. 'Can't blame him for enjoying the popularity, mind.'

A memory flashed in. *Sylvette* ploughing through the dappled river. The warm breeze stroking my bare arms and legs. Was Dad there? Or Joan? No, just me and Tom at the polished wooden wheel. A shiver running through me, I rubbed my chilly arms. Was it worry for the elderly couple or something else? I couldn't quite say, but discomfort was there.

'I'll go there now,' I said. 'I fancy a walk and I still have Tom's cap.'

Chapter Sixty

The wind buffeting my umbrella, I briskly walked down Lower Street and glanced up the driveway of the Petersfield Hotel. The last time I came this way I'd been so excited to meet 'George'. God knows what state my febrile mind had been in, but despite all the internal warnings, the pull had been irresistible. And now a miracle had happened; I could ogle and hug and even kiss the man I loved. Something pure and amazing had pushed through the gluey secrets and darkness. I was lucky, so very lucky. But I had to keep a lid on the elation I felt. In some ways Miles had been right: I had been self-obsessed for weeks. Everybody had been so loving and patient and kind; it was time I gave something back.

Noting Tom's Rolls on the driveway, I crossed the road to Bureside, strode to the porch and knocked. The rain spitting on my shins, I tapped my foot and waited for a minute before trying again. No reply. Perhaps he and Joan were on one of their river trips? That would explain Joan missing bingo...

I walked around the side and frowned. *Sylvette* was moored in her usual place. Taking in her imposing splendour, I continued along the path to the rear garden, stood by the lagoon and watched the sharp downpour dimple its glassy surface. After a few moments I turned back to the patio. Nancy was right; the house looked mournful and empty. Yet Tom's car was parked at the front. Something didn't feel right.

Alarm spreading, I peered through the windows. No one was in, that much was obvious. Not even the desk lamp was glowing. Sheltering under the canopy, I pulled out my phone, scrolled down to Tom's number and listened to the ringtone. A ghostly echo immediately came back. His mobile was ringing inside the house. Surprised and anxious, I squinted through the glassy door. When I tried the handle, it opened.

Oh God; this was how Tom had found baby me. Dread tight in my chest, I stepped into the lounge. 'Tom? Joan?'

Cold and shadowy, the room smelled dank, unused. 'Tom?'

Feeling eyes burn into my back, I snapped around. There were some indeed, but only the sleepy-eyes of Joan's antique dolls. Trying to remember their names, I took in each unique face, but when I reached the last one, I realised it was new. What had Nancy said about them? Something fanciful about them being a representation of Joan's lost babies. But she'd said the poor woman had six miscarriages and there were eight dollies here.

A jolt of guilt hit again. Such a tragedy; I hadn't really focused on how devastating that must have been for both her and Tom. And where the hell were they?

Resisting the urge to flick on lights, I fumbled my way through to the kitchen. No cooking smells, baking warmth or sign of life; I should just turn back. They were out, that was all; it was as simple as that. And yet… As though an invisible hand was gently guiding me onwards, something was sucking me in.

'Joan?' I called again.

Stopping at the staircase, my mind raced ahead, alarm jangling. Suppose I detected a geranium smell or heard the hum of busy flies? I took a deep breath. That was in the past. And what had I said to myself only five minutes ago? It was time to give something back. They might be upstairs, ill and infirm; these lovely people might need my help.

'Tom? Joan?' I called.

Remembering the rough wall of Ranworth tower, I groped my way up the dark stairway. Fearful of what I might find, my heart boomed, but when I reached the landing, I let out my trapped breath. The bedroom doors were ajar; it was just an empty house in broad daylight.

Intrigue overcame my nerves. I'd never been up here before, so I followed a sweet scent to the first bedroom and stood at the opening. The double divan was neatly made, Joan's nightdress spread lengthwise on one side of the bed.

Relieved all was well, I stepped back, but a gleam of metal caught my eye. Perplexed, I stared. What was I seeing? Not only a large key in an external lock, but two heavy-duty bolts, one topping and one tailing the outside of the door.

My mind sticky, I returned to the room to work it out. This was a bedroom, right? A large bed, an easy chair and a portable TV. A dressing table with a mirror, the glass half filled by an assortment of colourful snaps. Then why have a lock and bolts on the *outside*? I almost turned away, but a familiar face in the collage caught my eye. Stepping closer, I stared. This was not a collection of *people*, but one girl, the same girl – as a dark-haired, solemn toddler; a skinny, bespectacled schoolgirl; smiling in a pink tutu; holding a silver cup aloft with a grin. Then a cluster of the same pre-pubescent child in a swimsuit or shorts or a lifejacket – each smiling image with a middle-aged man, his fingers denting her shoulder, her arm or her waist.

Realisation bubbled up, almost making me gag. Then a loud creak on the stairs cracked the silence.

I spun around with a jerk and gaped. The pale, rheumy eyes of a paedophile gazed back.

'Alice?'

'Where's Joan?' I asked, my voice barely there. He wasn't the sentinel. *She* was. She'd been protecting me from him all these years. And even now as an adult, he'd been stalking me, hadn't he? Watching and peeping… God, yes, that white face at the bedroom window had been wearing glasses.

'Joan? She's at home, love. She's asleep.'

I heard the metallic click before I looked. Blocking the door, Tom's hand was on the key, turning it clockwise and back, clockwise and back. Oh God, I'd seen him do it before, hadn't I? Smiling with those teeth and locking me in?

Though I knew to keep calm, to reason and cajole so I could make my escape, terrified words blurted out. 'Don't lock me in; please don't lock me in.'

He straightened himself then, erect like a soldier. 'This is Joan's room. Why would I lock you in? You've done nothing wrong.'

Adrenaline finally overtaking terror, I looked at him properly. He was horribly gaunt, the gossamer skin tight on his face, his limbs like bones. He'd lost weight the last time I'd seen him, but this was even worse.

I inhaled slowly, in and out, in and out. 'Joan's room… Why did you lock her in here?'

'Once a copper, always a copper. She had to be punished.' He took a gulp of air, the words emerging as a sob. 'I loved her dearly, but she had to be brought to book.'

My arms tingling, I turned to the photographs. The top of the dresser was adorned with an old teddy, a foal ornament and other bits and bobs from… God yes, my childhood. I pictured the solid silver box engraved with the letter 'J', the other gifts which had been left in my bedroom, too. Mum wouldn't have bought those for a newborn. Joan, the real antique buff, had. Focusing on the blue inhaler, I remembered the dent in my duvet. The woman had been lying on my bed.

'Punished for what?' I asked.

He followed my gaze. 'She liked to look at you, remember you, smell you. You were the baby she'd never had.'

Oh God, the seventh sleepy-eyed doll, the only one with brown eyes. And yes, I'd seen it just now, the new one wearing a sailor's suit was a blond-haired baby boy.

Goosebumps spreading, I repeated my question. 'Punished for what, Tom?'

'I'm so sorry.' Teetering back to the mattress and sitting, Tom covered his face with trembling hands. 'She didn't tell me for two days.'

My fear of him all gone, I knelt by the bed. 'Tell you what, Tom?'

He tapped his ear like he'd done at The Lodge. 'The earring. I suddenly noticed she was wearing only one. "Where's your other one?" I asked. "The baby took it," she replied.'

Rocking his body, he sobbed. 'I ran there as though my life depended on it, burst in… There was blood and flies. Already blowflies. Too late; I thought I was too late. I picked up the baby, just to warm the poor thing and she whimpered.' He peered at me then. 'Oh Lord, such a beautiful cry.'

Sitting back on my haunches, I tried to breathe through the shock. My fist was clasped tight; I could feel the smooth pearls in my palm. Could it be an actual memory from that long ago? Yes, like the one of Tom – policeman Tom – turning a key in a door.

When my focus returned, he was looking at me intently, his expression beseeching. 'Joan was my wife and I loved her. It wasn't her fault, not really. She was deranged, that's all, just for a time. She'd lost six of her own. I couldn't let her go to prison, could I?'

Oh God. My mother's murderer wasn't the 'bad penny' or a stranger. It was Joan Hague; *she* was the white-faced phantom. Frowning, I went back to Tom. 'So you came to Norfolk and jailed her here instead?'

As though the walls might be listening, he lowered his voice. 'I had to get her away. She'd left that earring. When I went back to call the crime in, I searched but...' He sighed. 'So we came here for good, never went back. Not until...'

We were quiet for a time, then Tom abruptly stirred. Straightening his back, he nodded. 'Jailing her, aye, in a manner. To shield folk from harm, keep people safe. That's what counted. Protecting you, especially.' He nodded to Joan's display. 'She loved you very much; I don't think it was necessary, but I couldn't take the risk, could I?'

Almost too exhausted to move, I sat next to Tom. I'd already guessed the answers, but I asked anyway. 'You say Joan loved me using the past tense. Has she died?'

He nodded. 'Aye, asleep.' He cleared his throat. 'She always said she wanted to die at home so I drove her back to Walkley. Peaceful, it was. In her top bedroom until they took her away.' He smiled thinly. 'Freed from prison at last.'

I was certain he'd eaten no food since. 'Where have you been? On *Sylvette*?'

'Aye. I felt Joan there. Happy memories…'

'Young' uns think only of themselves. Think it's all right to just do as they like or take what isn't theirs. That's when they need to be brought to book,' I remembered. I took a big breath. 'Why did Joan kill Ella, Tom?'

'It tore her apart, never having even one baby. She blamed me after the operation; said I'd made her have it; that I'd made her barren. But it was the gynaecologist's strong advice; I just wanted what was best for her. But I suppose…' He put a hand to his chest. 'We took away even hope.'

He didn't speak for some time. Then he deeply sighed. 'The baby by rights should have been hers, that's the reason. I don't know why she didn't take her that night, but she wasn't in her right mind, so…'

His words confirmed what I had already worked out. What had Melissa said about my 'grandad's' car? Only this man wasn't my grandad; he was my father.

Tom pulled out a wallet from his inner pocket and fumbled through the contents. 'I didn't know Joan had found out about me and Ella. Ella had agoraphobia; she'd had the baby at home, never registered the birth. I provided for her as best I was able, of course, but I couldn't visit too often for fear of being noticed. But I loved that little bairn so much, I couldn't resist keeping this right next to my heart.' He held out a small photograph. 'Joan must have found it and read the back.'

Terrified yet compelled, I took his offering and studied the image of a dark-eyed young woman and her baby. They were the spit of me and Joe. Turning it over, I read the loopy scrawl. *To Daddy from baby Alice. Six months old today!* it said.

Tom reached for my cheek, but didn't quite touch it. 'Aye, my baby Alice from wonderland.'

Chapter Sixty-One

I eventually stood and found my voice. 'I need some fresh air,' I said.

Mixed emotions mottled Tom's face, but they seemed to add up to the same thing – apprehension, worry, alarm. He'd kept this secret for so many years and he wanted my response. He needed my approval, my blessing, my forgiveness, I supposed. But right now all I could think about was the photograph, and the obvious huge age gap between my birth parents.

He nodded. 'Right you are. I'll go down myself and put on the kettle.'

I returned the way I'd come, scooped up my umbrella and headed for the bench looking out to the river. Though it was wet, I sat down and listened to the rain splash the water as I gathered my fractured thoughts. She was so similar to me; there was no doubt the young woman in the snap was my mother. How old would she have been? Sixteen? Eighteen? Twenty? Certainly no older. And Tom? He'd have been in his forties. My skin crawled. Oh God; he was too like the celeb who'd pawed Laura at the village fete – Dave the landlord, too; men who had turned my stomach.

Then there was Joan. The truth was so staggering I had to remind myself the woman had committed a crime; she'd murdered my mother. At fifteen months old, I'd witnessed it. Her actions had stayed with me all my life, not just causing my insecurity and fear of abandonment, but they'd impacted my mental health and brought on psychosis, for God's sake. And that man, my father, had covered it up. Sure, he might have 'punished' her in his own way, but she'd had enough freedom to wander through Bureside and steal items like a magpie.

I breathed through the bubbling nausea. Tom Hague was my father. Save for Joe, he was my only living blood relation. Could I really give him the acceptance he craved? Even pretend everything was all right?

Sighing deeply, I looked up to the boats trundling by. My happiest memories had been here. Could I still own them?

Glancing back to the lawn, I pictured Mum and Dad in those stripy deckchairs. Tom wouldn't have disclosed Joan's involvement in the stabbing, but he must have told them he was my real father. Indeed, it made sense. They'd taken a huge risk for him and encouraged little Ali to spend time with him every holiday. They'd trusted him; they were his close friends. They hadn't shunned him or thought him a bad person. Eve and Doug were decent people; I valued their opinion.

As for Joan… She was dead, gone forever. I wouldn't ever need to face her again. Maybe that was why I was struggling to condemn her right now. And yes, she must have suffered horrendously from the loss of her babies and the finality of a hysterectomy. She'd been 'deranged for a time', Tom had said. Of all people, I understood that. And she'd meekly accepted her punishment, known she had to be 'brought to book'.

Noting a crack of sunshine in the clouds, I stood and shook away the chill from my limbs. My father wasn't a murdering 'bad penny' after all; he was a flawed but good-hearted man. Ella's note on the back of the photograph was clearly loving and sweet. When I'd absorbed the bombshell, perhaps the truth would finally give me a sense of belonging and help me feel anchored. As I turned back to the house, I caught a glimpse of *Ruby Jane* bobbing on the water. I smiled. Yes, Tom had brought me back to Oliver. I couldn't change the past, but I could have a happy future.

I found him in the kitchen, a forlorn and cowed figure, waiting patiently at the table. I held out my hand. 'Come on, Tom, let's drive home in the Rolls. We need to feed you up. I can't promise anything as tasty as Joan's, but I'll practice my Yorkshire puds, just for you.'

–

For the rest of the week I procrastinated, avoiding my conversation with Laura. But I figured I had excuses – worried about Tom's health, I'd insisted he stay at The Lodge until he felt stronger. With her questionable TLC, Nancy was a permanent fixture at his side. 'Like Velcro,' Oliver described it, 'poor old bugger.'

Then there was Miles. After his initial tetchy – and understandable – silence, he'd taken to calling me each evening, talking at length about Julia's demands and his irritation with his mother, who wasn't paying him enough attention, apparently. On reflection, I realised the poor woman had had a tough time with her self-absorbed son and even more egocentric husband. She'd given her all to her patients as well as them, but her needs had been ignored, so she'd turned to the booze for understanding, care and consolation. Though she was possibly a shrink who needed a shrink, she'd seen a vulnerability in me she'd wanted to fix – a fragmented mental psyche, no less – and I was grateful for that. And in truth, I had neglected her as much as anyone, so I was now making an effort to check in and ask how *she* was doing, listen to *her* worries and be appreciative of all she'd done. She'd still drive me nuts from time to time with her interference, I was sure, but ultimately she was a genuine person and she'd be a brilliant grandma to Joe.

The other distraction was Oliver. These days I could kiss and touch and gaze as much as I liked in theory, but we were stymied by etiquette. Tom and Nancy weren't stupid, of course, but other than a furtive peck when they weren't in the room, any intimacy at The Lodge felt wrong. He ate with Tom and me in the evenings, then went home to his cottage.

'Day off on Monday,' he said with raised eyebrows before parting each night. I knew what that meant and the anticipation was delicious.

–

On Sunday morning my preparations for a traditional roast were interrupted by the telephone.

'It's me,' Laura said.

I looked at my watch. 'You're early.'

'Late, actually. You've gone quiet on me. What happened to the visit?'

I heard her say something in the background. To Shelby, I assumed. 'Right; we're on the internet now before bed. November is good for Shelby. The fourth. I'm about to click "buy".'

'Don't!' I blurted. Then after a moment, 'Well do, but I might need another seat.'

I tensed. How would she react? She knew I was back in Norfolk and I'd briefly messaged her about Miles and Julia, saying it was a long saga, that I'd fill her in with that and other surreal stories when we met.

'OK, that's a date. Need to sleep now. Text me the details and I'll sort the tickets.'

I waited for a moment. 'Aren't you the least bit curious why I'm bringing a friend?'

She snorted. 'Ali, I know you. You wouldn't have split up with Miles unless you had someone else lined up. You always did need to be adored.'

I laughed. 'Love you too. Speak tomorrow.'

I turned away thoughtfully. I'd never seen it like that, but she was probably right. I hoped the bumpy journey of motherhood was making me a more complete person, *fixing* me, like baby Ali had helped heal my parents. At least until Dad had felt the need to end it all. My nose burned at the thought of his wasted life. Mum's too, from something so simple as her fleeting inattention at a road junction.

Resolutely pushing away the images both tragedies evoked, I returned to the dining room. To make room for the table in the centre, I had folded away Mum's travel easel, leaving just one. The canvas was no longer blank, nor was her chair vacant. Oliver was back in the land-scaping business, his first commission the plot he could see from the window.

I plonked down in the seat, absently swung it from side to side and studied the view. When I'd berated Tom for neglecting himself after Joan died, he'd chuckled: 'Roger wouldn't like me dying on him, that's for sure. He's been nagging me about tax and exempt transfers.' He'd patted my arm. 'Don't you worry, Alice. The paperwork's already been done, so we're not going to let the taxman take half. Roger's on the case and I'll be good for another seven years, just you see.'

Maybe he'd been referring to Bureside and his other assets, but gut instinct told me Tom didn't just own the woods and scrubland, he owned this house too. I'd never found any title deeds, and considering Dad's financial problems, it wasn't a surprise. Had he always owned it? Most likely – the trustee in bankruptcy would have sniffed out any quick transfer between him and Dad to avoid paying creditors. I was also pretty sure Tom had provided for Mum financially ever since, that those household direct debits came from his bank account, not hers. It made sense: Dad had been his surrogate son; Mum had brought up his child. Would we ever have a frank discussion about these things? Or why he didn't interact with me until I was five? But I suspected I knew the answer to that one: little Alice had been badly traumatised; she'd lost her real mother; she'd needed to settle in her new home.

In the main I was happy with not knowing chapter and verse. Most of the jigsaw had been completed by facts or guesswork, yet something was nagging at the back of my mind; something I'd seen or heard that had jarred. Like synchronicity, a soft breeze made me shiver. Silly though it was, I was sure Mum was still hanging around. Like the peculiar sensation I'd had at Bureside, I felt she was tugging me to find the missing pieces.

I heard Tom's whistle before he entered. 'Morning Alice,' he said, placing a tray with two mugs on the table. 'You look a little pale. Are you alright, love?' He looked at something beyond my shoulder. 'Thinking about your mum?'

This was a strange comment in many ways. My mum was a girl called Ella and he was my dad, but we both knew it wouldn't be mentioned again.

'Thanks.' I took the tea. 'I was, actually. How did you know?'

He busied himself with his *Sunday Times*. When he glanced up, his eyes seemed to flicker. 'Maybe because I do too.' He nodded. 'Aye, I think about her and… you know, that day, a lot and I feel so very—'

Not wanting to go there, I quickly interrupted and smiled brightly. 'You were up early for your newspaper. Any good news for a change?'

He took off his glasses, peered at the print and chuckled. 'Well I'm damned if I'll ever find out. Wrong pair for reading.'

I looked at my watch. The beef was a huge joint, so I had plenty of time before lunch. 'Tell you what, you keep an ear out for Joe and I'll fetch them for you. A brisk walk will do me good.'

Chapter Sixty-Two

Glad I didn't have to enter Bureside and see that spooky doll replica of my son again, I trotted past the garage towards *Sylvette*. His reading glasses were on the table in the saloon, Tom had said, so I'd be able to scoop them up and jog back before Joe awoke. Tom was capable and I trusted him, but he was still pretty weak, and Oliver hadn't yet appeared with a smile at the side door. I climbed onto the deck and shuffled around to the cabin doors. They were unlocked – a security risk, but not surprising; when Tom and I left on Tuesday, I hadn't anticipated him staying over at The Lodge. Not wanting to face the upstairs at Bureside, I'd asked Oliver to collect some of Tom's clothes and toiletries, but I'd clean forgotten he'd been sleeping on the boat.

Stepping down to the living area, I glanced around. There wasn't much sign of 'living' though, really – the room was neat, with only a water glass, two empty coffee cups, Tom's usual humbugs and a couple of banana skins to even show he had been staying here. No wonder he was so frail. But then he'd been mourning his Joan, and there was no doubt that despite everything, he still deeply loved her. I hadn't liked to ask what she'd died of – though cancer was my guess – and I sniffed at the thought of her funeral with only one attendee. It felt like a final punishment.

She'd taken a person's life, so maybe it was deserved, but even convicted lifers didn't serve a whole sentence.

What on earth had Tom done here for two weeks? Paperwork it seemed, and reading a book. I idly scooped up the novel, surprised to see it was *The Tenant of Wildfell Hall*. It seemed unlikely reading matter, but he loved all things Yorkshire and maybe he was a member of Mum's book club. Peering closer, I frowned. The two bookmarks... It was Mum's *actual* copy. And if I wasn't mistaken... I scooped up a small bottle from the window sill. Chanel No. 5. I'd smelled the scent on Joan, so it wasn't surprising of itself, but it was tarnished like the one I'd found in Mum's bedroom drawer.

Discomfort spreading, I slipped into Tom's chair and peered at what he'd been working on. His finances, it seemed. It felt wrong to look, so I put the ledgers to one side, revealing a buff folder underneath. Breath stuck in my chest, I stared at the cover. '*Norfolk Constabulary. Forensic Collision Investigation Unit.*' Oh God, it was the very thing I hadn't wanted to know about. I sat back and shook my head, but that invisible force was pressing me on. Swallowing, I opened it and peered at the first document. Yes: a fatal accident on an A road on the 30th June. The deceased one Evelyn Marie Baker.

Not knowing what I was looking for, I slowly turned the pages and scanned the witness statements. Damon, the driver of the other car: *the Mini came from nowhere; I tried to swerve away, but the front of my car clipped it and it started spinning, out of control...*

His front seat passenger: *I was turned to the window and saw the bonnet of the Mini at the junction, then it suddenly jerked out...*

I had no idea what I'd expected, but I sighed with relief. There was nothing there I didn't already know. I moved on to another witness. This account had been made later, after seeing the accident on the local news: *Though I'd already turned right before the crash happened, I remembered it because it looked like a road rage incident...* I frowned. Road rage? *The Mini was at the junction but the blonde lady was standing outside the driver's side, talking to someone in the car behind. I guessed it was an argument because of her body language.*

I nodded. It made sense of Mum's failure to put on her seatbelt. She didn't like confrontations; she would have been flustered when she climbed back into her car.

I read on: *Though she was turned away, she was gesticulating. I think the other person was still in his car and I don't know what make it was, but it was a lot wider than the Mini and it was silver in colour...*

Fumbling, I turned the page. Another youth from Damon's car: *The lady looked really shocked. As though her car had been shunted from behind.*

Dizziness hit and I reeled as I pictured the dent in the bonnet of the Rolls-Royce, the damage to its front bumper. And yes, when I'd walked past just now, the garage door was undamaged. I'd just made that assumption when I came here at night. That's what had been bugging me, the thing that had jarred – Nancy's comment about the 'repair' and Tom making Joan walk. He was very proud of his immaculate car. If he'd got nothing to hide, he'd have got it fixed straight away, not secrete it here until the danger period had passed.

My hands trembling, I covered my face. No wonder Tom had been so keen to be my 'liaison officer'. With his huge car, he'd shunted the small Mini into the path of a speeding vehicle before Mum had the chance to belt up. He'd been covering up his own crime. His *murder*. But why—

'Alice.'

The sound of Tom's rasping voice made me jump from my skin.

He lifted his palm and edged closer. 'Now Alice…' He glanced at the file. 'You've seen it, then. I'd forgotten it was here. As soon as I remembered, I came rushing.'

Putting a hand to his chest, he gasped to catch his breath. 'It was wrong of me, completely wrong, I know that but… Like before, it was too late.'

My heart thudded. 'What was too late?'

'I had no idea Eve had, that she'd—'

'She had *what*? What could my mum possibly have done wrong to deserve—'

'Nothing. She'd done nothing. Just trying to help, like you were, I suppose. She must have been worried Joan was ill, so she went upstairs and, well, saw what you did.'

I turned to the Bronte novel and pulled out Mum's note: *What do the pictures mean? The trinkets too? They must have been stolen. And the lock on the door?*

The final piece of the puzzle was nearly in my grasp. *This* was what Mum had wanted to talk to me about. She must have been concerned about Joan's clear obsession with me, seen the bolts and worked out the old lady wasn't what she seemed. Worried about my safety, she'd decided to come clean; perhaps even warn me against coming here.

I clenched my jaw. 'Mum saw Joan's room. Her prison. She was perturbed the… the shrine wasn't normal. She might somehow have put two and two together. So that meant you had to chase her in your car and what? *Silence* her—'

'Oh Lord, that wasn't me, Alice.' Stumbling to a chair, Tom shook his head. 'I couldn't keep her under lock and key day in, day out, could I? She had to use the bathroom and eat, go out with Nancy, to bingo and the like. She was a heavy sleeper, so then I could… well, keep her in. But she was stronger and quicker than she looked, and sometimes she caught me out when I was napping. She'd take the car when she fancied it.'

Joan. Oh my God, Joan. 'You told me she didn't drive it.'

'I know, and I'm sorry. I—'

'You what? You covered up a crime. Again?'

'Yes.' Tears shedded from his eyes. 'But like before, it was all too late. There was nothing I could do except think on my feet and… Maybe I made the wrong call, but your beautiful mum had already passed and Joan convinced me it was an accident, her foot slipping and the Rolls lurching into the back of the Mini. Like she said, she couldn't have known a car was coming on the main road at that moment. She was as upset as anyone, so I gave her the benefit of the doubt.'

He gazed pleadingly. 'I had no idea she was anywhere near the scene. I knew she'd been out in the Rolls and parked it back in the garage, but I had no inkling. Even when we heard the dreadful news, I didn't twig. Not until the penny dropped that she knew a lot about the accident, your mum's injuries and—'

'The collar. The lads drinking beer.' Nausea spreading, I lowered my head. Good God, Joan must have parked up in the shadows and watched the whole drama unfold.

'So then I went to look at the car and she told me about what had happened. Accidentally pressing the accelerator instead of the—'

'No Tom. You knew about the argument, the road rage.' I opened the police file and prodded the page. 'You knew there was more to it.'

'That statement came later. And by then I'd already... intervened.' He blew his nose. 'I didn't even realise your mum had been up to Joan's room until I saw the written note.' He glanced at the novel. 'I wondered why Joan had taken it that morning, so when we got back here, I had a look.'

Of course. The day of my 'date' with the gardener, Joan had slipped something in her shopper. I frowned. 'Why on earth did she do it? Mum couldn't have known anything for sure.'

Tom shook his head. 'I couldn't work it out. But...'

'But what?'

'That new German dolly arrived by special delivery two or so weeks ago, not long after Joan had popped in to see you with Nancy. "Special delivery, indeed," she said when the parcel came. "Our little Joe's arrived." And then I remembered how agitated she'd been when your Joe was born, desperate to see a photo, speculating when she might meet him, asking when I thought you'd come down after your mum... passed.'

An icy shiver trickled down my spine. 'What? You think she killed Mum so she could get her hands on Joe?'

'Lord, I don't know. In truth, I just thought she was excited. But after you'd arrived, sometimes she'd go missing and when she came back she'd say not to worry, that she'd only nipped to see you at The Lodge. That's when I started to panic; I didn't get the impression you'd invited her in.' He stood and moved to the window. 'She'd taken your mum from you… Did she want to do the same thing to Joe?'

Oh God. The sense of being watched, the car head-lights; the Peeping Tom at the window. Anger swelled. 'If that's what you thought, then why didn't you do some-thing about it, for God's sake?'

He flinched at my vehemence. 'I kept her in the house when I could. Made sure Nancy or Denise were at The Lodge when George wasn't around, so I knew you were safe.' He scooped up a plush cushion from the couch, held it to his chest and patted it like a baby. 'Then you came here on the Monday night and I knew that wasn't enough going forward. You were my Alice; I needed to do more.' He sighed. 'You were so upset that evening, love, crying like the end of the world had come. I promised you that nothing bad would ever happen to Joe or you and I meant it.'

Goosebumps spreading, I stared at the cushion. He looked at me intently. 'All's well now, love. She's at peace, asleep.' He nodded. 'And she's six feet beneath the ground.'

I took a shuddery breath to say something – God only knew what – but footfall on the deck broke the moment. Then Oliver appeared down the steps, carrying Joe's car seat.

'He's only just woken up.' He glanced from my father to me. 'I expected you both back sooner. Is everything OK?'

Tom tilted his head. 'Is everything OK now, Alice?' he asked me.

A breath of warm air seemed to brush my cheek, then the cabin door clicked shut. The men turned and looked at it in surprise, but I nodded in acknowledgement. My nose burned at the thought of a final goodbye, but I sniffed and smiled sadly.

'Yes Tom,' I said. 'Yes, everything is fine.'

Chapter Sixty-Three

Joe stirred on Oliver's lap and I kissed both their cheeks. The clutch in my belly was still there, a jolt of excitement and wonder when I gazed at my handsome man's face. I smiled. For a bloke who didn't sleep, he was doing a lot of it now. But then again, everyone on the flight was napping except me. I was gazing through the window and deliberating what I'd tell Laura. She'd be meeting her brother, so we'd be open about that, but the other discoveries I'd made felt more problematic.

Firstly there was troublesome little Ali; the girl who'd needed to be adored. Part of it she'd know, and in truth I was apprehensive – Laura was five when I joined the family; she'd still remember it and have her own tales to tell. I'd dipped into Mum's diaries and that taster was bad enough – the exhausting struggle to settle me, persuading me to eat, have a day without tantrums, a night without terrors. But at least the detail eventually lessened to one liners: *A first! Three hours solid sleep last night!… A smile, a real smile!… A whole night without screaming… Beautiful singing!… A proper Daddy's girl!*

From the moment that monster had sat on her daddy's knee, drunk her juice and eaten her food, my big sister had been usurped. How must she have felt when I flaunted the special bond between me and Dad? When I was clingy and needy and demanding attention? When I was praised and applauded, too? Yet Laura had loved me in her own kind of way; she'd looked out for me, cuddled me, let me climb into her bed. Save for the occasional 'gooseberry bush' or 'pixie' comments, she'd astonishingly kept the secret of my adoption.

As I stared at the cotton wool clouds, I knew I'd do the same about Dad. The painful truth about his financial problems, his arrest and suicide would only hurt Laura, so I'd keep them to myself. What about my own story? I wasn't sure how comfortable I'd feel about delving into my birth mother's death and the unofficial nature of my adoption, let alone the horrifying Joan revelations. And what about admitting Tom was my father? I chuckled to myself; it seemed only fair to explain his tickling and cuddles. I'd already mentioned I had a surreal story to tell. That's what I'd start with.

I sighed. My father, Tom Hague. We'd left him at Bureside in the questionable care of Nancy and Denise, but he was already so much stronger. His steadfast look in the saloon came to me from time to time. '*All's well now, love. She's at peace, asleep.*' That was the one thing I hadn't shared with Oliver. Had Tom smothered his wife when she was in one of her 'heavy' sleeps? Who knew, but it was the one secret I'd let pass. She was, after all, '*six feet beneath the ground.*'

–

My big sister was waiting for us at arrivals with an attractive bloke, a placard and a grin.

ALI BAKER, THINGY AND MYSTERY FRIEND it read.

After hugging me tightly, she stood back and studied Oliver. Almost jealous at the palpable connection, I watched their identical frowns as they took each other in.

'Have we met before?' she asked eventually.

Oliver held out his hand. 'I'm Oliver Newman,' he said easily. 'I'm the son your mother gave up for adoption before you were born. Which makes me your brother.'

'And you two are…?' she asked cautiously.

I laughed. 'Yes, scandalous, isn't it?'

A letter from C E Rose

Hello lovely reader!

Thank you so much for reading *The House on the Water's Edge*. I do hope you've enjoyed living on the River Bure, meeting Ali and George, Tom and Joan, and discovering their dark secrets.

If you'd like to read more twisty tales about relatable characters who get caught up in extraordinary situations, dilemmas or crimes, please check out my first CE Rose gothic-tinged psychological thriller, *The House of Hidden Secrets*, or my Caroline England domestic suspense novels, *Beneath the Skin*, *My Husband's Lies*, *Betray Her* and *Truth Games*.

Book reviews are extremely helpful to authors, so if you have the time and inclination, I'd be really grateful if you'd pop a short one on Amazon or Goodreads, or your other preferred forum. If you'd like to chat in person, hear my latest news or see photos of my moggies and other random things, my website and social media details are below.

Thank you again,

Best wishes,

Caroline

Website: www.carolineenglandauthor.co.uk
Twitter: https://twitter.com/CazEngland

Facebook: https://www.facebook.com/CazEngland1/
Instagram: https://www.instagram.com/cazengland1/
email: carolineenglandauthor@gmail.com

Acknowledgments

Huge thanks to:

My gorgeous family – Jonathan, Elizabeth, Charlotte and Emily.

Mary and Ron for the genuine love letters.

My parents, sister and brothers, for my own happy childhood memories of Horning.

Early readers Kate Johnson, Hazel James and Catharine Hughes.

Keshini Naidoo and Lindsey Mooney for inviting me to join the fabulous list of Hera authors.

Keshini and Jennie Ayres for the top-notch editorial input and advice.

Last but not least, my brilliant friends and writing buddies, the amazing bloggers and you guys – the fantastic reading public!

Reading group questions for The House on the Water's Edge

- What was your perception of Ali's parents in their younger days, as seen in their love letters? Do you think Ali takes after her adoptive mum, or her dad?

- Were you shocked when Ali still had romantic feelings for George despite knowing they were related?

- Did you think Tom was a kindly old man, or were you worried he might have darker motives?

- Did you have any sympathy for Miles at all? Do you think he'll end up with Julia?

- Did you identify with Ali's struggles as a new parent? Do you think the fact that she'd just had a baby impacted on her decisions at all?

- Did you like Laura? Did your feelings change when you discovered she'd kept the secret of Ali's adoption all her life? Out of the two sisters, Ali and Laura, which character did you identify with more?

- After finding out the traumatic truth about her real mother, how do you think Ali's life from now on will be affected?

- Would you like to live in a house like The Lodge? Has the book tempted you to visit the Norfolk Broads?

- What did you make of Madeleine? How would you feel about having a mother-in-law like her?

- Did Joan's dollies give you the creeps or did you feel sorry for her? Did you think Tom was right to 'imprison' her for all those years?